Other works by the same author

(Information for all works here: www.cathyace.com)

The Cait Morgan Mysteries

(Published by TouchWood Editions)

The Corpse with the Silver Tongue
The Corpse with the Golden Nose
The Corpse with the Emerald Thumb
The Corpse with the Platinum Hair*
The Corpse with the Sapphire Eyes
The Corpse with the Diamond Hand
The Corpse with the Garnet Face
The Corpse with the Ruby Lips**

Winner 2015 Bony Blithe Award for Best Canadian Light Mystery
**Finalist 2017 Bony Blithe Award for Best Canadian Light Mystery*

The WISE Enquiries Agency Mysteries

(Published By Severn House Publishers)

The Case of the Dotty Dowager
The Case of the Missing Morris Dancer
The Case of the Curious Cook
The Case of the Unsuitable Suitor

Short Stories

Steve's Story in 'The Whole She-Bang 3'***
(Published by Sisters in Crime, Toronto)

***Finalist 2017 Arthur Ellis Award for Best Short Story*

MURDER KEEPS NO CALENDAR

CATHY ACE

FOUR TAILS PUBLISHING LTD.

Stories and novella contained within the anthology 'Murder Keeps No Calendar':

Dear George
First edition copyright © 1988 Cathy Ace; second edition copyright © 2017 Cathy Ace
The Corpses Hanging Over Paris
First edition copyright © 2007 Cathy Ace; second edition copyright © 2017 Cathy Ace
Domestic Violence
First edition copyright © 2007 Cathy Ace; second edition copyright © 2017 Cathy Ace
Negroni
First edition copyright © 2007 Cathy Ace; second edition copyright © 2017 Cathy Ace
A Woman's Touch
First edition copyright © 2007 Cathy Ace; second edition copyright © 2017 Cathy Ace
The Corpse with the Fake Purse
First edition copyright © 2007 Cathy Ace; second edition copyright © 2017 Cathy Ace
Tea For Two
First edition copyright © 2007 Cathy Ace; second edition copyright © 2017 Cathy Ace
Shannah's Racecar
Copyright © 2017 Cathy Ace
The Corpse That Died Twice
First edition copyright © 2007 Cathy Ace; second edition copyright © 2017 Cathy Ace
The Trouble With The Turkey
First edition copyright © 2015 Cathy Ace; second edition copyright © 2017 Cathy Ace
Miss Parker Pokes Her Nose In
First edition copyright © 2007 Cathy Ace; second edition copyright © 2017 Cathy Ace
Tidings Of Comfort And Joy
First edition copyright © 2015 Cathy Ace; second edition copyright © 2017 Cathy Ace

DEDICATION

For my family, with love and thanks

CONTENTS

JANUARY

Dear George

January 1st

So here it is, the first day of the year I kill George. This diary will be a record of what I do this year, so that one day – when I'm long gone – everyone will know how clever I was.

I'll tell you, dear diary, absolutely everything. It'll be like we're partners. Yes, partners. No one else will know our plans. You see, it's time; after ten years of gradually hating dear, sweet George more and more, day after day, month after month, I'm going to do something about it. I'm going to stop him snoring. Stop his armpits smelling. Stop him scraping his knife on his plate. Stop him eyeing up young girls. Stop his palms sweating. Stop him picking his nose when he thinks I can't see him do it. Stop him dead.

I'll keep you hidden underneath my one and only frilly nightie. George never looks in that drawer, so no one will know you're there – except you and me. And we won't be telling, will we?

Today's been a big day; I decided to kill George, I found you, and it was sunny. Sunny on the first day of the year, in South Wales – not what you'd expect. I'll take it as an omen.

January 28th

I think I'm doing very well to find the time to tell you all about what's been going on every day. I make time to talk to you because you're so special to me. You understand me. Not like him.

He's out at his club again with his 'mates', tonight. I expect they'll all be sitting there cracking dirty jokes, and he'll be busy chatting up that new barmaid. We saw her on the High Street last week when we were going to the ironmonger. Said hello to him and everything, she did. Even called him Georgie. *Georgie!* Of course, he had to tell me who she was. Introduce us to each other. Little tart. All boobs and no brain. Mind you, I feel better knowing that I'll be at George's funeral in July.

Oh, that's right, I haven't told you yet, have I? I decided yesterday that I'd kill him on July 4th. It's Independence Day in America, you know. Good that, eh? The day I get rid of George will be celebrated by millions of people. And they won't have a clue.

February 1st

I've been thinking. I don't know how I'll manage when George is dead. We haven't got any money in the bank, no savings or anything, and I've never had a job. Not since we got married, anyway. George wanted me to give up work when we married. I don't think I could do anything really. Except awful things like working in a shop or a factory like I did in my teens, and I really don't want to do that again. It was horrible then, and it would be horrible now. I don't know how to get around this one at all. What shall I do?

Oh yes, that's a good idea. Get George to insure his life, then I'll get the money when he's dead. You're very clever. Almost as clever as me. I don't know much about insurance. I wonder if I could talk to Iris about it? She knows about lots of things; she's always surfing the net. Her son set it all up for her. She could find out for me. Or maybe I could use one of the computers George is always saying I should try at the library. Maybe he's actually made a useful suggestion. I'll think about it.

February 4th

I'm going to talk to George about life insurance tonight. When he comes to bed I'll raise the topic, all casual, like. We agreed a hundred grand, didn't we? That's how they say it, you know. 'A hundred grand.' It'll be grand when I've got it, I can tell you that much. Yes, I know you think that's greedy, but I'll want to live it up a bit when boring old George has gone. I'll tell you tomorrow how it goes. I've got to have a bath now. It's Saturday; we always do it on a Saturday, unless George doesn't feel like it. Knowing my luck, tonight he will.

February 5th

I had to tell George that I wanted us both to insure ourselves, just so I didn't make him suspicious. Joint life insurance, they call it.

He said we can't afford it, but I explained to him about how you can insure two people, and when one of them dies the other one gets the money. The one who's left hasn't got any life insurance on themselves, but I told him it's cheaper than us both insuring ourselves. As two separate people. Oh, you know what I mean. I understood when I explained it to him. He actually sounded impressed that I'd worked out how to use the computer in the library and print from it. See? Old dog, new tricks.

I ran into Iris today, and she said I looked tired. That's because George came in very late last night and woke me up. He never smells of drink, but I know he's been knocking it back, on the sly. Probably vodka. They say that doesn't smell at all. George says he's always busy at the Country and Western Club, but I know it's just an excuse to go out boozing to a place where he knows I won't follow him. Maybe next Saturday I'll go along with him, see what he really gets up to. That would blow his little cover story for late nights out.

February 12th

Sorry I didn't talk to you last night; I got all dressed up, and when George came in from doing a bit of shopping in town, I told him I was going out with him to his club. That shocked him. And you'll never guess what we did – we *did* go to the blessed Country and Western Club! Lots of people said hello to him as we went in, and then they kept coming up to him to ask him questions about all sorts of things. Lots of women, that is. But he didn't drink at all – only orange juice. He did that to make me think he never ever drinks, but I know different.

Anyway, even though he didn't drink, he still wanted to do it when we came home. Honestly, you sit in the corner all night not talking to anyone, listening to that awful racket, and you still have to come home and do it. Terrible. I don't think I'll bother again.

February 27th

We signed the insurance papers today. What an idiot. He didn't have a clue. Now, when I kill him, I'll be rich too. I can hardly wait. The 4th of July seems a very long way away.

Perhaps we should reconsider that date.

As soon as he's out of the way I can go on a lovely cruise; people would expect me to get away after all the fuss and the police and all that. I suppose it's the only way to do it; shoot George, then ring the police and give myself up, telling them it was a terrible accident. Besides, I want to see his face as I pull the trigger. I have to see the realization in his stupid eyes of what I'm doing to him; see him getting the point for once in his pathetic, miserable life.

It's all his fault anyway. For keeping the gun. If I hadn't seen it in his desk drawer last year I'd never have got this brilliant idea. It's probably illegal to have it; but that's alright with George because it was his high-and-mighty father's. I'm going to take it out onto Fairwood Common next week to check that it works. It's pretty quiet there, especially at this time of year. Who wants to wander about the Gower in the winter? Lovely it might be, but it can be bitter. And bleak up on the common. There'll still be buses running though. Not many, but some.

There are only three bullets in the gun, but I need to use one just to make sure I know how to make it shoot properly. I'll take the bus on Monday and wait until there's no one around. Just the sheep. As long as I don't point it at anything except the ground, it can't do any harm, can it?

Anyway, goodnight now. I'm sorry I haven't been writing in you as tidily as usual today, but that copperplate is very hard to keep going, and my hands are sore from wringing out the bedroom curtains this afternoon. Still, the washing machine man will be here tomorrow and then it'll be working again, I hope.

March 6th

I shot the gun today. I didn't realize it would make such a noise. It frightened the life out of me. Ha! What a funny thing to say; it won't frighten the life out of George, it'll shoot the life out of George. Oh, that does make me smile. It was so loud it frightened the sheep on the common. My word they can shift when they want to. No one heard me though; it was far too cold for anyone to be out on a day like this. I hurt my wrist a bit; I held the gun in two hands like they do on the telly, but it still pushed back a lot. It was very powerful. At least I know I can do it.

George didn't suspect a thing, of course; I'd put the gun back in the drawer by the time he got home from work. Not that he ever goes to the desk except to pay bills every month. Sometimes I wonder if he even notices that I'm here, let alone things around him in the house.

March 13th

I did the washing today; much easier now the machine's fixed. Even so, one thing I really hate is the way George refuses to use tissues, and will insist on using real hankies. I'm the one who's got to wash them. They're revolting. But he won't listen to me. I'd make him wash them himself, but he wouldn't get them clean, and I'm certainly not having her next door seeing dirty washing on the clothesline. Not that I could put it out today. Too wet. It'll all just have to hang around on the clotheshorse until it's dried off.

I was doing the ironing from yesterday's load when I tried to work out how many of George's shirts I've ironed since we got married – it's thousands. I feel as though I've ironed them all today.

I'm getting tired more quickly these days. Getting headaches too. George isn't at all sympathetic. He says I should get my eyes seen to. He'll find out if there's anything wrong with my eyes when I hit him with that little bullet.

April 27th

Our wedding anniversary. What a bundle of laughs today was, dear diary. I gave George a card and a pair of socks. He gave me a box of chocolates – then he ate all the soft ones. Pig. I hate him. Do you know he actually laughed at me as he ate the coffee cream? He knows it's my favorite.

Dear, dear diary, I know we agreed that we'd wait, but I can't any longer. He's horrible to me all the time. He hates me as much as I hate him, I'm sure of that, or he wouldn't have eaten all the soft ones, would he?

More than twenty years ago today I promised to love, honor, and obey him. Well, today I'm promising to love, honor, and obey myself. Please don't be upset, I'll keep you in the picture. I'm going to do it a week on Saturday, when George gets back from his big 'Annual Hoe Down' thing at his club. Then there'll just be you and me. And the money, too, of course.

May 6th

I know I'm early, but I had to talk to you – I'm so excited! I've smashed the glass in the back door, inwards, like we agreed, and I've put my big shopping bag in the middle of the living-room floor and filled it with all our bits of silver. It's already dark, and the gun is safe in my dressing-gown pocket. I'll tell the police I was in bed with a headache when I heard the noise. I'll tell them George kept the gun by the bedside – because he's just the sort of idiot who would – and I put it in my pocket and went downstairs.

I'll tell them how terrified I was when I saw a shadowy figure at the door coming toward me, that I thought it was a burglar or a rapist, and I shot at it. Then I'll tell them how I discovered it was my dear, sweet George.

They'll see how upset I am and I'll get away with it.

It won't be long now. He never puts the lights on when he comes home. I'll put you away for now. We may not be able to talk for some time.

The foreman of the jury rose from his seat.
'Not guilty.'
Clear and loud: NOT GUILTY.
It was An Accident. A tragic accident.
The past few weeks had been a tremendous strain; the newspapers had been full of it – photographs of 'The Accused' and 'The Victim' appeared everywhere, many of them none too flattering. But now it was over. The jury agreed with the general public: awful, but certainly not premeditated. The judge was saying something, then there were lots of congratulations being shouted from the gallery. Outside were more photographers and, thankfully, a taxi. Not back to the house; not to that hallway where it had happened. No, off to a hotel room; a bright, impersonal room with just a hint of luxury. Oh yes, that insurance money would come in very handy.

George Melrose turned on the television set, then bounced on the edge of the hotel bed. The afternoon movie crackled in monochrome and George smiled wryly at Katherine Hepburn in a dressing gown, not unlike the one his wife Joyce had worn as she had descended the stairs that fateful night.

George had looked at her disapproving eyes peering from beneath her curlers for the last time, had approached her, taken her hands in his, pointed the gun toward her heart and had pulled the trigger. The blood had ruined the dressing gown, of course. Then he'd put the gun in Joyce's dead hands and shot again, this time breaking the glass in the big old oak hallstand.

The police hadn't believed George that his wife had tried to kill him. He had never thought they would. After all, George was such an inoffensive chap, why would Joyce want to kill him? Unless she had a screw loose, of course. No, George was quiet and unassuming; a teatotaler who was hard-working, and happy to stay at home of an evening, watching the box. No one had ever known him to go out except to his country and western club, where he was a well-respected and diligent club secretary; dozens of members had come to the court to say so.

The police hadn't known what to believe, until they found the diary, tucked away in a drawer beneath one of Joyce Melrose's nightdresses. For months it had been hidden in the glove compartment of George's car, wrapped in plastic bags to keep it forensically clean. He'd carefully filled in each day's entry in painstakingly formed copperplate, copied from the calligraphy book the police had also found in Joyce's chest of drawers.

George rang for room service, and ordered himself a cream tea. The weather was brightening; George wondered if perhaps the summer would liven itself up a bit now. Joyce had actually liked summer, but of course it had made her sneeze. That woman had been allergic to almost everything. Possibly even life itself.

Miserable, boring, plain, whining Joyce. It really was incredible that anyone could believe she had been bright enough to think of what would have been a really clever plan. But then, as George often told himself, people could be unbelievably stupid.

That Inspector Glover they'd put on the case late in the day had been the only one sharp enough to spot that Joyce would never have got away with her plan. Indeed, he was the only one who pointed out it was clearly all a set-up, because of the silver in the bag on the living-room floor. After all, who could have put it there but Joyce herself, if she'd supposedly shot someone entering the house? No, George hadn't wanted them to think she was *that* clever.

Detective Inspector Evan Glover and his wife were finishing a late supper. They rarely discussed work, but the George Melrose case had aroused a great deal of interest nationwide.

As Betty Glover collected the dirty plates from the table and pushed them into the soapy water in the washing-up bowl she said, 'You look tired, Evan.'

'It's been a hard day. I won't be sorry to get off to bed.' Her husband's voice was heavy.

'Look, *cariad*, I know we don't usually talk about your cases, but if you want to chat about this one, you go ahead.'

Evan Glover finished his tea and carefully placed his cup in the center of the recess in the saucer. Betty didn't care for mugs.

'Don't worry, love, a good night's sleep will cure me.' He looked up at his dear wife of thirty years as she balanced the dishes in the rack to drain. Their eyes locked for a moment, then they smiled at each other; a smile of understanding, and sympathy.

Glover rubbed his tired face, hard, with both hands. He scratched his head and pushed his still-black hair from a furrowed brow. He sat quietly for a moment, hands clasped behind his head, rocking gently on his chair. Betty stacked the dishes, and waited.

Finally Glover spoke, his tone betraying his exasperation. 'I just haven't felt right about this Melrose case all along. There's something we've missed, but not something you can put your finger on. Forensics were inconclusive, and no matter how much of a gut feeling I've got, you can't convict someone on the basis of my indigestion. They call me an "intuitive copper", and my intuition says he's got away with murder. Anyway, he's cleared. That diary did it; all the experts said it was the work of someone missing a few marbles. Almost childlike. Still, she made it perfectly clear that she intended to do him in. Even covered the double insurance angle. You know, he's actually quite a nice chap. Quiet. Almost invisible. Colorless sort. Yes, that's it, colorless.'

Betty Glover wiped her hands on a tea towel, then spread the dishcloth across the taps to dry. 'Put some water in that cup before you come up, *cariad*. I'm going to make a move now. Don't you be too long. You need your rest.' Her voice was gentle, comforting.

'Night, love, I'll be up in a minute,' called Glover to the receding figure.

'They said in the papers she had her hair in curlers when your lot arrived at the house. Did she?' enquired Betty as she began to pull herself up the stairs using the banister.

Evan rubbed his eyes and answered nonchalantly with a sleepy, muffled, 'Mmm? Yes. Yes she did.'

His wife chuckled as she clambered toward the bedroom. 'Well, if I was going to bump you off, then give myself up to the police straight away, there's no way I'd have my hair in curlers. Who'd want to be arrested in curlers? What would you do with them at the police station? Ah well. Curlers? Yes, very strange that. She must have been potty, as you say.'

Glover was stunned. He stared open-mouthed at the china cabinet as though it had uttered the words itself. The curlers!

FEBRUARY

The Corpses Hanging Over Paris

I looked up from my desk to see a shock of green-and-blue dyed hair poke around my door. 'Professor Morgan, am I too early?' asked Paris Chow in a hesitant voice.

I assured him he wasn't, and didn't even bother to point out he was ten minutes late; since my migration to Vancouver from my native Wales several years ago, I've learned that ten minutes late is often viewed as being five minutes early by those who live here. Which still annoys the heck out of me.

Another reason I didn't mention his timekeeping was because it was the end of the week, and I had no particular plans for Friday evening, or indeed for the weekend, so I wasn't in a hurry to get away. But I'd imagined Paris would be running out of the place; it was the end of the Chinese New Year celebrations, and therefore the Lantern Festival.

'Come in, Paris, let's get on. I'm sure you want to get away.' He seemed to hold back, then stomped into my office room and pushed the door shut.

Okay, Cait, I thought to myself, *so he needs this to be private, and his entire being is screaming he's in turmoil.* I teach a course here at the University of Vancouver in reading body language, so it's fair to say I know my onions in that respect, and I steeled myself for what I feared might turn out to be an emotional conversation. All I knew for certain was that Paris had asked for an hour with me, as a favor. He'd taken a few of my courses in criminal psychology over the past couple of years, but I hadn't seen much of him recently. A hard worker with a good brain, he'd told me early on he wanted to work in criminalistics one day – so many of them do nowadays with all those shows on TV – and he stands a good chance; he's patient, listens well, attends to detail, and doesn't mind taking his time over something. I knew his finals weren't far off, so I thought he might want to talk about career plans, but now I was less certain of that original assumption.

Paris's voice shook with forced bonhomie as he spli
well, you know, like, I wanted to, uh, like, thank you
this time, professor.' Born and raised in Vancouver,
from the local disease – a seeming inability to speak ᵙ _
wasn't liberally sprinkled with the unnecessary, and frankly
irritating, seasoning of 'like', 'you know' and 'for sure'; another local
peculiarity I still struggled with. To be fair to him, Paris was always
polite, but on this occasion he seemed positively deferential as he
bowed his head to me; I'm used to a lot of my Chinese-born students
doing this, but for this Vancouverite, it was a first. With his ripped
jeans, Canucks' hockey shirt, and stripes of green-and-blue hair
down the middle of his head, he was hardly a vision of traditional
Chinese values.

'You're welcome, Paris. Off to the game this weekend?'

His eyes lit up and he bared two rows of gleaming white,
precisely aligned teeth in a grin that sparkled with excitement. His
parents had probably spent a fortune to ensure the perfection of
that smile. 'Yeah, Amrit and I got tickets in the nosebleeds. We're
gonna, like, thrash The Avalanche!'

I smiled too, seeing such passion. 'And what about other
activities? Finishing up the family celebrations?' I stayed cheery.

Paris stopped making eye contact, and his grin disappeared.
'Yeah, a lot of family stuff.' He paused, then added, 'That's why I'm
here. I want you to help me solve a murder mystery.'

I was speechless; which isn't something I can say about myself
very often. I gathered my thoughts – of which there were many.
'You're having some sort of family murder-mystery evening?' It was
the most likely of all the scenarios I was contemplating.

Paris Chow, or to give him his proper Chinese name, Chow Zhang
Yi, laughed nervously. 'In my family we keep our cultural traditions
alive in lots of ways. Every Lunar New Year, over the fifteen days,
we all meet to eat, give gifts, then eat some more. And we tell
stories. You know, like the way little kids here tell ghost stories
around the campfire?' I nodded. 'Well, we tell stories that are
supposed to engage and involve the rest of the family – all of them
from nine months to ninety years, which is about the age range in

my family. Of course, none of this is in English, and this year it's my turn to tell a story during the lantern-making party.'

'And you think I can help?' My skepticism must have been audible.

'Yeah.' He seemed convinced.

'Do you want some tips on presentations? Some ideas for props?' I was at a bit of a loss.

'Thanks, but no thanks. I just wanted to run the story past you so you can let me know if I'm telling it well. You said once that you try to tell a story to keep students interested – remember?'

Even with my eidetic memory, I couldn't remember exactly when I'd have said it in front of Paris, but I try to say it at the start of every course I deliver. I nodded in what I thought was a non-committal way, as I pictured Paris when I'd first met him; back then he'd been three years younger and dressed in a less outrageous manner . . . I recalled khaki pants, a blue-and-white golf shirt, and hair shaved almost to his scalp. He'd carried a red backpack, and had looked about fifteen. Within two months his personal presentation had shifted to be a little less like the way you'd expect to see a forty-year-old on the golf course, and much more as you'd expect to see a teenager at university. It was a process so many of them went through as they wriggled around trying to find their niche in a world where almost everyone was new to them, and the group dynamics had to be worked out. Those first few months at university are an incredibly trying time – psychologically – for youngsters; they suddenly find they are minnows in a vast sea, no longer at the top of the food chain as they were at high school.

He took my silence as approval, and continued, 'So I'm going to tell a story about Shanghai – which is where my family is from, so they'll all, like, know the places I'm talking about. The story's about star-crossed lovers. And I hoped you could help.'

I was puzzled. 'Well, that sounds interesting, Paris, but romance isn't really my strong point.' As I spoke I was thinking, *If only you knew how much it's not my strong point you wouldn't be asking me.*

He smiled timidly and said, 'Well, I don't know about that, professor, but crime is, and this is a story about passion, and jealousy, and murder – and that's your bag, eh?'

I was beginning to see some light but couldn't help asking, 'Do you think that's the sort of story that would go down well with a family group? Aren't you supposed to avoid the subject of death at the New Year?'

'Oh yeah,' he replied in a matter-of-fact way, 'for sure, it's supposed to be bad luck, but my family is a particularly gory lot; the more monsters, injustice, and tragedy there is in a story, the more they'll love it. Have you ever seen a Chinese opera? They all love them.'

Short of admitting that my one and only experience of Chinese opera had left me utterly confused and almost deaf, I didn't know what to say, so I countered with, 'So you think that a professor of criminology is your best bet for a useful guinea pig?'

Paris nodded, and pulled out a fat folder stuffed with paperwork, divided into sections with colored tabs. He leafed through it until he found the right spot. He didn't look up as he announced, 'I'll use my notes. I want to get the facts straight.'

I found his statement interesting. 'And this is a case you've created yourself, for this purpose?'

He nodded, not making eye contact.

I decided to not mention the fact I could tell from his micro-expressions he was lying, on the basis I wanted to find out why he would do such a thing. I encouraged him to try a run-through of his tale. He sat forward in his chair and began. He'd obviously decided to adopt a special story-telling voice; it was low and conspiratorial, and I soon found myself enjoying his dramatic style of delivery.

'Shanghai in the 1930s was a rough place, especially if you were poor, and Chinese. It was known as the Pearl of the Orient, and the Paris of the East.' He looked up. 'All my family know it's why I chose Paris as my western name.' He grinned. 'Anyway, at exactly the same time it was also referred to as the Whore of Asia, which tells you more about what the place was really like. Between the January 28th Incident in 1932, and the Japanese Occupation in 1937, Shanghai was demilitarized – but it was run by baron gangsters; some were Chinese, but most were Western. The wealthy, international residents known as the Shanghighlanders lorded it over the slums, and built their imposing Western-style finance houses and office buildings along the western bank of the Huangpu River. They got away with murder – quite literally – when they wanted, because of the extraterritoriality agreement which made them exempt from Chinese law. In truth, Shanghai was full of Westerners looking for easy access to everything that was illegal in the West, but which was available for sale on every street corner in a city of sin where girls came in from farms and villages looking to make quick money with their exotic looks.'

My right eyebrow shot up; it does that when I'm surprised, or cross, or trying to make a point, or displaying disbelief . . . to be honest, it's a multi-purpose eyebrow. This time it shot up with amazement. I had to interrupt. 'You're *quite* sure this is a suitable story for the whole family?'

'Yeah, they'll be fine,' replied Paris, using his 'normal' voice once again. 'The adults know, like, all this stuff; it's our heritage, see? But I have to frame the story for the younger ones. They'll love it, for sure.'

Paris seemed quite certain of himself, and I rationalized he was talking about *his* family, after all; my own family now comprises an urn at each end of my mantelpiece in my little house a few miles from the university, and a sister I haven't seen for years because she lives in Australia, so I couldn't really comment. I let him continue, interested to see where the tale would go; I suspected it would take me to some pretty questionable places.

'During this wild period, a young girl named Lily made her way to Shanghai from a small village hundreds of miles away. She went there to make money to send home; her father was sick, and couldn't work on the family's farm any more. Her parents had forbidden her to go, but she had sneaked off in the night. She was a good seamstress and brought samples of her work to show to what she thought would be the nice women who ran the shops where fine ladies' garments were made. But do you know what she found when she got to Shanghai?'

Paris stopped, and seemed to expect some sort of response from me. I furnished one. 'She found they were all horrible people and she was ensnared into slavery?'

Paris smiled, and added in his non-storytelling voice, 'Well, something like that, but that's how I plan to get the audience involved, see? I'll ask them questions and they can take the story forward themselves. Does that work okay?'

I smiled. 'It's a nice device. Where'd you come up with that one?'

Paris put his hands together and bowed mockingly. 'Oh Great Master – I see how you do it, and I, humble servant, copy you.'

'Ha! Very good. Well, if you think it works when I do it in my lectures, then feel free to use the technique yourself, oh humble servant,' I replied cheerily. 'So, come on then, what happens when Lily gets the awful job, in terrible conditions, for next to no pay?'

Paris took a deep breath, and was off again. 'The woman who runs the shop where Lily takes a job, Madame Chang, is horrible. Lily doesn't get paid at all, but she puts her mind to doing well and she gradually makes her way up the sewing hierarchy to become the seamstress who works in the back of the store, doing alterations and last-minute changes for the customers who come in for their final fittings. Lily's now receiving a little money, which she saves, and she uses every opportunity to listen to the English-speaking customers. She even learns to speak some English herself; she is a very clever girl, you see. One day, Lily is called into the store to pin up the hem of a dress for a wealthy woman; Mrs Eversholt is Chinese, married to a rich Westerner. She dresses in Western clothing, which is Lily's specialty. As Lily is hemming Mrs Eversholt's dress, the lady's son, Charles, comes into the store; he is young and handsome. Lily has never seen a wealthy young man of mixed race before, and she makes the mistake of letting her mouth fall open as she stares at him. When Madame Chang sees this she screams at Lily, and pushes her into the room behind the store. Mrs Eversholt and Charles can hear Lily being beaten. What do you think happens then?'

'Mrs Eversholt and her son rescue Lily from Madame Chang, and take her away with them?'

'Exactly!' responded Paris with glee. 'But there are some

complications.'

'But of course. What happens next?'

'Lily moves to the Eversholts' large mansion, where she looks after all her new mistress's clothes, and even makes her entirely new gowns. Mrs Eversholt discovers Madame Chang has paid Lily almost nothing in the whole year she has been working there, and she takes up Lily's cause, threatening to tell all her friends about how Madame Chang treats her workers if she doesn't give Lily the money she is owed. It takes months before Madame Chang finally agrees to give Lily's money to Mrs Eversholt; Lily thinks it is enough money for her to leave Shanghai, but Mrs Eversholt is really a selfish woman, and she convinces Lily to send the money to her family in the countryside in the care of a man employed by her husband. She does this because she wants Lily to stay with her to make a very grand gown for a special ball the Eversholts are due to attend. Lily agrees, because she is very grateful to Mrs Eversholt, and the man takes the money. When he returns, weeks later, he brings a letter from Lily's mother; Lily's father has died, and now her mother is very sick. The letter begs Lily to come home. Lily is very upset and tells Mrs Eversholt she intends to go back to her village; she would like to have her wages from Mrs Eversholt so she can leave. Mrs Eversholt agrees with Lily, and even offers her some extra money to be able to take a train a part of the way home, but the next day, something amazing happens that makes Lily decide to stay a while longer. Can you guess what it is?'

'Charles Eversholt invites Lily to accompany him to the ball?'

Paris looked crestfallen. 'I didn't think you'd guess.'

I reassured him. 'It's my job to understand this sort of thing. If you're asking a family group the same question, you'll probably get lots of different answers to add to the fun.'

Paris brightened. 'Yeah, I guess you're right. So, sure enough, Charles, with whom Lily has secretly been in love since she first met him, asks her to accompany him to the ball. Of course she agrees, and she stays to finish Mrs Eversholt's gown. She even makes one for herself from some leftover fabric in the house. All this time Mr Eversholt has been away on business, traveling around his oil wells in America, but he returns home just in time for the ball. That's when he meets Lily for the first time. When he hears about his son's plans to escort her in public, he becomes very angry. Eventually his wife calms him down, and Lily overhears the woman tell her husband that Charles's invitation was a trick to get Lily to stay. Lily is heartbroken, because she thought Charles felt something for her, but, after many tears, she decides she will make herself as beautiful as possible for the ball and make him notice – and want – what he cannot have. *Her*. The night of the ball arrives and Mrs Eversholt is very pleased with her gown. As she parades in front of her husband and son, who both look very handsome in their fancy evening suits, Lily enters the room and takes everyone's breath away; she is a vision of sweetness, innocence, and femininity. She is wearing an exquisite gown that mixes all the beauty and form-hugging allure of the traditional qipao dress, with the delicacy of lace and beadwork she has learned as a Western-style seamstress. Mrs Eversholt praises her work on both gowns, but secretly she is jealous of Lily's youthful beauty. She is also displeased that her son seems to have really noticed Lily for the first time. Do you think you can guess what happens at the ball?'

'Charles falls for Lily and the parents throw a fit?' I suggested.

Paris smiled. 'It is true that Charles and Lily are the talk of the ball, and they spend every moment together. Everyone wants to know who Lily is, so Charles makes up a story about her; they pretend she's the daughter of one of his father's managers. Mr Eversholt backs up this story, knowing this is just a one-evening liaison, and Mrs Eversholt is happy at first because people keep complimenting her on her dress; she tells everyone "a wonderful little girl who works just for me" made it for her. By the end of the evening she has a list of people who want to use her "wonderful little girl" to make dresses for them – so many, in fact, she could open her own dressmaking business. She becomes angry when Lily tells people her dress was made by the same "little girl" who made Mrs Eversholt's. The evening wears on, and Charles Eversholt becomes more and more entranced by Lily; they have never spoken much before, so it is the first time for him to hear her whole life story. He doesn't just fall for her, he wants to help her and her family back in their village. By the end of the night, Lily has forgotten how heartbroken she felt a few days earlier and is, once again, bewitched by the pale skin and almost-round eyes of the half-Chinese Charles. Charles too is under a spell; in Lily he sees hard-working innocence and a simple loving heart, not the idle scheming and primping of his mother, her friends, and their daughters. He tells Lily he wants to go back to her village with her when she leaves in a few days, and says he will help on the family farm. His father overhears this conversation and is very angry; he hasn't paid for his son to have an expensive education with a view to one day taking over his business empire, to have him run off with a Chinese peasant to work on a farm. But he keeps his anger hidden and, when they all get back to the house after the ball, he says nothing to his son, but tells his wife of his plans. Can you guess what they were?'

'To send the son away? To send the girl away? Depends which was more convenient, I suppose,' I answered.

'You're good, professor,' laughed Paris. 'Of course, I hope there'll be a whole bunch of ideas being thrown around every time I stop – and I know the older ones will tease the younger ones in the family, and vice versa – but you get the idea, right? So do you think I'm stopping at the right places?'

I gave him the reassurance he needed. He was an engaging storyteller – his voice was interesting to listen to, and he was using a pleasant, slightly archaic form of language that lent itself to the story and the time in which it was set. Bolstered, Paris continued.

'The following evening, Lily asks Mrs Eversholt for the money she is due from her time with the household. Now Mrs Eversholt is in a quandary – should she give the money to Lily knowing that Charles is planning to run away with her, or should she hold onto the money so Lily cannot go? Mrs Eversholt is a clever, sly woman, so she decides on a compromise; she tells Lily she will have the money for her in two days, and Lily does not mind this delay because, although she wants to go back to her mother, her main concern is to be with Charles. That evening Lily and Charles sneak out to meet in a small public garden in the French Concession, where they are unlikely to be recognized. They are very much in love and they cannot stop kissing each other on the hands, on the lips . . .'

I had to break in, 'Okay Paris, I get the idea – that's enough of the romance. When do we get to the murder?' I was mindful that, although I had no plans for the evening, I did actually *want* an evening.

Paris snapped back into student mode, apologized, then happily paraphrased for me, 'I can make that bit go on as long as I like – the women'll love it and the boys'll all shout and jeer because it's soppy. But nothing happens till the next day, so I'll pick it up then.'

'Okay,' I accepted, thankfully.

'The next morning, Lily is called to Mr Eversholt's study. When she enters the study she sees Mr and Mrs Eversholt, but no Charles. They give Lily the money she has earned by working for Mrs Eversholt, and they tell her she can leave when she likes, as they had promised she could. Lily is distraught, but cannot show her feelings, so she asks if she can say goodbye to Charles before she leaves. Mr Eversholt tells her that Charles has already left for America, where he will work at Mr Eversholt's oil wells and marry a beautiful, well-educated young oil heiress in Texas. The Eversholts are pleasant and helpful to Lily, and they pretend to be excited that they were able to get her money a day early for her. They also pretend to not notice her tears, and soon the distraught and brokenhearted girl is leaving the mansion, with a train ticket, the money she has earned, plus a big bonus. She walks to the railway station, sad, and crying all the way, and there she waits for the train that will take her most of the way to her village. As she waits, she paces up and down, and then she sees something she cannot believe – she sees Charles! He is across the tracks from her. Lily runs up and down the platform waving her arms and shouting loudly. Eventually Charles sees her. Lily calls to him "I love you", and Charles calls back that he loves her too. And with that he sets off to run across the railway tracks to reach Lily. Can you guess what happens next?'

'Oh good grief, Paris, don't tell me it gets *really* gory at this point. Does he get squished?'

'Charles Eversholt does not get "squished", but I am hoping for lots of unpleasant suggestions from the boys at this stage – and maybe lots of squealing from the girls. Do you like it?'

I nodded, it was a good way to keep the younger ones involved.

'Charles reaches Lily, and tells her he'll never let her go. His father has told him that Lily had run away, having stolen some silver from the house. Lily tells Charles how sad she was to hear that he will marry someone in America. They realize how Charles's parents have lied to them both, and take the train to Lily's home together, with high hopes of a future that will not be blighted by Charles's father or mother. A few days later they reach Lily's village, and discover Lily's mother is very weak, but she gives her blessing for their marriage, which takes place the very next day. Because China is such a large place, it takes some weeks for word to reach the Eversholts about what their son has done, but when they find out they decide to confront him at Lily's village. When they finally get there they stay at the local inn, and send word to their son – who is now living with his new wife on Lily's family farm – that they wish to meet with him in their rooms. When Charles arrives at the inn, their argument is heard by everyone – the whole village knows in moments that Charles will never receive a penny of his inheritance if he stays with Lily, and that the Eversholts are horrified by his marriage to a peasant. Furthermore, Mr Eversholt is overheard threatening to have "the whore" thrashed to within an inch of her life, until she confesses her cunning, gold-digging plans. Charles argues loudly on behalf of Lily's honor, but finally leaves his bitter parents at the inn, returning to the farm. There he tells Lily and her family of what has taken place.' Paris paused and said, 'Ready for the Big Moment?'

'Yep – let's do it!' I chuckled.

'The next morning, the Eversholts' servants find them both dead in their beds. They have not been injured in any way, so the assumption is they have been poisoned. They have also been robbed of their jewelry and money, but the local police discount this as a ruse, and immediately rush to arrest Charles Eversholt because news of the argument the day before has reached them, via the servants. But when the police arrive at Lily's family farm they discover the young married couple has fled. Lily's mother is dying, in her bed; she tells the police the young couple decided to leave before Mr Eversholt had a chance to carry out his threat of having Lily beaten. Lily's mother is clearly distressed by her daughter's flight and is failing fast; she tells the police that, very late the night before, her daughter and her son-in-law ran into the house within minutes of each other, they forced her to accept most of their money, and then Lily had told her she would never see her again. Lily and Charles Eversholt have disappeared, and are never heard of again. The very next day, Lily's mother dies.'

I found the set-up absolutely satisfying. 'Nicely told,' I said. 'And?'

'The question is, of course – who killed the Eversholts? Was it Charles, desperate to save Lily? Was it Lily, from a desire to rescue her husband from a tyrannical father? Was it Lily's mother who wanted to save her darling daughter, and allow her happiness? Or was it the work of unknown bandits or thieves, or even the Eversholts' own servants?' Paris stopped, and smiled.

'And that's as far as you've got with your story?' I was a bit exasperated to say the least.

'Yes,' said Paris defensively. 'And that's the problem. I want everyone to guess who did it, because that's the fun of it. But I need to know for myself.'

'You don't know?' I sounded as annoyed as I felt. He shook his head. 'How on earth can you begin to write a murder mystery without knowing who did it, Paris? Doesn't the entire tale hang upon the psychological profiles of the characters?'

'I guess,' he said, hesitantly.

I took a deep breath. 'Let's start at the other end, then. What was the poison? How was it administered? How easy would it have been to get it into the Eversholt's food, or drink? Who would have known about the poison? How easy would it be to get hold of? There are so many questions, Paris. I think you need a bit more work at the end; the romance stuff is all pretty well worked up – but I think you need to give the crime details a bit more attention.'

Paris pulled a lined notepad and a pen out of his backpack.

'That's just the kinda thing I need to know – so what should I tell them?' He waited with his pen poised.

I decided it was best to get it over with as quickly as possible, so I dumped the technique I usually employ when students ask me what they should do; instead of turning the question back to Paris and asking him what he thought, I just plain gave him my opinion.

'You need to give more information about the poison; tell them what it was, how it's come by, and how it could have been administered.' Paris was scribbling away. 'By the way, did you "research" that element?' I still didn't want to let on I knew he was lying.

'The poison used was a wild plant's root; the police knew that because of signs on the bodies. Everyone in my family will know it; it's often used in Chinese medicine, in tiny quantities, but, like so many of the things traditionally used, it can become deadly when taken in large concentrations. It's sweet when you eat it as a root, still not unpleasant when dried and powdered, but becomes bitter when mixed with water. Back in the day I guess they'd all have known about it.'

'Not all, Paris,' I pointed out. 'In many cultures, and certainly in Chinese culture, medicine is something that's dealt with by a small group of people who keep their secret knowledge just that – secret; those who possess such knowledge pass it on, but not to everyone – only to a select few. So the use of such a poison puts Lily's mother squarely into the frame, and maybe Lily herself; Charles wouldn't be likely to know about the poison, given his background.'

'But Charles's mother was Chinese,' interrupted Paris, 'she might have taught him stuff when he was little, and maybe he remembered what she'd told him when he needed to.' He didn't sound, or look, terribly sure of himself.

'It seems unlikely, Paris, but, okay let's assume knowledge of the poison itself doesn't necessarily narrow our field of suspects. How does it act, by the way – is it fast, or slow? What sort of time frame are we looking at for the deaths?'

Paris perked up. 'Now that's a good one. I could mention that; it all depends how much a person eats – the more they eat, the quicker it acts, but since no one knew when the Eversholts died exactly, other than at some time during the night, it doesn't help.'

I wasn't deliriously happy about how things were going, but I guessed he had a reason for being so cagey. 'Okay then, let's move on. What about opportunity? Who could have got the poison into the Eversholts' bodies, and how? You told me they weren't injured in any way, so they must have ingested it somehow, I suppose.'

Paris put down his pen and focused on the ceiling as he spoke. 'Right. The dinner and dessert were served by the Eversholts' servants in their first-floor rooms at the inn. However, the kitchens on the ground floor at the inn could have been accessed by anyone, and everything was left there unattended at some time or another. Also, there was a sort of balcony that ran around the entire first floor, so anyone could have climbed the external stairs and gained access that way. The food, the drink, the desserts – they were all available for tampering with at any time.'

I was beginning to get the picture, and his detailed knowledge of the setting for the murders was starting to reveal his duplicity. 'So you're saying any one of our list of suspects could have put the poisonous root into the food or drink the Eversholts consumed that night?'

'Yeah, that's right.' Paris was beginning to look quite excited.

I picked him up on it, deciding to be kind as I did so. 'I think there's some sort of plot afoot here, Paris. Are you trying to get me to solve a *real* case for you?'

He looked at his notepad, then studied his pen. 'It's just a story that I want to tell,' was his final, pathetic attempt to hoodwink me.

I decided to play along a little longer. 'Okay then, Paris – we've dealt with means, and opportunity, without eliminating anyone, and we're clear on motives, right?'

'I guess.'

Finally, I was beginning to get impatient. 'Paris, you've told the story in such a way that anyone can see Lily would have killed to free her husband, Charles would have killed to be free of his parents, Lily's mother would have killed to save her daughter and, possibly, the Eversholts' servants or an unknown thief might have killed for the stolen items – or some other reason you haven't told me about. Is that about it?'

'Uh huh,' was the only thing I got out of him as he dropped his head even further.

I pushed on. 'Research tells us that most murders are committed by men; however, when women do kill, they often use poisons and other things, like pills, which don't require physical violence. In this case, however, poison might have been used so the victims didn't have a chance to cry out in the night – drawing attention to their plight – so it could be the tool of either a female, or a cautious male. Everyone could have known about the poison and how to use it, anyone could have administered it into the food. Was there any forensic or medical information you haven't mentioned?'

'There was an autopsy, but the local guy did it, and all he told anyone was that the Eversholts had eaten the poison. He wasn't very sophisticated.' Paris was dragging his storytelling feet.

I could picture a rudimentary slice and dice being carried out in a mud-washed room in rural China back in the 1930s, and realized I was getting a bit ahead of myself. I reined in my desire to push ahead and tried to be methodical. First of all I had to get Paris to come clean about a few family facts.

'Will your grandparents be at the party this weekend?' I asked, all innocence.

Paris looked nervous and mumbled, 'Yeah' under his breath.

'Do you think they're going to like this story?'

'I guess.'

I decided this was the moment to confront him. 'Lily and Charles are real people and members of your family, aren't they? This is a real case from your family's history in Shanghai, isn't it?'

He bit his lip, and didn't make eye contact with me. 'Not exactly.'

'What do you mean, "not exactly"?' I pressed.

'You know Sandra Redmond?'

'Your girlfriend?' I knew Paris and Sandra had been a couple for years – they were hardly ever seen apart, had taken all the same classes as each other, and were generally thought of as an odd, but strangely well-matched couple. She was a pretty, blue-eyed blond, and a good Canadian girl through and through – the type who enjoys kayaking, and running the Grouse Grind – while Paris was whacky, off-beat, and enjoyed using his appearance to shock and challenge.

Paris nodded. 'Yes, my Sandra.' His face softened as he spoke her name. 'Charles and Lily were her great-grandparents, on her mother's side.'

I was surprised.

'So Lily and Charles made off to Canada, where they lived in poverty and happiness?' I asked.

Paris's voice was heavy. 'Kinda. It turns out they traveled across Asia and Europe by land, then got a ship to Canada. Lily gave birth to Sandra's grandmother pretty quick, and they all lived in Halifax for years. It was about as far away from China as they could get. And they *were* poor, and they *did* work hard, and then Sandra's grandmother married her grandfather, and they moved to Regina. Then they had her mother, and she married Sandra's dad, and they moved to Vancouver. We met here, at university.'

'Why this story then, Paris? Got some big plans, have you?'

Paris looked amazed. 'How did you guess?'

'Paris, I'm a psychologist first and foremost. Nowadays I apply my expertise to the field of profiling victims of crime, but you're not that difficult to read. You want to marry Sandra?'

Paris smiled and nodded with excitement. 'And she wants to marry me too. But . . .'

'Go on,' I encouraged him.

'You're right. This isn't just a story; it's a really famous unsolved case in Shanghai. In all of China. No one ever found out who killed the Eversholts, and everyone just sort of accepted it must have been Lily and Charles, or at least one of them. My whole family knows about the case, and when Sandra tells them about her family they'll know who she is. You see, her great-grandparents changed their names when they immigrated, but we can't begin our life together without telling my family everything. It would be very . . .' He hesitated before whispering the key word, '. . . dishonorable.'

I got it. One of the things I learned soon after my arrival in

Vancouver was that – in the Chinese community – honor, the integrity of the family unit, and the way that every generation of a family is linked to all the rest, past and future, were critical issues taken seriously by all. If Sandra was to be married to Paris, then all her ancestors would be coming along for the ride. Maybe it would be in her favor that she had Chinese blood in her, but I didn't think the Chow family would be leaping over each other to welcome the great-grandchild of probable murderers into their family.

'So you want to tell the story to convince your family it wasn't Sandra's great-grandparents who killed the Eversholts, is that it?'

Paris nodded, and added, 'But I want to prove it too. If I can. It has to be beyond doubt.'

'That's a pretty tall order, Paris. This all took place over eighty years ago; how can you prove it now?'

'I don't know. I thought, like, maybe you could help. I know you've worked on real-life cases in the past and, well, I guess I just thought, like . . .' He trailed off, audibly losing hope with every syllable.

I couldn't help but feel sorry for him; it seemed Lily and Charles weren't the only star-crossed lovers in this story. Given that I don't have a single romantic bone in my body, being a happily single forty-something-year-old, I knew I didn't want to help him for all the soppy reasons – I wanted to help him because there was a problem to be solved.

So I asked the only sensible question, 'Where've you been getting all your information, Paris? Is it all just hearsay from within Sandra's family, or do we have some real facts to go on?'

Paris passed me his folder. Inside it were newspaper clippings, articles downloaded from the Internet, photocopies of letters and cards exchanged between Lily, Charles, their daughter, and her daughter. Paris had done a thorough research job – I wouldn't have expected anything less from such a methodical and diligent student.

As I flipped through the plastic wallets protecting his treasures, I glimpsed a sepia photograph of all three Eversholts; they were posed stiffly in front of a spectacular staircase, ornate lamps flanking them. The Mr and Mrs were all I'd expected – he was upright, with slicked hair and a dress suit, she was Chinese only in her features, which she'd done her best to hide under heavy make-up and a tiara-like headdress. Charles was young, and I thought of Paris as I peered at the grainy picture. I guessed Charles would have been about twenty-two or so, and here was Paris sitting in front of me already older than that by two years, yet still in school. Charles was smiling and looking straight at the camera – he was obviously a confident young man.

As I was thinking this Paris piped up, 'That picture was taken at the ball I told you about in the story. That was the night Charles fell for Lily.'

So that was what I could see in the young man's expression – literally the first flush of love, of passion. That chemically induced state of euphoria that kids us into thinking we've found a mate for life; that rush of endorphins that makes us do the stupidest things, even if they are totally contrary to our nature, just because we believe the object of our obsession wants this of us. How stupid we become when we allow chemistry to take over our bodies.

I put the story into context as I continued to flick through the file. Two youngsters, passions boiling over, physical desires burning them up, hidebound by cultural taboos and controlling parents, the romance of a damsel in distress, the appeal of a strong, handsome young man. It really was an age-old tale.

Now to the murder; I could see a great deal of newspaper space had been given to the story in the English language newspaper in Shanghai of the day. Obviously it had been a great scandal, and much was made of the fact Lily had gone missing, and that her mother had clammed up. There didn't seem to be much of an outcry that Charles, too, had done a bunk, but I guessed that was to be expected.

Paris didn't seem to have left out any of the key facts of the story, and it was clear the local police – such as they were – had been baffled; they had no proof of any one particular person's involvement, so they couldn't bring charges against anyone, not even in absentia.

I moved on to some cards and letters Lily and Charles had given to each other over the years; obviously they'd been passed down in Sandra's family, and there were even little scribbled notes they had written to each other. It seemed that, when they'd married in China before they left for Canada, they'd become man and wife under the names of Lily and Charles Farmer, which struck me as a nice touch. It was also clear they'd spent every moment they could together, but with their working lives pulling them apart for what must have been about fifteen hours a day, their time together was never enough for the lovebirds – hence all the notes.

There were lovely little wedding anniversary notes, birthday wishes, and Christmas greetings – they wrote what was in their hearts, and seemed to share so much. Thanks to my ability to speed-read, I managed to get through the file's contents pretty quickly, then looked over at Paris.

I smiled knowingly as I asked, 'So, do you want to prove who *did* it – or do you want to prove *they didn't* do it? That's the real question – because I can help you with one, but not the other.'

I knew what his reply would be; he confirmed it when he answered, 'I want to prove they didn't do it. Can you help with that one?'

He was on the edge of his chair. All his hopes seemed to rest on my shoulders.

I tried to be as good as he thought I was.

'Look at this, Paris.' I pointed to a note that was written from a hospital bed in Halifax.

Paris read the note aloud:

> February 14th 1955. My darling Lily, I know it is difficult for you to come here and see me like this every day, especially when I have been such a strong man all my life. But we must face the fact I am dying, and you will now have to live without me. I hope you will stay with our darling daughter Joy for many years to come, and you know I will be watching over you both. She is a beautiful young girl, almost as beautiful as her mother, and you must be sure she marries that boy Ted. He's a sound young man, and will work hard to support her. I've given him my permission to ask for her hand, but I believe my illness has held him back. Don't let them wait too long; you know how it feels to want to be with someone you love. It seems strange to say goodbye to you – I feel as though you have been with me all my life, and I know the memories I have

of you will come with my soul when it leaves this sick old
body. So now is the time when I have to tell you that I forgive
you. You were stronger than me even then – I could not have
done what you did. We have never spoken of it, but I have
always known. God has blessed us with a happy life together,
and a wonderful, healthy daughter – he would not have done
that if he hadn't forgiven you. If God can forgive you, then I
can certainly do likewise. Indeed, maybe it was God's work
you were doing that night – for without your actions, we
would never have had this life together. I forgive you, and I
thank you, and I love you, my darling Lily. Charles.

'Wow,' exclaimed Paris, 'I've read that note before, but it never
clicked. I can see it now; she did it. Lily killed the Eversholts, and
Charles knew about it all along. Oh no. What'll I do? This is proof she
did it.'

Paris was distraught. I tried to calm him. 'Hang on a minute,
Paris. Read the next note, too. The one from Lily to Charles, inside
the big heart-shaped card.'

Paris flipped the plastic wallet and began to read aloud again:

February 14th 1955. Darling Charles, This will be my last
Valentine to you – we both know that, and I will not lie to you
at the end. I love you, Charles, and I have done so since I first
saw you in Madame Chang's all those years ago. You have
been my strength and my life – you have always been my
Valentine, in good times and bad. I cannot write very much,
you know how bad my eyes are these days, but I wanted to
send you this big heart and tell you that you hold mine in your
hands. I will hold your secret close to *my* heart forever. I will
never speak of it, not to one living soul. Only God knows, and
he will smile on you. Your Loving Wife, Lily.

Paris looked confused. 'I don't get it. Well, I do – I mean, I never
read it, like, *that* way before, but could she be telling him she knows
he killed his parents?'

I smiled. 'Exactly.'

Paris still looked puzzled. 'Exactly what?'

'Oh come on, Paris, you're sharper than that. Each one of them
obviously thought the other one did it. They both make that clear in
these notes.'

'So which one of them *did* do it?' Paris jumped to his feet with frustration.

'Neither of them did it, Paris. Charles knew he hadn't done it, but assumed Lily had; Lily knew she hadn't done it, and assumed Charles had. Neither of them did it – and here's the proof.'

Paris sat back down with a thump and took a moment to re-read the notes again. A smile lit up his face; his perfect teeth gleamed at me.

'You're right. It was there in front of me all the time; these two notes. I'd completely missed their significance. You're right – there's no other explanation. Sandra's going to be so happy.' He was on his feet again and grasped my hand with both of his. 'Oh Professor Morgan – I can't begin to tell you how important this is.' He had tears in his eyes, and I could feel my own begin to well up.

'It's okay, Paris, I'm really glad I could help.' I tried to calm him. 'I think you should also emphasize in your storytelling that, if Lily's mother was so sick she died just a day after the Eversholts, she couldn't possibly have done it either; so there's no chance that Sandra has a murderous ancestor at all. Play up the theft angle – I think there's a strong argument for the local authorities not taking enough notice of that. They were lawless times, Paris, and I'm sure news that a wealthy Westerner with a bejeweled Chinese wife were staying at the local inn would have reached some of the region's thieves of the day. The local police probably just didn't want to admit the murderers could have been still lurking in the area. I hope you and Sandra will be very happy together. So what will you do? Tell the story, then read the final farewell notes from Lily and Charles?'

Paris was gathering up his bits and pieces, stuffing them haphazardly into his backpack. He was distracted as he looked at me, bright-eyed. 'What? Oh yes, I'll do that. That's just what I'll do; I'll tell them a story like it's a chance to solve a crime, and when they've all worked out that the letters show both Lily and Charles were innocent, then I'll tell them who Sandra is. It'll be great; they'll all be very happy. *Gung Hei Fat Choi*, professor – Happy New Year!'

He waved as he rushed out of my office, and I could hear him speaking to Sandra on his cell phone before he'd even reached the end of the corridor. He was in for quite a life-changing weekend.

As I gathered up the mountain of scripts I needed to grade at the weekend, I could visualize the Eversholts eating their last meal together, full of anger and bigotry; I silently hoped the poison had given them as much pain as they had caused Charles and Lily – even though Paris had said it wouldn't have done so.

As I drove my old but beloved red Mazda Miata toward my little house on Burnaby mountain, I allowed my thoughts to turn to who had killed the Eversholts, rather than who hadn't. I discounted the notion of thieves in the night, and of the Eversholts' own servants killing their employers; thieves or bandits wouldn't have bothered with poison – they'd have simply battered the Eversholts to death, or – more likely – slit their throats, and the servants wouldn't have wanted to be out of a job even if they could have sneaked off with a bit of jewelry. No, since it clearly wasn't either Lily or Charles, it must have been Lily's mother.

The psychology was right; Lily's mother had a strong motive, and she'd have had both the means and the opportunity. She would certainly have risked it – and she'd have found the strength to push her feeble body beyond its normal limits for her daughter's sake. She was an aging widow, ailing, and probably under the care of a doctor, so maybe she'd had the poisonous root close to hand. I felt sure she'd have killed to ensure her daughter's happiness, knowing she was close to death herself. An old woman, maybe swathed in disguising headgear, wouldn't have been noticed sneaking through a rural inn's kitchen, or even stirring a pot, and, without a witness – and there had been none – no one would have been able to prove it was or wasn't her, either then or now. I wondered why Lily's mother hadn't given herself up to the police, in order to protect her daughter's reputation, but realized her untimely death might have prevented her from following through with any plan she had to do just that.

I was sure Paris would be able to convince his family that Lily's mother would have been too sick to do it, and to convincingly point the finger at bandits and thieves. After all, what harm was there in that? Lily's mother had wanted her daughter to be happy; I was sure she'd want her great-great-granddaughter to be happy too.

Having battled heavier than usual traffic on my short trip, I finally got home at the end of a long week and decided I deserved a drink. Just that day I'd ploughed through grading two midterms *and* solved an eighty-odd-year-old mystery, so, if anyone deserved a Bombay and tonic, it was me. As I slipped a slice of lemon into my glass I glanced at the copy of *The Globe and Mail* I'd tossed onto the kitchen table, still unread. I was amazed at the price of a barrel of oil, and my mind leaped to the Eversholt oil holdings. I wondered if they'd been left to Charles; he was the Eversholts' only son and heir, and they hadn't actually had time to change their wills before they died. I decided to mention it to Paris on Monday; after all, Sandra's family might be able to do something about claiming her birthright. She could be very rich indeed.

MARCH

Domestic Violence

The blood from Dominic's head wound pooled beneath his crumpled, dead body.

'Now, what are you going to do, Sharon Taylor?' I asked myself.

Bounty, the quicker-picker-upper flashed through my mind. Paper towels were not going to be enough; nothing would ever remove this stain from the floor.

'I hate you, Dominic. The grouting's ruined and you're bleeding all over everything. Typical.' I knew that shouting at him wouldn't help the situation, but it helped me. 'Come on, Sharon, pull yourself together,' I told myself.

If only Dominic hadn't kept going on about my hair. He certainly hadn't needed to laugh. He knew I was upset about the perm. I'll never go to that dreadful hairdresser again. I'd said that. And he knew I'd been crying all afternoon about it. So why did he have to laugh? It really wasn't necessary.

And now there he was. Dead in the middle of the den.

Maybe if I hadn't had the poker in my hand when he'd laughed at me, there wouldn't be this mess. But, as it was, I had no choice. I had to stop him laughing. I supposed at least I'd managed that.

If only I'd killed him in the bathroom; that would have been much easier to clean up – a couple of bottles of bleach and I'd be done. Now it would be much more difficult to get rid of the evidence.

I rolled Dominic onto his back with my foot.

It was real unfair of him to laugh at my hair disaster. Frankly, he was no oil painting himself. I looked at my reflection in the mirror above the fireplace. I thought maybe I *could* go back to Cynthia and ask her to cut my hair short. That would get rid of most of the perm, and it might even kinda suit me. After all, now that Dominic was gone I'd be getting back into the dating scene again.

But first, I had the floor, and the body, to sort out.

By nine o'clock I'd just about finished clearing up, except for actually burying the body; that would have to wait until later. I was just in time to sit down and watch a *CSI* rerun. Just as well I've 'wasted so much time' watching this 'rubbish' as Dominic always called it. Nowadays I know lots of stuff about all types of things that make it much easier to clean up properly after a murder. All I have to do this time is tile over the tiles that are already on the floor, and I'll be fine. Tiling is pretty easy, really; I don't know why men make such a fuss about it, and now's a good time of year to get supplies in the March Madness sales. I'll go for a neutral color; they always say neutral's best on those home makeover shows.

But the den will do for now; there's not a drop of blood to be seen with the naked eye – just the fresh smell of bleach, and a hint of citrus disinfectant in the air.

I wasn't always so knowledgeable about cleaning up after such an incident, of course. When Barry and I had that run-in in Saskatoon six years ago, I had to replace the whole back deck before I moved. That was a pain, and expensive too; I had to take the whole thing down, burn it, and rebuild a new one, because you just can't get blood out of wood, no matter how hard you try. That Luminol they have these days is too clever by half.

The entire project took me weeks, and all the time people kept dropping in with cakes and stews to tell me how sorry they were that Barry the Beast – my pet name for him – had run out on me. Little did they know that all those fires in the back yard hadn't just been to 'get rid of mold', but had been pretty good cover for burning the body parts too.

Of course, all this nonsense with Dominic means I'll have to start over. Again. It's not easy trying to move on. With nothing. Name changes cost good money. But, after Barry I did it all okay; I picked myself up, moved to Vancouver, and met Dominic. I guess we've been pretty happy. Until last week, that is. I should have seen this coming, then.

Dominic was like Barry in so many ways: demanding his dinner be on the table when he came through the door at night; scowling whenever I spent any money on myself. It's not as though he'd let me work, so of course it was all 'his' money. He'd even started to mention how much I was spending on cleaning products. He seemed to have no idea that a woman needs a well-stocked cupboard under the sink, just in case.

CSI was kinda disappointing – it was a real old repeat. It was the one where they find the woman's body in the sandbox, and Grissom flirts with the dominatrix madam. Not a bad episode, I guess, but I don't think they need to bring sex into it quite so much. Not everything's about sex. Sex is pretty unimportant when you compare it with companionship.

That's not what Dominic thought. I found all those magazines in the garage on Friday. Filthy beast. He tried to make out he was 'holding them for a buddy'. Yeah, right. I didn't think they even printed those things anymore. Maybe they don't. Maybe he's had them for years.

I'm no tart, not like the women in those magazines. He liked that about me when we met. He liked that I was quiet, and cooked him nice meals in my basement apartment. He liked that I insisted we got married before we did the full sex thing. And, to be fair, he did seem to go off it pretty fast after the wedding. Which was good. And then there are always headaches to fall back on. So we got by quite well, really.

I guess it'll be easy enough to get used to sleeping alone again; it's almost spring and the weather will be getting warmer, not colder. His feet were always freezing in the winter anyway, so at least I won't have to put up with that any more.

I'll need an early start in the morning; best set the alarm for 5 a.m. I never wanted to live on acreage in the back of beyond, but it was Dominic's money so I had to agree. As it all turns out, that's a pretty good thing now; I can drag his body behind the compost pile when it's dark, then put him under the flower bed I was planning for the far side of the septic field. All the plants are there, ready to go. We're pretty isolated out here, but if someone were to catch a glimpse of me from the road pulling his body from the house, that wouldn't be good. So I can do the rest tomorrow in daylight, but get him out of the house in the dark.

What a day it's been.

It all started when I got up and dragged Dominic's body out to the side of the house. By half past eight I'd dug a real big hole, covered him over, had my breakfast, *and* I'd finished the planting. It should look pretty nice by July – lots of yellows and oranges; I like bright flowers. And quite a few are perennials, so I won't have to keep replanting every year, which always saves a lot of work and expense.

Then they called from Dom's work, Webster's Wood Products. I'd been expecting the call. They wondered where he was, of course. I said he'd gone off to the office at the mill as usual that morning, and I hadn't heard from him since. Wouldn't expect to. They said there must have been a mix up. I said okay. That was that.

I don't know what they meant by a 'mix up'; he goes to work every day, so they must expect him every day. How can something so simple get 'mixed up'? Maybe they thought he was supposed to be at one of his Downtown meetings instead of at the mill itself. Maybe he *was* supposed to be at a meeting, I don't know, and I really don't care. But I did try to sound a little worried when the girl spoke to me; they often talk about 'affect and intonation' on the TV shows I watch, so I hope I got that bit right.

Once I'd got them off the phone, I drove Dom's truck along the back roads to the Canadian Tire parking lot where they don't have any cameras. Thanks for that handy hint, Mr Grissom. Just in case anyone saw me, I wore one of Dom's old shirts and his floppy old gardening hat; another thing I've learned from TV is they say people only remember shapes, not faces, so that's good.

After I'd dumped the truck, taken off his clothes, and thrown his keys into the river, I walked over to Cynthia's Salon. I cried a bit when I got there and told her that my husband hadn't been very kind about my new hair-do, so she cut my hair for free and we all agreed it looked much better. She said I can go back in a month for a tidy-up at no charge. She's not so bad really, just young, I guess.

I caught the bus home. I'd been wearing a bandage on my wrist to make out that I'd hurt myself gardening and that's why I couldn't drive, so if I bumped into anyone I knew on the bus I'd be covered. It's a decent walk from the bus stop, but it gave me time to think. I planned how I'd re-organize the closet when I got rid of all Dom's stuff; I'll use the bags from Big Brothers BC – they're always grateful for cast-offs.

But when I got home, who should be there but the police!

I must admit I got a shock when I turned the corner and saw them at the front door. For a minute I thought about just keeping on walking, but I realized that was plain silly, and that I should find out what they wanted.

And I'm glad I did. Well, kinda.

There was a cute young girl in casual street-clothes, called Sally, and a Staff Sergeant Broquet. Pleasant enough guy in his late forties. Kinda glum-looking. Well pressed uniform.

I let them in, and offered them tea, and cake or cookies. I asked them if they liked my hair because I'd just had it done, and they said they liked it very much. Then the guy in the uniform told me they'd come about Dominic.

I gotta admit, I wondered what they meant.

They asked me when I'd last seen him, and I told them he'd gone off to work as usual that morning. Then I told them that the folks had called from the mill to say he wasn't there, but that, no, I wasn't worried because I knew he often went into the Downtown area for meetings, so I assumed that was where he'd gone.

Then they hit me with the bombshell.

The cop in the well-pressed uniform spoke first. Nice voice. French speaker, so he was kinda formal.

'I'm sorry to inform you, Mrs Taylor, that we are urgently seeking an interview with your husband. Usually we would not divulge details, but we are concerned that you might try to shield him. Let me assure you that would not be a good idea.'

I noticed he looked over at the girl Sally as he spoke to me. He seemed to be urging her to carry on for him, but he didn't catch her eye. Finally he turned his face toward me again, but I noticed that his eyes weren't looking directly into mine. He cleared his throat. I couldn't imagine what he was about to tell me. Or ask.

'There's no easy way to say this, Mrs Taylor, so I'll just tell you outright.'

He seemed to pause for a whole minute. I actually felt my eyes open as wide as they could as I waited for him to speak.

Eventually he said, 'We have CCTV footage that shows a man clearly identifiable as your husband entering a hotel room in Downtown Vancouver with a known prostitute yesterday afternoon where, shortly after he left the room, she was found to have been . . . violently murdered.'

He let it sink in.

I must admit, it took a moment.

I sipped my tea and took another cookie – my home-made oatmeal with dried apricot, real tasty, if I do say so myself.

'You mean my Dom was in a hotel? Downtown? Yesterday?' I'm sure I sounded genuinely surprised. I gotta admit, I was.

'I'm afraid so, Mrs Taylor.' When she finally spoke, Sally had a sweet voice. Local girl. West Coast. Even so, I didn't think this was the sort of thing a girl of her age should be worrying about; she looked to be in her early twenties. 'It seems he was a regular client of this particular prostitute, ma'am.' She seemed real upset about it.

I sipped again.

'And you think he's murdered this . . . woman?' I didn't want to say the other word.

'I'm afraid so, ma'am,' the girl replied. She seemed kind, but too thin, of course. They're all too thin these days. She continued, looking at the cop, then me. 'We're really in very little doubt about this case. We know they went in together, at which time she was fine. We know Mr Taylor came out alone, and we have several of your husband's fingerprints on the –' she glanced at the cop – 'murder weapon, and inside the room.' Her eyes were big and round, and she looked real sad.

It sounded pretty damning. And I was sure there was more they weren't telling me. They always hold something back, don't they? Then they can catch out the murderer when they give themselves away by knowing something the police never told anyone.

The cop spoke next. 'Did you notice anything unusual about your husband when he came home last night? Did he maybe rush to change his clothing? Was he unusually excitable?'

I thought back to the previous evening. I tried to be honest.

'I guess he was a bit more picky than usual,' I admitted. 'We had a row about my hair. He thought the perm I'd had was a mess, so I went and got it all cut off this morning. He was right. But he didn't need to be so nasty about it.'

Sally and the cop exchanged a knowing look.

'Might we see the clothes your husband wore yesterday?' asked the cop.

I pictured the blood-soaked shirt and muddy pants clinging to Dom's body, buried beneath the soil close to the windows through which I was staring.

'Now that could be a problem,' I admitted. I put down my cup and looked them each straight in the eye – her first. Her eyebrows arched in query.

My mind whirred and clicked into place. 'After we had the row, I made Dom sleep in the spare room. When he went off to work this morning he had the same clothes on as yesterday because I wouldn't let him into the bedroom to get fresh ones.'

I picked up my tea; I needed a sip of something hot and sweet. They nodded. They understood.

'I'm real sorry,' I added. 'It sounds so horrible now.' I shook my head helplessly. *Intonation and affect. Intonation and affect.* I let the cup and saucer shake a little as I held it. Sally took them from me. She patted my hand.

They left pretty soon afterwards. Sally said she'd stay with me, but I said no, I'd rather be alone. They were real keen that I promised to get in touch with them if Dom were to contact me. I guess they'll tap the phone line now, and probably keep an eye on the house too.

It's just as well I buried him this morning, I'd never have been able to do it this afternoon.

They'll never give up looking for Dom, they say. It's been six months now and they still haven't tracked him down. Of course, they weren't surprised that he'd disappeared. They'd even expected it. The Victim Support people have been real nice; they see me as a victim too, you see, which is right in a way. I've had to get a job to support myself, which they've helped out with. Working in an office isn't so bad, but I'm still not sure if I can afford to keep the house on. It's a worry, I gotta admit.

Sally and I have become pretty friendly. *She* thinks it's fine for me to date now; tell the truth, she's encouraging me. She's always trying to get me to meet new people. In fact, I'm off to the Royal Canadian Mounted Police Fall Ball on Friday with a nice widower who used to work in the criminalistics office. Not out in the field like they do on TV, more on the filing side. We get along just fine. Brian's his name. He's almost bald, but he likes my cooking. Brian's real concerned about his teeth, which is a good thing when you're in your late fifties.

I might let him kiss me soon, I guess, but I'm still a married woman really. I have to wait before I can divorce Dom due to desertion, but Brian says that's okay; he understands that we are seeing each other under *very* unusual circumstances.

Brian loves gardening. He was real impressed with my new flower bed. He even helped me keep the weeds under control through the late summer. He's so good around the place. Handy. Three acres is a lot to look after when you're alone.

Brian has a cute little condo in New Westminster. He's mentioned that it has plenty of space for two, and I'll admit it would be much easier to keep clean than this old place, but I can't sell the house because it's joint property. All I can do is keep it and keep paying the mortgage, or stop paying the mortgage and they'll take it away from me. Now that would be a real shame. And, of course, someone might choose to dig up that new flower bed, and I can't have that.

I guess I'll have to stick it out at the place for as long as I can. If I do have to move Dom I'd rather do it when he's just bones; he'll be at the messy stage about now. I had to deal with one of those about twenty years ago, and I swore then I'd never touch the stuff again. Disgusting gloop.

Luckily, Brian has said he might move into my basement and help me out with the mortgage payments. Maybe we can talk about that again on Friday. I reckon I saw a gleam in his eye when he mentioned it; he might think we could share a room. But, of course, that would be out of the question while I'm still married. I'll ask him what he really meant when he picks me up to go to the ball.

I just hope he doesn't turn out to be like all the others. Dominic and Barry were bad enough, not to mention Ben and Ted. And Gordy, back East? He was a real pain. I hope Brian's different. I deserve a good one this time.

APRIL

Negroni

Doug Rossi considered himself a lucky man: he'd been born to a loving couple; raised in a small but caring community on the west coast of Scotland; married his childhood sweetheart, and ran a well-established family business – Rossi's Fish and Chips – with a prime location on the seafront.

Most other people in the village considered Doug cursed: he was the only child of five siblings to survive infancy; his fisherman father had been lost at sea when Doug was very young, leaving his mother to run a foundering chip shop alone, then she had died just weeks after his eighteenth birthday; his wife of seventeen years had recently been killed when her car hit a stray cow and – to top it all – the local council was insisting Doug make thousands of pounds' worth of alterations to his ramshackle chip shop, or be closed down.

As Doug always said: it was how you looked at a thing that made it what it was, and if you just took the bitter with the sweet, it would usually all work out for the best. In the end.

The one thing *everyone* in the community agreed upon was that when Doug won the lottery it was marvelous; he could get the building work done on his shop, afford to take himself off on holiday while it was being carried out, and he'd have a nice little nest egg when he returned.

And they were right; when Doug arrived at the bustling airport in Florence, he wasn't a sad or bitter man in need of a pick-me-up. No, Doug Rossi was a man on a mission; he'd gone to the City of the Lily to find his roots, his Italian-Rossi roots, and he just *knew* he was going to have a wonderful time doing it. Of course he wished his late wife could have been with him, but he'd been working hard on coming to terms with her loss, and had decided to make the most of his one chance to see the land his immigrant grandfather had always referred to with teary eyes and a wistful smile.

There was a lot he wanted to see – the Uffizi, the Duomo, and the Baptistery, just for starters; he'd heard stories about them all his life, and now he would get to see them for himself. But, more than just visiting the tourist spots, he wanted to taste Italy, to smell it, to *feel* it – he wanted to know what it was to *be* Italian. What he hadn't planned on doing was stumbling across a vicious murder and getting dragged into a blood vendetta that would threaten his very life. But then again, who would?

As the driver who'd collected him at the airport zigged and zagged through the frantic suburban traffic, Doug wondered if he'd done the right thing booking a place so far outside the center of the city. However, when the car finally swept into the gardens that surrounded the Hotel Villa de Luca, Doug was comforted; the faded, yet clearly once-grand ochre façade of the hotel made him feel strangely calm, the symmetrical windows either side of the portico entrance glittering in the spring sunshine. It was an inexplicable sensation; everything felt 'just right' to the recently widowed Scottish chip shop owner. He was treated with the utmost respect and gentility by the staff, who welcomed him with flawless and charmingly accented English.

Once settled in his room, Doug sent out a silent 'thank you' to the nameless girl at the travel agents' in Scotland who'd all but forced him to book a deluxe double room, rather than the single that had been his first choice; his room was opulent, yet homey, with an extraordinary mix of ancient and modern furnishings. He surveyed the view from his private balcony, entranced; all of Florence lay before him, just across the river – a medley of shadow-strewn red roof tiles, ochre stone, soaring towers and, above it all, that wonderful ribbed Duomo, of which his grandfather had always spoken with such affection. As Doug breathed in the sweetness of the fresh spring air he could hear bells chiming in the distance, and birds singing joyfully in the trees beneath him. The chip shop in Scotland seemed to exist in another lifetime for Doug, and the mellow light settling on the gardens around him reminded him of . . . nothing; it was all unique to that moment, and place.

Doug had feared he'd be too tired for dinner after a long day of traveling, but realized he was quite peckish. He wasn't, however, feeling terribly adventurous, so unpacked his meager supplies of clothing into a massive antique wardrobe, and decided to eat at the hotel itself, before returning to his room for an early night.

Outside the grandly-chandeliered ballroom that housed the hotel's restaurant, he noted with annoyance that it was closed that evening for a private event; an arrow pointed to the bar, promising a full menu from seven o'clock. With two hours to kill before the possibility of having something to eat, Doug toyed with the idea of taking a walk around the hotel's gardens, but decided to go to the bar first and have a cup of coffee, to give himself a bit of a lift. He perused a selection of brochures about the attractions of the city displayed on a large pod in the entryway; reading them would give him something to do to pass the time before dinner.

As he contemplated the choice of leaflets, he couldn't help but notice a tall, slim, dark-haired woman standing just inside the front doors of the villa. She was screaming in Italian into her mobile telephone, and gesticulating wildly with her free hand. Impeccably dressed in a flowing fuschia trouser suit, she seemed to fit her surroundings perfectly, whereas Doug felt a bit like a duck out of water.

Wandering uncertainly into the bar, he ordered a cappuccino, then watched with fascination as the barman engaged in a ballet of activity that resulted in the production of a frothing beverage. Doug felt he should have applauded as the young man set the drink on the tiny glass table in front of him with a flourish, but his attention was grabbed by the woman he'd seen earlier, as her heels clattered across the bar's intricately inlaid marble floor. She threw herself into a chair close to Doug's, then shouted something at the server in a rich, deep voice that was both commanding and soothing. She spoke to Doug in rapid-fire Italian as she lit a long, slim cigarette. He had no idea what she'd said, but decided the best course of action was to smile politely and drink his coffee.

As Doug replaced his cup on the table – having finally found a drop or two of liquid beneath a pillow of foam – the woman started to laugh. It was a throaty, joyous sound. Once again she called out to Doug, and this time he knew he had to acknowledge her in some way other than just grinning inanely.

'I'm sorry, I don't speak Italian,' he shouted – slowly – to allow for the fact she was foreign.

'You face – you face!' she called back.

Doug made the international sign of not understanding – he held up his hands and shrugged his shoulders, while smiling and shaking his head.

The woman unwound herself from her chair. She strode to the bar, picked up a napkin, then waggled it in front of Doug.

'You face – you have cappuccino here,' she shouted, pointing at her own face.

Doug crossed his eyes to look down; sure enough, a little mound of cappuccino foam was sitting on the tip of his nose. He wiped it off, and felt himself flush with embarrassment.

'*Mille grazie,*' he said, then added, '*Grazie mille,*' just in case he'd got the words the wrong way around.

'You welcome.' The woman shouted her response despite the fact she was just inches away. 'You English?' she asked as she folded herself into the chair opposite Doug's, uninvited.

Doug straightened his back. 'No, I'm Scottish, not English.'

The woman puffed out cigarette smoke as she spoke. 'This is very different, I know. I have met Scottish guests before. They tell me.' To the server, she called, 'Mario, I have my drink here with Meester . . .' She paused and looked at Doug.

'Rossi,' supplied Doug.

'With Meester Rossi,' she shouted. Dropping her voice a little, she spoke directly to Doug, 'You have an Italian name, Meester Rossi. It is for red, like you hair.' She smiled broadly at Doug's copper waves, then added, 'You have family here in Firenze? In Florence? You are Fiorentino?'

Doug replied as clearly as possible, 'I know it's where my family came from, but I don't think any of them are still here, now.'

'So why you come?'

Doug wasn't used to anyone being as direct as this woman, and her truncated use of the English language made her seem rather brusque; he felt as though she was telling him off all the time. But he felt oddly freed from what would have been his normal, polite reserve, and saw no harm in talking to an unknown, beautiful woman in a hotel bar. And beautiful she was; he'd noticed that immediately. To his eyes, in any case. She reminded Doug of a champion racehorse; all perfectly proportioned and sleekly put together, but if you studied each feature, she wasn't what you'd call pretty.

As Doug was wondering how to explain why he'd come, and why he'd been able to come, he looked at his coffee and decided not to risk another mouthful. When the server brought the woman's drink, which chinked refreshingly in a fancy crystal glass, he asked what it was.

'It is a Negroni – you will like it!' She spoke to the boy, 'Another Negroni like this, with soda.' She turned to Doug and declaimed, 'In the daytime it is better with soda, it will take long to drink. You will like it. It is invented here, in Firenze, in the 1920s. At Casoni Bar. You must take mine. Cin Cin!'

Doug felt he had little option but to take the glass she was forcing upon him. He sipped the reddish liquid with care, unsure what to expect. His taste buds felt as though they were about to burst; the drink was fragrant and, at first, sweet at the front of his tongue, and on his lips. Then, as he swallowed, a wave of intense bitterness hit him; his mouth felt cleansed. The singed orange peel balanced on the edge of the glass gave the experience an extra dimension, the pungent oils settling in his nose and making the flavor of the drink even more complex.

'It's like a wee work of art in a glass,' he said quietly, addressing the drink itself, more than the woman opposite.

She sat back and looked at Doug through narrowed eyes. 'You understand what is difficult. Complicated. This is good. So, why you come here, in Firenze?'

Once again the woman was challenging Doug to give an answer he wasn't sure of himself. So he just let loose, and told her everything that was whirling about in his head.

'My wife just died, and then I won the lottery. I had to leave my business for a while because otherwise it would be closed down. I own a fish and chip shop. A *ristorante*.' He was pleased to show off another Italian word. 'I thought I'd come to the home of my ancestors to see what it was my family left behind. Oh, and the art here – I'd like to see some art too, and I know there's a lot of that. I've never had much time for art, and I'd like to put that right. In fact, I've never had much time for life; it's all been work, work, work, and I'd like to put that right too. So, here I am.' He paused and sipped his drink, enjoying the sweet-bitter flavor once again.

'Ah,' said the woman, lighting another cigarette, 'you come to fill emptiness. It is a good place to do this. But first you have to learn what is empty, so you know how to fill it up correctly.' She reached up and took the drink the barman was offering her, and once again 'Cin, Cin-ed' then drank.

Doug smiled. He felt wonderful.

'A wee work of art in a glass? This is good,' she reflected, returning Doug's smile.

Doug rested back into his chair and allowed the Negroni and the late afternoon light to wash over him as the woman spoke.

'Me, I am Antonia – Antonia de Luca. I am from here.' She waved imperiously, and Doug took her words to mean she was from Florence. 'I leave when I am young, but I come back, and now I cannot leave again or they change the place, and I do not want this. I must stay now to find my inheritance from my family. If they change the house my chance will go away. I must not let them do this.'

Doug was confused; deciding he should be as direct as she'd

been, he asked, 'Do you mean you come from this villa? You own the hotel?'

Antonia laughed her throaty laugh. 'Ah, if only I owned this place.' She smiled and put her drink onto the glass table that lay between them. She leaned toward Doug. 'My great-grandfather, he build this house for my great-grandmother around one hundred and fifty years ago – they are very wealthy people. My grandfather and my father, they are born here, just above us –' she pointed to the ornately painted ceiling – 'but my father he is only good at spending money, not like my grandfather who is good at making money. So my fortune is not so good. But my father, even though he is not good at business, he is still a clever man. Like a fox, yes?' Doug nodded. 'He pretends to spend all his money so the government cannot get it in taxes. They want it, they chased him for it – but I know that somewhere here at the villa, he leave something of value for his little ones. I can live here if I want to, because of the contract my father signs with the people who buy the villa, and if I live here I can say what can and what cannot be changed. But, if I do not live here, they can do as they wish. So it is my home, but it is not my house. Maybe it is a little like my prison. Do you see?'

Doug thought it was a very odd arrangement, but said he understood. He couldn't imagine what it must be like to live in a place that had once been your family home but now housed strangers. Especially since the poor woman didn't sound as though she really wanted to be there at all.

'Does it bother you to have your home being a hotel?' he asked, feeling like an interloper.

'Not when the guests are handsome and interesting like you, Meester Rossi.' Antonia smiled and winked at Doug as she sipped her drink. Doug felt hot. She continued, her voice running like treacle over Doug's senses, 'Tonight I have friends here for my birthday. You join us.' It didn't sound like a question or an invitation, it sounded like an order.

The thought terrified Doug. 'Oh thank you, but I don't think I could,' he spluttered.

'Do not *think*, Meester Rossi, just *do*. Life is too short to think too much. We waste too much time thinking.' She paused, then added, 'I think this!' and laughed at her own little joke.

Doug laughed too; she was funny. As they were both laughing, like old friends, the manager who'd greeted Doug upon his arrival approached and whispered something in Italian to Antonia. She nodded and pushed herself out of her chair.

'*Pronto*,' she barked at the manager, who sped off. She turned to Doug, who had sprung to his feet, and said, 'I go. Arrangements for tonight do not go well, and I *must* have all things as I want them. I will see you in the ballroom at eight – this is when we begin. Formal dress, of course. I see you then.' She held out her hand in front of Doug and, unsure what to do next, he shook it vigorously. This seemed to amuse Antonia, who made her way toward the main foyer, trailing a long chiffon scarf behind her.

The only clear thought in Doug's head was that he didn't have a thing to wear to a formal birthday party for an impoverished Italian woman of high birth, that would take place in an ornate gold-and-marble ballroom in just a few hours' time. He cried plaintively to the barman, 'Do you know where I can rent an entire formal get-up for this evening?'

'*Si*,' said the barman, and – for some reason – Doug wasn't at all surprised.

The next couple of hours passed in a blur. First, Doug was packed into a car at the steps of the hotel and delivered like a parcel to a tiny shop in a narrow side street somewhere on the outskirts of Florence, which the hotel's manager had arranged to stay open until he arrived. The two assistants there spoke little English, yet outfitted him perfectly with evening attire, and somehow managed to convince him to buy some slacks and shirts, as well as a linen suit, which they insisted flattered him. While his purchased clothes, and rented ones, were being prepared, he was directed to a nearby antique shop where he selected an apparently ancient Venetian glass perfume bottle as a birthday gift for Antonia.

By seven thirty, Doug was sitting on the edge of his hotel bed, bathed, shaved, dressed, and ready to go. He found himself as nervous as a bridegroom, and almost as excited. He didn't understand why he was acting as he was, everything was so out of character for him, but he was enjoying every moment.

As Doug entered the ballroom, at eight o'clock sharp, he saw Antonia some distance away, kissing a short, bald man on the cheeks. As Doug's eyes met hers, his hostess called in her deep voice, 'Meester Rossi – my friend. Welcome!'

The twenty or so pairs of eyes in the room that turned to look at Doug saw a slim, red-headed man of average height, stunningly attired in a narrow-lapelled, double-breasted evening jacket, bearing an elaborately packaged gift box, and wearing a beaming smile. They watched him cross the room, hardly aware there was anyone in it except their guest of honor. Had he been able to understand it, Doug would have been surprised at the discreet buzz of exchanges in the room – all of which were variations on the theme that Antonia had been keeping some sort of secret.

Antonia kissed Doug on both cheeks, something that had never happened to him before, and he caught her scent as she did so; it was a heady bouquet that reminded him of the roses in his grandmother's garden, and it suited her exotic dark looks perfectly. It even seemed to have a hint of wine about it, which matched her sheath-like, claret evening gown. She smiled as she took the gift he offered and said, 'You should not give me a gift – but I thank you. I will open all gifts later, after dinner. See, I put it here.' She steered Doug to a long, low table where she placed his gift with several other packages.

'Champagne, Meester Rossi – or do you have another name?'

He replied almost breathlessly, 'Douglas, or Doug – whatever you prefer,' even though no one but his mother had called him Douglas since he was a child.

'Doog? Darg?' Antonia pronounced his name awkwardly. 'It is not a good name – I prefer Doo-glass – I will call you Doo-glass,' and it was settled; Doug was introduced as Dooglass, with a heavy emphasis on the second syllable. With his freshly minted name, Doug felt like a different person, and acted like one. His presence was taken as an opportunity by those he met to practice their English, and he found himself entranced by the varying accents and amusing difficulties with translation. All the time Antonia was at his side, allowing him to be at ease with these people, who were obviously weighing him up with every glance, and each question.

Within thirty minutes he'd met everyone, and a mixture of poor translation and fevered gossip had established him as a recently widowed Scottish restaurateur, who was independently wealthy and had come to Florence to search out impoverished ancestors whose lives he wished to improve. Blissfully unaware of this misrepresentation, Doug chatted as best he could to everyone he met; he even dared to hope the expression on Antonia's face meant she was impressed by his manner as he did so. When the gong sounded for dinner, his hostess scooped him up and insisted he sat beside her. An array of magnificent dishes were brought to the grand table, where they were consumed slowly, and with much conversation. Each course pleased Doug's increasingly appreciative palate, and was paired with a wine that heightened his enjoyment. As they ate and drank Antonia explained each dish for him, telling him how it was prepared, and in which ways herbs and spices had been used to give layers of flavor . . . and Doug fell deeper under her spell than he could ever have imagined. By the end of the sumptuous meal Doug was a little tipsy, and head over heels in love with Antonia de Luca. He knew, with certainty, he was experiencing the most perfect night of his life.

After leaving the table, Antonia's great pleasure and enthusiasm upon opening Doug's gift caused raised eyebrows around the room, but not quite as many as when she pulled a shawl about her shimmering claret gown and guided Doug out of the ballroom, into the chill air of the garden. The moon was full, as was Doug's heart. He didn't question Antonia as she steered him toward a small grotto set to one side of the garden.

'It is not the Pitti Palace, but it is my own lovely grotto,' she told Doug as she struck a match to light an oil lamp that hung at the entrance to the carved and bejeweled cavern. 'My father have men make this for me and my brother when we are children, but my poor little brother he is always scared of the dark cave. Me? I like to hide inside. He would call to me – "Toni, Toni, come now and play!" – but I would wait until he was gone, then run out to laugh at him in the sunlight. Ah, poor little Gianni, he is gone from here now and controls a big company in America, in Chicago. I miss him so much. He left here after my father died. He is what they call an Internet Giant. He sells Italian clothes, and Italian things for the house and the kitchen, to American housewives – he is very good at this. Maybe one day I visit him, but I cannot leave my home for now, because I want to find what my father leave here for us. Gianni, he says my father has spent all the money that the government does not take, but I believe my father when he says he leaves wealth for me and Gianni.'

Doug didn't really understand what Antonia was talking about; he found the sound of her voice almost hypnotic, but had to admit to himself that following what she was saying wasn't uppermost in his mind. Doug had seen photographs of the famous grotto at the Boboli Gardens, and intended to visit it, but he knew nothing would ever compare with Antonia's grotto: the light from the oil lamp bounced off thousands of tiny shimmering stones, lumps of multi-colored glass, and mirror-chips that had been set into the man-made coral-like finish of the walls. Doug was entranced. But even more than being bewitched by his magical surroundings, Doug knew that at any moment he would reach out to take Antonia in his arms and kiss her in this other-worldly place, and that his life would never be the same again.

Antonia took Doug's hand, and pulled him deeper into the cave-like structure. They turned a corner so that the view of the garden, and any light from the moon, was lost to them. This was it, Doug knew it. *This* was his moment. Antonia's hand was still in his, and he squeezed it. She turned to face him. Her skin glowed in the lamplight, and the corners of her lips curled upward with a hint of a smile. Her eyes sparkled. She glanced down, to rest the lamp safely upon a stone bench beside them, and Doug waited for her to look up again, to gaze deep into his eyes . . . but, instead, she let out a guttural wail that pierced the night, and his aching heart.

Letting go of his hand to clasp her face, she wailed, 'Gianni! Gianni!' and ran out of the grotto, screaming, leaving Doug standing in the dim lamplight, peering down at the floor where she had seen whatever had horrified her. There, lying in a pool of something that glistened black, was a man's contorted face, eyes staring. A thick, shining gash encircled his neck. Doug couldn't see the rest of the body beneath the stone bench, but he didn't need to; he bolted into the night air where he found Antonia was howling in agony at the top of her voice.

Antonia looked at him, her beautiful face contorted by anguish. 'Is my brother. Gianni. My brother.' She shouted something in Italian while shaking her fist at the heavens. Doug had no idea what to do – Antonia didn't seem to want to be comforted; she was like a madwoman, and she started to tear at her shawl. All he could make out were the words *'eliminare'*, *'immondezza'* and *'ambrosi'* which she kept repeating over and over. He had no idea what the words meant, but he knew she wasn't singing someone a love song.

Within seconds a tall, slim, grey-haired man, Doug knew to be named Paulo, arrived on the scene. Doug assumed he was asking Antonia in Italian what had happened. Paulo looked blackly at Doug, and shouted at him to keep back. It hadn't occurred to Doug for one moment that anyone could imagine he might be the reason for Antonia's distress, but he soon realized this was exactly what Paulo, and several of the other men running toward his screaming companion, suspected.

Doug was all but held back as Antonia screamed at Paulo; the man's expression changed to one of shock, then he let go of Antonia's bare arms and ran into the grotto. When he emerged, he looked grim; he walked away with sagging shoulders, pulling out his mobile phone. He gathered the people who were coming toward the grotto as he walked and talked. Doug noticed him trying to drag away one man in particular – the short, bald man Doug had seen Antonia greet earlier in the evening, whose name he couldn't recall.

Upon catching sight of the small man, Antonia flew into an even greater rage; she screamed '*assassin*' at him, threw her shawl to one side and began to run at the man, clearly intending to do him harm. Even though he didn't really understand what was happening, Doug knew he had to stop Antonia from hurting anybody, herself included, so he rushed to catch her in his arms, and gathered her into his body. As he looked at her tear-stained face, and saw the anguish and anger in her eyes, it pained him that *this* was how it should be as he held her close for the first time. He was sharply aware of the loss of a moment that had never happened, and it shocked him to realize he felt even more helpless than he had on the day of his wife's funeral. He couldn't begin to comprehend how that could be, but he knew it was the truth.

'Gianni, Gianni,' sobbed Antonia onto Doug's shoulder. Her body shook, and she let out cries of pain that cut through the night air. Dogs began to bark in the distance.

'Antonia, I am so sorry,' was all Doug could muster. He didn't know how to say anything that mattered in Italian, so he pulled back, and nodded toward the grotto. 'That's your brother in there? Gianni?' He wanted to be clear.

She nodded and sobbed. 'Why he is here? And why is he dead?' Doug reflected on the same questions.

'I am so sorry, Antonia,' he whispered. He wiped away her mascara-laden tears with the silk handkerchief one of the assistants in the rental shop had placed in his breast pocket. 'Don't worry, we'll get to the bottom of this. I believe Paulo has phoned the police. They'll be here soon.'

'I do not need the police. I *know* who has killed him,' she hissed, turning toward the bald man, who was being held back by some of the other partygoers. 'This man, this viper, he has done this. Ambrosi! *Assassin! Essere dannato!*' she screamed.

'What are you saying?' cried Doug, 'I don't understand what's going on – who is that man? What are you saying to him?' If ever there was a time Doug wished he could speak Italian, this was it.

Antonia spat out, 'He must die. This murderer must die; his family has *vendetta* with my family. He has killed my brother because of my family's treasure. He must die, Genovese scum. I kill you!' She shook her tiny fist, and reverted to Italian. Doug was locked, once again, within his dark world of incomprehension.

As the night air grew more frigid he waited, holding Antonia close to him; finally the police arrived and illuminated the garden with lamps that bleached everything white, or threw it into inky shadow. He held her as they took away her brother's body, and as she sobbed her account of their evening to the detectives. He could tell, through a few words in Italian and Antonia's translations, that she continued in her insistence that her brother had been assassinated by this Alessandro Ambrosi, from Genoa, whom she had invited to her birthday party despite the fact she claimed that the Genovese Ambrosis and the Fiorentino de Lucas had a vendetta that dated back to her great-grandfather's day.

'I believe it is right to have you enemies closer than you friends, but if I have not invited him, then my baby brother Gianni is alive now,' she wailed.

Finally it was Doug's turn to answer questions; Antonia helped, still weeping, with translation and interpretation, and he was able to confirm her account of the evening. When the police made ready to leave, Antonia finally agreed to return to the house, which, though it blazed with the same chandeliers as it had at her birthday dinner, offered no comfort to the implacable woman, or Doug.

When he knew Antonia was safe, the door to her apartment on the top floor of the hotel locked and bolted, Doug finally went back to his own room, where he fell onto his bed. It was almost dawn, and he was utterly exhausted. Just twenty-four hours earlier he'd been standing at the front door of his cottage in Scotland, wondering if he'd packed enough socks for a two-week sightseeing holiday in Italy. Now, as he stared at a painted ceiling that told a symbolic tale of redemption, he was totally spent, and too tired to even organize his thoughts. He fell into a fitful sleep, his dreams populated with glittering ballrooms and threatening shadows. At one point he saw Antonia fall from a cliff that had appeared at the front steps of the hotel, then saw himself, strangely disembodied, running along a pathway he believed led to a museum that housed religious relics – but found it to be a never-ending bar piled high with pirate gold, and he was surrounded by policemen who kept shouting at him in gibberish. They kept screaming, and screaming, and screaming . . .

Doug awoke to the sound of birdsong after an hour of sweaty sleep with his heart pounding, a full bladder, and a desperate need to know that Antonia was safe. He was horrified to see the crumpled mess his rental suit – which he'd slept in – had become, and decided he'd better get himself cleaned up before he did anything else. A shower partially revived him, and he donned the linen suit he'd rather cavalierly purchased the previous evening. As he checked his new self in the mirror before leaving his room, he realized he might feel exhausted but at least he looked fresh.

He grappled with the temptation to telephone Antonia, then wondered if he should check how she was with the hotel manager; finally he decided to simply go to her rooms and see her, face to face, for himself. Doug was nervous, unsure what sort of a state she'd be in; he hoped he'd have the strength she'd need to feel supported. He knocked timidly at first, then more heartily, then, having received no response, with complete panic.

Finally Antonia pulled open the door and stood before him. She looked magnificent; no bleary or puffy eyes, no blotchiness of complexion. Doug couldn't get over the fact that she looked perfect; her hair was coiled in a bun at her neck, her make-up was flawless, and she wore a vivid orange outfit that both fitted beautifully and complemented her dark coloring. She had told him the night before that she was turning forty-five, mocking his mere thirty-seven years, but at that moment she looked younger than Doug by a decade, his baggy eyes and strained expression adding years to his appearance.

The sobbing woman he had held close to him in the chill of the night had disappeared. Doug had come to Antonia to be her hero, her rock; he almost felt a little disappointed that here was a woman who needed no support – she was completely in control of herself, and, he suspected, would soon be completely in control of everyone about her.

'Caro mio, Dooglass,' Antonia cooed, and she reached out to Doug, pulled him toward her and kissed him slowly and softly on each cheek. Doug's stomach flipped; he tried to convince himself it was because he was tired and hungry, but he knew it was an even more basic instinct at work.

As Antonia pulled back from him, he whispered hoarsely, 'You look wonderful. I thought you'd be . . .' He didn't quite know what to say.

Antonia replied sharply, 'I look this way because I must. If I am a mess, then no one takes me seriously. No man respects a woman when she is in pieces – no man will do what I ask if I cannot master myself. I need to prove Ambrosi is a killer; today the police will believe me when I tell them this. Last night I am weak; they see a woman screaming, crying. They ignore her. Today they see that Antonia de Luca is in control, and she is right. I hope Ambrosi he has not already escaped. The police said he must stay at his home, that they will watch him, but I think he will go away somewhere. No Ambrosi listened to anyone else, ever. They are trouble. All of them.'

As Antonia talked, she marched down the carpeted marble staircase that led to the main entrance. Doug followed in her wake. She greeted the manager and a couple of the employees with kisses and comforting gestures – Doug assumed she was assuring them that she was quite well – then the manager led her to a small car parked beside the main entrance.

'Dooglass, you come with me.' Doug knew he couldn't have left her even if she'd not invited him to join her, so he slipped into the passenger seat. He was still grappling with his seatbelt when Antonia sent gravel spraying from accelerating tires.

Doug let out a little cry.

'Do not worry, Dooglass, I am a very good driver. No one else can drive but Italians.' They shot out of the hotel grounds and onto the road without the slightest hesitation, screeching around the corner. Doug was terrified, but, as she threw the steering wheel this way and that, he had to admire Antonia; she didn't so much drive the car, as ride it. She was almost at one with the vehicle, and she kept her eyes on the road even as she talked to him and rooted around in her handbag for cigarettes and a lighter. As she talked, and drove, and smoked, her mobile phone rang. She answered with one hand, her other holding the steering wheel and the cigarette, '*Pronto,*' she answered, then listened, shouted a curt, '*Si, fra mezzora,*' and dropped the phone back into the little cubbyhole beneath the handbrake.

'We see the police in half an hour, Dooglass, but first I will see Ambrosi. I will bring him to the police with us – or he will pay the price.' Antonia revved the engine and the little car shot forward at an even faster pace; Doug gripped the sides of his seat with anxiety. They crossed the River Arno within a few minutes; Antonia clearly knew where she was going – and how to get there – but at every turn there seemed to be innumerable lanes of traffic to cross to reach the next street which she'd race along, before becoming all but immobile within another knot of vehicles.

They flew past glorious Renaissance buildings at an alarming rate, their route circumnavigating magnificent piazzas filled with people enjoying their breakfast coffee, and taking them along cobbled streets Doug knew were hundreds of years old, but which now became no more than a nuisance, causing Antonia to skid as she cornered, cursing in Italian as she did so. As he held on for dear life, Doug felt he should speak his mind.

'You can't just face down this Ambrosi man, Antonia. What's the point? Let the police do their job. Let *them* bring him in. Besides,' Doug had a flash of brilliance, 'it can't have been him who killed your brother, because he was with us at the dinner table all night. You know it and I know it – *we* are his alibi. The police doctor said Gianni had only been dead a couple of hours when we found him. It can't have been Ambrosi.'

Doug felt rather pleased with himself, but Antonia shouted, 'If not this Ambrosi, then another Ambrosi, or someone they pay. You do not know them. They stop at nothing. They destroy my father. They tell the government about him and he lose everything in taxes and fines. They destroy life for me and Gianni, and now they kill my poor Gianni.'

'But why?'

'*Vendetta*,' was Antonia's angry reply, as though that one word communicated volumes.

For Doug, it didn't; he didn't really understand the whole concept of a vendetta, except in the broadest sense. True, they'd read *Romeo and Juliet* at school, but at the time he'd thought it was all a bit soppy and hadn't paid much attention except for the bits where there was fighting, or the odd slightly smutty joke.

'But what does that mean?' he begged.

Antonia slammed on the brakes to stop at a traffic light. She looked across at Doug and narrowed her eyes. 'You Scottish. Is not the same for you. For me and my brother, it is life, and death. The de Luca family hate the Ambrosi family. The Ambrosi family hate the de Luca family. It has been this way for a long time. Me? I try to be a friend, I try to stop the *vendetta* because it is not a good way to live today, in this century. But the Ambrosis are all mad men, they will not stop. They will kill me too, if I do not kill them first.'

With that threat hanging in the air, the lights changed and once again they were tearing through the streets until Antonia finally screeched to a halt in front of an unimpressive, yet clearly ancient, brick building. 'We are here. You come now – or stay. If you come, then you are in *vendetta* with me. You cannot go back from that. But I have only one gun, and this gun is for me.'

Doug was horrified. Where on earth had she got hold of a gun? He couldn't imagine knowing how to go about getting one. Good grief, it might be Antonia herself who lost her life! Doug had to stop her. The seriousness of the situation had finally dawned upon him; this was a *real* blood feud – whether Alessandro Ambrosi had killed Antonia's brother or not, Antonia was about to embark upon a course of action that could result in another life being taken, and he couldn't risk her doing that.

Pretty sure that gentle persuasion wasn't going to work, Doug grabbed Antonia's arm as she started to unbuckle her seatbelt, then he pulled her toward him and kissed her, forcefully. It was all he could think of doing. She returned his kiss with equal passion, and, as his moment of heaven was complete, Doug's heart thumped in his chest, making him worry a little about how healthy he really was.

Doug was determined to tell Antonia that – whatever it meant – he would stand by her, but that he really believed going after Ambrosi with a gun was not a good idea . . . but, before he could say a word, he felt something hard and cold being pushed against the exposed part of his neck. Antonia's eyes looked past him, and widened with shock and fear. Doug's heart continued pounding, but now for a different reason; he had no idea how he knew it, but he was quite certain someone was pushing the barrel of a gun into his flesh.

He turned his head slowly, and saw the weapon was being held by Alessandro Ambrosi himself; Doug could see Ambrosi's hand was sweaty – he hoped his fingers didn't slip.

'Get out, now!' demanded Ambrosi.

'No I won't get out – I am not leaving you alone with Antonia for one moment,' replied Doug, not knowing what had prompted him to be so courageous in the face of a firearm.

'Get out, *now!*' squeaked Ambrosi, and he prodded harder at Doug with the gun. 'I don't want your precious Antonia – I just want to get into the back of the car. Move now – *pronto!*'

'Do it,' whispered Antonia. Doug's mind raced as he unbuckled himself and opened the door; he kept his body within the doorframe and his face to Ambrosi, as he fiddled with the seat-lifting mechanism, finally tilting it forward out of the way. Ambrosi warned him not to try anything as he wriggled his short, portly frame into the rear passenger seat, then Doug slammed the seat down and jumped in before Ambrosi had a chance to force Antonia to drive off without him.

'Where you want me to drive, pig?' shouted Antonia, staring at the little man in the rear-view mirror.

'Do not worry where we go – just drive and I tell you where,' Ambrosi barked at Antonia.

She turned and sneered at him, 'And you do this at the end of a gun? Like a coward?'

'Coward or not, I am the one in charge – now drive!'

Antonia did as she was told; the tires screeched on the glassy cobbles as the little car sprang to life again. Doug was thrown against the headrest, and scrambled to pull on his seatbelt as he tried desperately to think of some way he could get Antonia and himself out of their predicament. He no longer even saw the history whizzing past them, instead, scenes from films he'd watched on television over the years flashed in front of his mind's eye; sadly, all the films had one thing in common that was most definitely lacking in the current situation – an action hero.

He kept trying to work out how he could defuse the situation, but nothing came to his frantic mind. As Alessandro Ambrosi shouted directions at Antonia he wondered if they'd be able to leap from the car – without getting shot – during one of the periods when they hardly moved, grinding through pockets of gridlock, but he quickly realized there was no way for him to communicate any such plan to Antonia without Ambrosi knowing. Doug had lost his sense of direction entirely, and began to be convinced he was seeing palazzos and piazzas for the second and third time. Maybe Ambrosi was trying to throw off a possible tail? Antonia had said the police were supposed to be watching him. At that thought, Doug's spirits lifted – if the police had been watching Ambrosi, they must have seen him grab them and force them to drive off. His heart got another boost when Antonia's phone rang and she told Ambrosi she'd have to answer it because it would be the police, wondering what had become of her.

However, to Doug's great dismay, this information led to Ambrosi grabbing the phone, answering it himself, in Italian of course, and barking at the police. Antonia's eyebrows rose and she said, 'Why you want us to meet the police at my villa?'

Doug was glad Antonia had thought of this method of letting him know what was going on.

'I will *prove* I did not kill Gianni,' replied Ambrosi roughly, 'this is why, Antonia – now drive!' and he poked the gun toward Doug with a threatening gesture.

Eventually they arrived at the villa, and Antonia drove slowly through the formal gardens that surrounded it. Doug knew he should have felt relieved when he saw the police cars and the armed officers adopting positions from which they could shoot, without being shot at, but he didn't feel more secure – in fact, he felt a great deal more concerned; what if gunfire broke out? He or Antonia could easily be hit by one of the dozens of men who were all now aiming their weapons at the little car.

'Be calm,' shouted Ambrosi as they arrived at the entrance to the villa. Doug could see nervous faces peering from behind curtains on the upper floors of the hotel, and could imagine the staff and guests had been told to make themselves scarce. In all his experience of life, which he was beginning to realize wasn't that great, he had nothing to help him out at this juncture; he had no reference point, no role model, nothing to go on at all. All he knew – that Ambrosi didn't – was Antonia had a gun in her handbag; but Doug couldn't reach her bag. Even if he could have reached it, he wouldn't have known what to do with a gun, so Doug resigned himself to that knowledge being useless.

As the car crunched to a halt, there seemed to be a moment of complete stillness. To Doug's mind, even the birds stopped singing. It might have just been a few seconds before Ambrosi spoke, but to Doug it felt like a lifetime, as he turned and stared into the potentially deadly barrel of the small gun.

'Get out, English!' he barked.

That did it; something in Doug finally snapped. 'I'm a Scot actually, not an Englishman, thank you very much, Alessandro, and I'll get out only when I am sure Antonia is in no danger whatsoever – which means I'll get out when you chuck that gun away.' Doug felt as though someone had commandeered his power of speech; he had no idea what he would say next, so even he was surprised when he added, 'Look, Ambrosi – there are more than a dozen marksmen training their weapons on you right now, so you're not going to get away from here. Who holds a gun to a defenseless woman's head to *prove* his innocence? It makes no sense. You've brought us here. You knew the police would be here. You even told them you had us at gunpoint – so what the devil are you planning? It can't be to shoot us, right here, with all these people as witnesses. So just throw the gun out of the car window, and let's get on with being civilized human beings.'

None of Doug's stomach churning terror could be heard in his tone, or seen in his manner; he knew this because he noticed Antonia's eyes flicker with . . . he wasn't quite sure what, but he hoped she was impressed. He certainly was.

Ambrosi's shoulders sagged, and Doug saw his chance; he grabbed the barrel of the gun, levered it out of Ambrosi's hand and threw it out through the open passenger window. As it landed on the gravel with a light clatter, Doug shouted, 'Run!'

In a matter of seconds, Antonia and Doug were both out of the car and running toward the police who, in turn, all rushed toward the car. Once the police had hold of Ambrosi, Doug grabbed Antonia and pulled her to him.

'Are you alright?' he panted.

'Si,' she replied quietly, 'I am.' She straightened her blouse, tucked a stray strand of hair behind her ear, and smiled warmly. The couple watched the police drag the handcuffed Ambrosi across the gravel driveway toward them.

The policeman with rather more elaborate fittings on his uniform than the others – the one Doug suspected was in charge – spoke rapidly to Antonia, who responded in a low voice. Doug didn't recognize any of the uniformed police as having been in attendance the night before, but did see a couple of faces he knew – two plainclothes officers who'd returned, literally, to the scene of the crime. A few brief exchanges in Italian followed their arrival, then Doug's hand was taken by Antonia as she, the handcuffed Ambrosi, the two detectives, and an armed officer, all began the short walk to the grotto.

No one spoke; Doug reflected on all that had happened since he and Antonia had walked the same path the night before, and he found it hard to comprehend that what had occurred had actually involved him – Doug Rossi. The Doug Rossi who had always truly believed that if you took the bitter with the sweet, everything would turn out for the best in the end. He had to admit he was, for once, in a situation that could never turn out for the best; Antonia's beloved brother lay dead in a police morgue and there'd be no bringing him back, even if they did discover the truth about who had killed him, and why.

Doug was astonished to realize the situation hurt him because it hurt Antonia; he was grieving because she was grieving. He couldn't help himself; her loss was now his loss. She'd never be whole again without her successful businessman brother, whom she'd clearly loved a great deal. Nothing could change that – it was all bitterness and loss, and it always would be. Doug felt a bit overwhelmed.

The grotto seemed to have shifted position in the gardens; the walk to it the previous night had seemed a long and wonderful one, now they were there before he knew it. Its appearance had also diminished; as Antonia had lit the lamp the night before, the grotto had shimmered and sparkled with tiny points of light that made it look magical and mysterious, now Doug could see it was built almost like a little cement igloo. Even the niche area set off to one side – that had held so much promise, but had so tragically hidden a dead body – was no more than four or five feet in length. Doug felt he was in a theatre with all the lights on, with scenery stacked at the back of the stage; all the illusion was gone, and only artifice remained. Doug felt the disappointment in the pit of his stomach.

As he grappled with the loss of the previous night's dreamworld, he reminded himself that at least he'd seen it and felt it, and that for a few moments, it had been real; that would have to be enough for him. Then another, nameless, worry crept over him, and he looked at Antonia with alarm. Thankfully, he saw no change in her; just warmth and glowing skin, strength and vulnerability, and the smile at the corner of her full lips as she looked at him with her disarmingly direct gaze. Doug's moment of panic was gone. Once again he could concentrate on what was happening around him – and he needed to focus, because most of it was taking place in staccato Italian, with hands being thrown about all over the place, and Antonia shooting rapid translations at him.

Ambrosi was shouting; he was protesting something – Doug assumed his innocence. Antonia was holding her own in her deep, strong voice; Doug assumed she was continuing her assurances that Ambrosi was somehow connected to her brother's death. The detectives looked bemused, letting them get on with it, and the uniformed policeman was clearly trying to work out how to light a cigarette while holding onto his gun. He finally holstered the weapon, lit a cigarette, then took out the gun again, training it on the handcuffed Ambrosi. This set off the two detectives who also lit cigarettes, and finally Antonia paused and did likewise. Unfortunately the little silver gun she'd been hiding in her handbag fell out as she retrieved her lighter. Every member of the group drew a surprised breath as it fell, but it was gathered up nonchalantly enough by the younger of the two detectives. Its appearance led to a vicious stream of invective from Ambrosi, who also seemed to be aggrieved that everyone but him was puffing away as they shouted at each other.

Doug couldn't believe it when the younger detective lit a cigarette for Ambrosi, and stuck it into the corner of his mouth. Ambrosi exhaled smoke through his nose as he continued to talk and, unable to follow what was being said, Doug became fascinated by the length of the ash that refused to fall from the accused man's cigarette, no matter how violently he shouted at Antonia and the policemen. It seemed that, for a few moments, Doug's world was reduced to that lengthening, and gradually drooping, pillar of grey ash. It fascinated him. He couldn't take his eyes off it. He barely noticed the detective hand a small brown bag to Antonia, or that she poked about in the bag, cursing.

What finally drew all of Doug's wandering attention was Antonia's triumphant shout of '*Assassin!*' as she held aloft what looked like a tiny diary or notebook.

She pointed accusingly at an entry. 'See Dooglass, Gianni writes he is to meet with Ambrosi – last night. It is here in his book – see detective – see?' She thrust the book under Doug's nose, then, before he'd had a chance to even focus on the page, she pushed it toward both Ambrosi and the detective. 'Ask Ambrosi, why does Gianni write he is to meet him?' she demanded of the detectives in a low, commanding voice.

Doug noticed that Ambrosi, whose cigarette ash had finally fallen onto his otherwise immaculate tan wool jacket, looked worried. He shook his head and said, 'I do not meet Gianni.'

'Liar – *li odio!*' shouted Antonia. Doug could feel her frustration. Here was a clear sign that Ambrosi was lying; the entry in Gianni's diary seemed damning.

'I do not lie,' said Ambrosi in a pleading tone. 'He want to meet me. I say no. I refuse to meet him, but he insist. He know I come to your birthday party. I believe he comes here to try to see me after I say I do not wish to meet with him.'

One of the detectives spoke to Ambrosi in a low, menacing voice. Ambrosi's shoulders dropped further with each sentence. The detective translated for Doug. 'I have told this man we do not believe him. I have told him I believe he *wants* to tell me the truth.

He thinks he cannot tell me the truth because it will make clear he is a criminal in other ways. I tell him we know this already, so he should tell the whole story.'

As the detective spoke Ambrosi spat the cigarette end from his mouth and ground it into the dirt with his heel. He looked at everyone in turn, slowly shook his head in resignation, and said, 'I tell the true story. I speak in English, for the English.'

'I keep telling you I'm a Scot,' interrupted Doug, but he got stern looks from the detectives, so thought it best to shut up.

Ambrosi spoke quietly, his features softening. 'Antonia. Your brother Gianni, you love him, I know. But he is not a good man.' He shrugged.

'Liar!' shouted Antonia.

'*Contessa, per favore*,' retorted the young detective sharply, and Antonia fell silent.

'It is as I say. When he was a child he was wild, yes?' said Ambrosi.

Antonia looked at her feet as she replied, '*Si*, but this is normal for a boy – he runs, he plays, he fights, he gets into trouble with the police. He is not a bad boy.'

'Maybe not a truly bad boy, but he is a truly bad *man*, Antonia,' said Ambrosi. Doug thought he sounded disappointed. He wondered why.

'At the end of his life, your father, he called me to him –' Antonia seemed ready to interrupt again, but the older detective raised his hand in warning – 'it is true. I come to this villa to see him when he lies dying in his bed. We agree then, no more *vendetta*. It is over. Done. I learn some history about my grandfather and your great-grandfather, and it is not so good. I think my family is wrong, I tell your father this. The *vendetta* is false. Unfair. So I promise to look after you and Gianni for him when he is gone. You?' He looked fondly at Antonia. 'You want nothing from me – you think of me as an enemy, so you keep me close. This is good because I can see you are always safe.'

Antonia glared at him, but he continued, 'Your father, he *knows* that I have not betrayed him to the government, but we both agree to let the world think I have done this. But I promise your father I will find out who has really done this, who has told his secrets, and who has given the government information about him so they can take his money. I promise I will find out who has robbed you and Gianni of your future. You must understand, Antonia, I would not betray your father to the government – I too hate the taxes we must pay. If I want to hurt him, I do something that does not benefit the crooks who run this country. I have no time for them. They walk with smiles on their faces when they want you to vote for them, but they carry knives behind their backs, and all have bank accounts filled with money from those they say in public they are against.'

Doug thought it was bizarre that every member of the little group shrugged their shoulders and nodded at this statement; it seemed they'd all found some common ground at last.

Ambrosi continued, his tone subdued, 'For many years I keep trying to find out who gives your father all his trouble and, finally, I hear from someone I trust very much, it is your brother, Gianni, who has given the government the information about your father, to get himself out of big trouble with the police. Bad trouble, Antonia. The police – they know this.'

Antonia looked pale. 'No, *non e allineare* – it is not true,' she whispered. She glanced at the detective, clearly wanting him to deny it, but he nodded in a way that showed his acceptance of these facts. Doug saw Antonia's shoulders droop, her back bend just a little; she moved closer to him, leaning heavily upon his arm. All the attention was on Ambrosi, who Doug was beginning to see in a slightly different light. It was also clear to him Ambrosi had more to say, and was determined to say it.

'Antonia – my dear child – the government, those crooked men, they let Gianni stay here while your father lives, but when your father dies, they tell Gianni to leave Italy. He did not choose to go, as he told everyone. He was told to live in another country, so he goes to America, to his cousins. There, with money I give to him – yes, it is true – he begins a business. At least, this is what he says. But, Antonia, he is a liar. All the time he say we must send the clothes, and the shoes, and the leather goods, and all the other items he says he will pay for, but he does *not* pay. Now – this year, after all these years – I say "No more money. Enough." Nothing more is sent to America for him to sell, and keep all the money. Whatever I promise your father, Antonia, I am sorry, it is enough now. It is done. My own business interests, they are suffering. Now I must look after my own family.'

'Even if I believe what you say, why does Gianni come here, last night?' pleaded Antonia. 'And why should I believe you did not kill him? If it is true he has stolen all this from you, you have even more reason to kill him.'

'Antonia, I am with you, all night,' replied Ambrosi, evenly. 'You know that. And I tell no one about Gianni coming to Italy because I do not believe he is here. I think they stop him at the border, or at the airport – it is the authorities who made him leave, why would they let him return? And why should I think he comes to the villa, if I think he cannot get into Italy? But last night, when I see what has happened – and I know he is not dead by my hand – I leave here, I make phone calls to America, to Gianni's business partners, and they say that it is not just from me that Gianni buys his products. Now, I know he does not *buy* them from me, he *steals* them from me. So I believe he steals from others too. I find out the other people he is supposed to buy from – who he steals from – and I know one man he has been stealing from is a very bad man. Here, detective – in my pocket – I have his name.'

'Why can't you just say his name?' shouted Doug, frustrated by the sense of melodrama that was beginning to overtake matters. Ambrosi shook his head and pursed his lips.

The uniformed policeman fumbled in Ambrosi's jacket pocket until he found a piece of paper. He showed it to the detective who whistled.

'You know the name there? What is it? Who is he, this man? What's it all about?' asked an increasingly agitated Doug.

The detective passed the paper to Antonia. 'He has our interest for a long time.' He turned to his colleague and said something in Italian. His colleague nodded. 'We see the same style of killing of a man last month. Luigi Bianco was killed this way – with a wire garotte. Professional, silent; no prints, no forensics. Bianco did bad business deals with this man also.' He nodded at the slip of paper in his hand. 'This man does not kill for himself, you understand; he buys killers to work for him. He has a great deal of money, so he is able to keep his hands clean. And he likes to give big bribes to many important people who can help him to wash his hands if they become dirty. But, although he has much money – more than any man could ever need – it is known that if you steal even a little from his pocket, you will pay the highest price for your sins against him.' It horrified Doug that the detective scratched his finger across his throat as he made this last statement.

Doug could see Antonia was holding back tears. He knew instinctively she felt she was losing her brother all over again; the brother she had loved, and thought she knew, hadn't really existed. Doug squeezed her closer to him, and knew there was no way back

– he'd face it with her; it all had to come out. Now.

He said to Ambrosi, 'So you're telling us that Gianni de Luca was killed by a professional hitman who was hired by a wealthy gangster, from whom he was stealing? And that all these years you've been secretly looking out for Antonia, and funding her brother's crooked business in America, to make up for your grandfather starting a *vendetta* against Antonia's family?' Doug could hardly believe he had found himself in a situation where those words could even be used. Ambrosi nodded sadly, and Doug knew it was all true.

Looking deep into Antonia's eyes he tried to let her know by his expression that it hurt him to speak as he did. 'I know you don't like to think of your brother this way, but the police back up at least a part of Ambrosi's story, and it might be that it's true.' He paused, then decided to push on. 'Be honest, have you ever known Ambrosi to do anything to hurt you, or to act against you in any way?'

Antonia pouted like a small child, dropped her head and shook it. She was angry, Doug could tell. Then she looked up at him, her eyes flamed, and she hissed, 'He had a gun at your head, Dooglass – why this? Why would an innocent man do this?'

Ambrosi answered for himself, 'Because I have to get you all to where I know the police will be. I must put my case to them, and to you. The police might believe me – but I think I will not live very long if you do not believe me, Antonia.' His voice sounded tired.

Doug knew what he meant; he'd been in no doubt that Antonia had meant to kill Ambrosi, so he felt Ambrosi had read the situation pretty accurately. Doug said, quietly, 'He's got a point.' He let his comment hang in the warming spring air, and said no more.

Antonia sighed. It was a long, shaky sigh. She straightened her back, and said to the assembled crowd, 'The person who kills my brother is not here.' She nodded at Ambrosi. 'If the police will allow you, I think you should go to your family now. The *vendetta* is over. We will speak and meet soon, but not until after I bury Gianni. You will not attend his funeral. That would not be correct.' She turned her attention to the detectives and spoke so calmly that it shocked Doug, 'You will not find out who kills my brother because I have no money, and the man you speak of has much money, so you will not be allowed to discover Gianni's killer. But I think, if you are real men, you will try. I will take my Gianni and bury him, and I will telephone you every day to find out what you have discovered. This I promise.'

As the police walked away with Ambrosi, toward the villa, removing his handcuffs as they did so, it seemed to Doug that Antonia was in control once more.

She looked at Doug and spoke softly, 'Walk with me?'

Doug nodded, and they set off along a little path that arced between two formal beds full of low-growing spring flowers.

'I'm so sorry about Gianni,' began Doug. He meant both because Gianni was dead, and because he had not been the man she had thought he was. He knew Antonia understood he meant both things when she squeezed his arm to stop him.

She turned, and looked at him, smiling. 'Dooglass, you are a good man,' she sighed. 'From nowhere you have come . . .' She stopped herself and smiled more widely. 'From *Scotland* you have come, and you have saved me. For all my life I have wanted a man like you, and now, when I really need one – you are here.' Doug could feel his face flush as she continued, 'You are handsome, funny, and brave. You can be strong, and you can be weak. You are perfect. You understand sweet, and you understand bitter. You understand life. You are a clever man, Dooglass, and any woman would be lucky to have you. But me? I am old, I am poor. I am a prisoner here at this house until I find – I do not know what it is, even! And if my father lies about the *vendetta*, maybe he lies about my inheritance. He never tells me why I must stay at the house. He says in the contract that they cannot change the house and they cannot change the gardens until I say so – and I do not really care what they change – it is just a house.'

Fat tears rolled down her cheeks. She looked and sounded like a small child as she wept, her lips and chin quivering as she spoke. 'All I care about is my little grotto, and now . . . now I think I will never feel safe there again. It is now a place of death – not of happiness. I have lost my father, and my brother, and now my only truly happy place.' She wept uncontrollably.

Doug wasn't surprised that she could cry, he'd seen her do that the night before, but what took him aback was *how* she cried; guttural sounds wracked her body so forcefully that he thought she might fall. Blinded by tears as she was, Doug led Antonia toward the grotto, where he ripped away the police tapes and pulled her through the opening so she could more or less collapse onto the bench seat inside.

'Not here – not here,' she managed to mumble through Doug's

handkerchief.

He tried to calm her. 'It's alright, darling, I'm with you. It's just a place – I'll keep you safe.' He held her shuddering body. After a long time, Antonia's sobbing subsided and she looked up at him, bleary eyed. Every trace of her make-up had been washed away by tears; Doug noticed tiny freckles on the bridge of her nose. She looked so fresh – and totally vulnerable.

'Now then,' Doug tried to sound jovial, 'is that a bit better?' Antonia gave a small nod and a weak smile. 'So tell me, what's all this Contessa business? I heard the policeman call you Contessa and I wondered if there was something you weren't telling me. Am I wiping the eyes of a titled lady?' He grinned madly, desperate to take Antonia's mind off everything.

'Ah Dooglass, it is nothing. Almost everyone in Italy has some sort of title. I am Contessa Antonia Marcella Luiga de Luca di Fiesole.' Doug's eyebrows shot up. 'For years I have sold myself.' Antonia smiled as she reassured him. 'Don't look like this! I mean I sell my name – it is how I live. I have clients who pay me to take them about Firenze, arrange parties with my friends, they like my title – the Americans like it a lot. And if they stay at the villa then it is like they are at my home. It is good for me, and I think it is good for them. But I still am selling myself; my ancestors would not care for it, I think.'

'And here's me just a chip shop owner with a few quid,' said Doug sadly. 'What chance do I stand?' This time it was his turn to sag, and Antonia's to support.

'Stay with me, Dooglass? I know you can be here a little time more, and maybe we bury Gianni soon. But, you stay with me after the funeral? Yes?' Her eyes were begging Doug to agree, but what could he do? Didn't he have to get back to the shop when his fortnight's break was over?

'I could stay a bit longer, I suppose,' Doug answered slowly, almost thinking aloud as the words left his lips. 'The shop won't actually be ready for a month – but I think I'd better stay somewhere a bit cheaper than the villa.'

'Oh, *stupido* – you stay with me, as my special guest, Dooglass – this is not a problem,' was Antonia's matter-of-fact response, which made Doug's stomach churn, as he thought about what it might mean.

'Umm, okay,' was all he could manage.

Antonia smiled at him coquettishly. 'I like you, Dooglass. You are the most *real* man I have known. And, as I tell you last night, I have known many.' Doug remembered some of the stories she'd told him at her birthday dinner about millionaires who had wanted to have Antonia as their own, and all he could do was mentally applaud their good taste and pray this wasn't a dream. Antonia changed the mood by pointing at the wall of the grotto beside them.

'Look, it is midday – see how my name sparkles? My father, he puts our names here so at noon the sun shines on us!' A childish smile spread across Antonia's face.

Doug looked where she was pointing and, sure enough, the sunlight was reflecting off a clearly defined 'ANTONIA' made out of little brownish pebbles pushed into the cement wall. Below it, he also saw 'GIANN'.

'Oh no! Some pebbles have fallen from Gianni's name,' wailed Antonia. This discovery set her off into sobbing again. Doug gently removed his arm from her shoulder so she could mop her tears, and he reached out to the place where there was clearly a letter 'I' missing from the end of Gianni's name. Three small pebbles had been levered from the cement – Doug could see the marks where they had been worked out with a knife. The cuts in the cement were fresh; Doug was in little doubt someone had purposely removed them. He wondered why anyone would do such a thing.

He almost chuckled as he rubbed his fingers over the remaining stones. 'You know, not far from where I live in Scotland there's a place called Creetown, where they have a gem museum. I used to go there as a boy, and the one thing that always fascinated me was a small rough stone they kept locked in a special cabinet; it was an uncut diamond. It looked just like this – brownish, dull, and absolutely unpromising. Boy, oh boy – I haven't thought of that place in years.'

'This was my great-grandfather's business – diamonds. My grandfather too. It is how they make their money.'

A moment of silence passed. When Doug could bear it no longer, he blurted out, 'You don't think this could be your inheritance, do you?'

'Oh Dooglass, in the bag they give me from Gianni's pockets – I think – here!' Antonia thrust her hand into the brown paper bag and rustled about, finally pulling out three little pebbles – clearly the three that had been removed from the wall. Her eyes opened wide.

'Gianni must have known – he must have guessed – he must have come here to take what was his.' Doug knew she didn't want to admit her brother might have planned to take a good deal more than what was rightfully his, so said nothing. 'I will take these stones to a man I know. He is very old, but knows much about diamonds. He works for my father many years ago. He is like an uncle to me. If we are right, oh Dooglass, imagine . . . I am rich. We are rich. We can stay together forever. I can buy back my home, or I can be free of this house, I can be free of everything – we will travel. You can leave your *ristorante,* we can be together and enjoy our new life. I will not have to sell my name. You can see art and beautiful things around the world, and I can be with you and love you.'

Doug felt tears of joy prick his eyes and he knew, even if these weren't diamonds, Antonia wanted him like he wanted her. He also knew the man he'd become over the past couple of days could make it all work out – somehow. The chip shop faded away. He could sell it. No one would really miss him in Scotland. They could gossip about him all they liked in the pubs, what did he care? All he cared about was the promise of Antonia's lips, and all he could hear were the noon-day bells chiming across the Arno. Never had an April day held so much promise. Never had Doug felt so full and happy.

Of course he knew life wasn't *perfect*; he'd suffered the tragic loss of his wife, but, there again, he and Antonia had found each other. They might have just discovered a healthy inheritance, but they would always feel the touch of Gianni's ghost . . . and who knew if his professional killer would ever be caught, or the man who had paid him brought to justice?

But Doug looked at it this way – nothing was ever *perfect*. Nothing. And he reflected that, maybe, without the bitter you wouldn't even recognize the sweet. And at that moment, life was sweet.

MAY

A Woman's Touch

Detective Inspector Evan Glover was comforted by the sight of his wife's face smiling at him from his phone. Sadly he knew that was probably as close as he'd get to her until who knew when; he had a suspicious death to investigate, and they could take time.

He'd just received a call from Dr Rakel Souza, head of forensic pathology at West Glamorgan General Hospital – or West Glam Gen, as everyone referred to it – who'd informed him that a Mrs Emily Kitts had been poisoned. Paramedics had failed in their attempts to resuscitate the woman at her home six days earlier and had – quite correctly – ascribed her death to a massive heart attack. However, Dr Souza was now able to confirm the heart attack had been precipitated by a pretty hefty dose of nicotine. When Glover asked why it had taken six days to discover this interesting fact, Souza's tone changed from her usually gently professional manner.

She sounded testy as she replied, 'It's not my fault. The body came in as a heart attack, and we're swamped here; it might be May, but that late cold snap was the last straw for a lot of the old ones who'd hung on through the winter. I had no way of knowing she was a suspicious death. Have you got any idea how many bodies we get through here in a week? There's a lot more of them turning up their toes than go through your hands, and I've got to deal with them all. This one? An otherwise healthy woman of fifty keels over with an assumed heart attack; her own doctor's on holiday and the locum doesn't want to sign a death certificate, so it's over to me for a poke about to find out what killed her. I can see she's had massive heart failure, but I can't understand why. The team in the lab tells me there's nothing showing up on the initial toxicology results, but I don't like it, so I get them to do some more tests. That's when they tell me she's got nicotine in her. I can see she's never smoked a day in her life, so I get some more tests done and find she's got *loads* of the stuff in her. All that back and forth takes time. I'm only one person, you know. And don't tell me I should have alerted you when I had my suspicions, because we had that conversation before and I have, obviously, taken to heart the advice you gave me – which was to not waste your time until I was sure. Well, I'm sure now. So there.'

Glover and his wife Betty had known Dr Rakel Souza, and her

husband, for more than five years, and he admired the fact she'd worked her way to the top of her professional tree given that she, like him, had been raised in a tiny terraced home in a less-than-salubrious part of Swansea where expectations of greatness were few and far between. Both of them had bettered themselves through years of diligence and application to their chosen professions.

Souza, like Glover himself, was well-known for her patience. But now? Glover had never heard her so close to the end of her tether. 'Hang on a minute, Rakel,' he countered, his voice calm and even, 'you're right, I don't know what you go through down there, especially in the mortuary.' He pictured the stark white rooms where he'd spent many hours standing by as post-mortems were carried out on bodies in which the police had an interest. He hated the place. 'What I was trying to do was understand the situation. If you're telling me we've got a suspicious death on our hands, and we might have a six-day-old crime scene, then I'll work with that. Just give me all the facts you've got, and I'll take it from there. It might be that the delay won't matter in the long run.'

Souza confirmed the poison had been ingested through the victim's mouth, and there were trace amounts on the skin of the dead woman's hands. Emily Kitts had somehow taken in the poison over a lengthy period of time – probably hours – in small doses, allowing the poison to build in her system, finally resulting in a massive heart attack. The fact the woman still had sufficient mental capacity to dial 999 and report her condition was a surprise to Dr Souza.

Glover also managed to elicit the doctor's suspicions that the victim would have been feeling the symptoms of nicotine poisoning for several hours; they would have included feeling dizzy and nauseous, and probably profuse sweating. 'Given her age, and general condition, the deceased might have believed she was experiencing menopausal hot flashes,' added the medic. 'They're a bugger, I can tell you that much from personal experience; you convince yourself you just have to work through them. She could have ignored, or at least rationalized, her symptoms for many hours.'

Glover confided, 'Betty tells me she's convinced her personal thermostat's packed it in altogether; she's not having an easy time of it.'

'I know exactly what she means. Tell her she has my sympathies, and send her my best, Evan,' said the doctor.

'Will do. She keeps telling me to ask you and Gareth over to our house. And I do, as you know. Please let's try to work out a date?'

'You know we'd love to come, Evan, but you of all people understand how difficult it is to set a date for something as simple as a dinner. But let's try. You, me, our calendars, and a promise of Betty's lamb ragout, and we should get something sorted within the next month or so, right?'

Glover chuckled ruefully. 'We'll see, eh? Anyway, Rakel, back to the matter at hand; what exactly is a large dose of nicotine, and did she eat it, or drink it?'

'We're talking about the woman taking in about a teaspoon full of pure nicotine. Someone could have boiled down cigarettes to produce a horrifically bitter potion, or maybe they could have got her to swallow one of those bottles of nicotine liquid you can buy almost anywhere these days for those vaping devices. Of the two – if I were a poisoner, or someone contemplating taking their own life – I'd go for the latter; spending a few quid on a bottle of colorless, tasteless liquid that can kill someone is a lot easier than boiling up packets and packets of ciggies for hours on end. But I cannot yet tell you which method was chosen by our killer – if that's what we're talking about. You see, I cannot say for sure the woman didn't do this to herself, then phone for an ambulance when she had second thoughts. What I *am* certain about is that her stomach contents – the remains of some biscuits and what I believe was a ham sandwich – were negative for nicotine when tested, so I think it's unlikely she ate or drank the poison in one hit. I believe it was absorbed gradually through the lining of her mouth.'

'Sounds like a conundrum,' observed Glover, his heart sinking. 'Isn't there anything you can tell me that might be helpful?'

Souza swore in Welsh; she was well-known for doing so when talking to monoglots, and Glover was certainly one of those – though his years of playing rugby meant he was more than passingly familiar with Souza's exclamation. 'The skin's the most efficient way for the poison to enter the body, but the amount on the victim's hands was pretty small – far too small to have done the damage, and there weren't large patches of the stuff painted onto her, or anything like that. No puncture marks, either. She definitely ingested it. I'll admit I'm puzzled, but there are still a few tests I can do. I'll get you whatever I can as soon as possible. But you can't rush science.'

Glover recognized one of Dr Souza's favorite ways of shutting down a conversation, but he decided to add, 'Listen Rakel, you've just caught a suspicious death – feel proud. Who knows what happened here – that's up to us to find out – but without your diligence, we'd never have known a thing about it. So, thanks.'

He hoped Souza was mollified, but was also aware that a six-day-old trail to what might be a murder – or possibly an intentional overdose – meant a long day, or week, lay ahead of him. Even though it was only Monday, he sighed as he visualized the weekend trip to the Brecon Beacons he'd planned with his beloved Betty disappearing over the horizon, maybe never to be retrieved.

He weighed the idea of stopping to grab a quick coffee, but realized if he could get away from HQ quickly he'd stand a better chance of missing the afternoon school rush, when the streets of Swansea became a nightmare knot of traffic. So, instead of bothering to sit down behind his desk, he patted his pockets to check he had all his communication devices, and called into the cramped office across the hallway, 'Stanley, with me right now, please.'

As he continued toward the staircase a youthful blond head popped out of the office door into which Glover had shouted. 'Sir?'

'Suspicious death, Stanley. Drop everything. I'll drive, and you can gather all the salient details as we go, okay?'

It wasn't a question, and Detective Sergeant Liz Stanley knew it. The Welsh habit of finishing a statement of fact with what *sounded* like a question was something she'd quickly noted after moving to South Wales from her native Bristol; it had been bad enough being an Englishwoman in a Welsh police service, to not understand the way her colleagues used the language she'd always assumed they shared would have been an affront she'd never have overcome.

Stanley gathered up her jacket and followed her boss to the small car park behind the police station. They sped from the courtyard with Glover driving, passing information to Stanley as she made notes. She also opened the files Dr Souza had emailed, and read them aloud to her boss.

Glover wrapped up their exchange as they parked. 'So we'll talk to the husband who has no idea we know about the poison. I want to keep it that way for as long as I can.'

'Yes, sir.' This was Stanley's standard reply to pretty much all of Glover's statements and questions, not just because Glover was her boss, but because she had enormous respect and admiration for him; he was an instinctive detective, rather than a slave to procedure, but he also managed to retain the support of his bosses by doing just enough to keep on the right side of the politics at HQ.

Having been assigned to Glover for about six months, Stanley was still in awe of him as she watched him swoop down on the facts of a case and make sense of them in a way no one else could. There was no question about it, the man saw connections and disparities that escaped his colleagues, and he was able to draw the right conclusions from what it seemed he alone had observed. Stanley knew she'd been lucky to be put to work with him, and she always hoped some of Glover's 'magic' would rub off on her. But she doubted it; she knew she was bright, but accepted she was a slogger – a woman good at keeping facts straight and following up on leads, but somehow she couldn't make sense of them the way Glover could.

'You ready for this then, Stanley?'

'Yes, sir,' replied the DS as they stood at the door of 65 Plasmarl Park Terrace.

'Say next to nothing, follow my lead, and look as thick as possible, right?'

'Yes, sir.'

'Not that looking thick should be a problem for a Bristolian, eh?' joked Glover. He quickly added, 'Don't tell HR I said that unkindly. I meant it as a witticism – you understand that, right? We just had that seminar on respect in the workplace, didn't we? Sorry.'

'Not a problem, sir, I get it,' replied Stanley, stifling a smile.

Glover rearranged his features to look suitably grave when a short, balding man, aged somewhere around the mid-fifties, opened the door to them.

'Mr John Kitts?' Glover and Stanley showed their official IDs, which the man peered at through thick-lensed spectacles as Glover introduced himself and his DS. Glover cut across the man's hesitant 'Yes' with a businesslike, 'We're here about your wife, Mrs Emily Kitts, sir. Our condolences for your loss. I wondered if we might have a few words? Just wanting to get the facts of her demise straight. I'm sure you understand – an unexpected death in the home and all that . . .' Glover's voice trailed off into a warm yet polite smile – a smile that disarmed most people.

John Kitts invited Glover and Stanley into the house, where Glover detected the nauseous bouquet of any number of cleaning products. He wondered whether Emily Kitts had been an 'obsessive compulsive deodorizer', which was how his wife referred to women who just couldn't stop trying to make things smell like something they weren't; Betty hated toilets perfumed with citrus fruits, and carpets redolent of summer florals.

Considering John Kitts' generally unkempt appearance, Glover suspected personal hygiene hadn't been top of the list of things the man had attended to in the past several days, something he reckoned the late wife would never have let him get away with. He spotted a mound of dirty dishes peeping over the top of the kitchen sink, and half-full mugs were dotted on every available coaster in the living room.

'I'd offer you tea, or coffee, but I'm out of milk.' Kitts sounded as though he couldn't have cared less about the tea, the coffee, or the milk.

Glover was running all the standard questions in his head as he took the seat he was offered. Had this man killed his wife? Might he have wanted to? Could he have? How would her death change his life? Glover had to find out the answers to all those questions, and more – and without letting on he knew that anything untoward had happened. He'd have to tread a fine line, with care.

'Don't worry about us, Mr Kitts – we're just fine without a cup of anything, aren't we, Stanley?' Glover beamed at his sergeant, who nodded and beamed back – inanely, as requested. 'I'm sure you've got much more important things to be thinking about than buying milk, Mr Kitts,' continued Glover. 'I understand your wife's death must have been a terrible shock for you. Might I ask what happened, exactly?'

Kitts seemed to be immediately engaged, excited even, and leaned forward in his chair as though to take the officers into his confidence. He looked around the room before he began to speak, and when he did so it was in not much more than a whisper. Glover wondered just how controlling Emily Kitts had been.

'It's been awful. I never imagined being without her, you see. She's been the love of my life since we were fourteen. Well, she was fourteen, I was a few years older. We met in school and we've never been apart since. And now? Well, I don't know, really.' The man seemed deflated, genuinely despondent, and confused.

Glover had to admit that, if Kitts was acting, he was doing a good job of it.

'You see, I wasn't here when it happened,' Kitts continued, bleakly. 'I could have helped her if I'd been here, I'm sure of it. I'll never forgive myself. If only I hadn't forgotten that stupid newspaper. I always buy the newspaper on my way home from work.'

'And where exactly do you work, Mr Kitts?'

Kitts seemed surprised by the question, but answered promptly, 'I work in the City Archives down at the Brangwyn Hall. I've always been an archivist – it's fascinating work, you know.' He seemed to be about to try to convince Glover that poring over old papers and filing them away was an intriguing job, but Glover helped him get back to the point.

'So you usually get the newspaper on the way home, you were saying?' he pressed.

'Yes, that is my habit,' replied Kitts breathlessly. 'I pass the shop at the end of the road on my way from the bus stop, so it's no trouble, and it means we don't have to pay that silly paper boy a weekly delivery fee. Anyway, I forgot it; I remembered I'd forgotten it just as I got about halfway up the road. I knew how disappointed Emily would be, because she loves – *loved* – to keep up with the local news, you see, so I turned around and went back to get it. One thing led to another, and I suppose I was in the shop for a fair bit, just having a general chit chat. When I came along the road the second time, there was an ambulance at our front door, and a bit of a crowd had gathered; all the neighbors were trying to find out what was happening. I rushed in, and there was poor Emily white in the face on the floor in the kitchen, and they were trying to get her heart to start. But they couldn't. They tried and tried, but they couldn't make it work. And then I couldn't get hold of Dr Jenkins, because he was on holiday, and the young lady doctor they sent instead of him wouldn't sign the death certificate. It was all most upsetting.'

'I know this must be difficult for you, going over it all again, but I'm sure you understand we have to make some sort of investigation in the case of an unexpected death.' Glover thought he'd leave it at that and see what happened.

Once again, Kitts scanned the room before he bent his head forward and whispered, 'Yes, I understand, and so you should. I can't understand it, you see. Emily was never ill a day in her life. Never complained of anything ever being wrong with her whatsoever. She was as healthy as a horse. Ask anyone.' Kitts leaned even closer to Glover and added, 'But you do hear about these things, don't you? You know, an apparently healthy person dropping dead with no warning, then you find out they've been living with some sort of undiagnosed condition hanging over their head all their life, unbeknownst to them. I expect to hear something like that when they've had a chance to examine poor Emily. Mind you, I wish they'd hurry up – there are so many things to plan, and I still don't know when I'll be able to have the funeral. They seem to be terribly slow at that hospital.' Kitts reached out a hand and laid it upon one of Glover's. 'I don't suppose you could help with that at all, could you, inspector? I'd be ever so grateful. There's such a lot to get done, you see.'

Glover withdrew his hand from Kitts' moist grip, which made him think of damp putty, and straightened in his seat. 'I'll do what I can, of course, Mr Kitts, but I need to clarify a few things first. Now, about your wife; do you know what she'd been doing while you were out at work that day?'

Kitts reflected for a moment and stared hard at Stanley, who sat with her pen poised above her notepad.

Licking the tip of his thumbnail, Kitts replied, 'Well, it was Tuesday, so I suppose she'd have cleaned the bathroom, then she'd have done the ironing and starching. That was Tuesday, Monday being laundry day.'

The widower obviously felt he'd answered the question fully, but Glover followed up with: 'Might I see the bathroom, and wherever she'd have been doing the ironing and starching, please, Mr Kitts?'

The man seemed puzzled, but answered politely, 'I don't see what good it will do, but you're more than welcome.' He led the two detectives up the narrow, steep stairs to the bathroom. Other than a couple of globs of toothpaste in the bowl of the sink, and a few items being out of place, it was dazzlingly clean and exuded some sort of sickly scent Glover couldn't place. Kitts then led them to what would have been a spare bedroom, had it not been turned into a repository of what Glover assumed to be the epitome of clothing care; a large ironing board with a fierce looking iron sitting upon it dominated the center of the room, beside which stood two smaller boards that seemed ready be to locked into place on top of the larger one. Beneath the net-curtained window that looked across to the terrace of houses opposite was a low rail, upon which hung a wide selection of men's shirts – mainly white or blue – and a veritable rainbow of women's blouses. On the right-hand side of the room was a rail carrying an assortment of dresses, skirts and trousers; all perfectly pressed, each item was covered with a clear plastic bag to protect it from the non-existent dust in the house. The final wall, to the left, was filled from the floor to the ceiling with an open-fronted organizing system comprising small cupboards, cubby holes, and shelves bearing plastic bins with labels that read 'Black Shoes', 'Brown Shoes', 'Canvas Shoes', and 'Evening Shoes'. A further array of shelves was filled with piles of immaculately folded garments. Glover smiled inwardly at what Betty would think of all this; anal was a word that came to mind.

'Your wife seems to have been an admirably well-organized woman, Mr Kitts,' commented Glover, wisely keeping the sarcasm out of his voice.

'Indeed she was,' gushed Kitts, 'like I said, I don't know what I'll do without her – she kept me so well-turned out.' The front door bell pealed in the hall below; Kitts seemed uncertain about what he should do.

Glover spoke casually, 'Why don't you see who's at the door, Mr Kitts? We'll be just fine here. You'll know where to find us.' He smiled his special smile.

Kitts bowed his way, backwards, out of the room and Glover and Stanley could hear vague sounds coming from the hallway. Stanley quickly and quietly pulled out plastic bins, poked around in and behind the hanging clothes, and made a dash for the other bedroom. At the same time Glover was making himself at home in the bathroom, checking the contents of the medicine cabinet, and of the alarmingly well-stocked cupboard full of cleaning products beneath the sink.

By the time John Kitts rejoined them they were both standing in the laundry room nonchalantly admiring the view of the houses across the street.

'A neighbor calling?' asked Glover, as he watched the woman who had just left the Kitts' home enter a house across the road.

'Yes, Mrs Roberts. Mary. She's been such a help, I don't know where I'd have been without her stews and pasta dishes. I've never been much use in the kitchen; Emily always said I got under her feet. I only know how to make bacon and eggs, and I'm not very good at the eggs. You can't live on that, can you?'

Glover knew it was best to refrain from making a crack about hardening arteries to a man who possibly believed his wife to have died of a heart attack, so asked, 'Were Mrs Roberts and your wife good friends?'

Kitts considered his answer briefly, then said, 'I don't think Emily had any real friends, in the normal sense of the word. She didn't like to be close with anyone except me. But I know Mary always came here for tea and so forth on a Thursday morning. Wednesday was Emily's baking day, so Thursday was the best day to have someone over, you see.'

'I do,' replied Glover. As the threesome descended the stairs he considered the regimented way in which the Kittses had lived their lives. He wondered if there might be a list of daily duties hanging on a noticeboard somewhere in the house, or whether the routine had been so well-known by the couple after years of endless repetition that one wasn't needed.

They arrived back at the kitchen, which had obviously proved too much for Kitts; as Glover had suspected, Kitts wasn't a washer-upper, he was a stacker, and the stack had reached toppling point.

'That's what Mary was after – her casserole dish,' said Kitts pointing at a ceramic pot caked with something brown, half-poking out of the sink. He looked sheepish as he whispered, 'I told her I hadn't finished it – I suppose I'd better give it a bit of a rinse before I give it back. She's been so solicitous these past few days, but Emily always said she was a bit overly fussy about that sort of thing.'

Glover wondered how a woman to whom cleanliness was clearly such a priority could say that someone else was 'overly fussy', and decided he'd like to meet this Mrs Mary Roberts, so it was with the information that she lived at number 64 that Glover and Stanley took their leave of John Kitts, with Glover promising the man he'd telephone him as soon as he had any information about the release of his wife's body.

As they ambled across the road Glover and Stanley compared notes.

'Anything useful or notable in the laundry room or bedroom, Stanley?' asked Glover hurriedly.

Stanley, a woman of few words, answered succinctly, 'Nothing out of the ordinary, sir,' then added with an eye-roll, 'well, not for that type, anyway. The bed was poorly made, but I suspect he doesn't even know how to do that much for himself.'

Glover nodded his agreement. 'Nothing in the bathroom either, except enough Vim to kill a horse. But she didn't die of Vim, she somehow got nicotine into her system, and I didn't see any phials of that lying about anywhere. The kitchen seemed to be clean, too, in our sense of the word.'

They'd arrived at the front door to Mary Roberts' house; Glover spotted the remnants of movement in the net curtains at the window, and the door was opened before he had a chance to knock.

Mrs Roberts was a slim, angular woman in her early fifties, with chestnut hair suspiciously free of grey, and a liking for a shade of lipstick Glover thought had gone out of fashion in the Forties – it was the most vivid red he could remember seeing since they'd done away with the old telephone boxes. When she smiled, Mary Roberts looked as though she'd like to eat a person. Whole. Glover suspected it was the redness of her lips and the strange length of her teeth that made him conjure up the wolf from Little Red Riding Hood, and he couldn't shake the image as he took the woman's hand; her long fingers wound around Glover's, and her talon-like red fingernails dug into his flesh.

'Detective Inspector Glover and Detective Sergeant Stanley, ma'am,' said Glover. He knew a certain type loved to be ma'am-ed, so he laid it on thick. 'We understand from Mr Kitts that you were friendly with his wife, Mrs Emily Kitts, and we wondered if we might have a few words?' Glover knew that sometimes the less he said, the better.

'But of course, inspector, would you both like to come in? I'm sure we'd be more comfortable in the parlor than on the doorstep.'

As Glover recalled that 'parlor' had been his own mother's preferred term for the largely unused front room of their tiny family home, Mary Roberts ushered the detectives into her version of heaven on earth. As in the Kitts' home everything was spotless and gleaming, and the smell of deodorizing chemicals hung in the air. But there the similarity ended; this house was a symphony of monochromatic beige upon beige, all presumably in the best possible taste, and all probably horrifically expensive. It was like seeing the before and after in a home make-over show – with the Kittses favoring the floral, flounced before, and the Roberts house showing what 'good design' could achieve in essentially the same space. Glover had felt overwhelmed by detail and pattern in the last house, now he was under-whelmed and uncomfortable – everything seemed to be bland, yet sharp and angular. Even the chairs upon which he and Stanley perched, rather than sat, seemed to be inadequately upholstered.

When Mary Roberts thrust a square cup sitting atop a square saucer into his hands, Glover wasn't surprised.

'Now then,' she gushed, as she offered a square plate of custard creams, 'tell me everything.'

Glover placed his tea upon the rectangular glass table in front of him and smiled. 'Well ma'am, we were rather hoping you could tell *us* something. We're trying to get a clearer picture of Mrs Kitts' life and habits. You understand, of course – sudden death, and all that.' He beamed his special smile at her, and she flashed her frightening teeth back at him.

'Of course I understand. I mean, we all watch the telly and that, don't we? But it wasn't such a surprise, you know. She was never a well woman; she was always complaining about her indigestion, and her back, and her head. She said it was a miracle she got out of bed some days.'

Glover found it interesting that the husband and the friend should tell two such different stories about Emily Kitts' health; he wondered which one was telling the truth.

'Of course,' clucked Mary Roberts, as if she'd read Glover's mind, 'she never told John anything about anything. She said she never wanted him to worry about her. But she wasn't a well woman. They say it was her heart. Is that right?'

It was clear to Glover that Mary Roberts wanted to be *the* one with the news in the area – he could almost feel the net curtain brigade twitching with excitement, knowing they'd get the inside story from Mary the minute he and Stanley left her house.

Play it safe, Glover, he told himself. 'Well, at this stage I can't say too much, of course; we're just trying to get a fuller picture of Mrs Kitts' routine. Who she saw, where she went, what her habits might have been. That sort of thing.'

Not a mention of 'Might someone have wanted to murder her?' or 'Was she in the state of mind to take her own life?'

Mary Roberts' teeth gleamed. 'Emily was quite the local character, Inspector Glover.' She laughed lightly, then added in a more somber tone, 'It's why we'll all miss her so. You see, you could tell the time by Emily; if it was ten o'clock on a Monday morning, she'd be hanging out the washing; unless it was raining, then she'd use her dryer. If it was nine o'clock on a Wednesday morning, she'd be off to the shop to get her baking supplies, and if I was so much as two minutes late for our ten thirty appointment on a Thursday morning she'd sulk through our coffee and cakes until I'd apologized at least three times.'

'How interesting,' Glover responded. 'Did she have many friends?' he asked.

'Oh no, Emily didn't have friends – she just had people who served her; you know, the people she met in the shops. I was the only "real" person she had anything to do with. She and John have been over here for dinner a few times, and I've been there to dine too, of course, and I'd go to hers every Thursday, but that was it. The whole of the rest of her life revolved around her house, and making John look good. Emily didn't have time for anything that took her attention away from those priorities. And of the two, I'd say the house was more important to her. Yes, what people thought of her house, then what people thought of poor John. Though, you see, no one ever really saw her house. So there's that. I don't think she actually cared about John, as such, just what people thought about the way she turned him out for work every day, and how he looked and acted when they did the shopping in town at the weekend. She dressed him like he was a doll, you know. I heard her telling him once to change before he came down for dinner one evening – she'd laid out all his clothes for him and instructed him on how to dress as though he were three years old.'

Glover had suspected Emily Kitts had controlled her husband; maybe this was an insight into just how far she had taken that role. Might her cowed husband have fought back by somehow getting her to take a lethal dose of poison? Might he have sought his revenge for years of being browbeaten, and killed to obtain his freedom?

'Does Mr Roberts know the Kittses too? Might we have a word with him?' asked Glover.

Mary Roberts studied her fingernails. 'There hasn't been a Mr Roberts for about two years now, dear. He was a smoker and a drinker, and it finally got him – had a heart attack one morning and that was that. Sixty-one and didn't look a day over fifty-five they all said. A good-looking corpse he made. We even had an open viewing at the funeral directors'. He'd have liked that, Harry; always very proud of his looks was my Harry. Mind you – they got him into trouble more than once. But I'm sure you know what I mean, being a good-looking man yourself.' Her expression had changed from sad to coquettish, and Glover tried to stop thinking *all the better to eat you with* as he smiled politely across a sea of beige at the woman with the frightening teeth and the fetish for right angles.

'So Mr and Mrs Kitts took you under their wing, so to speak?' Glover tried to keep the conversation going.

'Not really, dear, it was more the other way around; I felt sorry for him, and she was tolerable, I suppose. She might have kept a clean house and baked a nice Victoria sponge, but it was all about Emily, Emily, Emily if you ask me. She'd probably have been happier if John hadn't been there messing up her house.'

Trying a slightly different tack, Glover asked, 'Do you happen to know if Mrs Kitts was taking any medications?'

'She told me she'd come off the pill last year,' volunteered Mary. 'I don't know why she was even on it, if you know what I mean, but she did make a big deal of coming off it. Went straight into menopause, of course, and I got all the gory details. I know she never told John about any of that stuff, because she thought it was all something to hide under the carpet. Goodness knows what century she thought she was living in, but there you are. More tea?'

Glover declined, not having touched his first cup, and asked, 'Was she maybe taking something to help her through the change?'

Mary Roberts sipped her tea and chuckled. 'Ah, "The Change", these men are so sweet, aren't they?' She winked at Stanley. 'You lot don't know what to say when it involves anything below a woman's waist, do you? Well, not when you're in polite company anyway. But, to answer your question, I believe she used sage tea to help with the flushes, but that would be it. She tried to get me to drink the stuff once, but I told her to forget it; I've heard it's disgustingly bitter. Besides, I'm well past all that now; I put all that behind me at a very early age.' Again, the dead woman's neighbor grinned alarmingly at Glover; he did his best to ignore it.

'So you don't know of anything out of the ordinary that might have impacted Mrs Kitts' health just before she died?' he pressed.

Mary Roberts reflected for a moment then answered bluntly, 'Not a thing – she was a miserable, controlling woman, but she wasn't any more ill than she usually was. I suppose she'd been looking a bit peaky for a few days; I thought it was just one of those down weeks she got, but maybe it was more. Perhaps I should have paid more attention when I saw her sweeping the front step on Monday, looking a bit pale, but I didn't. And that was the last time I saw her. Very sad.'

Mary Roberts didn't seem to be full of regret, but Glover had to admit she seemed pretty genuine, and possibly accurate, in her assessment of Emily Kitts' character. As he and Stanley walked across the street to their car he had a suspicion the telephones would be singing along Plasmarl Park Terrace for some hours to come, but he was beginning to feel there wasn't much more he could do that evening. Not without something else to go on from Dr Souza in any case.

As the detectives were opening the car's doors a woman called to them from some way along the street. She rushed toward them.

'Excuse me, are you the police?'

Fearing some sort of emergency, Glover approached the woman rapidly. 'Indeed we are the police, can I help you at all?'

'Are you here about Emily?'

'May I ask who *you* are, ma'am?' asked Glover politely.

'I'm Beryl Hughes, from the shop at the end of the road. And I want to know if you're here about Emily.' The short, stocky woman looked cross for some reason, as though she was about to live up to the promise – or threat – of her red hair.

'Well, it's difficult for me to comment, Ms Hughes, but I can tell you we have to undertake certain enquiries in the case of all sudden deaths in the home.'

'Sudden death in the home, my eye!' snapped the woman. 'We all know she came down with a heart attack. Good God, man, she phoned for the ambulance herself and *they* told me that's what she'd had before they left.'

The red hair must have been natural, surmised Glover, or else this woman had colored it to match her temper.

Beryl Hughes continued her diatribe at the top of her voice. 'Just 'cos her doctor was on holiday doesn't mean you can go hounding that poor man. A locum not signing the death certificate? Have you ever heard of anything so stupid? And don't you go believing a word that one over there tells you; she was over in Emily's house herself on Tuesday morning, likely as not telling Emily what for, as usual. Dropped in on the off-chance, she did. Who does that? Just dropping in is so rude. She couldn't leave Emily alone. Couldn't leave him alone either – I reckon she fancies him, see, but then I dare say she fancies anything in trousers. Give you the eye, did she?' She tutted in disgust. 'I bet she did – she's always flirting with my husband, and with me there in the shop too. She's got some front that woman, I'll give her that. She's on the prowl for certain I'd say – you watch, she'll be all over poor John now he's on his own.'

Glover never ceased to be amazed at the amount of vitriol that seemed to lie just below the surface of every community. He didn't want this woman to make a scene for all to hear, with him at the heart of it, but he did want to find out what she might know, so he used his quiet, calming voice when he replied. 'As I said, Mrs Hughes, whenever there is an unexpected death and there's no primary healthcare provider able to sign a death certificate, we have to conduct certain standard enquiries. Under such circumstances it would, of course, be normal to talk things over with the spouse, and anyone who they felt had been close to the deceased. Do you think that would include you, Mrs Hughes? Were you close to Emily Kitts?'

The woman's fire seemed to be somewhat quenched. 'No, not really,' came the much quieter response. 'I mean, she'd come into the shop a few times a week and we'd talk a bit, like you do, but I wouldn't say I really *knew* her – not like a person, you know? But John, now, he'd always stop for a real chat when he came in at night for his newspaper. Bless him, he's a hard-working man, you know, and ever so nice. I just think he should be allowed to grieve at a time like this. He must be feeling it very bad. They were like lovebirds, he always said.'

Glover noted the point she'd made and asked, 'How do you happen to know that Mrs Roberts visited Mrs Kitts on Tuesday morning? I understand it was their normal routine to meet on a Thursday, not a Tuesday.'

The woman raised her eyebrows and pulled Glover close to her. 'Emily came in to buy some biscuits on Tuesday morning. Now there was a surprise; Emily always baked all her own stuff, but it seemed *that* woman had just strolled across the road and as good as invited herself in for a cup of coffee, if you like. Well, of course Emily didn't have anything to offer her, hence the dash to my shop for some emergency biscuits. I don't know why the Roberts woman was there, but you're right, Thursday was their day as a rule. Rude thing that she is; dropping in, my eye. Sticking her nose into something that didn't concern her, more likely.'

Glover thanked the shopkeeper, and promised to keep her in mind if he wanted to know anything more about what went on in Plasmarl Park Terrace, as she assured him she would be the one who would know. He didn't doubt her for one minute, and said as much to Stanley as the two finally pulled away from the kerb and drove toward HQ.

As Stanley negotiated the early evening traffic, Glover popped one of his favorite strong peppermints into his mouth and crunched loudly. Stanley knew her boss was concentrating, she also knew better than to interrupt with questions or observations. After a few minutes, when the peppermint had been decimated, Glover spoke.

'So it seems we have an uncomplaining, caring childhood sweetheart who's left behind a bereft husband, and a moaning, controlling biddy from hell who's not got a friend in the world . . . and they are both the same woman. I wonder which one was the real Emily Kitts? The husband believes she doted on him, the "friend" thinks she treated him like a child. And the friend lied about seeing Emily alive for the last time on Monday – though we only have it second-hand that she was actually at the Kitts' house on Tuesday. The shopkeeper seems to think *he's* the one we should feel sorry for, and that the Roberts woman is after him for herself. The women in this man's world all seem to think he needs looking after in some way. Why do you think that is, Stanley?'

'I think some men just bring that out in women,' replied Stanley in her matter of fact way.

'True, and quite profound, Stanley,' agreed Glover pensively, then he added, 'I didn't see it myself, did you? He seemed a pretty inoffensive chap, not the good-looking type with the puppy-dog eyes or anything like that. Now *that* I could understand. But him? Just a bit of a nondescript type. Horrible hands – damp and clingy. Don't know how he'll keep the house up with her gone. Pretty clear she did everything there. But that's not our problem. Our problem is: did she jump, or was she pushed, so to speak.'

'Nothing to suggest she took her own life – no note, no pattern of depression. Even if we believe the friend about the menopause thing, they don't *all* go around topping themselves, do they, sir? Menopausal women, I mean,' added Stanley.

'Delicately put,' replied Glover, 'for someone in their thirties.'

'And if she was going to do away with herself,' continued Stanley, seemingly oblivious to Glover's barbed comment, 'why use something as elaborate as nicotine poison? Surely an overdose of something you can buy in the chemists' would have done just as well? Nicotine is a pretty exotic way of doing it, wouldn't you say, sir?'

'Well, exotic is one word for it, Stanley,' agreed Glover, 'and I think you're right about the suicide theory. I never thought it was likely to be the case anyway, given the poison, as you say. So it's good old "foul play" then, eh?'

'Seems to be, sir,' replied Stanley. She dared to add, 'Any thoughts yet, sir?'

Glover smiled across at his subordinate. 'You know better than that by now, Stanley. Cards close to the chest, that's me. But what about you? Let's see what you think.'

Stanley shifted behind the wheel. 'I think it all hangs on how the poison got into her system, sir. Kitts wouldn't have had the chance to give her anything specific to eat or drink that day; he was at work – Wilks just texted to confirm that. But it could have been something he'd left in the house for her to suck on, you know, something that would dissolve like boiled sweets or something – no problem with access there. He could have put something into the herb tea mix maybe? That way might it have absorbed into the stomach lining and not shown up in the stomach contents? But motive? Well, Wilks says there's no huge life insurance policy on the dead woman, and they seem to get by on his income quite well. They have a savings account with a couple of grand in it, but that's it. It seems to me he'll lose out by her death, especially if we go with the "lovebirds" theory. It could have been the Roberts woman – sounds like she lied about being there that day, but I can't imagine the motive. It can't be because she thought he was a catch, surely? And it doesn't seem as though anyone else ever went into the house, if we believe Kitts himself, and what the Roberts woman said. Maybe the Hughes woman in the shop hated Emily's guts and poisoned the biscuits?'

Stanley chuckled, but Glover didn't, instead, he stared grimly at the road ahead of them as he asked, 'Who stands to gain by this death, Stanley? That's what I don't understand. When people kill it's usually to get something they want, or to stop something happening that threatens their lifestyle or their standing in the community, or maybe threatens someone they love. What could Emily Kitts have done to someone, or what could she have threatened to do to someone, to make them do this to her? Or what does her not being around any longer give someone the chance to have, or do? Kitts will be "free" if we disbelieve his "lovebirds" idea, or Roberts can get her hands on him now he's a widower – those are the simplistic choices.'

'Or what if the shopkeeper has some plot to get rid of Emily, then her own husband, and run off to Spain with Kitts?' offered Stanley.

They both chuckled, then Glover crunched another peppermint as they crawled toward HQ. By the time Glover was behind his desk again it was almost 7.00 p.m., but he put in a call to Dr Souza on the off-chance he might catch her before she left for the night.

Souza answered the call herself. She sounded elated, yet concerned, as she told Glover what the path lab had told her. 'The nicotine definitely got into Emily Kitts' system via her mouth – that's where the greatest concentration was found, but she didn't drink it, or eat it. The best we can come up with is that she licked it, or sucked it.'

Glover shared Stanley's idea about boiled sweets, which Souza agreed might be a possibility. Then he asked, 'What do you mean she could have licked it, if she didn't suck it? Do you mean like it was on postage stamps, or a whole load of envelopes, or something?'

Glover could hear the smile in Souza's voice as she replied, 'You could be right, but she'd have had to have licked a lot of postage stamps or envelopes over about three or four hours to arrive at this pattern of saturation.'

Glover hadn't seen anything in the Kitts' house to indicate that Emily Kitts had spent her day licking hundreds of stamps, but she might have been sending out some sort of mailshot for some reason. He'd check that. 'Anything else?'

'Yes,' replied Souza, twittering with excitement, 'I can tell you the poison was made from cigarettes, rather than being a formulation manufactured for use with a vaping device. We found chemicals in her tissues that come from cigarettes – not when they are smoked, but when the cigarette tobacco is in its un-burned state. I think someone took quite a bit of time to literally cook up a potion from maybe hundreds of cigarettes, probably warming the tobacco in as little water as possible to extract the nicotine, then reducing the liquid to make it more potent. They'd have ended up with a dark brown, extremely bitter liquid. We can't tell how strong the solution was, only that a good deal of nicotine entered the woman's system via her tongue and the walls of her cheeks. As for the amount we found on her hands, well, it was high, but as I told you earlier today, it wasn't enough to kill her.'

Souza let Glover absorb the information. She waited for the detective to ask the inevitable question. It came within about three seconds. 'How would someone know how to do that? I mean – how does a person find out about boiling cigarettes to make nicotine poison?'

Dr Souza was ready with her answer. 'You know, Evan, years ago I'd have said you'd be looking for someone with a good working knowledge of chemistry, but nowadays it's the sort of thing you can find out about on the Internet.'

Glover himself used the Internet as a valuable research tool, but he always wished it could be policed better; like blunt instruments or knives, it wasn't the tool that was to blame, but the way people used it. In this instance it meant anyone could have worked out how to make a particularly nasty poison.

'Doc, is there anything about this woman's body that might give you a hint as to how or why she might have licked the poison – anything that might give me a lead as to what she might have licked it off?' Glover was fishing, hoping that Souza had something more up her sleeve, but he was disappointed.

'I'd like nothing better than to be able to help, Evan – but there's nothing there. There's nothing to suggest that any other substance entered her body *carrying* the poison, so I can't give you a clue, I'm afraid.'

Glover knew he'd have to work with what he had. He thanked Souza and popped his head around Stanley's door as he pulled on his jacket and made his way toward the exit. 'I'm off, Stanley – anything for me before I go?' Hope against hope.

'Nothing much, sir. Wilks has been checking the system for records connected with our cast of characters; nothing on anyone. Well, not living anyway; Mary Roberts' husband, Harold, was once had up on indecent exposure charges, but it seems it was a Rag Week thing when he was up at Cardiff Uni back in the Seventies. Otherwise they're all clean, not even a parking ticket outstanding on any of them. I spoke to Kitts' boss in the City Archives; he wasn't happy that we reached him at home, but he was quite forthcoming. Kitts is well-respected at work and they all say he's quiet, diligent, and highly professional. Apparently a clever man, they say. The victim never worked, so no pool of disgruntled ex-colleagues to look into. They own the house outright – paid off the mortgage about five years ago, and all the bank accounts seem to be in order. And that's about it, sir. Any more news on the poison?'

Glover passed on the information he'd gleaned from Dr Souza, and Stanley agreed it didn't help much. Preparing to phone Betty to warn her he was on the way home, Glover's parting words to Stanley were spoken as he marched along the hallway, 'See you bright and early at eight – get some sleep!'

'Hello?' Betty Glover sounded out of breath when she answered the phone.

Glover was immediately in a better mood just hearing his wife's voice. 'How are you? You sound puffed!'

'Oh I'm fine – just running up- and downstairs with the clothes I've been ironing. How about you, *cariad*? Coming home tonight, are you?'

'That's why I'm calling, I'm just leaving now; home in about twenty minutes. Do you want me to pick up anything on the way?'

Betty promised him a beef stew, so Glover was able to concentrate on the drive home, knowing he'd get his favorite food when he got there – how could you beat meat and veg in a bowl full of gravy?

Half an hour later Glover was dunking chunks of a batch loaf slathered in salt butter into a steaming bowl of deliciousness. For a few moments he couldn't have been happier, but the sensual pleasure was short-lived, and his mind turned to the day that lay behind him. He knew he should really pay attention to whatever it was that Betty was talking about, but he didn't seem to be able to tune in properly.

'. . . and all I can say is I'm glad it's nearly all done now, and I won't have to do it again for another six months or so . . .' was all he caught.

He realized he should have known what Betty was referring to, so tore his mind away from the case and asked her outright, 'What was that, love?' Experience had taught him it was best to not pretend he'd been listening.

Betty Glover raised an eyebrow and patted her husband lovingly on the arm. 'I'm sorry, here I am rabbiting on about the blinkin' ironing, and I'm sure you've got a lot more on your plate than that. I'll be glad when I've managed to finish it all – that's all I was saying. But it's not important. What about you? Rough case?'

Evan Glover was not one of those detectives who liked to bounce ideas off others; he preferred to gather the facts, think about them, consider the people involved, work through all the information methodically, then try to let it all flow freely through his mind, attempting to make sense of it as he did so. But, since the Melrose case, he'd realized it could be useful to have another opinion – and that, sometimes, an outsider's was the best type of opinion to get. But in order to get an outsider's opinion he'd have to divulge facts that were not for public consumption, so the only outsider he could discuss his cases with was Betty, who absolutely understood the situation, and would never break his confidence. Also, Glover knew his wife to be an intensely intelligent woman, as well as being a trained counsellor with a background in psychology and sociology. These days she put her skills to good use at the local community center where she worked part time as a member of the Citizens' Advice Bureau, thanks to a windfall inheritance from her late Great-Aunt Barbara.

He weighed where to start, and what to tell her; he decided to begin with the most difficult problem. 'A suspicious death came in today . . .'

Betty nodded as she slurped joyfully at the rich stew.

'. . . it seems the woman died by licking nicotine poison.' Glover noticed his wife's eyebrows rise in both surprise and query. 'Yes, she licked the poison – she didn't drink it, or eat it, and nothing else went into her body with the poison; she must have licked it off a hard, non-transferring substance – and over a period of time – hours Rakel said. It would have tasted incredibly bitter, so something must have masked the taste. I know if I can work out how that was done, then I'll stand a much better chance of solving the case.'

Betty wiped her mouth with a paper napkin and asked, 'The husband?' in a muffled voice.

'Could be; he could have had had the opportunity, could have had the means – the doc tells me anyone could find out how to make the poison by looking it up on the Internet. But I can't see a motive. He'd have us believe they were soulmates, and that she doted on him. To be honest, he seems gutted. I don't think he was putting it on. But I have been wrong before.' He knew Betty could point to at least two cases in his background where Glover had come unstuck and the culprit had turned out to be the very person he'd believed had been the least likely suspect. Even *he* had to admit that sometimes he got it wrong . . . to begin with.

'Anyone else?' came Betty's next obvious question.

'She had no enemies we know of; she was a housewife, so no workmates wanting to do her in.' They chuckled, both thinking of the people Betty had frequently mentioned she'd like to throttle at her office. 'She had no real friends it seems, except the woman across the road – who reminded me of the wolf in Little Red Riding Hood; grasping, I'd say.'

They sat and ate a little more, then Betty asked, 'Would I have liked her? The woman who died, that is.'

Evan reflected as he chewed. 'Hard to say, but I think not. She was one of those women who had lace and flounces throughout the house; everything was frighteningly clean and ponged of chemical sprays. Fabulous laundry room, mind you – though I reckon you'd think it was a bit over the top.'

Betty was intrigued. 'What do *you* mean by over the top?'

'Lots of cubby holes with plastic bins with labels on them; a humungous ironing board all set up and ready to go; rails and rails of pressed shirts and stuff; a whole bedroom set aside just for ironing and starching, and so on. For a woman who apparently didn't go anywhere except the shops she certainly had a heck of a lot of clothes. It was like a shop itself – all sorts of stuff there.'

'If you'd been here this afternoon you'd have probably thought the same thing. There's a lot to do in May,' replied Betty, sounding tired.

'Okay, you've got me there. What do you mean there's a lot to do in May? What's May got to do with it?' Glover was genuinely puzzled.

'The change from winter to summer clothes, silly. Any day now you might decide you want all your lightweight stuff – you know, thinner shirts, lighter colors, even the odd short-sleeved shirt or two. So I pull everything out, sort through it, do the washing and ironing, then swap around the wardrobes – I bring some summer stuff into our bedroom, and some winter stuff goes back into the spare room. It's a busy time for a laundress, don't you know.' She winked.

'But, surely you didn't put everything away dirty at the end of last summer, did you? Why's it all got to be washed and ironed now?' Glover was still puzzled.

'Look, I might not be the type who moves all the furniture to vacuum under it every week – I'll pull the sofa out every month or so, but that's it. But when it comes to clothes that have hung around in the back bedroom all winter – well, they just aren't fresh. I like to wash them out to freshen them up a bit, then of course they all have to be ironed, and moved around the house. That's why I've been running up- and downstairs all day. My so-called "day off work" has been anything but.'

They both returned to their stew in silence. Evan wondered if he'd been told off. When the bowls in front of them were emptied, Betty picked them up and pushed them into the sink.

Evan got up and cuddled her as she stood at the counter. When Betty turned to face him he could tell by her expression she wasn't cross anymore; she was smiling warmly, and happily announced, 'There's spotted dick for afters. With custard, if you want, or syrup if you prefer, which I expect you would.'

Evan Glover was beside himself – beef stew *and* spotted dick? It was almost too much for one human being to cope with. He poured Golden Syrup over his portion of the steamed pudding and tucked in gleefully. He'd almost spoiled his appetite with a huge bowl of stew, but he'd make room for this. He was halfway through his bowl when he realized Betty wasn't eating.

'None for you?' he mumbled through a mouthful of syrupy

sweetness.

Betty patted her tummy and shook her head sadly. 'Got to watch this.' She giggled, then added, 'Another thing about it being May is that the possibility of flashing around a bit more bare flesh than usual in summer clothes is on the horizon. I'll just finish ironing these last two shirts, and then I'm done.' Evan nodded and continued to devour the pudding.

Betty poured hot water and washing up liquid into the dirty dinner bowls as the iron warmed, then chatted to Evan as he ate, and she ironed.

'So, if there's no one standing out as a suspect in this case, where do you go from here?' She didn't wait for her husband to answer, instead she added, 'I suppose you could check if the husband has any enemies – maybe someone meant to kill him, not her? Or maybe there's a deep, dark secret in the dead woman's past, or even her present. You know, some of the most boring people aren't boring at all – they're actually leading a double life. Trust me, if I've learned anything during my time working at the CAB it's that people can be hiding some incredible secrets.'

Evan respected her opinion, but reckoned Betty was clutching at straws.

'I don't know what more to say really, *cariad*,' she continued. 'I think you're right, it seems the poison thing is the crux of the matter.'

Evan nodded in agreement and wiped his mouth as he pushed away the empty dessert bowl. Betty had finished ironing the first shirt and was buttoning down the collar. As she arranged the shoulders on the hanger and fiddled with the little buttons Glover watched, grimacing; she had the metal hook of the coat hanger clenched in her teeth, allowing her to use both hands for her task.

'Careful, you could chip a tooth,' he warned.

'*Uch a fi*! I hate that metal taste,' exclaimed Betty as she removed the coat hanger from her mouth and placed it on the hook on the back of the kitchen door.

Evan was transfixed. 'Do you always do that?' he barked.

'Do what?' Betty looked taken aback.

'Put the coat hanger in your mouth like that?' Evan was even more brusque.

'Of course,' was Betty's cautious and curious reply. 'Doesn't everyone?'

Evan leaped out of his chair, pounced on his wife, and planted a kiss on her forehead. 'Don't wait up, I might be late,' he shouted as he made for the front door. Betty knew if he'd been a dog his nose would have been down, and his tail up.

'Good luck, *cariad*,' she called toward his back as he made a dash for the hallway and the jacket he'd left hanging on the banister. As Glover pulled on his coat and opened the car door with his beeper, he speed-dialed Stanley on his phone.

'Yes, sir?' responded Stanley after two rings.

'Stanley I need you and a Forensic Investigation Team over at the Kitts house immediately. Use your charms to get him to let you all in, I know you have them when you need them, though they're usually well-hidden under that sensible gray suit you always wear. I need the FIT to be able to carry out tests on the spot for nicotine. While they do that, I need you to find out if Mary Roberts got any sort of payout when her late husband kicked the bucket. In fact, I need to know what his post-mortem said – if they did one, that is. I need everyone to arrive without lights, and keep the whole thing as low-key as possible – tell the FIT lot no bunny suits out in the street before they enter – and I need them to do some very specific tests for me. Right?'

Stanley listened, puzzled, as Glover continued with details of the tests he wanted performed; she took notes, made a few phone calls, and sped toward Plasmarl Park Terrace. There she met up with the FIT sent from HQ and they all strolled as nonchalantly as possible toward John Kitts' house. Glover arrived a little later to be met by a bemused Stanley who confirmed the tests for nicotine that Glover had asked for had all turned out to be positive. Stanley could hardly contain her admiration, and couldn't work out how Glover had guessed what to look for.

She went on to answer Glover's other questions: 'Harold Roberts died in August two years ago, sir. Dropped dead with a massive coronary at the local tennis courts. There was a post-mortem, and no funny business, it seems.' Stanley looked up at Glover who was popping a peppermint into his mouth. 'Wife got the life insurance – it was a couple of hundred grand. No problems there either. It all seemed above board, sir.'

Glover chewed and crunched. 'Do you happen to know what the man studied at Cardiff Uni – where he so happily exposed himself all those years ago?'

Again, Stanley referred to her notes. 'Here we are, sir – it seems he graduated from the School of Pharmacy. The late Harold Roberts was a dispensing chemist at a shop in Bonymaen for almost thirty years, and died just before he was due to take an early retirement.' Stanley closed her book and added, 'Always a shame that, when they go before they've had a chance to enjoy some time to themselves.'

Glover crunched, arched an eyebrow, and muttered thoughtfully, 'Alright, I suppose it might come to it that we have to dig him up – if he wasn't cremated, that is, which is most likely – but, for now, just tell the FIT folks they can get all that stuff out of there and bagged for evidence, and then you come with me to see our lupine friend.'

'Sir?'

'Mrs Mary Roberts of 64 Plasmarl Park Terrace. I'm looking forward to this.'

The two detectives crossed the road; most of the street's residents were shut in behind closed curtains, probably drinking their cocoa and watching TV, or maybe some were already sound asleep, but Glover could see the light shining through Mary Roberts' front bedroom curtains. She took a few moments to respond to the ringing of her doorbell, and Glover could tell she wasn't pleased to see them.

'Oh, detectives, it's late. And I'm not really dressed for visitors or I would invite you in, but if you don't mind––' She clutched her dressing gown around her throat.

Glover cut her off and interrupted with: 'I realize it's late, ma'am, but we are here on the most urgent business. It's about poor Mrs Kitts, you see. We really do need to speak to you, in private.'

Glover could see the turmoil in the woman's eyes. She seemed to make some internal decision, then her gaze settled upon him and she became her gracious self – the woman they had met earlier in the day reemerged, this time without the benefit of make-up.

Once again ushered into the beige parlor, Glover was unsurprised to discover it wasn't granted any softness by its lighting – the angular overhead fixture blazed with hundreds of watts, and the overall effect was to make the room look even more stark than it had by daylight. Mary Roberts looked older and less vibrant than she had that afternoon – the lack of thick make-up and vivid lipstick accounted for most of that difference, but Glover wondered if she had an inkling about why they were there. If she did, she was putting on a good act, offering tea, coffee and even 'something stronger', all of which were declined politely by Glover.

'Mrs Roberts, I don't want to beat about the bush – you strike me as the sort of woman who would prefer I come straight to the point.'

He paused, to gauge her reaction.

Her response was to relax into a chair and arrange her dressing gown as flatteringly as possible.

Ah well, thought Glover, *here we go then . . .*

Aloud he said, 'Mrs Mary Elizabeth Roberts, I am here to arrest you on suspicion of murdering Mrs Emily Kitts. You do not have to say anything, but it may harm your defense if you fail to mention when questioned something which you later rely on in court. Anything you do say will be given in evidence. I am going to ask you to accompany me to the police station where you will be questioned, and I am bringing in a Forensic Investigation Team to search your house for possible sources and preparations of certain substances that relate directly to the death of Mrs Kitts.'

The woman looked surprised, but didn't lose her composure. She asked if she could dress.

The next couple of hours were a blur for Glover and Stanley; taking anyone into custody requires an amount of paperwork that would be off-putting if it weren't for the fact it's the only way to bring a possibly guilty party to a point where they can be interviewed in a way that's acceptable to the courts, so they ploughed through the reports, and waited for the solicitor their suspect had requested to attend her interview.

It was just before two in the morning by the time Glover and Stanley – with Roberts and her solicitor – were as settled in an interview room as it's possible to be, and Glover was ready to begin his interrogation. He could tell the woman wasn't going to be an easy person to break so, rather than asking questions, he decided to confront her outright with his suspicions, and see where that got them. The recording equipment was switched on and Glover listed all those present, for the record.

He looked the woman straight in the eyes and began. 'Mary Elizabeth Roberts, I put it to you that you killed Mrs Emily Kitts by means of nicotine poisoning. You prepared the poison, an art you had gleaned from your pharmacist husband, and took it to Mrs Kitts' home when you visited her on Tuesday morning. You arrived unexpectedly at her house and invited yourself in for coffee, knowing she would likely have no baked goods left from the week before to offer you, necessitating a visit to the shop at the end of the street to buy some biscuits. While alone in her house, when she ran to the shop, you took the poison you had prepared and transferred it to the metal hooks of all Mrs Kitts's coat hangers, which were hanging in the laundry room. You knew that, being a woman of extreme habit, Mrs Kitts would be doing her ironing that day and further surmised that, it being May and the time when both summer and winter clothes are being prepared for wear, she would be ironing more than the usual amount of clothing. You left after your refreshments, allowing her to get on with her duties, and waited for the hours of her inadvertently licking the nicotine when she placed the hangers in her mouth to take effect.'

'What a very clever idea, inspector,' replied Mary Roberts coldly, 'but, even if you were to discover that all her hangers had been treated in such a way, there can be no connection with me, because I didn't do it.' And that was the response she stuck to, for two extremely long hours.

By four a.m. Glover was frustrated, Stanley was beside herself with annoyance, and Mary Roberts was still smiling her wolfish smile, clearly convinced her story would hold fast. Finally, the two detectives broke off the interview and got themselves a couple of cups of gritty coffee from the machine in the hallway.

When Glover went to relieve himself, Stanley popped into her office to see if there were any messages from the FIT. A few moments later she hammered on the door to the gents' toilet shouting, 'We've got her, sir.'

Glover pulled open the door with a grin on his face. 'The FIT lot found something?' he asked.

'They certainly did, sir.'

'And why am I only finding this out now?' was Glover's bear-like reply.

'The report's just come through on e-mail, and they rang the front desk to tell us to check what they'd sent. They've only been on it a few hours really, sir.' Stanley was doing all she could to placate her boss.

'Alright, alright, Stanley, let's give the little pointy heads the benefit of the doubt. What have they found to help us out?'

Stanley smiled. 'Believe it or not, sir, they have found a small pastry brush in one of Mary Roberts' kitchen drawers with heavy traces of nicotine at the base of its bristles; it seems she didn't wash it out thoroughly enough. Hers are the only prints on it.'

Glover nodded and looked pleased. 'Pretty good, Stanley, but is it good enough? Is it enough to break her? I don't suppose there's anything else is there?'

'Yes, there is, sir.' Stanley was almost bursting.

Glover smiled. 'Go on then; you've saved the best till last, haven't you?'

'Oh yes, sir. How do you feel about a saucepan with trace amounts of nicotine, found in her kitchen? It was one of those old enamel pots and the nicotine was found underneath a couple of chipped bits in the base. Strong stuff, they said. And again, only her prints.'

'Am I allowed to pat you on the back, without it being misconstrued?' asked Glover with a smirk.

'I believe so, sir,' replied a beaming Stanley.

Returning to the interview room, Glover formally charged Mary Roberts with the murder of her neighbor, then outlined the new evidence for the benefit of the woman and her solicitor. He hoped she would confess, but could tell by her expression this was not her plan.

'Your fingerprints on the pastry brush, and ditto for a cooking pot with nicotine in its base? It's damning, Mrs Roberts. No jury will believe you didn't do it.' Glover hoped she'd break.

'Well, I'm afraid your evidence is wrong,' replied the accused woman tartly. 'I am a fastidious person in the kitchen, and I am particularly so when it comes to enamel – it's a tricky surface. There won't have been anything for you to find on the pot. Because I didn't do it.'

Glover pounced. 'Now isn't that interesting, Mrs Roberts; I don't believe I specified it was an enamel pan, and all your others are stainless steel.'

He knew he had her.

Around nine o'clock in the morning, Mary Roberts finally told her full story. When Glover asked what had made her think of the coat hangers, her straightforward answer was: 'Well, it's pretty obvious really, isn't it? I mean, what *would* she put in her mouth that tasted awful? I did think about the sage tea, but she never drank it when I was there, and I couldn't be sure she still used it at all.'

However, even with the benefit of her confession, it was difficult for either Glover or Stanley to fully comprehend the woman's motive, despite her explanation.

When Glover asked why she had killed Emily Kitts, Roberts smiled as she replied, 'People never see beneath the surface, do they? John is a lovely man, and Emily treated him like dirt. She went on and on about how inadequate he was, about how boring he was; but he isn't – he's a funny, intelligent man, and I would have looked after him a treat. We could have sold one of our houses and lived off the proceeds from that for a while; we'd have been very happy. Personally, I thought we should sell his, because her taste in décor was shocking, but then, mine might sell better because it's so lovely. What do you think?'

Glover could tell she had imagined that by killing Emily she could take over running John Kitts' life; she honestly believed she could make him happy, and truly believed she would be happy too. She'd completely lost sight of the value of a human life – she was simply driven by the desire to get what she wanted.

So the shopkeeper had been right in a way, and John Kitts had been right too – in that Mary Roberts was a woman to whom he could turn in his time of grief. The problem was that she was the woman who had killed his wife and caused his grief in the first place.

By eleven, a bone-weary Glover was on the phone to Dr Souza, who was eager to hear his news.

'I hear you got your man – or rather, your woman, Evan. Congratulations. Now tell me – I'm dying to know – how did she do it?'

'Coat hangers,' was Glover's cryptic reply.

'Coat hangers?'

'I tell you what, Rakel, I've got to come to see you about the paperwork on the post-mortem findings anyway, so how about I buy you a coffee and tell you all about it? You can also tell me if you think there's any chance this woman killed her first husband too. I wouldn't put it past her; she hinted he might have strayed, at least with his eyes if not with his entire body, and I don't get the impression she'd have taken to that very kindly.'

'Well, I'm happy to do what I can, of course, but you can forget the coffee, thanks. You can buy me a nice green tea instead; have you *seen* what coffee does to your insides?'

'No, and I don't want to. I'll be there in about an hour.'

Glover pulled on his jacket and called to Stanley as he walked past her office, 'With me, right now, Stanley.'

'Yes, sir,' replied Stanley as she caught up with her boss, 'where to, sir?'

'We're off to see Dr Souza and I might treat myself to a pint later – so you're driving, right?'

Once again, Stanley knew this wasn't a question. 'Yes, sir,' was her only possible reply.

JUNE

The Corpse with the Fake Purse

The applause was polite rather than thunderous, but I supposed it was the best I could hope for from a group of police officers who'd rather be anywhere in the world than in a university lecture theatre at eight o'clock on an unseasonably warm evening in June. I'd reached the part of my presentation where I was wrapping up. They seemed to have stayed with me for the last hour and knew we were on the home straight. I noticed people trying their best to not fidget and forcing themselves to look attentive as I brought up a new slide on the screen behind me.

Then I spoke what I suspected would be my most popular words that night, 'So, in conclusion –' I could sense the relief in the room – 'the concept of victimology allows us to better understand a crime by better understanding the victim. As we grow to understand the victim and their lifestyle and habits, so we are able to infer where the victim and the perpetrator might have crossed paths, if they possibly knew each other socially, or intimately, how they came to know each other, and why the victim might have become a victim in the first place. None of this places any blame on the victim, of course; it's simply one more tool in our detection arsenal. Victimology, together with forensic pathology, information sharing and management, and, of course, good old interrogation of both the facts and any suspects, can all work together in harmony, to help law enforcement professionals such as yourselves with successful crime detection, and maybe even prevention, in the twenty-first century.'

I left it at that, smiled thankfully through another, slightly more enthusiastic ripple of applause, then stepped aside while Chief Superintendent Dufray stood to make his closing comments. He rocked on his toes and looked smug as he read from his prepared notes.

'Thank you very much, Professor Morgan –' he nodded in my direction and smiled like a shark – 'for an enlightening glimpse into what the School of Criminology here at the University of Vancouver is doing in terms of victimology research, and theory building.' He emphasized the word 'theory' rather too much for my liking. 'Thank you, too, for allowing us to use these delightful premises. It's nice for us all to get away from our own buildings and breathe the slightly fresher mountain air up here, especially on such a delightful evening. But before I release all these eager young officers back into the wild . . .' He paused for a laugh, and eventually got a chuckle out of one of the youngest in the crowd. 'I have a bit of a surprise for us all.'

I was half expecting someone to step forward with a bunch of flowers or maybe, if I was really lucky, some chocolates or a bottle of champagne, but that wasn't the case. Cory, the chap who sets up the AV equipment for lectures in the part of the university we were using, pushed a trolley through the door. He smiled at me as he fiddled around with a piece of kit he'd wheeled in. I had no idea what was going on. Dufray, too, was smiling, and in a way I didn't like at all.

'Tonight we have a special treat for Professor Morgan.' Dufray's tone made the word 'treat' sound like a threat. I felt apprehensive as the projection of the slide being fed from my laptop was replaced with a vision of a young freckled face, twenty feet across, beaming at us from the screen above my head.

Dufray took a microphone from Cory, and spoke into it loudly and precisely, smiling as he did so. 'Constable Webber, can you hear me?'

The eyes on the screen opened wide, and the young man looking down upon us answered, 'Yes, sir, I can hear you just fine, sir. Can you hear me?'

'Indeed we can, Webber.' Dufray looked triumphant and turned to Cory whom he dismissed from the room with a curt, 'I think I can handle it from here, young man.'

I still didn't have a clue about what was going on. And I don't like that. Dufray addressed the room full of police officers – who were not only as puzzled as me, but were now beginning to panic they might never escape.

'I know you've all enjoyed tonight's talk about the theory of victimology, and I'm sure we're all pleased Professor Morgan was able to give us case examples from around the world where the techniques she spoke of have been used on an experimental basis. But tonight we have a unique opportunity to give her a chance to put her theory into practice, and to apply it to a real, current murder case.'

Dufray was clearly expecting some sort of reaction, but what he got was a room full of blank looks and a smile from me that could have frozen Hell. My head was whirring; what was this man talking about? My stomach was sinking; this had all the hallmarks of Professor Cait Morgan – me! – being put on the spot and made to look a right twit. And why would Dufray do that, I wondered? Then I mentally answered myself; because, despite the fact he'd gone along with the idea of tonight's lecture, I knew he had about as much use for the idea of using victimology as a day-to-day detection tool as I have for a Martha Stewart book on baking – all well and good in theory, but not really of any practical use.

When no one reacted, Dufray continued, 'Holding the camera, and ready to take direction from Professor Morgan, is Constable Webber. Indeed, we have at our disposal what one might call a "Webbercam".' Dufray paused for guffaws but only drew a polite titter from one or two in the room. He filled the empty space with his own manic laughter, then pressed on, undeterred and smiling broadly. 'Webber is at the home of a recent murder victim. Professor Morgan won't have heard about the case, because, as far as the public is concerned, we're working it as an accidental death, though we have been in no doubt the victim was murdered. I thought it would be an excellent opportunity for Professor Morgan to show us how her theories work in practice. How about it, professor – are you game?'

If I could have killed him on the spot I'd have been happy. If I could have run him through a woodchipper, alive and screaming, I'd have been happier. This man was the epitome of smugness, and a perfect example of the tendency of the inept to float to the top in the politically charged world of the modern police force. I hated him, but I kept smiling. If there's one thing I know for certain, it's that you don't let an animal with bloodlust smell fear. I stepped forward; I didn't want anyone to see me shake with anger in case they thought I was scared by this slimy little toad, and his sneaky plot.

I beamed my most professional smile, and spoke as graciously as I could. 'Gosh, chief superintendent, what a treat! You've obviously gone to a lot of trouble, and I really appreciate it. Hello, too to Constable Webber, and his "cam" –' not even a titter this time – 'but I don't want you to think of this as a party trick or a parlor game. Victim profiles can take days, sometimes weeks, to build. I think we have less than half an hour left tonight?'

Dufray grinned back at me; he thought I was wriggling on the hook, and was moving in for the kill. 'I'm sure there's something you can show us in thirty minutes or so, professor.' He hissed my title at me as though it was an accusation, not something I'd spent years earning.

'Please, call me Cait,' I replied, smiling. 'I ask all my students to use my first name.' I knew I was sinking to his level, and had to stop myself, so decided to give the little creep a run for his money.

'Okay then folks – here we go – a lightning-fast victim profile.' I decided to try to get some of them in the room on my side, but could tell it would be hard going. 'I promise I won't keep you longer than half an hour, so let's see what we can do in that time. I'll work through the victim's home, then tell you a story about their life after we've had a look around. How about that?'

It was like drawing teeth; without an anesthetic for them, or me. There was nothing left to do but get on with it, so I did. I stomped up the flights of stairs that led to the back of the amphitheater-style lecture room and took an empty seat in the middle of the back row. I had the best possible vantage point and, despite some wobbling, I had to admit the picture from Webber's camera was pretty sharp. He was standing beside a fairly nondescript front door, which obviously led to a flat – something I've now learned to refer to as a condo.

I spoke into the microphone, 'Can you tell me where you are, Constable Webber?'

Dufray answered in a shrill scream at the front of the room, 'No, he can't tell you the address, Cait, but I can tell you it's a Downtown condo, on the twenty-third floor overlooking Coal Harbour. Over to you now, Webber.'

As Webber pushed open the front door I had already worked out the condo in question must have cost somewhere between $600,000 to well over a $1 million, depending on its size and when it had been purchased, so already I knew we were talking about someone with, probably, a pretty healthy income.

The doorway led to a stubby entry hall; to the left the open-plan living, dining, kitchen area enjoyed a floor-to-ceiling wall of windows. As Webber moved inside I asked him to go to the windows and sweep the view. It was the first chance I'd ever had to see what the people who lived in those condos saw, and it was amazing; when they put 'Beautiful British Columbia' on the license plates around here, this is certainly what they're talking about. There, on a perfect early-summer's evening, we all saw the snow glistening on the tops of the mountains, the trees of Stanley Park magnificent against the skyline, and restaurant- and bar-going knots of people wandering happily through what is some of North

America's most expensive real estate. I could almost taste the calamari and the Granville Island Ale; but the stark reality was that I had to perform like a circus animal to get us out of this dreary lecture hall.

'Thanks, Webber – you've made us all as sick as pigs!' I called out, raising an unexpected wave of wry laughter from the room. Now *there* was a double entendre I hadn't intended. 'Oops!' I chuckled, and asked him to take me around the rest of the apartment. We moved from the open-plan living area into the hall, then across to a gleaming grey marble bathroom and a bedroom that seemed to be mainly bed, then we were back at the front door again.

'Thanks, Webber, now we've got the lay of the land, could you take me into the bedroom please, and let's have a look into the closets.'

The camera wobbled into the bedroom and there was a bit of a kerfuffle as Webber pulled at the sliding mirrored doors. Inside I saw a row of well-organized women's clothes; a few dresses, some lightweight business suits, blouses, and smart casual pants took up most space. Everything was arranged in color blocks. It was a single female's apartment; what sort of a woman?

'Could you pull out an item and check the label and size for me please, Webber?'

'Size eight,' he called back, 'and it's Diane von something.' The poor constable seemed baffled. I put him out of his misery.

'It's okay, I recognize the print and those two other dresses are by the same designer. Can you show me her shoes? Hold up a couple of pairs, would you? Also her bags and purses; can you do the same, please?'

He did, and I swallowed hard. She must have spent thousands on clothes and accessories; they were all classic, yet bang up to date. This woman had some serious money tucked away in her closet. Knowing she was dead made it all seem so pointless; being a size eight didn't mean she necessarily had to starve herself, but being a comfortable size fourteen I knew that if I'd ever wanted to look good in those things I'd have to go without pretty much everything that I loved, for a long time. And even then I wouldn't be able to afford them. I rationalized maybe she was an 'eat to live' person; so, not like me at all – I'm definitely a 'live to eat' type.

'Can you go through the undies drawers please, Webber?' We saw La Perla, Victoria's Secret, Marks & Spencer's, and Rigby & Peller labels. There were a few pairs of socks and packets and packets of unopened light tan hosiery. There were a couple of silky nightgowns, a few sets of tees and shorts, and a few sets of fleecy pajamas.

'Thanks, now can you go over to the bedside table?'

There we saw a frighteningly complex and modern alarm clock, an unopened bottle of spring water, and a tiny pewter elephant, sitting so his trunk pointed toward the window. The bed linens were clean, the bed well-made. The chocolate-brown suede headboard made the room look like a hotel, but its sweeping height balanced the tall windows quite pleasantly. The drawers of the table were empty.

'Have you removed anything from the scene?' I asked Dufray.

'Yes, but nothing that would prevent you from forming an impression of the victim,' was his pompous reply.

'Great,' I replied, loading the one word with as much disdain as I could muster.

The other bedside table was both empty and bare, so I asked Webber to move into the bathroom. Once again, everything was ordered and clean. Her make-up box didn't hold the sort of clutter my own little squashy bag does – no half-used palettes of cheap and cheerful powder shadows for this pretty miss – she had a box with a magnifying mirror set into its lid with special lighting fitted into it too; it sat up on a glass shelf. I asked Webber how far from the ground it was – he said about five feet. Within it were expensive cosmetics, all clean and fresh-looking; the woman favored a neutral palette, and her lipsticks were in the beige to brown range. Her blemish stick was medium, her mascara brownish-black. At the bottom of the box were a few aged condom packets.

Beside the bath were lavender and chamomile bath salts, but it was clear she used the shower more often than the bath – loofahs, scrubby net balls, and salon quality shampoos and conditioners were all ready to go inside the glass cubicle. Her towels were white and fluffy. The room looked like a spa.

'Thanks Webber – now back to the main living area, please, via the hall closet?'

Webber pulled open the hall closet to reveal wet weather outerwear and a couple of cardboard boxes on the floor.

'Can we see inside the boxes, please?'

Webber hauled them out and opened the first one. He rummaged around and we were able to see a collection of old and battered items: a teddy bear; a catcher's mitt; a couple of golf balls;

some cocktail umbrellas that read 'Duke's'; a couple of swizzle sticks from a bar called 'The Onion'; a pretty pathetic looking rosette from a bouquet of flowers with no card attached; lots of napkins from various eateries; a faded old folder that contained school projects, reports, and a yearbook. The other box offered up much of the same – though this time the detritus seemed to be neither as ancient nor as dusty, in fact, stuffed into the top of the box was what appeared to be a particularly expensive, classic brown and tan handbag. My interest was piqued.

'Give us a closer look at that purse, can you, Webber? Can you have a look inside?'

Inside were a few receipts from a bar I knew to be located just below where this apartment must have been, on the waterfront. They were dated about six months earlier. There were also two lighters, a book of matches from one of the highest-end restaurants in Vegas, a couple of low-value casino chips from a casino in Downtown Vegas, and a collection of pull-tab cards and Keno slips. Otherwise the bag was empty; the insides were clean and the outside seemed to be in good condition. I wondered why it was stuffed into a box in the hallway, and not on the little shelf in her closet with all her other designer bags.

'Webber, can you hold the bag in front of the camera for a moment, and turn it very slowly, please?' The young officer managed to juggle the camera and the bag quite well, and I could see what I needed.

'Thanks, now let's dig into this box some more.'

Webber's delving revealed a small plush grey hippopotamus that wore a purple T-shirt bearing a telephone company logo, an empty bottle of a local micro-brewery's Christmas Ale, a tackily-romantic glossy birthday card that said, 'It's not fair you're not catching up' and had a handwritten message that said, 'And it's not fair you only get one gift – but you do'. It was signed Don, and there were lots of Xs and Os. A handful of matchbooks from strip clubs and questionable bars were next. Finally, Webber came out with a pack of playing cards which he immediately dropped; they scattered and slithered across the dark hardwood flooring. Webber lay the camera on the ground as he tried to collect up the cards; I knew I didn't have much time, so I asked him, instead, to get into the tiny kitchen as quickly as he could. A peek into the fridge showed it to be almost empty, except for a bottle of Veuve Cliquot champagne, and an unopened jar of cocktail onions.

'We've emptied this out, Cait,' interjected Dufray. 'We removed all opened food items from the home. We also took away the garbage from under the kitchen sink, and from every other room.'

That helped me somewhat – at least I knew what *not* to look for.

As Webber moved around the kitchen I noted some implements I'd have expected to see there were not on show; upon his pulling open the dishwasher I saw it had been run – no dirty dishes here. Inside it were two plates, two wine glasses, two bowls, one larger bowl, various serving and eating implements, and a couple of tumblers.

The island counter was clear except for two simple holders with burned out votive candles inside them; the narrow dining table was bare, save a large glass bowl full of seashells and small stones.

The compact seating area was furnished for style and comfort, with a tan suede couch sporting beige throws, a couple of suede half-cube floor cushions, and a glass table that was clear of clutter. Along the end-wall of the apartment was ranged a large ultra-thin television, an expensive music system, and an elaborate dark metal shelving structure that had a couple of photographs tucked into two of its many square display pods. I asked Webber to show us the photos. One showed a little girl playing on a lake beach, holding a shiny quartz pebble to the camera, the other showed a family wedding group where the fashions suggested the ceremony had taken place in the 1970s; the bride was wearing a voluminous not-so-mini mini-dress and the groom had longer hair than his new wife's. There were some books, but not many.

As Webber turned back toward the couch I spotted a small table tucked between the wing-end of the sofa and the window. I asked him to take us there. On a little leather-covered table was an untidy pile of magazines; it was the only part of the apartment where perfect order didn't reign supreme. Before allowing him to touch the pile I asked him to zoom in; we saw a jumbled pile of women's magazines, and they all seemed to have little yellow sticky-notes poking out of them. I asked Webber to pick up a few and flick through to the pages where the notes appeared. In every case he turned to an advertisement – for everything from cars to shoes, from make-up to clothing, and jewelry. Sometimes the sticky paper had a note on it – 'Damn!', 'Typical!', 'So wrong for them!' were some of the comments. After a few minutes I thanked Webber and told him to sit and take a break for a minute.

All eyes turned to me, and I was ready. I walked back down the steps to the front of the room, and could see Dufray had a twinkle in his eye. His micro-expressions told me he was just waiting for me to screw up, and that feeling had infected others in the room; whereas they'd been politely attentive during my talk, now every eye was piercing me with real interest. I knew I'd better be good. I took a big breath, and began.

'Well, that was an interesting fifteen minutes, don't you think?' They smiled and nodded. 'Being a naturally nosey person I for one think it's great to get a chance to have a look around one of those swish apartments, and on my salary that's about as close as I'm going to get!' There were some sympathetic nods around the room.

'I'm sure your boss wants me to tell you about both who was murdered *and* who did the murdering –' I smiled sweetly at Dufray and raised one eyebrow in as threatening a way as I knew how – 'but, to keep you all in suspense, I'm going to talk about the victim first. Is this the victim's only home?' I tilted my head in Dufray's direction and he nodded. 'Good. Then the victim was a single, professional woman aged thirty-five. She was of medium complexion with naturally brunette hair, cut somewhere between her shoulders and her ears, and which was – at the time of her death – colored with high- and low-lights. She was fairly fit, but didn't work out. She walked the sea wall often, but never jogged. She was slim, about five feet eight inches tall, with an athletic build. Her job was as an advertising sales manager for an up-market glossy magazine. She worked on a mixed salary and commission basis, and was good at it. Very good. She frequently traveled on business to London, Toronto, and New York, and had visited all three cities within the last six months. For vacations, she dreamed about returning to Hawaii one day, and recently went to Vegas. When she took a gap year between school and university she traveled around Thailand. She drank – possibly just a little too much at times – but she always had done; she started young, and enjoyed brew pubs, but latterly frequented fancier restaurants and wine bars. She graduated university in Vancouver, in either business or the arts, possibly even a strange mixture of both because she couldn't decide what she really wanted to do. She stayed here after graduation, but she's originally from a small town in Alberta. She was definitely heterosexual and sexually active, has had a live-in lover in the past, but she'd been living alone now for at least five years. Not much action on the man-front since then, I'd say, but she did have a relationship which lasted at least six months, that she broke off in early February this year. Her birthday is in late December, and she has a brother, who doesn't live in Vancouver.' I drew breath. I'd been concentrating hard on recalling the contents of the apartment, and hadn't really noticed what was going on around me – I do that sometimes when I'm on a roll, I sort of zone out; now I zoned back in again.

'Is this the sort of thing you wanted to know?' I asked cynically of Dufray. All eyes turned from me to him; the poor man was a picture.

He managed to clamp his mouth shut, just in time to open it again and say, 'Whatever you think you can tell us, Cait – please, continue.' Was that a little shakiness in his voice? I hoped so.

I did as he asked. 'The woman didn't own a car, she worked in the Downtown core about ten to fifteen blocks from where she lived. She'd never be seen on a bus or the SkyTrain, and had access to a car service, rather than having to take cabs. For business entertaining, which probably took at least three of her evenings a week when she was actually in town, she'd entertain in Yaletown and maybe some of the up-market ethnic places Downtown. For her own amusement, she'd go to the pubs on Robson and the clubs in Gastown. She loved Sinatra, Bublé, and Beyoncé. Oh, and by the way, she gave up smoking in, approximately, March, and was trying to cut back on her wine consumption at home. She hated to be alone, and used work as an excuse to side-step real life. She was lonely before she died, mainly because she found it difficult to trust people. You'll probably find she had many acquaintances, but few real friends, and all the people she knew will agree she was always good company, but they'll each know a slightly different person. She'll have talked to them about what *they* were interested in, never pushing a personal agenda. They'll tell you she was generous and thoughtful; always happy to buy a round at the bar, and probably the one who encouraged people to go on to a club afterwards. She would have been good at sending birthday and anniversary cards on time, and she'd have chosen them thoughtfully, to be suitable for the recipient. Any gifts she gave would, likewise, have always been carefully chosen. She didn't attend church, but was raised within an actively Anglican family.'

I stopped again, and weighed how I should continue. I couldn't resist it. 'So, shall I tell you now who killed her and how? I'm assuming you know.'

This time Dufray stood to reply. He smiled at me, but the shark-teeth weren't on display this time. 'I think we must all congratulate

Professor Morgan on an excellent job,' and he started applauding. The rest of the officers were as confused as me; was this Dufray's way of closing down the session, I wondered? The applause grew throughout the room, then Dufray announced, 'Thanks for being here – see you the next time.' And that was it; the officers were dismissed, and started to head for the door. They'd seen their chance to get out, and they were taking it; I was nonplussed, and more than a little annoyed.

Dufray and I remained at opposite sides of the room as the officers drifted out into the empty corridors beyond the lecture hall. When the last one had gone, the door slamming behind him, Dufray turned to me and let me have it with both barrels.

'That was very impressive, professor. I suppose you think you're very bloody clever. I've had a team of ten on that case for a week – and you just pretended to know it all in a few minutes. I won't stand for it. I will not be made fun of in front of my officers; I want to know who gave you your information, and I want to know now. Someone will pay for this.'

He was somewhat pink in the face; I counted to ten before I answered, telling myself to be calm when I did, but my blood was boiling too. He really wasn't a terribly nice person; I don't like bullies or hypocrites, and he was both.

I took a deep breath and forced myself to relax my shoulders. 'Chief Superintendent Dufray, all I can do is assure you I know nothing about the case you're working on. Everything I've told you is what I've deduced from what I saw via that camera, then interpreted using my knowledge, insights, and training. No one is trying to make a fool of you, chief superintendent,' I concluded. Inwardly, I was thinking he was quite capable of doing that for himself; outwardly, I smiled as genuinely as I could.

His face screwed up in what I judged to be a torrent of swirling thoughts for a few seconds, then he looked me in the eye and said simply, 'I don't believe you. I don't believe you could deduce from the scene what you just did. And, as for making out like you know how she died and who did it – there's no way you could know that just by looking at what you saw.'

I responded a little more sharply, 'If you don't believe me, I can take you through everything I've said, and tell you what I saw and how I interpreted it so you can understand the process better. As for how she died, and who did it, I agree I don't know exactly who did it, but I can tell you the man's name; it was Don. I can also tell you she was probably strangled or smothered by him after she had dinner with him at her home. Don was the ex-boyfriend she'd dumped in early February; he's probably quite a large, powerful man, and when you find him you'll discover that, although the apartment looked undisturbed, he stole all her jewelry and a few other small, high-value items. Oh – and he also probably drives a leased, high-end SUV, that won't be subtle in any way. Probably lots of spinning rims, that sort of thing. He's a wannabe gangsta-type, though I don't believe he'd have links with the gangs hereabouts.'

Dufray got even redder in the face. 'That's it! I'm out of here. I never want to see you again, young woman, and I never want to hear you've been trying to push this victimology crap to any of my officers. I will find out who has been leaking information to you, and I will have them up on disciplinary charges. You academics are unbelievable – you'll do anything to make us think your weird ideas work so you can keep getting government money and grants, just so you don't have to get a real job. Just you wait till I find out who did this to me; you haven't heard the last of this.'

He slammed out of the room and I was left alone, shaking with anger and frustration.

I've always been used to being a woman in a man's world, and all I've ever done is act like a human being, and treat others the same way – regardless of their age, gender identity, sexual orientation, ethnicity, or religion; at least, that's what I've always tried to do. But the veneer of political correctness is still just that, merely a veneer, for so many people, and Dufray had just shown his true misogynistic colors as well as his own insecurities, and his total inability to believe anyone else's way might actually work. That said, there I was with a boost of adrenaline running around my body, and the huge anticlimax of having no answer to my burning question: was I right about any of this?

I sat down for a moment to try to calm myself, then nearly jumped out of my skin when a loud, disembodied voice called out, 'So have you finished with me now, Professor Morgan?' In a nanosecond I realized I was hearing the voice of Constable Webber, who was smiling into the camera and much larger than life on the screen above me.

'I'm so sorry, I completely forgot you were there,' I exclaimed.

'Has the chief gone?' he asked sheepishly.

'Oh yes, he's well and truly gone,' I replied with a sigh.

'Good. You know, he had no right to speak to you like that,

professor. But it's how he is with everyone. They all say he's got a heck of a temper on him, but that's the first time I've seen it – or I guess I should say heard it, because I can't see you there, of course. Did you really work out all that stuff for yourself, or did someone tell you? I mean, we only just arrested the guy today and I don't think anyone on our team would have said anything. You *did* do it all on your own, didn't you?' He sounded as though he wanted me to be right, and his boss to be wrong.

'Yes, Constable Webber, I did do it all on my own. No one in your team told me a thing; I was totally in the dark when you and your camera-feed came up on the screen. I'm sure Dufray's annoyed this little experiment of his has backfired. Or has it? I don't even know if I was right.' I suspected the young officer could hear the hopelessness in my voice.

He replied with a gleeful, 'Well, I guess I get to be the lucky one to tell you everything. You were right about *everything,* I mean it was so *cool.* The woman, what she looked like, what she did, where she worked, how she lived her life – *everything.* How did you know that stuff? How? Like – how did you know she dumped the guy in early February? How could you know that?'

'The greetings cards in the box – you know, the box with the birthday card?'

'Yeah?'

'There was a birthday card that said that one gift wasn't fair, so I worked out she had a birthday near Christmas which meant she often only got one combined gift for her birthday and Christmas, and the guy who signed himself as Don gave her a card for that, but there was no Valentine's card from him, which she'd probably have kept if she kept the birthday card, so they'd split up by then.'

'And how do you know she dumped him?'

'If she'd been dumped she'd have kept more bits and pieces from times they'd spent together; she'd obviously cleared out most things connected with him, except a few items. The female dumper does that; the female dumpee keeps everything. The guy she lived with earlier – back in her past – dumped her; hence the little drinks umbrellas from Dukes in Honolulu, and the swizzle sticks and all those napkins and so forth. The littlest things mean a lot; you don't throw them away until you can't remember why you kept them in the first place, and – when you get dumped – you remember the happy times together for a long, long time.'

'Okay, I guess that makes sense, but what about all the other stuff?'

'Constable Webber, do you have a first name?'

'Dave.'

'Okay, Dave, do you want to sit down and settle yourself, and I'll tell you all about it?'

Dave Webber jumped up, jiggling the camera about, and smiled broadly into it. 'I'd love it, prof. Have you got time?'

Of course I had time; what else was there to do on a lovely June evening but grade papers? Also, if I'm honest, I just can't help myself when there's a chance to educate someone who wants to learn.

'Indeed I do, Dave, and please call me Cait. Ready?'

'Ready.'

'Looking around it's clear to see she lived alone, agreed? Nothing male at all about the place, or in the place.'

'Yep – agreed.' He nodded into the camera.

'Her physical description? Age is easy; the yearbook date allowed me to work that one out. Figure? Size eight clothes, no bathroom scales, that's pretty straightforward; she's slim and doesn't worry about weight, so probably a natural ectomorph not an endomorph. Height? Heels are mid-sized, not flats or huge stilettos, so she's tallish, and the height of the make-up mirror would suit someone about five eight. Hair? All her clothing and make-up colors tell me she's a brunette; she's always well-turned out, but there's the fact she's probably got a few greys coming in – she's the kind of woman who'd cover that up with both high- and low-lights. Length is deduced from her shampoo which is for flyaway hair – you'd never have that type of hair cut too long, but she wouldn't want the tomboy look of a crop. How am I doing?'

There was a slight pause and I thought Webber was somewhat distracted, but then he beamed and said cheerily, 'Spot on, prof – just keep going, this is great.'

I was enjoying it; it's such fun to show someone how something's done, knowing there's at least some chance they might learn something.

'Background next. The family wedding has to be her mum and dad – take a look behind them in the photo – there's a sign that tells you they're in a Kiwanis Lodge in somewhere I've never heard of in Alberta; I know the cities and larger towns in Alberta, so it wasn't much of a leap to work out they're in a small town. My socio-economic and historical knowledge tells me people stayed pretty much where they married to raise their children in those days, plus, of course, there's the same town name, with the name of the school, on the yearbook, so that's where she's from. I infer a university education from her management position, and suspect she'd have wanted to get away from small-town Alberta, hence university in Vancouver. Maybe the family had come here to see Expo in '86 and she'd decided to come back some day? A brother? The catcher's mitt, a memento of backyards and summer days – it's not her dad's, it's too small, so a brother – but there's nothing else, so they don't see each other often. A gap year? She's the sort of girl who doesn't really know what she wants to do – you don't wake up one morning and say "I'm going have a career in advertising sales", you sort of drift into it, so I'm sure she'd have taken a year off with itchy feet. The little Thai elephant next to her bed shows she cherished that place, and she'd spent enough time there to know elephants always have to face out of a room to bring good luck into it. Her job? The magazines you showed us; she's not reading the magazines, she's researching them. All the titles are up-market, and she's looking at where her potential clients are advertising. She's taking an overview – no category specialization, so she's management – that knowledge comes from the times when I worked at an advertising agency in the UK. So she's an advertising sales manager for an up-market magazine, and I happen to know that means her target advertising agencies and media planners will be in Toronto for Canada, New York for the USA, and London for Europe – hence her business travel pattern. And there's some nice underwear from the UK – she'd have bought the Marks & Spencer's stuff, and the Rigby & Peller items there – which confirms the UK business trips. Mixed salary and commission compensation package? Again, management will draw a salary, but she was a hard worker and she'd be driven by big commission opportunities. All that stuff in her closet has to be paid for, you know; any woman with thirty-three pairs of five-hundred-dollar-plus shoes needs to know she can earn big bucks.'

'Hang on a minute,' interrupted Dave, 'how do you know she's got thirty-three pairs of shoes?'

'You took the camera into the closet, and I saw them all lined up on the racks.'

Dave jumped in again, 'But how do you know there are exactly that many pairs? Do you know what colors they are too?' He was almost taunting me, and I knew I'd have to come clean about my 'gift' – but I didn't want to sound weird.

'Okay, I confess,' I laughed, 'I have what they call a photographic memory. The proper term is an eidetic memory, and many people believe there's no such thing; sometimes when I find myself standing in my kitchen wondering why I went there, even I question if it truly exists. But I do have a special ability to encode and remember all types of stimuli and recall them in great detail at will – so it is somewhat like looking at a photograph, but for every one of my senses. It's awfully hard to explain, and I prefer to not do so, to be honest, Dave, so I'd be grateful if you'd keep that confidence for me. And the shoes? There were eight black pairs, five brown or tan, two navy – do you want me to go on?'

'No, I guess not. That must be cool, eh? Have you always been like that?'

'It's not like having a second head, Dave; it's something a lot more people could do well – or at least better – if only they trained themselves. If you wanted to learn some helpful techniques, I could always suggest some reading for you.'

Dave chuckled. 'I think it's kinda over my head, prof, but I bet it's pretty cool to remember everything. I'd do great at my exams if I could do that.'

'Yes, it's pretty cool to be able to remember everything,' I agreed, but didn't add that with it went the problem of not being able to erase images you'd rather you'd never seen. Instead I continued, 'So, onto her lifestyle – I imagine you're getting the picture now; her shoes tell me she doesn't drive – no scuff marks, but she does walk – some of them have been repaired and some need a bit of work. Given her income and the quality of clothes she wears she's not going to use public transit or even a normal cab, and the media companies do so like their car services. There are no workout clothes, but she's got shoes you could walk in; however, there are no running socks, so she walks on fairly even ground, and doesn't jog. Thus I deduced she walks the sea wall; she'd have easy access given where she lives. Her job means she'll have to entertain a lot, no stretch there, but her natural preference is for the lower end of the market; the matchbook from The Onion tells us that. We all know what that place is like, don't we?'

Dave nodded. 'Yeah, it's a bit rough even for me.'

'The drinking? She's from small-town Alberta so she'd have gone to pubs – and she likes pull-tabs and Keno; definitely a pub girl. Look around you. See all the spaces there for wine bottles? See how few bottles there are? She's been used to having a lot around, now, not so much; so she's trying to cut back. And the smoking? Lighters and matchbooks in the discarded handbag, the one she was given by her ex, Don, I believe. It's a fake, by the way; you can tell by the way the material is cut through the LV logo – that's exactly what they won't do with the real ones, and she knew it. For a girl with class and money, she must have had a difficult time dealing with knowing she was in a relationship with someone who thought she'd be happy with a knock-off. The music likes? Just look at the CD collection. One of her few books is a copy of the *Anglican Order of Service*; she'd have been given that at her confirmation, so I know she was brought up as a churchgoer – but I suspect she'd be too tired and hungover to make it to church on a Sunday for many years.' I paused, thinking about what to say next. 'And that's about it, I suppose. Does that explain how I did it?'

'I guess so, except for all the personal stuff. I mean, how can you know what she was like with her friends, and all that stuff about being lonely?'

Immediately I saw a line rushing toward me I didn't especially want to cross; I didn't want to tell this young man I recognized and understood the life of a workaholic single woman, living in a world where everyone wants something from you, and where every time you trust someone they turn around and hurt you. How it becomes natural to compensate by having lots of people with whom you do things, but to whom you aren't truly attached. How life is lived so you're always in demand as the one who can make a party go with a swing, but who knows the bleak reality that everyone always lives alone, no matter how much of a crowd you try to mix yourself into. I'd lived it; he didn't need to know that.

Cover up Cait, curl and roll; bounce back, every time. Thicken that shell.

I gritted my teeth. 'I'm a psychologist first and foremost, Dave; I've turned my training in psychology to focus upon criminal psychology in the past decade, and more recently on victimology, so I can draw on what I know about general patterns of behavior for certain personality and social types, when I need to.' I left it at that.

Then I heard another voice, and the camera was showing me another face. 'Hello, Professor Morgan – Bud Anderson here, head of the Integrated Homicide Investigation Team. They call me Mister I-Hit. You can call me Bud.' He chuckled. 'I've been listening in on your explanations to young Webber here; don't blame him for not telling you I was in the room, I wouldn't let him say anything, and he's an obedient young constable.'

'Sorry, prof, he *is* my boss,' came from Dave in the background.

'I've been fascinated,' continued Anderson. 'I wanted to get to your lecture tonight but I was tied up with a little interrogation we had to finish. The guy we've picked up for this job, in fact. What I'd be interested to hear more about is how you made your deductions about him; that would be quite something.'

Once again I was pushed off balance; prove yourself, then prove yourself again. No one ever said life would be easy, but it can become totally annoying sometimes.

'Welcome, Bud. I'll be brief, it's getting late.' I didn't mean to be rude, but I was getting thoroughly cheesed off. 'So, who dunnit? It wasn't a robbery gone wrong; the expensive bedside radio clock, and all the music and TV equipment remaining untouched prove that. Clearly she'd had someone around for dinner; the dishwasher tells me she prepared food for two, it was eaten, cleared away, and she ran the dishwasher, so it wasn't a hot and heavy date. No, her guest was someone she felt comfortable inviting to her home, and someone around whom she could clear up. Not a new man in her life, but an old one. She dumped him, she can invite him for dinner. And nothing says "the evening's over" like putting someone's wine glass into the dishwasher, and running it. This man – the "Don" who signed the birthday card – he wasn't what she'd thought he was; he showed her a façade. She might have met him at one of the lower end clubs she liked to go to, and I believe at first he seemed to be just like her – maybe an ordinary background, now earning a lot of money, and happy to spend it on a newly-acquired taste for fine clothes, foods, wines and vacations. Remember the Vegas matchbook and chip? I believe he's the gambler, and I suspect they went there together. Also, a chip from a low-end casino but a matchbook from the high-end? Probably he did the gambling and she bought the dinners.'

There was still no input from either man, nothing to tell me if I was on the right track or not, but I carried on, regardless. 'He gave her gifts – some small, like the plush hippo – but he showed her his true self when he gave her the knock-off handbag. I have a suspicion that did it for her; it showed he didn't understand her at all. She'd have been worried by that; I suspect it was his birthday-slash-Christmas gift to her, and it didn't go down well. For her, it was the beginning of the end. He strikes me as a chancer – a guy trying to slither up the social ladder, not climb it. A classier man wouldn't have been taking her to strip clubs, no matter how "high-end" they might be. Show him a shortcut and he'll take it, even if it means breaking or bending the law. Probably makes his money in something like "imports and exports", or some other catch-all phrase that means he can do some shady deals. I would suggest he's never really come to terms with her dumping him; he probably thinks of himself as a real ladies' man. He's at the apartment for dinner, something goes wrong. Maybe he's turned up thinking they'll even have a one-night stand for old times' sake, or maybe he tries to win her back, or gets a bit too close for comfort. Possibly she says something he doesn't like.' I tried to calm myself as I recalled how a single wrong phrase used to be able to set off my ex-boyfriend Angus – how I'd never known what might turn him from a normal person into a ranting, fighting machine. 'Something sets Don off, and she's taken by surprise. He quickly overpowers her, and strangles or smothers her. There was nothing broken or knocked about, so it probably wasn't an accidental, deathly fall. Psychologically Don's a bully – he almost sneers that she's only getting one gift for both her birthday and Christmas in the card he signed; being a bully doesn't necessarily mean a large stature, but often does. I wouldn't be surprised if Don works out quite a bit – playing to his narcissistic tendencies – so maybe he surprised himself that he actually killed her. I don't know enough about Don to be able to say if he went to her condo with deadly intent, but, as I said, he's a chancer, so – even though he possibly hadn't planned to kill her, once she was dead, he knew where all her good stuff was, so he reckoned he might as well take it. A woman as well-turned-out as this one would have had a good stock of both real, and good quality dress jewelry – and there was none in the apartment. She'd also have probably had a few good art pieces about the place in those empty niches in the wall unit, for example, possibly from local galleries; I can tell from her clothing she has an eye for design, and art was strangely absent from her home, so I suggest he took such items too. But, without more information, I couldn't have told you more. I would have had no way of finding out who this Don person is. Sorry.'

I was looking at a huge, smiling face on the screen; it was so big I couldn't really make it out, Bud Anderson had pulled the camera close to him. 'You can see me, right?' he asked.

'Yes,' I confirmed. *I can almost see what you had for dinner*, I thought.

'Then this is for you, Professor Cait Morgan,' and he kissed the lens. It looked disgusting. As he pulled back from the smeared glass – which he made worse by rubbing it with a tissue – Bud said, 'I can't see you, so I guess you could be a wizened old gargoyle, but I don't care. You deserved that kiss. What I've just heard is amazing; you're so on the money it's spooky! We picked up the ex today; the idiot was trying to sell some of her possessions – locally carved First Nations' masks, as you surmised – and we had the insurance records. I want all my officers to come and learn how to do what you just did – well, okay, not all of them, but some. How much do you cost to hire? Can I afford you, I wonder? Can I *not* afford you? Anyway – give me your e-mail address and I'll get in touch tomorrow, right?'

Impressed by the man's perspicacity and ability to make an instant decision rather than waffle about, I gave him my e-mail address, but thought it only fair to warn him about Chief Superintendent Dufray's outburst earlier in the evening.

'Don't worry,' replied Anderson, 'I'm used to him dumping on me. And he doesn't run the I-Hit anyway; he'd like to, but we report directly to *his* boss, which the poor man hates. So if I want you, and I can justify the budget, I can have you. And you know what? If Dufray goes off on one about this tomorrow, he'll just be helping me prove my point that you're good, and you can help us. Think of all those man-hours we could have saved, if only we'd used one woman-hour – so long as that woman was you.'

I had to chuckle and couldn't resist. 'But any woman-hour is worth ten man-hours, Bud.'

'Just what my wife's always saying,' he replied amiably. Then he added, 'By the way, just so you know, Don Waverly – that's the creep's name – won't get away with it; he had the rest of her stuff in his place, and we'll nail him with DNA in any case. Her fingernails hold the key to his conviction, I'd say; she put up a fair fight as he smothered her, poor woman. He's still covered in the scratches she made. Sounds like there was a screaming match, and he was trying to shut her up; he keeps saying he didn't mean to do it. But to take all her stuff like that after he'd killed her? That sort of callousness won't play well with a jury. Her parents are in from Alberta, and they're going to clear her apartment tomorrow, they're pretty much emotionally shredded, of course, and, you know what, Professor Morgan – here's something I think you'd understand – *that's* what pushes me to make sure we do the best we can at I-Hit. We're here to represent the victims, and those they leave behind, and I'd be really glad if you could maybe help us out, professor. It's about justice for those who've gone, and those left behind.'

'Please call me Cait,' I asked, 'especially if we're going to work together, which I'd love. I echo your sentiments about justice needing to be served; it's what's driven me to develop the theories I have. I look forward to hearing from you.' I meant it.

'I'll be in touch, soon – over and out, professor.' The screen went black.

And there I was, all alone in the lecture theatre; it seemed suddenly very quiet. The adrenalin rush was still coursing through my veins, but I had nowhere to direct my energies anymore. It had been quite an evening. It was almost ten o'clock; time for home, a bit of TV, and a large Bombay and tonic – refreshment in a glass on a summer's night, for a forty-something workaholic woman with no one to talk to but a remote control, and a frozen burrito or two.

I realized too late that I hadn't asked the name of the victim – the woman herself. I wondered about that as I drove home; why I hadn't asked? Had I been dehumanizing her, as much as her killer had? Had my analysis been just a game – a puzzle to solve? Had I begun to lose my connection with reality? Just the usual sort of things you mull over while driving home from work of an evening.

When I finally walked in through my front door, I couldn't help but wonder what someone would say about me if they performed the same analysis of my home as I had of the nameless dead woman. Given my general lack of interest in domestic chores, and knowing my own quite individual taste in interior décor, I shuddered. I decided to clean out the fridge the moment I entered the kitchen, and promised myself I'd make an effort to fold my laundry and wipe down the bathroom counter before bedtime. I also made a mental note to find out the victim's name from Bud, and to ask if there was to be any sort of memorial service for her in Vancouver; even if I didn't know her name, I almost knew what it was to have lived in her skin, and I wanted to say goodbye to a stranger I now felt I knew so well.

JULY

Tea for Two

Edna Sweet had known from the age of ten that she wanted to own a tea shop. By the time she was fifteen and a half she'd further decided that since she didn't really like boys, and they didn't seem to care for her, she would probably never have to change her name, so her shop would be called The Sweet Olde Tea Shoppe. She liked the way it sounded; it spoke to her of a genteel clientele and gingham tablecloths. English through and through, like her, it would be a sign that the times had not left behind the manners and expectations of a more chivalrous age.

With a specific vision before her, and the family recipe for teacakes as her only inheritance, the sadly and suddenly orphaned Edna left school the day after she turned eighteen and promptly buried her parents, who had both, tragically, been run down at a bus stop by a drunk driver a week earlier. She got herself a job at the checkout in Tesco's by day, and two other jobs by night – one as a barmaid in a pub during the week, the other as a nightclub server at weekends. She literally worked every hour she wasn't asleep. While earning as much as she could, she spent as little as possible on what passed for a life at her meager bedsit in Finsbury Park.

By the time she was twenty-five Edna still hadn't saved up enough money to realize her dreams. Then, although she had given up all hope of it happening, she finally received a payment in compensation for the loss of her parents; thanks to a thoughtless man from Edmonton who couldn't say no to just one more pint, Edna was finally able to leave North London to hunt down an opportunity to start her new life.

After much searching she purchased a small, rundown roadside café on the edge of a village just outside Oxford. The village was pretty, though not pretty enough to draw the tourist coaches that clogged the streets of other local market towns, and, although it had four pubs and two churches, it had nowhere for 'ladies' to take morning coffee or tea.

Having moved into the little flat above the café, Edna spent an entire month scrubbing, cleaning, bleaching, and fitting out the grease-pit she had bought. She couldn't believe the previous owner hadn't killed anyone; everything was filthy. However, with maximum effort, and minimum expenditure, Edna proudly flipped the sign on the door at ten a.m. sharp on Monday the 2nd July. The Sweet Olde Tea Shoppe was open for business.

It was, without doubt, the happiest moment of Edna's still relatively short life. As she turned to survey her world she grinned with satisfaction, because it was exactly as she had imagined it, all those years ago: white walls and paintwork; small, round, dark wooden tables; traditional Windsor-backed chairs with little blue cushions for comfort; and, set against the farthest wall, a large, darkly reassuring Welsh dresser bedecked with willow pattern china. Fresh blue-and-white gingham cloths covered every table, each of which was laid with sparkling white cotton napkins and gleaming cutlery.

The walls bore cross-stitched panels of floral arrangements, or homilies such as 'Home is where the heart is', all executed by Edna herself over the past several years during her 'spare time'. The very air itself was almost edible, being full of the aroma of Edna's special toasting teacakes, which she had promised, in her advertisement in the local newspaper, to serve free to anyone ordering a pot of tea between ten a.m. and five p.m. on her Grand Opening Day!

As she looked about her, Edna told herself not to blub with excitement, and she certainly couldn't stay still, so she busied herself straightening the already thrice-straightened tablecloths, and made imperceptible adjustments to the positioning of the polished cutlery. The tinkling of the bell on a spring that Edna had placed above the door sent a shiver of anticipation through her entire being; she was about to meet her first customer. Edna swung around to see two ladies enter. They were perfect! Both had probably already celebrated their seventieth birthday, had gloriously unruly gray hair and each was wearing a well-pressed, lightweight, open-necked blouse atop a cool cotton summer skirt, artlessly gathered around a spreading waist. To Edna's great joy they both sported tights with their sandals; an arrangement that she felt spoke of proper county ladies who would never go about barelegged, whatever the weather.

'Welcome to The Sweet Old Tea Shoppe. My name is Edna Sweet, I'm the owner.' She bristled with pride – she was so excited to hear those words fall from her own lips. 'Please come in and make yourselves at home.'

The ladies cast their eyes about Edna's establishment and seemed to be satisfied.

'Let's sit here in the window, Betty,' suggested the one wearing the pink blouse above a pink and blue skirt.

'That'll be nice, Joan, yes, let's,' replied the one in the yellow blouse and green skirt.

'Do you have a lavatory?' enquired the lady in pink.

'Indeed I do,' replied Edna, waving her arm toward two discreet doors in a small corridor that led off from the main tearoom. Years in the hospitality business had taught her that the quality of the 'facilities' would attract, or repulse, certain types of customers. Edna had installed new white bathroom fittings, within white-tiled cubicles, and had decorated with soft lemon gingham curtains, silk flowers, and dishes of pot pourri. She had ensured that both the Ladies' and Gentlemen's washrooms were designed to be able to be kept spotlessly clean, and delicately fragranced, at all times.

Edna noted the lady in pink was gone for no more than thirty seconds – hardly enough time to wash her hands, let alone powder her nose – before she returned, and nodded approvingly toward her friend. Edna knew instinctively that her shop had just passed an Important Test.

'Tea for two please, Edna – and make sure it's piping hot, mind you,' said the lady in pink.

'But of course,' replied Edna, gushing, 'and would you like some teacakes? I bake them myself, then lightly toast them under a real grill – not in one of those machines. I serve them with butter on the side so you can choose just how much you want, and I can bring you a selection of jams and preserves.'

The two ladies made eye contact with each other and the one in pink replied on their behalf, 'That would be excellent, Edna. Thank you.'

As her customers settled themselves into their prime window seats, and began to discuss the décor and the facilities, Edna made sure she was able to present her first customers with the best tea and toasted teacakes ever served in the British Isles. Her hands shook a little as she carried the tray toward the table. She placed the tea pot, cups and saucers, side plates, and serving plate bearing the warm teacakes, lightly upon the table. 'I'll be right back with the preserves and the hot water,' promised Edna, and was as good as her word.

'Oh Edna?' called the lady in pink.

'Yes,' replied Edna, 'what can I do for you?'

'My friend Betty here . . .' began the lady in pink.

'Hello, Betty – pleased to meet you,' nodded Edna.

'My friend Betty and I – I am Joan by the way,' she paused.

'Hello to you too, Joan – and thanks for being my first customers,' said Edna.

'We were wondering where you're from. You're not a local, are you?' Joan made the statement sound almost like an accusation.

'No,' admitted Edna, wondering whether all those stories she'd heard about villagers being unhappy to admit strangers into their midst were true. 'I was born in Willingdon, but I grew up in Finsbury Park. Mum and Dad died when I was eighteen, and I stayed on in the area. I moved into the flat upstairs here about a month ago when I bought the café. It's a very nice village – not too much traffic and lovely people.'

'I see.' Joan looked at Betty with one eyebrow raised. 'We were just wondering if that was a London accent we could hear.'

'Very perceptive, I'm sure,' Edna replied. If she'd had a forelock, she'd have tugged it.

Joan sailed on regardless. 'Betty and I were wondering where you were from because the name Sweet is so unusual, and there was a girl by that name in our school, wasn't there, Betty?'

Betty seemed to jolt to life and took up her cue. 'Oh yes, indeed there was – Emily Sweet. Though she wasn't, was she, Joan?'

Edna smiled. 'I know my dad didn't have any brothers or sisters, and there weren't even any cousins that I know of, so I don't think we could be related.'

'Of course not, my dear,' interrupted Joan, rescuing Edna as she floundered, 'it was just a co-incidence that you have the same name.' She seemed to change the subject. 'And such a suitable name for a Tea Shoppe!'

They all laughed and smiled, and Joan and Betty proceeded to heap upon Edna general compliments about the strength of the tea, the delightful way the milk jug didn't drip, the taste, texture, and correct toasting of the teacakes, and the décor.

When they left, about an hour later, Edna had gone so far as to refuse to let them pay a penny for their refreshments – as a recognition of their being her first customers. It wasn't like Edna to baulk at asking for money, but this was a special day – she was beginning to develop genteel ways for a genteel village, where people lived genteel lives in genteel homes.

Around noon, an elderly married couple came in and took tea and teacakes; around two p.m. a couple of young mums popped in for a quick coffee on their way to collect their toddlers from kindergarten, then took up Edna's offer of stopping in on their way back to pick up some complimentary teacakes for the kiddies themselves. At four p.m. sharp – the time at which most people think that everything stops for tea in England – a young man with a ruddy complexion and a panicked expression almost fell in through the door, making Edna wonder if the clattering bell would fall off it's wildly-bucking spring.

'Are you Edna Sweet?' he enquired breathlessly.

'Indeed I am. Do I know you? Can I help you?' Edna wanted to cover all eventualities. She couldn't help but notice the young man was very nice looking in a freckle-cheeked, sandy-haired sort of way, with even features and a few beads of sweat on his forehead. He looked to be about Edna's age, or maybe a little older.

'You don't know me, but you can certainly help me, Edna.' He beamed. He was rather like an enthusiastic puppy, thought Edna, and she couldn't help but return his smile as he explained, 'I'm in a spot of bother. I work for the local rag, and I'm a bit late with some copy. Gran was here this morning and said I should come to take some photos and write a bit about you. She said I'd love the place.' Edna realized he was looking her up and down. She pulled self-consciously at her white collared shirt and her gingham apron. 'What she didn't say was that you were a girl. Well, she *did* call you a girl, but she calls everyone under sixty a girl and I didn't imagine that someone your age would be setting up a tea shop.'

He paused and pulled a large camera from his shoulder bag. 'How about it? I could get you on page three by Thursday!' He gave Edna a cheeky wink.

Edna smiled coyly as she playfully flicked a tea towel in his direction and grinned. 'Oh, get on with you – you are wicked.' Then she thought about what he'd said. 'What'll it cost me?' she asked in a matter of fact way.

'Cost? There's no cost. In fact,' the young man drew conspiratorially close, 'I'll owe you a drink, Edna, if you do this for me right now.'

Edna couldn't have imagined such an opportunity falling into her lap – a story about her Tea Shoppe in the local newspaper, for free, the week she opened; she reckoned she'd better make the most of it. She struck a foolish pose and asked mockingly, 'Where do you want me?' and they were off.

The young man arranged teapots, cups and saucers, and plates piled high with teacakes, along the edge of the Welsh dresser, and, as Edna changed into a clean apron and tidied her hair in the Ladies, he called out, 'My name's Stephen by the way – Stephen Halyard to be precise. Well, okay then, Stephen Henry Charles Halyard to be perfectly precise. And Joan is my father's mother. I've already interviewed her, of course, so I've got some useable quotes. But for now, speed is of the essence; my deadline is six o'clock, and if I'm quick I can get all this e-mailed off and the editor won't know I've been skiving, so,' he lowered his voice as Edna emerged, 'if you're ready.' He took in Edna's freshly washed and brushed appearance and smiled as he said, 'Splendid – what more could a chap want?'

Edna blushed; she knew she wasn't pretty, but she also knew that if she looked clean and fresh, her clear skin, bright eyes and neat figure allowed her to look at least respectable. That said, Edna didn't have bags of confidence about her appearance, and she battled nerves and shyness as the young man snapped her. Stephen kept up a good flow of banter-like conversation; he jollied her along with encouraging words, and the odd anecdote about assignments he'd been sent on by his boss that had gone horribly, and hilariously, wrong. Edna poured endless tea, held plates of teacakes, offered them to the camera and, at one point, courageously offered both a teapot and a plate of teacakes in the photographer's direction.

Finally, as Stephen was checking the shots he'd collected on the little screen of his camera, Edna asked, 'Do you want to interview me at all?'

'Interview you? But I just *have* done, sweet Edna; couldn't you tell I was squeezing every ounce of truth out of you? Didn't you feel the weight of my interrogative skills? I'm shocked. Shocked and dismayed that you missed entirely the majesty of a man operating at the peak of his capacities.' They laughed again, and then he was gone.

After all the excitement, Edna quite forget she was due to close at six o'clock, so it was almost seven before she dragged herself up the narrow staircase to her little flat. Once there she plopped down into the old armchair she had bought at the nearest charity shop and mulled through the day's events; not too much business, but those who'd been in had been complementary. She could hope for a busier day tomorrow and then, on Thursday, the local newspaper would be out and hopefully there'd be a photo and a bit of a story about The Sweet Olde Tea Shoppe.

All in all it had been a good day, and that Stephen Halyard was – well, Edna blushed at what she thought he was.

Even before the local newspaper article appeared, Joan had clearly been busying herself on Edna's behalf, and it seemed as though every member of the Women's Institute, of which Joan was the treasurer, all the members of the church choir, in which Joan was the leading contralto, and every parent and grandparent of every Girl Guide – Joan was heavily involved with the Guiding movement – had decided to visit The Sweet Olde Tea Shoppe. Thankfully, they all seemed to be big eaters. Teacakes, Chelsea buns, fairy cakes, scones, ice-cream, sandwiches, pop, tea, and coffee were consumed in gargantuan quantities, and Edna found herself having to make an emergency visit to the wholesaler's very early on Thursday morning to purchase more supplies.

Although hard work had never frightened Edna – indeed, it had almost become her reason for being – she was already exhausted by the time she flicked the sign to 'Open' at ten o'clock on Thursday morning. She actually screamed aloud as, two seconds later, Stephen Halyard once again flung himself through the door – with that same grin plastered across his freckled face that she had dreamed of during the few hours of sleep she'd snatched the night before. He waved a newspaper triumphantly above his head, then gathered Edna and tried – without much success, given the space constraints – to spin her about.

He started singing, 'Tea for two, and two for tea . . .' then subsided into 'dum-de-dums' for the rest of the well-known song.

Taken aback, Edna found she was more abrupt than she'd meant to be when she snapped, 'Stephen, put me down and stop messing about, I've just got all the cloths straight, and my pinny sorted.'

Stephen immediately let go of her, and his whole face fell. Once again he looked like a puppy, but this time Edna was reminded of one being admonished for happily running into his master's study with just half a slipper hanging out of his mouth. His eyes grew wide as he apologized, 'I'm so sorry, sweet Edna Sweet – I didn't mean to mess up your nice pinny.' He attempted a cheeky grin and a wink, then added, 'I'm so excited. Have you seen it? My boss put the whole thing in, word for word – no changes. And it's a huge photo – he's never given me so much space before, and he's always changed my copy. Oh Edna –' he looked as though he were about to grab her again – 'I'm so blinking chuffed!'

He thrust the newspaper toward Edna who opened it to see a huge photograph of herself, standing in front of her Welsh dresser pouring tea, beneath the headline 'Sweet Olde Tea Shoppe: A New Local Treat'. Edna read the article; it filled the rest of the page, and not only did it list the entire range of her offerings, but it also talked about her whole life story. Edna thought she sounded like someone she would admire, and The Sweet Olde Tea Shoppe sounded like somewhere she'd like to visit.

Joan Halyard, Stephen's grandmother, couldn't have been more flattering with her comments – she even mentioned the cleanliness of the lavatories – and when Edna raised her eyes to meet Stephen's, she knew they were full of tears. She was overwhelmed; her exhaustion got the better of her and she felt dizzy. She put out her hand to try to find something that would steady her, but instead of grasping a piece of furniture, she found Stephen. He took her arm and steered her into a chair. A look of concern crossed his boyish face.

'I'm not even going to ask if you're alright, because you're clearly not. You sit there – I'm going to make *you* a cup of tea – and you'll take it with four sugars, young lady.' He motioned for Edna to remain seated, which she did without any argument.

Luckily, no customers arrived until a good fifteen minutes later, by which time Edna had been fortified by an extremely sweet cup of tea, and a rather clumsy, but equally sweet, hug from Stephen. Even more fortunately, the first customer of the day was Stephen's grandmother, Joan, who offered to step into the breach and insisted that she be allowed to help in the kitchen should the need arise.

Edna felt enormous gratitude to this pair; she knew that because of their combined efforts on behalf of a complete stranger, her business stood the best chance of success she could have hoped for. She dared a firm handshake for Joan, and a friendly pat on the arm for Stephen, and the offer of free pots of tea for both of them for life – an offer which Stephen pooh-poohed, but which Edna noticed Joan did not decline.

By the time Edna's first paying customer arrived, she was ready to step into the fray herself – which she did with alacrity and a winning smile. Joan and Stephen shared a pot of tea and some rock cakes, and it was clear to Edna that Joan was keeping an eye on her. Dared she hope that Stephen was doing the same? She thought probably not and tried hard to focus on getting through what turned out to be a bumper day, with many people dropping in to try out the newly-famous little tea shop. And so it continued into the weekend.

By the end of the month it seemed Edna had hit a rhythm; The Sweet Olde Tea Shoppe had become an integral part of village life – and she played her role as hostess to the hilt. She loved every minute of it all. There was a morning crowd, a lunchtime crowd, and an afternoon crowd.

Joan and Betty were, of course, daily regulars – except for a Sunday, when they spent their day at St Michael and All Angels, the large Anglican church that dominated the center of the village. If she'd been pushed, Edna would have confessed this lack of an appearance by Joan was a nice change for her; working seven days a week had been something she'd been used to for years and being on her feet twelve hours a day was something with which she was equally familiar – she'd even got used to seeing the same old faces across the bar at the pub where she'd worked night after night. What she wasn't used to was the way Joan would wait until the place was empty, then call across and ask Edna very directly about some sort of controversial topic. What worried Edna was that, as she got to know more about Joan from Stephen – who dropped in several times a week – she developed a picture of a woman who almost single-handedly held together the strands that wove the fabric of the traditional life of the village. Edna was in no doubt it was Joan's very public support of her venture that had guaranteed its success, and, while Joan didn't exactly have power within the community, there was no question her influence ran deep, and probably held more sway than any actual power base could.

Given that influence, Edna always felt as though Joan were testing her; Edna became nervous that if she gave responses Joan didn't like, she might withdraw her very visible support of the tea shop, and may even take negative action. Edna made up her mind to broach the subject when she next spoke to Stephen alone, though she knew this would be tricky; she didn't want to offend Stephen, or even his grandmother via him.

On Monday 31st July, something happened that would make the idea of such a conversation leave Edna's mind forever. It was on that day, during a little pre-opening 'One Month in Business' celebration, to which she had invited Joan, Betty and Stephen, that she left Stephen fiddling around with something 'top secret' in the kitchen. She wanted to check on how the ladies were doing with their toast and marmalade and, as she approached them from behind, Edna quite clearly overheard Joan say to Betty, '. . . but of course we'll have to put it in the tea – that's the only way he won't taste it. It's a very bitter poison, you know, and we can't have him not drinking the full dose . . .'

At that precise moment Stephen burst into the room, stopping Joan in her tracks, and lighting up the whole space with his inimitable brand of happiness by declaring that the 'suspense was over' as he pushed a tiny birthday cake bearing one little candle under Edna's nose.

It was just as well Edna was supposed to look surprised, because her mouth was still agape from having overheard Joan. She gathered herself enough to be the gracious recipient of well-wishes, and even managed to summon enough wind to blow out the candle.

And then another extraordinary thing happened; Stephen gathered her up in his arms and gave her a fleeting kiss upon the cheek, gushing, 'Listen – I've learned all the words now.' As he broke into a loud, and fairly tuneful, rendition of the whole of 'Tea For Two', Edna tried to not look embarrassed. Joan and Betty exchanged a particularly meaningful look when Stephen warbled 'a boy for you, a girl for me'.

Edna didn't know what to think; she couldn't even process her feelings for Stephen because she was still so caught up in the earlier moment. What should have been an opportunity for meaningful eye contact and bashful lash fluttering became a moment when all Edna wanted to do was run into the street and escape the atmosphere she suddenly felt was suffocating her.

She must have looked like a deer caught in headlights because, as he took his bows after his big finish, Stephen passed the cake to his grandmother and asked Edna, 'You're not going all wobbly on me again, are you?'

As Edna looked into his face she noticed for the first time he had wrinkles beneath his lovely, happy eyes. For some reason, she burst into tears.

Stephen was distraught. 'I'm sorry, I'm truly sorry, Edna – I thought you'd like the little cake. I didn't mean to overwhelm you. Or was my singing really that bad?' He clearly didn't know what to say or do for the best.

'Stephen, it's not your fault. I was up early this morning and I haven't eaten yet – it must be a sugar low. I'm sure I'll be fine once I eat something.'

Stephen brightened. 'I'll get a piece of cake ready for you in a jiff.'

Edna's smile broadened and became less forced. 'I'll be fine – and a piece of cake would be great. You go and get that organized.'

She gave him a friendly wink, and gathered her thoughts. She told herself to not be silly; she had misheard Joan's comments. She straightened her pinafore, flicked her stumpy ponytail in defiance, and turned to face the anxious Joan and Betty with a broad smile on her face.

With cake and hot, sweet tea to sustain her, Edna was able to cope with opening up at ten a.m., but Joan lingered alone after Betty and Stephen had left.

That night, as Edna sat on the edge of the bath soaking her feet in hot water and brushing her hair absentmindedly, she tried to focus again on what she had heard Joan say that morning. She rationalized that Joan couldn't really have been talking about poisoning someone, but then wondered how her words could be interpreted otherwise. If she'd been talking about poisoning wasps, or ants, or something creepy-crawly like that, she wouldn't have mentioned that the poison was so bitter that it had to be hidden in tea, or that the person in question needed to drink a full dose.

As Edna mulled over this problem, she realized she'd brushed her scalp sore and that her toes had gone all wrinkly, so she wiped off her feet, put away her brush and fell into bed, where her dreams were unpleasant.

When Edna woke the next morning she knew she had to try to find out what on earth Joan had been talking about. Despite her feeling that, somehow, everything would work out for the best just because of Stephen's presence, she had never been a person to rely upon others; it just wasn't in her nature. So she set her mind to finding out more about Joan from other members of the community, rather than just from her grandson who – however wonderful he might be – was bound to be biased. She would also keep an ear open for all Betty and Joan's future conversations.

With these resolutions in place she got herself dressed for what looked as though it would be another hot, sunny day, and hoped her success would continue. She followed her plan of trying to find out about Joan from other villagers, and reassured herself that everyone spoke so highly of her she must have misheard Joan's bizarre conversation with Betty.

It was the 24th of August when it happened again. The morning rush had started late that day, and Edna was grateful for it. Usually by eleven she was full of the early gossiper crowd, but that day it was just the obligatory Joan and Betty, plus Charlie and Ivy from the almshouses down the road. They were a delightful little couple of whom Edna had become quite fond; she thought of them as 'the little couple' because they were so diminutive. Both in their early eighties, with a stack of grandchildren and a diamond wedding anniversary on the horizon, whenever she saw them together Edna felt she'd happily trade her youth for a taste of the happiness and contentment they seemed to share.

As Charlie patted his wife's hand, and they murmured about some family get-together they were looking forward to attending, Edna strained to hear every word that Joan and Betty were exchanging in their prestige seats at the window. She'd already been over to refresh their hot water, bring more butter, a new selection of jams, and had hovered at the next table as much as possible without seeming to be listening. After years of learning how to block out inane bar conversations, Edna had retrained her ears to pick up on key words she had previously been unwilling to catch; she still needed to convince herself what she'd overheard the previous month was rubbish.

It was while she was polishing a knife at a table behind Joan's back, that, once again, Edna caught the word 'poison'. Every nerve in her body immediately reacted. She heard Joan say, quite clearly, '. . . you see, my dear, once the poison has worked and he's gone, we'll have to have someone to help us move the body, because if we kill him there, everyone will know it was us. And we can't lift him on our own – he's far too heavy for that. We're not as young as we used to be.'

Edna was listening so intently she was startled by the arrival of Vera and Gwen, a couple of church choir members; she always thought of them as two naughty schoolgirls – the type who'd head for the back of the bus on a school outing, but never really cause much trouble. She knew their order by heart and was genuinely pleased to greet them, though she knew it meant she'd either miss the next part of Joan's conversation, or their arrival would stop it altogether. She brought tea, toast, and raspberry jam for two as quickly as possible, and could tell the pattern of conversation between Betty and Joan had moved back to the conspiratorial after some general greetings, their heads being bent close together over their almost touching teacups.

She'd missed something. Drat!

To hear anything now, Edna knew she'd have to get extremely close, so she returned to polishing knives, which had seemed to go unnoticed before. This time she needed her most heightened hearing to catch the whispers passing between the two women. She was quite sure about what she heard, but she found it almost impossible to believe.

For once it was Betty who was speaking, and she seemed to be pleading with Joan, '. . . but don't you see, my dear, if we involve someone else to help us, it'll make everything so much more complicated. In fact, we'd end up having to kill them too. Unless *he'll* help us out again. Remember Ruby, last time? I didn't want anything to do with it, but you insisted she had to go because she'd seen too much, so you had to kill her as well. I can't see why we can't just kill this one in his front parlor and be done with it. Then all we have to do is walk away. Who's to know we've even been there?'

Edna realized with horror the significance of Betty's words. Joan and Betty had killed before, and not just one person. Someone called Ruby was dead, and she hadn't even been their primary intended victim. Edna didn't have time to process this information before the next sentence sent her reeling.

This time it was Joan who spoke. Her tone was icy. 'Oh Betty, grow up. It doesn't matter how many we kill, so long as I – I mean *we* – get what we want. In fact, sometimes I think the more the merrier; the world's hardly going to miss a few old scroungers and moaners, is it? I ask you – who missed Ruby? No one. She wasn't even mentioned after a couple of weeks. And if we'd let her live she would have tittle-tattled to everyone; she never could keep a secret. And as for the old boy himself? Did you see anyone shed any tears when he went? Not one, Betty, not one.'

Joan's voice snapped off as Charlie and Ivy scraped their chairs away from their table to leave. Before Joan had a chance to turn around, Edna made sure she was fully involved in helping Ivy to her feet; she suddenly realized it might not be healthy to be caught overhearing Joan's conversation.

After she'd sent the beaming couple on their way as cheerily as she could, Edna cleared their table slowly, in a piecemeal fashion, allowing her more opportunities to pop back into earshot of Joan and Betty. But, after about ten minutes, it was clear she would hear no more from them about killing people, as they were now discussing the new awning being hung above the Post Office entrance, declaring it an eyesore and a blight on the High Street.

The choristers Vera and Gwen, ever the yea-sayers in support of their doughty lead contralto Joan, were supporting her in her idea of going along to Mrs Vickers, the postmistress, to Have A Word With Her Right Now. As all four ladies rose to take their leave, Edna rushed about collecting payments, pulling at chairs, accepting used napkins, and almost bobbing as the group left on their expedition.

Just as the little huddle left, Stephen arrived. As ever, he seemed to be in a terrible rush; he was looking pink, and glowing with a slightly sweaty luster that Edna found most appealing.

Of course she was delighted to see him, but her mind was in as much turmoil as the blender she was using to make him an iced latte. Should she – could she – say anything to him? If she did, what on earth would she say? She knew Stephen quite well by now, but in a 'polite company' sort of way; they'd only ever met in the tea shop. How attached was he to his grandmother? For one fleeting millisecond she even questioned whether he might know about her penchant for poison, but dismissed it immediately. He couldn't know; he wouldn't stand for it. She was quite sure of that.

As she handed Stephen his drink, Edna decided to take the bull by the horns; the tea shop was empty except for them, and she sat down beside him at his table, a move that prompted him to get up as she took her seat. Edna liked how that made her feel.

'Stephen,' she looked at him seriously, 'I have to do something that's very forward of me, and speak to you about something that's rather awkward and . . .' She hesitated, searching for the right word '. . . personal.'

Stephen sucked hard on his straw, then wiped his brow with a snowy napkin. He placed the tall glass on the table and returned Edna's serious gaze. 'I have to talk to you too. I can't put it off any longer. I have to tell you . . .' He, too, hesitated. '. . . it's awful, and I can hardly believe it, but I suppose it had to happen one day. I just wasn't expecting it to happen now.'

Edna was relieved. He knew. He must have overheard something too. He was also nonplussed and anxious; they could Do Something About Joan *together*!

'Oh Stephen – how did you find out? I overheard them here – Joan and Betty were talking about it quite openly – I couldn't believe my ears . . .'

Stephen looked puzzled.

'What do you mean? I haven't told Gran. I haven't told anyone.

Good grief, I'm only just telling you, and I wouldn't tell anyone before you. Mind you –' he nodded sagely – 'Gran's good at that sort of stuff – knows a person better than they know themselves, as she always says. She told me when I was just seven that my nanny was no good, and she was right; nanny just upped and took off one day without a by-your-leave, leaving me all alone in the house, if you please. And Fred Wilmslow, who ran the Scouts a few years ago, she spotted him as a bad 'un, and sure enough all the Scouts' funds disappeared at the same time he and Ruby Smith did a runner.'

'Ruby Smith? Who's Ruby Smith?' Edna pounced on the name.

Again, Stephen looked puzzled.

'Ruby Smith? She lived in Acre Lane. Retired schoolteacher. Never married. Bit of a gossip if you ask me, but harmless. At least, that's what we all thought until she ran off to Scarborough with Fred Wilmslow, and all the money from the Scouts' bank account. A couple of years ago. Gran always gave her a bit of a wide berth, too. So you see, Gran really does know people better than they know themselves. So, maybe she knew how I felt, even before I did.'

Edna cut across Stephen's wistful voice with a sharp, 'How do you know they went to Scarborough? Did someone see them there?'

Stephen seemed more than puzzled; he seemed to be getting frustrated. 'Well, yes, Gran saw them when she was on a weekend break there with Betty. But, look, why are you so interested in old Ruby Smith? She's nobody. She left ages ago. *You're* the important one, Edna. *We* are important.' He pushed back his chair and stood, looking down at Edna. Then he went down on one knee. 'Edna Sweet – I am in love with you and I want you to marry me,' he declared.

Edna stared at him. Stephen placed his hands over hers where they lay on the table. He felt very warm, and comfortable. Somewhere in the distance Edna heard bells, and in his eyes she saw a future. But what sort of future?

'I don't know what to say,' she muttered, suddenly dry-lipped.

'I'm thirty-two years old, healthy, wealthy, and I want at least two children,' announced Stephen proudly. Then he faltered, 'But if you don't want children then we could talk about that, but I really do want children. And I am healthy – I got a check-up last week. And I am wealthy – I own the big house where Gran and I live and all the fields behind it and the orchard, and I own a row of cottages at the back of Acre Lane. I own all the stables and the houses on the farm – oh, and the farm too, of course. In fact, if Great-Grandad hadn't sold it off, I'd have owned the whole village. Now I only have about a thousand acres – we've been here since the *Domesday Book* was written, you know. Isn't that great?'

'The *Domesday Book*?'

'You know – the book they did in 1060 -something to find out who lived where.'

'Yes,' replied Edna calmly, 'I know what the *Domesday Book* is. But why are you telling me this?' Her mind was in a whirl.

'Because I love you, silly, and I want you to know you won't go short; I can look after us both. My family is established. We're reliable; we've been here forever. I don't have to worry about money, and nor will you. This job with the newspaper is just to keep Gran off my back about being a rich layabout. I'm not really a layabout – I just haven't found out what I'm good at yet. But I know I'd be good at loving you, and you'd be the making of me, Edna Sweet. All your energy – all your vision – that, and my money, and there'd be no stopping us. It would be wonderful.'

Had anyone else been there they'd have been treated to a tableau, the type of which is rarely seen: a true English gentleman, down on one knee, proposing marriage to a woman he has yet to kiss properly.

Edna knew exactly what to do. In fact, she knew it was the only thing she could do. She burst into tears. Stephen stood and dug in his pockets for a handkerchief, which Edna took from him. She had to give herself time to work out what on earth to say. Tears were a useful device, and they were having the desired effect on Stephen; he was now begging her to take her time to answer him, reassuring her that he understood how sudden all this was, that she needed to think. She agreed to talk with him on the phone that evening, then a couple of customers arrived, and he left.

Eventually the day was over, and, as she flipped the sign on the door to read 'Closed', Edna could feel the weight of the day lift somewhat, only to have that weight replaced with another, greater load; thinking about Joan and Stephen, and murder and marriage.

She dragged herself upstairs and flopped onto her bed, her face buried in her pillows. She didn't want to think about it all, but knew she had to. It wouldn't go away if she ignored it. Indeed, it could only get worse, because now she knew two things for certain that she hadn't known when she woke that morning: Stephen Halyard loved her and wanted to marry her, and Joan Halyard was a cold-blooded killer.

The question was – did Stephen love Edna *enough* for them to be able to deal with the fact that she knew his grandmother to have killed already, and to be planning to do it again?

As she flipped onto her back and kicked off her kitchen clogs, Edna turned her mind to Stephen; he was attractive, funny, gentlemanly, and the fact he turned out to be wealthy as well didn't hurt. Not that she'd ever marry for money, but, coming from where she did, she certainly didn't underestimate the value of it. She didn't know one single negative thing about Stephen; indeed, no one in the village had a bad word to say about him. He obviously felt strongly about her, loved her, and it had been so wonderfully chivalrous when he'd gone down on one knee.

Edna dwelt upon that image for a moment and almost entirely forgot about Joan. But, with Stephen being Joan's grandson, it would never be possible to forget about her altogether.

Edna had to face facts. She'd heard Joan talking about a murder plot, and was convinced that Joan had killed before. What should she do? Should she confront Stephen? Would that break his heart? Would he rally to his grandmother – the woman who had all but raised him after his parents had died – or would he support Edna – the woman he had known only briefly, but with whom he wished to spend the rest of his life?

As she dragged herself toward the bathroom, for a revitalizing, cool shower, Edna made a decision she knew would change her life forever; when she phoned Stephen that evening she would accept his proposal, not mention her suspicions about Joan, and continue in her efforts to listen to Joan and glean information about her and her possible victims over the next weeks.

She clung to the hope she might be wrong about the woman. She rationalized that, if she was wrong, and she gave up Stephen because of a partially overheard exchange, she would regret it for the rest of her life.

The decision was made; why threaten her own future happiness on the basis of what might prove to be a misheard phrase or two?

The news of Edna and Stephen's engagement flooded the village within half a day. Almost everyone who came into the tea shop had heard, and immediately congratulated Edna; if they didn't know when they got there, they certainly knew before they left. Edna was overwhelmed by the kindness being shown toward her, but was not the only person to note that Joan and Betty were not in their usual window seat at their usual time.

By noon Edna was beginning to get nervous; she suspected there might have been words between Stephen and Joan – after all, she wasn't a girl with the sort of background that a legendary family like the Halyards might want within their ranks. Of course, 'their ranks' was comprised solely of Joan and Stephen these days, so it might be a fifty-fifty vote. What could Joan's absence mean?

By four o'clock Edna was also concerned that she hadn't been visited by her fiancé that day; usually Stephen would have found some reason to pop in for a refreshing drink or a sustaining bun, and on this day – of all days – Edna had rather expected to see him. But there was no sign of him. Edna knew it wasn't copy day for the newspaper, so where could he be? Of course, she was so busy that the rest of the day slipped by, and it wasn't until she'd closed up for the night and was taking a well-deserved bath, that she could turn her whole attention to worrying about the non-appearance of Stephen and Joan.

By the time she was dry and curled up on the sofa with a salad and a cold drink, Edna had decided to finish supper then telephone Stephen – after all, they were engaged now, why wouldn't she phone him?

Edna picked up the receiver, punched in Stephen's number and the telephone rang out at the other end, but all she got was the recording of Joan barking that she should leave her name and number after the tone. Edna did so, in a somewhat hesitant voice, and left a feeble message telling Stephen that she'd like to hear from him, when it was convenient. Edna padded around the claustrophobic little living room, not knowing what to do next. All her chores were completed, she had cleaned and fed herself, and she had no idea where Joan or Stephen were, nor how to reach Stephen. The clock told her it was nine thirty. She thought she might as well try to get some sleep, and face the next day at least refreshed.

But Edna couldn't find sleep; she tried reading, listening to the radio, then she played some soothing music designed to help those who, like her, could not relax into a restful night. When she finally did sleep, she did so fitfully, and by five thirty the next morning Edna was exhausted, sweaty, feeling decidedly wobbly, and totally unprepared to face the day.

She operated on autopilot preparing the tea shop for the day ahead, turning the sign to 'Open' bang on time. As she was walking back to the kitchen the door flew open and there – as so many times before – stood Stephen, his face glowing with perspiration. Edna's first reaction was of genuine joy – but that initial response was immediately replaced by something else; Stephen's face didn't show his usual, puppy-like mixture of happiness and eagerness, instead his eyes were truly panicked, his face about to break into a tortured grimace, not a smile. Edna knew something was horribly wrong.

'Stephen – what is it? You look awful.'

'It's Gran,' he cried. Edna saw a tear roll down his cheek as he sprang toward her. He gathered her tight in his arms and cried like a baby into her hair, his sobs mixed with words, 'Oh Edna, it's Gran. She's dead. The brakes on her car went. They couldn't save her. Yesterday. Bottom of Long Hill. Her and Betty.'

Edna held Stephen tight. His whole body shook. She stroked his hair and, when he was able to pull back, she wiped his bloodshot and swollen eyes; they were still the most wonderful eyes she had ever seen. She knew right then that it had been perfectly correct of her not to say anything to him about her suspicions regarding Joan. Terrible though it was that she was dead, at least it meant Edna didn't have to worry any more about her possibly being a murderer. She realized this was an entirely selfish response to Joan's tragic demise, but, after all, it was a blessing in many ways.

While Edna felt relief and compassion in equal measure, and set about delivering the sympathy she felt for Stephen as best she could, she could tell he was devastated. She locked the door to the shop and turned the sign to 'Closed', then pulled all the gingham curtains shut, so that no one could see inside.

She suspected Stephen had been up all night, and that proved to be the case. Over several cups of fortifying tea she discovered Joan and Betty had decided to visit some friends from a neighboring group of the Women's Institute. The village being about thirty miles away, they had decided to make a day of it, so Joan had gone off with Betty, leaving Stephen to busy himself making arrangements for the forthcoming wedding which – although Edna had agreed it should be soon – seemed to be something Stephen envisaged as happening in a matter of weeks.

Putting her surprise about that particular matter to one side, Edna poured more tea, and let Stephen talk. Apparently he hadn't begun to worry about Joan until about six o'clock in the evening; usually home from any trip by around four, it was unheard of for her to miss her six o'clock sherry. Stephen didn't know who she'd gone to visit exactly, and got no answer when he telephoned Betty's house. Ringing around a few of the other church ladies he'd managed to discover the telephone number of one of the women Joan had planned to visit. Upon phoning them he'd been told that Joan and Betty had left for home at around two thirty.

A call to the local police had finally brought a visit from PC Wymans, who had informed Stephen of the fact Joan's car had been found smashed into a wall at the bottom of Long Hill, a part of the back-road route she would have favored from the village she was visiting. The PC had driven Stephen to the hospital where Joan had been taken, but their arrival only allowed Stephen to have it confirmed by a doctor that both Joan and Betty had been dead upon arrival. He'd stayed all night with her body, ravaged though it was by the accident. It was a duty of love he hadn't been able to undertake for his parents, who Edna knew had died in a car accident while on holiday without him in Spain. It was a heavy burden to bear, to lose two parents and a grandparent all to car accidents, and Edna wasn't surprised to hear Stephen swear he'd sell his car and walk everywhere for the rest of his life.

She held his hand and patted his arm as the tragic tale tumbled out of him; she didn't know how to give him any real solace. All Edna could do was to, literally, stand by her man over the weeks that came; first at Joan's funeral, and then at their wedding.

It was the biggest wedding the village had seen in many years; almost the entire local population was in attendance and, as the early September evening light glowed upon the happy couple at the end of a wonderful reception held in the church hall, Edna knew she had found the happiness she had so long desired. She looked into Stephen's eyes – her husband's eyes – and knew she'd made the right decisions in life: the right decision about where to have her dream tea shop, the right decision about not mentioning her suspicions about his grandmother, and the right decision to marry him.

Edna popped Harry's little feet into the snuggle suit he wore for bed; she could hear Joanie giggling as she played with her father in the next room. Stephen's head appeared around the door, swiftly followed by that of his daughter, who clung precariously to his ears as she steadied herself upon his shoulders.

'Come on now, Joanie – let Daddy put you to bed, you know it's time,' called Edna, smiling. 'Harry's ready – look,' and she held her wriggling son toward his father and sister as if to prove that his being ready was a sign it was time for all playing to end. When both children were snug and sleeping, Edna and Stephen made their way downstairs to the drawing room, where a roaring fire in the far-from-modest hearth was taking the chill off the night air.

'Oh Stephen, you built a fire, how lovely.' Edna kissed her husband and gasped as he pulled an ice bucket replete with champagne and glasses from behind a leather wing chair and proudly shouted, 'Happy Anniversary!' He flicked the switch on an old cassette player and the familiar strains of 'their' song filled the room.

'Ssh, the children,' stage-whispered Edna as she closed the door to the hallway. She hugged her husband as he popped the cork on the glowing green bottle and poured the golden froth into two delicate champagne flutes. Toasting themselves, they fell onto the antique rug that sat before the fire, and cuddled. They certainly had good cause for celebration; five years of happiness and almost never a cross word. Edna now owned dozens of 'Sweet Olde Tea Shoppes' across England, and even sold her own line of tea paraphernalia and home décor items online, while Stephen was a very happy stay-at-home father. How lucky Edna was to have found him; how pleased he was to have discovered that his role in life was to be a father.

Edna's entrepreneurial mind and Stephen's initial investment had allowed her to become wildly successful in terms of business; his love, and their children, had allowed her to become all she could as a woman and a mother. She was complete. And she knew it. She blessed it every day of her life. Certainly she wished she could spend more time with the children, but she worked from home as much as possible and knew that, even when she had to be away, Stephen was with Harry and Joanie every moment, cherishing them as she did, and keeping them safe and happy.

The couple cuddled and reminisced about the years they'd spent building their life together, and talk turned, inevitably, to how Edna had chosen this particular village for what had turned out to be her first shop, then to the first time they had met, and then – of course – to Joan.

It was always at this point in their otherwise happy reminiscences that Edna felt awkward; she still had a lingering discomfort when she thought of Joan. Unfortunately, she'd not been able to come up with an acceptable argument to prevent naming their daughter for the woman who had raised Stephen, but the use of 'Joanie' rather than 'Joan' helped Edna to come to terms with it. As the years had passed, and little Joanie had developed her own personality, Edna was able to almost erase the connection with Joan from her mind. But, at this time of year, the conversation always turned to Stephen's grandmother, and the role she had played in their coming together.

Edna had never mentioned her concerns to Stephen; Joan's death had removed all reason for her to say anything. Indeed, Edna had almost convinced herself that her suspicions about Joan had been groundless, so there was really nothing to mention in any case.

The couple kissed, and Stephen said dreamily, 'I love you, Mrs Edna Halyard. Or should I say, Miss Edna Sweet, as the world knows you?'

'I'm so much happier being Mrs Halyard than being Miss Sweet, but we both know what works best for the business.'

'I know,' he reassured her. 'Just as well they named you for your father's mother, not your mother's mother, or you'd have been Etta Sweet.' He giggled. They giggled together. They'd often giggled about it before. 'Now you'd be Etta Halyard, but then Etta *anything* is a bit tough, don't you think? They wanted to name me Gascoigne after my great-grandfather. Can you imagine going through life being called Gascoigne? That's even worse than Etta, you have to admit it.'

Edna smiled. Stephen looked so beautiful with the firelight flickering on his skin. She stroked his face, lovingly. 'I don't care what I'm called, so long as I am your wife. And I'd have married you whatever your name, whatever your situation in life.'

Stephen took a swig from his glass and looked at Edna with a curious glint in his eyes. 'But you wouldn't have, would you? You wouldn't have married me if Gran hadn't died, would you?'

Edna was taken aback; Stephen had never said anything like that before.

Her eyes must have betrayed her surprise, because, before she had a chance to respond, her husband added, 'I knew it, of course – I knew you'd found out about her. I knew that, although you said yes, you would have ended up saying no to me. If I hadn't acted, we wouldn't be here today. You wouldn't have married me and become Mrs Halyard, and there wouldn't even *be* a Joanie or a Harry Halyard.'

Edna took it all in. 'What do you mean I found out about her? What did I find out?' Edna was scared, but she blurted it out anyway.

'You found out about Joan killing people.' Stephen spoke as if he'd made a mere throwaway comment, not as though he'd just hurled a grenade into their happy life.

Edna gulped at her champagne, to give herself a moment to think as much as because she needed the drink. How to respond? Honesty was the best policy, she decided.

'Okay, Stephen, I'll come clean. I overheard Joan and Betty talking one day about poisoning somebody, and then she mentioned Ruby someone or other, whom she'd already killed. You told me about that Ruby woman and the Scout master disappearing, and I thought Joan and Betty must have done something awful. Of course, I didn't know whether to say anything to you about it. I didn't know if you'd believe it because – frankly – I didn't know if I believed it myself.' She finally drew a breath, then hissed, 'Oh my God, Stephen, do you mean Joan really did kill people?'

'Yes. She really did.' Stephen sounded quite calm; Edna felt anything but. Until that moment she'd almost managed to convince herself that it was all a fiction.

'What do you mean *exactly*?' pressed Edna – hating to believe, but needing details.

'Ruby Smith and Fred Wilmslow, it was them. When you mentioned Ruby's name I knew you must have found out something; Gran was never as discreet as she thought she was. You probably overheard her saying something in the tea shop one day. She nearly got caught out like that several times; what Gran thought of as a whisper wasn't terribly quiet at all, and she'd never admit to having a hearing problem, of course.'

Edna's eyes widened as her husband continued to speak as though he were having a very ordinary conversation about some everyday topic.

He continued, 'But they weren't Gran's first. I believe she killed my nanny when I was a small child. I'm not sure how she did it, but she told everyone that the girl had simply gone away, which – upon mature reflection – I think was unlikely. And Gran also mentioned several things which led me to believe that she somehow tampered with my parents' car causing it to crash and kill them both.'

Edna interrupted – aghast and puzzled in equal measure, 'But didn't your parents die when they were on holiday in Spain? That's what you told me.'

Stephen airily waved his arm. 'Oh they did, but Gran had been visiting them there right up until a couple of days before they died. I believe she fiddled with the car they'd hired. Of course, all she ever really wanted was to raise me herself. She hated my mother, you see, because she felt my father had married beneath him, thereby betraying the family name. The family name was very important to Gran – she'd have done anything to defend it, to allow it to reach its full potential.'

He finished his champagne, and topped up Edna's glass as well as his own. Edna was stunned, but sipped.

Stephen continued nonchalantly, 'Before that – before she even married Granddad, in fact – I believe she killed her own brother; he was a bit of a bad 'un, and someone whose reputation she felt wouldn't let her rise to meet the requirements of the Halyard family when she decided she wanted to marry into it. My father was conceived out of wedlock, and Granddad had to marry her PDQ. Of course, that was all hushed up too; Gran managed to wriggle herself into one of the oldest families in England by seducing the son of the house. Believe it or not, apparently she was quite a looker.'

Stephen guffawed, and Edna had to admit this statement surprised her as much as any of the others. She sipped her champagne as her mind raced.

Stephen was on a roll. 'Once she'd got into the family, Gran made it her business to become guardian of the Halyard name. When Granddad died, she became the sanctimonious old biddy you met. I think she might have killed him too, because he went a bit gaga, and she wasn't very keen on that – then he died. Unexpectedly.'

Stephen paused for a slurp of champagne, but continued in the same matter of fact way. 'Gran put the Halyard name before everything else. And I mean everything; when I was growing up, she instilled in me that your family and your name are the most important things you have in life. And, to be fair to her, I'm convinced everything she did – in the early days, that is – really was to protect the family name. But I could see she was getting more emboldened about killing. That Ruby woman was a case in point; Gran only meant to kill Wilmslow himself, you see, because he'd called her a stuck-up something or other and implied she wasn't up to the Halyard name – just about the worst thing anyone could say to Gran. She bashed him over the head with a coal shovel. You wouldn't think to look at her that she'd have had the strength, but she did it sure enough. And Ruby Smith heard something going on in his back garden next door to her cottage – which was where it happened – put two and two together when he "disappeared", and made the mistake of telling Gran her suspicions. So, of course, Gran had to kill her too. By stealing the Scouts' money Gran was able to make it look as though Fred Wilmslow had run off with both the cash and Ruby, and Gran let it be known that she and Betty had spotted them in Scarborough.'

'But what did she do with the bodies?' asked Edna, grappling with the vision of the tiny septuagenarian Joan trying to move anything more hefty than a footstool.

'I buried them in the orchard.'

'*You* buried them?' Edna was stupefied.

'What else could I do?' Stephen seemed genuinely surprised that Edna should have asked. 'Gran was in trouble, so I had to help. She couldn't move them herself, so I carried them into the orchard one night, and buried them. No one ever goes to the orchard, there's nothing much there worth picking, as you know, so it was an ideal place.'

Edna felt as though maybe she was going mad. She felt compelled to ask, 'Was there anyone else?'

'Only them, that I know of.'

'So – to be clear – you know for a fact that Joan killed two people, and you believe she killed five others, four of them family members?'

Stephen nodded. 'Yes, that's right.'

'I overheard her talking about poisoning someone. Who on earth was that?' Edna felt some relief she'd finally been able to say the words.

'Well, that was the problem, you see, because she was planning to kill the vicar.' Edna's eyebrows shot up even further. Stephen evidently picked up on her surprise. 'Exactly – you can't go around killing vicars and expecting to get away with it. I'm sure questions would have been asked about the vicar.'

'Really?' Edna wasn't sure if she'd added enough sarcasm to her tone for Stephen to spot it; his response showed she hadn't.

'Totally. The rev's a lovely man, and everyone knows him. I'm sure he didn't mean it when he told Gran she wasn't a real Halyard; he only meant that she'd married in, which she had, of course. But Gran didn't see it that way; she said he'd slighted her, and she said she'd decided to kill him. However, it seemed she and Betty were at odds about how they should do it.'

Edna couldn't help herself, 'What about Betty? Why was she

involved in all this?' She was morbidly intrigued.

'Betty happened to be with Gran when she whacked old Wilmslow, so she got involved from then on. She wouldn't dare give Gran away; she liked being Gran's special friend. And I think she was a bit potty too, of course.'

Edna's, 'Uh-huh,' was laced with irony, but Stephen missed it as he continued his narrative.

'I was getting worried about Gran; I was pretty sure she'd get herself into trouble over the vicar, and I couldn't talk her out of it.'

Edna's heart sank. 'So you discussed this with her?'

'Oh yes, Gran and I talked about everything, all the time. She really liked you, you know. She said you'd give the Halyard blood a lot of new energy, which it needed. She was right, of course; Harry and Joanie are real live wires, and Joanie is just as beautiful as her mum.'

Edna couldn't believe Stephen's conversation was able to move from murder to compliments so easily.

Her husband grinned cheerily. 'So that – and because I worked out you'd somehow twigged something about Ruby Smith – was why I had to kill her.'

Edna couldn't speak; she swallowed hard, and let her husband continue.

'You'd said you'd marry me, but I knew you wouldn't go through with it; not if you suspected Gran of killing someone. You're so tenacious; the writers in the business pages say that about you and they're right, you are. You'd never have let go; you'd have worried about it, and you wouldn't have known whether to say anything about it or not, and you'd have ended up not marrying me. So I mucked about with Gran's brakes – it's pretty easy to do on older cars. I knew she'd come back down the Long Hill way, and I knew she'd end up smashing into that big wall at the bottom. I was pretty sure she and Betty would die outright, because Gran always drove too fast. I couldn't be certain, of course, so that ride with the PC to the hospital was a bit hairy, but when they said they were both dead on arrival, I knew everything would all be alright. The car was a real mess, thank goodness, so they never knew it wasn't just an accident caused by poor maintenance and an older driver.'

'Right,' said Edna, feebly.

'So there she was, gone, and there was no reason for you to not marry me. So you did, and here we are.' Stephen raised his glass to his wife and added, 'Cheers!' as he downed the last of his champagne.

Edna suspected she was in shock, especially as she too raised her glass and responded with her own 'Cheers!' Then, for some reason she couldn't fathom, her mouth said, 'So what now, Stephen?'

'What do you mean, "what now"? Nothing now. We're doing just fine, aren't we?' Her husband sounded genuinely surprised.

'Yes, I suppose we are . . . but, you've killed two people, Stephen. And you've buried two more in the orchard. Don't you think we should . . .' Edna realized she didn't know what to say next.

'Should what, darling? No one missed the widow Betty; she spent all her time with Gran and had no children. Gran was going to kill someone who didn't deserve it, and I stopped her doing that. The other two? As I said, I had to help Gran, and everyone thinks they're having a great time living in sin in Scarborough. Where's the harm in that?'

Edna dwelt on her husband's words for a moment. What *was* she proposing? That her darling husband give himself up to the police for a crime he'd committed five years ago, which had actually saved the vicar's life, and which had drawn no suspicion at all? Or maybe that he should announce to the world he'd been an accessory after the fact to two murders committed by a woman now dead?

She had to agree with Stephen; it seemed to make little sense to do anything but carry on as though nothing had happened. After all, maybe even she was complicit; she'd had her suspicions and had kept quiet – maybe morally that was as bad as actually doing the deed itself. What would be gained by owning up now? Nothing. Her children would lose their father to a long prison term, she her husband. And he was such a *good* father.

Edna reached over and patted Stephen's hand. 'I love you, darling, and I agree we should let sleeping dogs lie.'

'Good,' Stephen responded in jolly tones, 'after all, I couldn't bear to see our name dragged through the mud in all the newspapers. It's our children's name too, you see, and they are so important to me. They are the ones who will carry the Halyard name forward. *They* are the ones who matter. But there, enough said. Fancy a cuppa? That champagne has gone straight to my head.'

They each helped the other rise to their feet. 'I'll make it, and you carry the tray through?' said Edna, almost brightly. It was their usual division of labor.

'Okey dokey,' was Stephen's jovial response, and they headed toward the kitchen.

Edna no longer knew what to think about anything; she was married to a murderer, who had been raised by a murderer, and she was rapidly coming to terms with the fact that sometimes, once it starts, murder is difficult to stop. Indeed, she was beginning to think that sometimes it might even be better to keep it going.

As she followed her tipsy husband she reminded herself she was now as much a Halyard as Joan had ever been, and that she too had a responsibility to the name her children bore. She wondered if she'd ever have to take action to protect that name in the way Joan and Stephen had done; she quickly told herself that was a silly thought – *she* wasn't a killer.

But what if Stephen let something slip? He didn't seem to understand that most people thought of murder as heinous; the way he'd just talked about it had proved that. What if he felt comfortable enough with the topic to discuss it with someone else? What if he had one too many glasses of port one night and said something, to someone? How could she ever be sure he wouldn't say or do something to ruin their children's futures?

As she pottered about in the kitchen a thought popped, unbidden, into Edna's head: what if Stephen thought *she* might not be doing all she could to uphold the family name? What would he do? He'd killed already, and didn't everyone say it got easier the more you did it? As Edna watched her husband kick up his heels and sing 'their' song, with a childishly happy grin on his face, she wondered how safe she was in her own home, her own car, or even when she was walking the dog.

Edna caught a glimpse of the rat poison tucked at the back of the highest cupboard, she noted the pill bottles pushed out of the reach of little fingers behind the tea caddy, she remembered the little wood axe in the woodshed. She suddenly realized she was surrounded by potentially lethal objects, none of which had ever seemed threatening before. By the time the tea tray was ready, her mood was black, and her soul deeply troubled.

Edna Halyard lay wide awake at the end of her fifth wedding anniversary with her beloved children sleeping peacefully in their own rooms, and her husband snoring gently on the pillow beside her. The outward signs of her life were the unchanged, but now she saw them from a totally new perspective; a perspective brought into sharp focus by the certainty she was married to a murderer. A perspective that made her question her own security. A perspective forcing her to totally re-evaluate her view of murder as being always a bad thing.

Stephen had been right in his assumption that she probably wouldn't have married him if Joan hadn't died, so she was already living a life facilitated by a couple of dead bodies. So what if, one day, there had to be one more little murder to allow her to hang onto her new life, her new name, and a secure future for her children? It would only be *one* more, after all.

As the sleepless hours passed, she felt with increasing certainty that Stephen couldn't be trusted. She loved him, but he could be very irritating sometimes; more often than not, actually. That 'man with the soul of a child' thing could become terribly wearing; he was clearly *never* going to grow up. And his blasé attitude toward his murderous roots would always be a threat because of that childlike quality.

Edna stared bleakly into the darkness and finally realized that, after five years of bearing the name, she'd have to face up to becoming a fully-fledged Halyard. And probably sooner, rather than later. She wondered what poison Joan had been talking about putting into the vicar's tea. She turned over and plumped the pillow; she'd do some research in the morning – if she knew anything, it was tea and, after all, it was what had brought her and Stephen together. Wouldn't it, therefore, be the most appropriate way for her to get rid of him?

AUGUST

Shannah's Racecar

Is this the end for me? For us? *Us*? Come off it, Sam, there's no *us*. There's me, lying in a pool of blood, and there's Shannah, looking like a pile of crumpled clothing bundled in a corner of this ruined hangar. Is she even alive? Has he murdered us both? Surely not. But there's all this blood; I never knew there was so much in me. Is that why I'm feeling so light-headed? As though everything is slipping away from me?

Why won't this nutter just take the car and go? It's what he's come for, and good riddance to it. If I could find my phone I'd ring the police, but it's slithered out of my pocket somehow. He's still shooting at us, for crying out loud. I've never even seen a gun before today. Not in real life. This is so frightening, in so many ways. Why me? Why us? It's all because of that blessed car, that's why.

I only met Shannah for the first time this morning, and I've never seen the wretched car before today either. This whole situation would be almost ridiculous, if it weren't for the gun, and the fact I'm bleeding like a stuck pig. It's the sort of thing you hear about on the BBC news, and wonder how it could ever happen in England's green and pleasant land. They never tell the whole story behind the headlines; nothing about the lives, hopes, or dreams of the victims. It's just a shocking sound bite about a violent killing, usually with more said about the murderer than those murdered, then they're onto the next thing. I don't want my entire life to be summed up in a couple of cryptic sentences, followed by a list of which local roads will be closed for repairs next weekend. My life means more than that, doesn't it?

But who will tell my story? No one else knows it. Not all of it, anyway. My choice. My fault. And who'll explain to Pete why this happened on my first real job for him? Who'll give the name of the bloke with the gun to the police? Maybe Pete will work it out. He should; he's bright, sharp. Even so, I don't want to become a name on a printout of statistics, with nobody caring that this happened just because I wanted to help a woman have a little fun. Doesn't that mean something – that I did this to help someone? Maybe I chose to help the wrong person? Even if I did, who will speak for me, now?

If I can just get myself up off the floor, I can see how Shannah's doing. If only this idiot would get into the car he seems to want so badly – and actually leave – then maybe we can take his vehicle and get back to my place. He can't drive two cars at once; maybe I can still save us both from this madness.

I turn my head. Everything hurts. Beyond the hangar, on the horizon, I can see a rose-tiled oast house. I adore oast houses; their conical rooftops have been part of my life since I was a kid. Like our famous white cliffs, they're what people always talk about when they think of the landscape here in Kent – a landscape that's drawn me back to where I was born and raised, after so many years.

I can see the sky outside, too; it's so big here – we're known for it. So many blues. Every blue. I love the part of the day when the light's changing. It's like time's at a point where it can go either way; as though you can go forward, or back.

All I have to do is stand up. But I can't. I can't move at all, now.

I know in my heart this is what ends it for me. As the last of my precious life-blood fills the fissures in the concrete floor, I think back about it all: Shannah's racecar.

Only moments have passed since Shannah was able to speak. 'Sam? Help me.' Her voice was no more than a dry croak.

I stumble toward her as fast as I can. I can still run in spite of the wave of pain in my lower back; I have to help her. This was supposed to be a simple job; that's why Pete gave it to me – his newest employee. The bloke shooting at us is Pete's client – *my* client – Bert Sampson. Shannah's not our client; I know, it's confusing. And scary.

All this for a car? It's just a thing; we're human beings. That's a big difference. Granted, my life might be pretty inconsequential, but it's mine, and I've a right to live it as I please. Just because I was born to a mother with a drop or two of royal blood in her veins doesn't mean I can't control my own destiny, be my true self, does it? That alone has been difficult enough over the years. Now this?

I shout, 'Take it. Go.' I don't know if Bert hears me; I hope he does. I finally collapse beside Shannah and grab her arm. It's a hot evening and her skin's wet with sweat, but cold.

I have to get us out of here. But first, I need to rest – just for a minute. I let go of her, and roll onto my back, I need to catch my breath.

We arrived half an hour ago for a good run around the tarmac in the car; it's the second time we've been here today, but I don't know how Bert knows about the place. Shannah must have mentioned it to him, even though she said she didn't. Her 'secret place' clearly isn't. I suppose he must have got fed up waiting for me to bring the car to Pete's office for him. Or maybe he followed us. She said he wouldn't be trouble, but he's here now, and he's all business. I see his face as he drives past me. There's real hate there. Does he hate me, or her? Or does he just hate anyone who's got his property? Maybe that. Then there's the gun. The shots ringing so loud my ears hurt.

'I don't want any trouble,' I shout.

I just want to get home. This was supposed to be a fresh start.

When Shannah was asleep on the bed in my flat that afternoon she'd looked so vulnerable. Appealing. I couldn't look at her any longer, so I stood at the window, to smoke a cigarette, enjoy the afternoon sun on my face.

Best view in the world, this; I live on a hill overlooking Dover. Everyone thinks they know Dover – white cliffs, coastal paths, and a view of France on a clear day. But they don't know it like I do. Dover – the 'key to England' for a thousand years; that creates an interesting city. They say history makes a place, and a place makes its people who they are. I am most definitely one of Dover's people. Born and raised here, until I was a teenager anyway. And now I'm back. It's in my blood, see? It's part of me, like I'm part of it.

When you grow up in Dover you learn about how incredibly bloody the protection of property can be; every war involving Europe and England – since before those names even existed – has left its mark here. And our local schools make sure you learn each key fact. It's something you take for granted as a Kentish teen – you know why Dover Castle's medieval fortifications were needed, how Napoleon was repulsed, and why the secret tunnels and chambers beneath the castle walls were a-buzz with activity during the last war.

'I'm hungry,' mumbles Shannah, still groggy. 'Got any food?'

I check the fridge; inside it there's a collection of take-away containers with rancid dregs.

'The fridge is empty,' I lie. 'Pizza place down the road's not bad.'

'So I see.'

Ten greasy boxes piled on the table tell a tale.

'I'll go,' I say.

'Good.'

'What do you fancy?' I ask, checking I've got some cash.

'No meat. Anything veggie. Extra cheese.'

I buy the Carnivore's Feast to compensate for the apology of a pizza I get Shannah; we eat our separate meals in silence, and drink a couple of cold beers. I make another trip to the shower, alone this time. I run the water cold. It helps, but not much.

'Fancy going for another ride?' she calls.

She knows I'm not going to say no. For once I don't hear my mother's favorite saying, 'Just because you can, it doesn't mean you should.' Why not, Mother? Why not?

The first time I ever saw Shannah, that morning, we were on the seafront. Just where the string of plastic-tabled cafés and seasonal ice-cream shops peter out there's a row of houses that stalwartly face the English Channel, built when Edward VII was on the throne. Somewhat bedraggled these days, they were the sort of place my mother would have called 'middle class' a couple of decades ago, while looking down her nose at them.

There's a road in front of the houses, then a wide grass verge dotted with weathered benches; it leads to the sand, then the sea. I stare at that last narrow strip of England, thinking of all the blood that's been shed over millennia to protect it, and there she is – Shannah, standing beside the car.

I focus on the car first; not because it's more important than a person, but because it's why I'm here. It's a classic American beast – a 1969 Chevy Camaro Z28. Probably worth thirty thousand, or more. I bet it looks good under the bonnet. V8s do.

Shannah's quite a picture herself. Her dress matches the car's paintwork – red with black stripes and trim – and there's a lot of thigh on display; she's clearly no shrinking violet. As I draw close, she pushes a pair of cat-eye sunglasses onto her face. Her nail polish and lipstick match the car. Even her hair's a vivid red.

I tell her why I'm here. She understands.

'So, Sam, how about we take her for a spin? I know a secret place where I can let her rip.' She makes it sound exciting; her voice growls, like an idling V8.

'Sorry, but I've got to get it to the client at PI Pete's office,' I say. She pouts, peers at me over her sun-specs. I check my watch. 'How long would you need, do you think?'

Her cheeks dimple. 'A couple of hours, tops.'

I sigh and shrug. '"Just because you can, it doesn't mean you should." My mother used to say that. My ex-wife too.' I lie about my ex-wife saying it, but it allows me to tell Shannah all she needs to know about me.

'Your ex-wife?' Dark eyes flash at me over rhinestone-studded frames.

I nod. Am I trying to be the true professional my new boss tells me I should be? 'PI's don't muck about with anyone involved in a case,' Pete's warned.

'I'll drive,' I say.

'No, I'll drive. My car.'

'For now.'

'Then I'll drive, for now.'

The coast road is clogged with the morning's tourist traffic. We rumble past a car with screaming kids in the back seats. They're heading for Dover Castle, of course. I suspect the fact the fortifications there go back to the Iron Age will be lost on the children, who'll probably end up clambering over the massive cannon balls used during the Napoleonic Wars. Us? We're heading up the coast to who knows where.

Once the traffic thins out, Shannah presses the accelerator, and the car throbs beneath us. She tells me about Pete's client – the bloke who wants the car from her. She explains how he's lumpen, and treats her like he owns her. She's no one's to own, she says. I wonder.

I know the man's name, and something of his reputation; Pete told me. She must have known at least the same about him before she got involved with him. Bert Sampson is an unforgiving local loan shark who preys on those who inhabit Dover, which – although I love it – is admittedly a place which gathers to itself more than its fair share of the displaced and vulnerable. Always has, always will. That's how it goes with ports; gateways from – and to – Hell, for so many.

Her eyes never leave the road as she regales me with every detail about what she did to get her hands on the car. It represents a victory of some sort to her, it seems. I'm sad for her; a thing like a car shouldn't mean so much to a person.

She keeps talking; I'm happy enough to listen. Nowadays, she says, she has a respectable life, teaching pole dancing at various gyms. She even does it for some housewives who live out on the nicer estates; they hold private parties in their perfectly primped houses, she takes along her pole, and struts her stuff. They do their best to copy her. She sells them naughty undies to wear when they show off their new moves to their husbands, who commute to London all week.

Ah, the joys of suburbia. One of the reasons I left Dover was because I didn't want to be gradually suffocated by the atmosphere that exists here – it can be toxic. The name of your street, or who your parents are and their role in the local community, outweigh your potential value to society. So terribly, terribly British.

Mother could never see how it was for me – that I couldn't be truly myself if I stayed. Poor Mother. I certainly didn't want that life. For a place with such expansive skies, the horizons in Dover felt – for me, back when I was a teenager – frighteningly limited.

We arrive at the place where Shannah can put the car through its paces. It's not much more than an open field, with a few crumbling buildings dotted about. I recognize it as an old aerodrome. So many places like this existed here once – airfields used by fighter planes in the 1940s. The remains of tarmac where Spitfires taxied before roaring off to bob and weave in dogfights over the English Channel to save humanity from the Nazis now mean no more than that Shannah has a place where she can play with 'her' car.

The societal-memory of men who sacrificed their youth for their country overwhelms me, as Shannah slams down her stilettoed foot, and we take off. She's vibrating with life. Maybe those young men who died felt the same way when their engines roared across this place. I thank heavens she's a good driver, because otherwise the corners would eat us up; the car wasn't built for them. Finally, we grind to a halt, both breathless from the ride. The smell of hot rubber lingers in the heavy air as we rumble to a standstill outside a long-abandoned hangar.

'Let's drive in there for some shade. I'm hot,' she says. The engine pulses.

'You certainly are,' I say.

I'm around six feet, and she's no pocket Venus. The car's too small for us. I suggest somewhere more conducive to a good time, so we decamp to my flat. Fast.

Before I headed out that morning I'd opened a window; my flat needs a good airing now and again, especially when the forecast is for higher than usual temperatures. From the vantage point my window offers the cliffs aren't white – they're a jagged green mass set against the glittering sea beyond. Like the ripped edge of England.

Perspective is everything. Take me, for example; my mother would have a fit if she could see me now – though I think I could be doing a lot worse.

I've been a private eye for about three weeks. My boss, Pete? He's been one for thirty years – almost my whole life. He's learned a thing or two in that time, he says. Took me on because he doesn't have anyone like me on his team; more options for him when it comes to new jobs, he hopes. He's impressed with the way I've applied myself so far.

Pete says I need a selection of hats, jackets, and sunglasses in the boot of my car, so I'll be able to follow someone without them knowing it's me, possibly for days. That's all people notice, he says; the big picture, not the details.

He's probably right. I know no one ever notices the stuff that really matters about me. Why would they? I'm just Sam. Big Sam. Sam who used to stand at the door of a club late at night, when the drunks and the weirdos want to get in. Sam with the growing beer belly. Sam with the failed marriage.

This new job with Pete'll be good. A job where I'm supposed to be invisible. Invisible means no one pays any attention as I pass them on the street, or sit opposite them in a pub. Never make eye contact, Sam, never connect; connections are a way in. I don't want anyone taking up space in my life; my life is mine. I've managed to tear myself away from the rest of humanity, and now I've found a job where that's a good thing. A perfect fit.

Pete sounded relaxed when I phoned him about this job. 'Easiest money we'll make this week,' he says.

'For you,' I say. 'You don't do anything yourself.'

'I've trained you up, and I get us the jobs. You'll get your cut.'

'Cash? Today?'

'When I get mine.'

For him it's just another case he's handing off to one of his team. For me? It's my first case out on my own. No more shadowing an experienced co-worker. It's a new life. A chance to start over. Show the world what I'm made of.

Pete says it's just a repossession, and he doesn't know why the client wants us to do it, but he does, and he's not the type you argue with. He tells me why; Bert Sampson doesn't sound like the sort of bloke whose wrong side would be appealing. Or healthy.

'Shouldn't take more than a few hours,' he says. 'Decent enough address to collect from. Some woman's got it. Just get the car from her and bring it here. Pronto. The client's coming to collect it here at the office. Shouldn't be any trouble. Easy job to start you off. Easy money, Sam. See you later.'

'Right-o,' I say. Easy money sounds good, because there isn't much of that about these days. And I certainly need some cash; the rent needs paying, I need ciggies, and pizza, and beer of course. It all costs. Maybe I can get myself a gym membership. I miss the gym.

I signed on with Pete because I'm apparently getting too soft-looking to be an effective bouncer. Too many youngsters think that challenging the 'beef' at the door is sport. It wasn't like that years ago, when I started. Then I got some respect. Awe, even.

'You're big,' they'd say.

'Indeed I am,' I'd say, 'and I know how to use every ounce. So watch it.'

That would be that. Being good on the door means you should only need two muscles – your brain and your tongue. I never was much use in school, but I've always been sharp. Even my ex-wife said that.

Recently, I found I wasn't getting as much respect; it's more difficult to diffuse a developing situation with a rapier wit when there's only blubber, not muscle, to back it up.

'You're getting soft, Sam,' says the club's owner Zach a while back. 'I've got to find someone harder, more ripped. Like you used to be. Whatever happened to that wife of yours? She kept you fighting fit.'

'Traded me in for a younger model,' I say. It's true.

'That'll happen if you let yourself go, Sam,' says Zach. He doesn't understand.

Zach gives me Pete's number because he reckons I'm still sharp, even if I'm not ripped any more. I phone Pete; he's got a good reputation in the area. With all the questionable characters a huge port like Dover attracts, there's a fair amount of work here for PIs, he says. Pete and I sort out a deal. Ta-daa! New life for Sam.

PI Sam doesn't have the same ring to it as *PI Pete*, which is what all Pete's adverts scream in big, bold letters. When we met for the first time face to face we laughed about Sam Spade; we both agree I'm nothing like him.

When I woke this morning my head hurt. Too many beers mean a hangover, I know that, but they were in the fridge, and it was hot. Very hot, for Dover; usually the sea breezes keep it cool. But not this August.

I towel-swat flies off week-old pizza boxes and think about clearing up, but don't. Instead, I sit on the settee, light a cigarette, and enjoy the way the smoke and dust dance in the first shaft of early-morning sunlight. Swirling. Shifting. I smoke another cigarette just to keep watching.

I chug, then push out thin streams, and pop circles with my tongue. The smoke reminds me of a family trip we took on an old steam train, when I was little. Then Daddy died, and we never did anything like that again. Mother's new chap didn't believe in family jaunts. He really didn't care for me at all. Probably a good thing. I was always tall and stocky, even as a child. Maybe he thought I'd be able to take him on if he came for me, instead of her. Poor Mother; keeping up appearances and protecting the family name from the merest hint of trouble took its toll on her. Sherry was her answer. Harvey's Bristol Cream, to be exact.

When I turned sixteen I broke her heart; I didn't follow the path she'd imagined for me.

That Cirque lot over in Canada started a trend, and I became a catcher for a troupe based in Brighton where they did the same sort of thing. I started in a novelty kids' act, then applied myself to the weight-training, got myself some of those special injections for a while, and beefed up nicely. They finally let me join an adult act when I turned twenty-two. The men who ran the business knew about the injections, but they didn't care as long as I got bigger, and stronger. Fine by me.

It's a good thing most people around here know nothing about my old job. Admit to wearing face paint, wigs, and all sorts of weird get-ups? Wouldn't help my image at all. But it was a good life. And there was Lena, of course.

Lena and her sisters shipped in from Leipzig; did one of those specialty spots folding themselves around each other in sparkly costumes until the audience thinks they're about to snap. Lena was the youngest in her family, and her mother got her doing all sorts of bendy stuff from the time she was a baby.

To be honest, I never thought I'd be her type, but it turns out I was.

It all began with me helping her with her English. Not a lot of folks along the south-east coast warm to Germans, even now; too many tales handed down within families of land-mined beaches, night-time bombing raids, and – of course – the Little Ships of Dunkirk. The English who live in these parts have never forgotten those mini-flotillas which set out from local harbors and beaches, especially in Kent, returning over-laden with battered, bloodied troops, and a total loss of innocence for the boaters who'd wanted to help their fellow countrymen. They never seem to talk about the death, the horror, the loss, only about the way they'd helped. That's important.

Lena and I would sit at the end of Brighton Pier, among the gaudy Victorian sideshows, and talk about all sorts. There was her with a heavy German accent, and me with my clipped public-school tones; her so tiny, and me so protectively large beside her. We got a few odd looks, which puzzled and annoyed me in equal measure; why can't people live in the twenty-first century, for goodness' sake?

As time passed, she and I grew closer. You know how that goes. Neither of us had any real friends; it was just us. Her mother – 'Mutti' she called her – was still back in Germany, so that was the easy part. It was her sisters we had to avoid, especially the eldest one, Erma. That woman hated me; once she worked out what was going on between us, she screamed at me in German whenever she saw me. Threatened Lena with dropping her from the act if we kept it up. But Lena stood firm. Besides, Erma knew the act would fail without Lena anyway, because she was the most lithe and flexible of all four sisters.

It took a long time for us to get married, but we finally tied the knot – which, in Lena's case, was something she could do with most of her body parts. We sneaked off to the Registry Office in Brighton, just the two of us. She thought it was romantic, and I loved seeing her so happy that day. But it was the beginning of the end for us.

Everything was tickety-boo until we got that piece of paper, then it all went to pot. So many of my dreams died in that marriage. No one but me knows how many.

First, I lost my career; I seriously damaged my knee trying to make a catch during rehearsal. It was a catch that was bound to fail, for someone; turned out that someone was me. I was laid up for two months, then hobbled about on crutches for a few more. Lena said I shouldn't have attempted the catch at all; that I should have let the safety mats do their job. She went so far as to say I made it worse, that I caused trouble by trying too hard to help.

That's when I began to work the door at pubs and clubs. Even though I wasn't as strong as I once was, I still looked the part because of all the physio workouts I'd done, and I kept on going to the gym as often as I could. But I wasn't happy. We weren't happy. We screamed and fought our way through another year, then we finally agreed on something – that it was time for me to leave. So I did.

She kept the child.

Leo, she named him. Lena and Leo; awful. Never told me who the father was, and Leo and I certainly never bonded. Best thing was for him to stay with her; I had no choice in the matter, anyway. He was two months old when I left; it'll be his second birthday soon. I hate it when I admit to myself how much I miss her. Him, too. That could have been a great life – a real family. But it wasn't to be.

'Just because you can, it doesn't mean you should.' Thanks, Mother. Okay, maybe I shouldn't have tried to make that catch.

So I cut my losses, and left my wife to raise the kid on her own. Maybe it's still just the two of them, I don't know. She made it clear as I left that she didn't want anything from me, so I promised her I'd give her as much of my nothing-ness as possible. And that was that – except for signing some divorce papers, which her solicitor told me would allow Lena to move on. Always willing to help, that's me.

I stand at my flat's grimy window and watch the seagulls swoop, thinking about how they're free to steal treats from the hands of Brit kids here in the morning, and from French children across the Channel, if they so choose, in the afternoon; how they're able to look down on humanity's little idiosyncrasies, like who 'owns' what.

'Come on, Sam, get focused, get ready for work,' I tell myself.

But I can't. I look toward the horizon, my broken dreams pulling me there. The sky is so many blues. Every blue. I love the part of day when the light's changing. It's like time's at a point where it could go either way; as though you can go forward, or back.

I shower, then poke around the heaps of clothing on the floor with my toes. I don't find anything that's fit to wear, so I shift the end of my bed to pry open the wardrobe.

I glance out of the window just one more time; the light's stopped changing now – the point when time might go forward or back has passed. The day isn't a . . . *thingy* . . . any longer.

What's the word? Something that's the same, both ways round. I concentrate. I can see Mrs Beynon, my fourth form English teacher, writing it on the board for us to read aloud. PALINDROME. That's it.

'Why isn't it one itself?' I ask her.

'You're too sharp by half, Samantha Barraclough-Gordon,' she says.

'The word should be the same from both ends, like what it means,' I press.

'Stop being such a cheeky girl, or I'll send to you to the headmistress's office,' she replies tartly.

'Why can't it be the same both ways?' I grumble.

'Nothing ever is,' she snaps. 'The odd word works that way, but nothing else. There's always something that changes the story of an event, or a life, or even a day when you tell it from the end to the beginning, instead of from the beginning to the end. It's called perspective. One little thing changes the way you see everything.'

Mrs Beynon; I'd forgotten her. I hated her. I suspect the feeling was mutual.

Finally, I find clean panties and a relatively fresh bra. It still fits. Just. Even my boobs are starting to sag. I do a few half-hearted palm clenches in front of the mirror to see if there's still enough muscle tone to help them bounce back, one day. I notice my waist is almost as thick as my hips, though I still haven't got a big bum. Lena used to laugh at me in my various glittery unitards, with no rear end to fill them out. Lena had a great smile.

I pull on a pair of jeans, and a shirt that I think I washed relatively recently. I check myself in the mirror, flattening a sprout of hair.

'You're flaccid, Sam, but you can do something about it. You know you can. Work out. Eat properly. Build the muscle back. You did it twice before. You can do it again – bad knee or not. Maybe find somewhere to get a few of those special injections. That should do the trick. Just to get yourself moving in the right direction.'

I agree with myself, and I'm finally ready to face the day; the first day of the rest of my life. A new life. A fresh start. Platitudes a-plenty.

Upon reflection, my life could have been easier, I suppose: the butt of jokes at school, where even the exorbitant fees for day pupils weren't able to insulate me from the other girls who would point and laugh at my lack of grace and lumpen appearance; Mother's sadness and desperation after Daddy died, and how she never seemed to recognize my loss, just hers; striking out on my own when I was really too young to do so, knowing I was 'different' and that – back then – that would never do in polite society.

And then, of course, there was Lena's crushing decision that she wanted a child more than she wanted me, or us, after all.

'Buck up, Sam. Remember the spirit of Dover – never let them grind you down. Be brave, courageous. Face your fears. Stiff upper lip, and all that.'

I pick up a two-word note I wrote for myself when Pete phoned the night before to tell me I was getting my first job to do on my own for him; I'd drunk several beers by then and I can't remember much about what he was saying other than that. I'll phone him back; he'll tell me what the note means. I chuckle; quite a coincidence – two of those palindrome things right there . . . two words that say exactly the same thing both ways around. But, like Mrs Beynon said, life's not like that; something always changes a story when you know the end. I put her out of my mind because this is the beginning, isn't it? Two words that mean I'm starting afresh. 'Shannah's racecar'.

SEPTEMBER

The Corpse that Died Twice

When the University of Vancouver offered me an opportunity to become an Assistant Professor of criminology I more or less jumped at the chance; being arrested on suspicion of murder can be a good catalyst for migration. Apparently being released and never charged doesn't mean a jot to the British tabloids, who'd hounded me – Cait Morgan, Associate Professor of criminal psychology, an irony they just couldn't ignore – long after the police acknowledged I had nothing to do with my ex-boyfriend Angus ending up dead on the floor of my flat in Cambridge one morning. It must have been a quiet summer for the journalists; they made my life unbearable. They didn't even let up when my parents died in a horrific car accident back in my homeland of Wales a few months later; instead they used the opportunity presented by Mum and Dad's funeral to snap long-lens shots of me in tears, which they later used as they pleased. It was a nightmare.

The opportunity of a fresh start in Canada – to say nothing of a tenure-track promotion – meant I could stop being who I had been, and start to become the person I wanted to be; I could leave behind bad memories, and tragic ones, and reinvent myself . . . to a certain extent. It was a way to put down some of my personal baggage – or at least to store it out of sight until I was ready to examine it. When you're in a new country you can show people only the parts of yourself you want them to see; you don't run the risk of bumping into someone who knew you twenty years earlier and still judges you on what you were back then before you've so much as opened your mouth in the here and now.

When I got the offer of an interview from the university where I now teach, I checked out some websites about Vancouver, and got the initial impression it was the sort of place you'd love if your desire was to go yomping up mountains before breakfast, yachting through lunch, then golfing before tea – followed by a dinner of salmon cooked four ways. All of which, with the possible exception of the salmon, is just not my cup of tea. Then I found some photographs of Harrison Hot Springs, and I began to see there were other ways to enjoy the wide-open spaces; just sit there and look at them.

Since I moved to British Columbia, Harrison has become my

'secret place'; I go there to escape the busy Downtown core of Vancouver itself, and even the bustling areas around my home and workplace in Burnaby. This being a stunning September Saturday – when the light has a mellowness you just don't see any other time of the year, and the air has some warmth but also a freshness you're glad to feel after the oppressive heat of the summer – I'd decided to head to Harrison for a little bit of R&R.

I'd been working, off and on, with Bud Anderson and the Integrated Homicide Investigation Team for the past couple of months; he'd call me in whenever a case came along where he felt understanding the victim might help, or simply speed up, his team's efforts. I'd also given a couple of talks to his team on the use of victimology in their investigations; it didn't pay a great deal, but any extra income was always welcome, because university pay is pretty pitiful.

As I drank my coffee that Saturday morning, and looked forward to my time in Harrison, I felt annoyingly thick-headed. The case that had caused me an almost sleepless night – and had me reaching for the bottle of Bombay just once too often – was a sad and puzzling one. A seventeen-year-old girl had been found wandering at the side of the highway that cuts through Maple Ridge, a now suburban, though once more rural, community nestling in the shadow of the Golden Ears Mountains, about forty miles east of Downtown Vancouver. When initially questioned the girl had claimed her boyfriend had just killed her father, at her family home. A comprehensive search of the home, and other possible locales, had turned up nothing; there was no damning forensic evidence, and neither the boyfriend nor the father were anywhere to be found. By that time the traumatized girl had been too heavily sedated to be of any further immediate use, so Bud had called on me to help his team by finding out whatever I could about the girl herself. I'd spent most of Friday at the girl's home, then the entire evening and night interpreting my findings, and writing up my report. I'd finally sent an email to Bud around midnight, pointing him and his team in the direction of the city of Kelowna – about three hours away – where it was clear to me, from some cryptic notes in the girl's diary, that her boyfriend had links. After being hunched over my laptop beside a pizza – with extra cheese and pepperoni, of course – for hours, I was frazzled. After that, there hadn't been much I could do but gulp down a few Bombays and worry through the night. So I decided I should take two bottles of water with me on my road trip, instead of the usual one; a breakfast of bananas, water, and aspirin meant I set off telling myself the weekend could only get better.

The drive to Harrison from my little house in Burnaby is quite something, and pretty much sums up my experience of my new home; preferring to not take the highway, I crawled through knots of traffic until I reached the back roads through Mission to Hatzic, and finally found myself in the delightfully lush Fraser Valley. The corn growing in the fields on both sides of the road was as high as Oscar Hammerstein's elephants' eyes, and I promised myself I'd stop at one of the roadside stalls to pick up a couple of dozen ears on the way back home.

When I arrived I parked in my usual spot, just opposite the Java café on the lakefront, and pushed myself out of my little red Miata. It was about eleven, and I felt justified in getting a coffee before I did anything else; besides, I needed a loo break, and that was the best place to go.

Fortified by a large mug of tooth-coating mocha with whipped cream – and a chocolate dipped biscotti, of course – I crossed the lakefront road to the paved walkway bordering the sandy beach. I planned to wander along the front as far as the hotel beyond the lagoon – an area created to allow for relatively safe bathing at this end of the lake.

As I set out I heard a voice behind me calling my name, 'Cait? Cait Morgan?'

I turned to see a figure some yards off that was vaguely familiar, but I couldn't put a name to the face; despite the fact I have an eidetic memory, that's not unusual for me, because I've seen a lot of people whose names I've never been told, having given so many lectures and presentations over the years.

The woman was waving excitedly and heading right for me with a big grin on her face, so I felt I had to do the same. It's usually at this point in an encounter I try to come up with some witty way of saying, 'How lovely of you to remember me – who on earth are you?' but my wit wasn't working terribly well, it seemed, so I said, 'Hello, nice to see you,' and left it at that.

The woman was about my height – short – and about my girth – overweight. She, like me, had long dark hair pulled back in a ponytail but – unlike me – she was wearing a sensible all-weather jacket. She was predictably weighed down by what seems, these days, to have become the omnipresent backpack. As I squinted at her I realized another summer had slipped by without me getting my eyes tested.

'Let me re-introduce myself,' she beamed. 'I'm Lottie Wentworth, from Black and Wentworth Public Relations Plus; you worked with one of my colleagues in London on a campaign for a new brand of vodka back in the Nineties. Remember?'

In a flash I was back at the advertising and PR agency I'd worked at in Soho all those years ago; the campaign she was talking about – to launch Valkyrie Vodka – had been the one that made me decide to give up the marketing communications game and go off to get my master's degree in something useful – criminology. The 'colleague' she mentioned was as memorable as the campaign itself, given she was the most vacuous nitwit I'd ever met; Jemima Hetherington-Knox could hardly spell 'cat', yet was supposed to be their best writer. She drove me nuts. After an interminable month, struggling to get her to come up with three acceptable stories about why trendy young things-about-town should drink this allegedly smoother vodka, it dawned upon me I could no longer cope with the pointlessness of my life, so I put together the best proposal I'd ever written, and it got me into Cambridge, and out of the agency world forever. If Lottie Wentworth had been the woman to employ the grammatically-challenged Jemima, then she was indirectly responsible for my current life, for which I supposed I should be grateful. Of course, if I hadn't gone to Cambridge I'd never have met Angus, nor suffered a truly psychologically and physically damaging relationship – so I supposed I could blame her for that too. On balance I decided to play nice.

'What a small world,' was about all I could muster as I smiled through gritted teeth, and screamed internally, *I thought I'd escaped from all you lot!*

She bowled along regardless, as all these PR types do. 'I was just saying to Jeremy that I recognized you, but we were never introduced properly. I was sure you wouldn't have known me, but I remembered you from the television and the newspapers, of course. All that bother you had in Cambridge.'

And there it was; less than a minute had passed, and she'd already mentioned the nadir of my life. Great. What would she do for an encore? Introduce me to her 'significant other' as the person who'd been accused of beating her abusive lover to death?

'Ah,' I replied, probably looking suitably sheepish.

She came closer and almost whispered, 'I'm so glad that all worked out for you; a terrible ordeal, I should imagine.'

I was pretty sure Lottie Wentworth didn't possess sufficient imagination to come even close to countenancing what I'd endured, but I let it pass. That was all behind me; I reminded the woman in the bathroom mirror each day that the police never charged her, and her character was never truly besmirched. Of course, given that Britain is ruled by the 'no smoke without fire' brigade, I suspected that, in Lottie's mind, I was as guilty as Hell.

I didn't know what to say to the woman; she seemed to expect some sort of exchange, so I put my 'be nice to the client' face on and asked the obvious question, 'Are you two on vacation here?'

As I spoke I asked myself, *Why do you always play up a Canadian accent when you talk to British people, Cait? Is it because you're trying to distance yourself from them? Trying to show you've changed, moved on?* I replied to myself, *You're the psychologist, Cait – shrinker, shrink thyself.*

'Oh yes, we're having such a lovely time – isn't it all so pretty around here?' Lottie's entire persona bubbled with energy. It annoyed the heck out of me.

'Well, I guess we call it "Beautiful British Columbia" for a reason,' I replied.

'Are you on holiday too?' she continued.

Haven't I just given you a big enough clue for you to deduce I live here? was what I thought, but out of my mouth came, 'No, I live here now,' in what I hoped was my most reasonable-sounding voice.

She gave me a knowing glance that riled me; I knew she was thinking I'd simply run away from the UK to hide from the journalists, because her nasty little micro-expressions were shouting as much at me. I added tartly, 'I'm a professor of criminal psychology at the University of Vancouver. Have been for some years now. It's a wonderful place to live and work – there's so much more space and room to breathe here than in London.'

Sometimes I find that letting out just a little steam means I can keep the rest of it in, and when you're dealing with a particularly stupid person, they never seem to notice anyway. The Lottie-person certainly didn't.

'Oh absolutely,' she gushed, 'if only we could get away and run the agency here, eh Jeremy?' They both literally snorted with laughter; it was like something out of a comedy sketch poking fun at the nouveau riche, English, upper-middle classes. Sadly, Lottie and Jeremy were alarmingly real, and they were spoiling my Harrison Saturday. I wasn't happy about it. All I could think about was how to escape.

'But surely you'd miss the bright lights of London, Lottie?' I ventured.

'Well, yes,' she continued to gush, 'I suppose you're right. I mean, where would one be without the theatre, and all those marvelous restaurants and so forth? And London is so *happening* these days.'

I wanted to get away. Badly.

'Well, don't let me hold you two guys up – have a great vacation. Nice to bump into you,' I lied. I gave them a little wave as I began to move away.

From behind me, a familiar voice called, 'Cait? What are you doing here?'

I turned to see Bud Anderson walking toward me, pulling Marty – his rather overweight black Labrador – on a leash behind him. They were both all smiles. They were also both panting.

'Hi, Bud,' I replied, with genuine warmth this time. I was nonplussed; Harrison is supposed to be 'out of the way'.

'Who's this then?' asked Bud in his usual direct manner, nodding at the couple who were still standing beside me.

'This is Lottie, and Jeremy. I did some work with Lottie's public relations company back in my London ad agency days in the Nineties. They're here on vacation and they're just off to explore,' I said, hoping they would be.

'Hi Lottie, Jeremy,' said Bud as he shook hands vigorously with each of them in turn. 'I'm Bud Anderson. Cait's doing some work with me right now – but of a rather different nature. She helps me find murderers.'

Lottie looked alarmed. I smiled inwardly.

'I'm a cop,' added Bud, by way of explanation.

'So they're still keeping an eye on you, Cait?' said Lottie, snorting again.

I wanted to stab her, and rip out her tongue. 'Not exactly, Lottie.' I smiled as broadly as I could.

'We don't need to keep an eye on Cait,' said Bud as he put a strong arm around my shoulders, 'she's the one who keeps an eye on us, aren't you?' He beamed almost manically at me, then at Lottie. 'In fact, she's helping me on a case right now, but you know –' he tapped the side of his nose conspiratorially – 'I can't say too much at this stage,' and he winked at the somewhat taken-aback Jeremy.

'I tell you what,' added Bud before anyone else could draw breath, 'if you knew the "old Cait", I think you should get a chance to see the "new Cait" at work. Why don't we all get a coffee across the road and I can show you what I mean. My wife's gone off with a group of her friends to walk around the lake a-ways, so I said I'd hang out with Marty. He's not up to hiking any more, poor guy.' And with a look from Marty that intimated he might be ready for a bit of a lie down, Bud steered us all toward a restaurant's rooftop terrace overlooking the lake where dogs weren't merely allowed, but were actively welcomed. Bud ordered a round of coffees, and some coffee cake, while doing a gentlemanly job of settling us all with just the right amount of sun shining on our faces, and only the slightest breeze at our collars.

I was puzzled; Bud had something up his sleeve and I didn't know what. I'd already had a few surprises and it wasn't even noon; how could the day possibly become any more complicated? I just hoped Lottie didn't come out with any more smart remarks, and begged everything that was holy to not let her bring up the subject of my dead ex, Angus, at all; I'd never discussed it with Bud, and I didn't see it as appropriate to have it raised now in front of the man who had the right to hire or fire me from potentially lucrative contracts.

'I don't know if you know it,' announced Bud once we were all comfortable, 'but Cait is quite a star; she's a leading light in victimology theory development and application around the world, and she's doing some great work for us. But there's a puzzling case she knows nothing about; it happened around here. It's the sort of thing I know Cait excels at helping my team with; how about it, Cait? Fancy hearing about a strange one?'

Unusually for Bud, he was being really annoying; I tried to show my confusion and irritation as I half-smiled at him and sulkily replied in the affirmative.

Bud carried on regardless, and I was beginning to feel more than a little uncomfortable. 'Around here, you see,' explained Bud, as though talking to two five-year-olds, 'crime is investigated by the RCMP,' he pronounced the letters as though it were the first time Lottie and Jeremy would have heard them. 'And, as we all know, the Royal Canadian Mounted Police – the Mounties – always get their man.' He paused for a laugh, but poor Lottie and Jeremy weren't at all clued in, and I suspected they'd both had a sense of humor bypass at an early age in any case, so he quickly moved on. 'I head up an integrated team, where we pull together people from all the local-operating forces to focus on homicides – it's an excellent, innovative model.'

I felt disappointed for Bud – a well-known champion of the approach – that this drew nothing but the slightest smile from Lottie.

Bud continued, 'About three months ago there was a fatal car crash just around there.' Bud pointed to the shore of the lake that ran away to the right of us. 'A young man, a youth really, was found dead in his car. He was alone, and he'd burned to death. Very crispy.' Bud was enjoying Lottie's expression almost as much as I was, and Jeremy gripped her hand in horror. I could tell Bud was doing his best to not smile as he spoke, and, to be fair to him, he was succeeding, for the most part.

He took a deep breath and explained, 'Despite the level of degradation it was quickly established the young man was a local, from Agassiz just along the road, and we discovered he'd actually been dead before his car hit a tree and burst into flames. It was all really sad because it was during grad celebration week here, and he was seen as yet another victim of what we call Grad-Madness. At least that's what we thought . . .' Bud paused for dramatic effect, and because the coffee and cakes had arrived. As we all tucked in I was still puzzled about how this case might involve me; I didn't have to wait long to find out.

'So, Professor Morgan – Cait – if you were to approach this from the victim-profiling point of view, what would you be trying to find out, and what would you deduce from that?'

I almost choked on my coffee cake. True, it was a bit dry, but that wasn't why I choked, and Bud knew it. His eyes were glinting and I could see the devilment in them. He was being playful, but I hoped his wicked game would be more at the expense of Lottie and Jeremy than myself, so I decided to go along for the ride.

'Okay.' I took a slurp of coffee and cleared my throat, 'Forensics – cause of death?'

'Massive dose of warfarin,' stated Bud baldly.

'How did it get into the body?' I queried.

'Booze. Giant bottle of American bourbon found at the scene; bottle broken, contents largely gone, but residual stomach contents told the story.'

'Age?'

'Eighteen.' Bud's shoulders heaved and he shook his head sadly as he spoke. 'Barely.'

'So where'd he get the illegal booze?'

'Why is it illegal?' interrupted Lottie.

'Legal drinking age is 19 here,' answered Bud, in a delightfully patronising voice.

'So?' I pushed.

'Seems a barman at one of the hotels back there –' he stubbed a thumb over his shoulder indicating the streets a block back from the lake – 'sold it under the counter to him.'

'Question the barman?'

'Yep. Swears he knew nothing about the warfarin. We believe him.'

'So how did the boy know the barman?'

'The barman's only 22 himself; they went to the same school in Agassiz. Knew each other from there.'

'So, the victim is a loner,' I observed.

'Why do you say that?' asked Jeremy.

I smiled. 'It's grad week, the victim's out on his own, drinking and driving at the lake – it doesn't sound like he's the center of a social whirl.' Then to Bud I said, 'He's a loner, knows older kids well enough to get booze from them. If the barman stole the booze from the hotel stock, then there might have been other intended victims, possibly many. Potential act by an annoyed customer at the hotel, or an ex-employee with a grudge?'

'The booze was not from hotel stock,' replied Bud.

'Curious,' I replied thoughtfully, then asked the obvious question, 'so where'd the barman get the bottle of booze?'

'Now this is where it gets interesting,' whispered Bud conspiratorially. We all drew closer to him.

'The barman claims to have accepted the bottle in exchange for a pair of his old sweatpants.'

'Interesting,' I said. 'With whom did he do the swapping?'

'Pete the Bum,' replied Bud.

Lottie, Jeremy, and I all looked at each other; for once we were all in the same place – completely in the dark.

'Who's Pete the Bum?' I asked. Lottie and Jeremy nodded, their mouths full of cake.

'Pete the Bum is a local character; he's lived here for years. He left behind the hurly burly of Downtown Vancouver, and pushes himself about this place in his wheelchair, living off the kindness of the locals, and generally making himself a gentle nuisance. The locals put up with him in the winter, then he pays them back by not annoying the tourists in the summer. In truth he's pretty mobile, but prefers the wheelchair; it lends him an air of authority, he claims.'

I was puzzled. 'So, Pete the Bum somehow acquired a bottle of bourbon—'

'*American* bourbon,' interrupted Bud.

'*American* bourbon –' I nodded at Bud – 'and he swaps it with a barman for a pair of sweatpants. Presumably Pete saw the sweatpants as being more useful than a bottle of booze, which is interesting. The barman then sells the *American* bourbon to a local youth who drinks it, and dies of an overdose of rat poison. Correct?'

'Correct,' replied Bud.

'So I'd say it's safe to assume the eventual victim was not the original target, and that the barman and the clientele of the hotel were not the targets. That is, if Pete the Bum didn't put the warfarin into the bottle.'

'He didn't,' confirmed Bud.

'And we know that because?' I asked.

'Because he wouldn't have had access to the form of warfarin found in the boy's system.' Bud looked as happy as his canine companion; Marty now had his own bowl of water to drink from, and was chewing his third of the treats supplied by our server.

'And what's so special about this warfarin?' I asked. Lottie and Jeremy looked eager to hear the answer too.

'It's American warfarin,' replied Bud, smiling and patting Marty's head.

I took a big slug of coffee, wishing it were something stronger, and went for it. 'So there's a special type of warfarin that you can only get in the USA?' Bud nodded. 'And that warfarin is used for what exactly?'

'Same as here, rat poison; but the US FDA has some rules about colorings they say have to be in the poison, and that's where it differs from our own Canadian stuff – the color-chemicals are different, so that's how we know it was American. Of course, you couldn't see the bourbon was a funny color through the brown glass of the bottle, so all the colorings in the world wouldn't have put someone off drinking it.'

'So the warfarin was American, like the bourbon?' I asked.

'Yes, like the bourbon,' replied Bud.

Lottie and Jeremy looked as though they were watching a tennis match as their heads turned to look at me and Bud in turn; goodness knows what anyone seeing our odd little group would have imagined was going on.

'But look, Bud, this isn't really fair; you know I consider victims and how they might be connected to the person who killed them. This boy was several people removed from whomever it was put the American poison into the American bourbon. How can I tell you anything about this case?' I was starting to run out of patience.

'But you are, Cait; you're following a path that your training sets ahead of you – whether it's about the victim who died, or maybe about the intended victim – you're on that path, just keep going.' Bud seemed genuine enough, and I could see the desire for closure in Lottie and Jeremy's eyes.

I gave in. 'Right. So the question is, who was the intended victim of the American poison in the American bourbon, and why is the fact both those items are from south of the border important?' I gave it a moment's thought. 'There are lots of cabins around this lake, right?' Bud nodded. 'Some of them must be owned by Americans, and more Americans must come here to board at the various B&Bs and hotels in the area, right?'

Bud nodded again. He turned to our rapt audience and said, 'We're about an hour from the border here, so Harrison is a popular spot with the Americans.'

I continued, 'I would suggest the bourbon and the poison were brought from the States, separately, and weren't intended to be used to kill. Initially. Have any Americans died unexpectedly in the last few months around here? In other words, did someone screw up in this instance and have another, more successful attempt, at their intended target's murder?' I hoped this was a good line of reasoning.

'No dead Americans, I'm afraid,' replied Bud. Realizing what he'd said, he added quickly, 'You know what I mean,' with a shrug.

'Any suspicious deaths at all?' I was reaching.

'Nope.'

Dead end. 'So did Pete the Bum tell you where he got the bottle?'

'He says he found it.' Bud raised an eyebrow, and I did likewise.

'So do we know where he stole it from?' I asked. I was beginning to feel the need for another couple of aspirin and hoped I wasn't sounding as exasperated as I was feeling.

'He wasn't saying. In a pointed way. And if you think anyone around here is going to report the theft of a bottle of booze – be it laced with poison or not – then . . .' Bud didn't have to finish.

'Yeah, yeah,' I admitted defeat on that one. I tried a new tack. 'Have there been any odd happenings around here at all, maybe in the month or so before the boy's death?'

'Some cabin fires. The local volunteer fire department had to run out a few times to douse small fires before they got to the trees. It can become a tinderbox around here.' He nodded at the expansive forests, and Lottie and Jeremy seemed to understand.

'One cabin more than once, or more than one cabin affected?' I asked.

'A few different ones, but one particular cabin was hit twice,' Bud replied.

'And was that cabin owned by an American?' I was seeing that path again.

'Ironically, the cabin is owned by a group of retired firefighters from Bellingham, just over the border. Being old pros they pooh-poohed the idea of having fire extinguishers and such like out there; thought they could manage just fine if there was an emergency. Idiots. It wasn't until after the second fire that they smartened up their act and got some firefighting equipment supplies on the property. They only ever use the cabin for the odd fishing trip, May through September, usually. They stay south the rest of the year.'

'Firefighters, eh?' I could see some light. 'They might not take too kindly to someone setting fire to their cabin, and would certainly not be happy about the locals having to help them out,' I added carefully. 'Have they been around much since the car accident?'

'Now there's another irony – or maybe a coincidence . . . though I generally don't care for them; they were first on the scene of the car accident. The dead boy's vehicle crashed into a tree not far from their cabin; they heard the noise, saw the flames, and put out the fire before anyone from around here could get to it, with the equipment they had by then. They called it in, and the locals came a-running to take care of any hot spots.'

'Since then?'

'They were around through June and into July, but haven't been seen at all since the boy's true cause of death was eventually made public.'

'Wow,' I said.

'Yeah,' replied Bud.

'So how's Pete these days?' I asked.

'Fine; they've found him a place at a residential home in Chilliwack,' replied Bud.

'And he has no idea?' I asked.

'Nope,' replied Bud.

'No one pointed out the error of his ways to him?' I couldn't believe it.

'I don't think there's much point – I mean, everyone keeps saying he's harmless, but he's not well-connected to reality.'

'He's lucky he's connected to it at all; he should be dead,' I concluded.

Bud nodded sagely, then raised his coffee mug. We both chinked and said cheers as though beer were involved.

We sat in silence for a moment, sipping.

Eventually, Lottie could contain herself no longer. 'Jeremy – do you know what they're talking about? Why have they stopped? What's the end?' She looked at her companion, her eyes searching his face for an answer.

Jeremy looked at Bud and myself with a stare so blank we might as well have been conversing in Greek – if Jeremy didn't understand Greek, that is.

'I'm sorry, Lottie darling, I have absolutely no idea what just happened. I say, Bud –' Jeremy's clipped tones made me smile inwardly – 'what's it all about? I don't get it.' Bertie Wooster couldn't have sounded more confused.

'Would you like to explain, Cait?' Bud was being gracious.

Two pairs of stupefied eyes turned toward me, and I took center stage. 'It's pretty obvious, really,' I said, annoyingly for Lottie and Jeremy, no doubt, because it clearly wasn't obvious to either of them.

Lottie tried to stare me down. I didn't flinch, instead I said, 'Pete the Bum likely holes up in some cabin or other shelter around here whenever he feels like it; he probably doesn't do much damage, but he thinks of every cabin as a potential home for himself. If the American firefighters aren't here often, chances are he'd settle himself in and be a bit miffed when they do show up. If Pete is – as Bud puts it – not well-connected to reality, he's going to feel slighted that he's been moved out of "his" home, and he might retaliate. Fire-starting is known to be relatively frequently connected to those who are homeless; it might be accidental, and the result of them trying to keep themselves warm in cold weather, but – psychologically – some of those who are homeless see property damage as the best way to hurt those who have what they don't. Please don't think I'm saying arson is widespread among those who have no home, however, the sad truth is many of those who live on the streets suffer from mental health issues, as well as facing the challenge of addiction. I wouldn't be at all surprised to find that Pete had started a couple of fires at the firefighters' cabin; since the fires happened when the owners were in residence, the chances are they weren't accidentally caused by Pete, but intentionally. I would further suggest the cabin owners suspected Pete, or maybe they even spotted him doing something related to the fires, and they decided to get their own back on him.' I paused, Lottie and her equally dim-witted companion were still transfixed.

'And this is where it gets nasty,' I continued. 'It sounds to me as though the American firefighters set out a bait bottle of booze for Pete, with something in it they believed would make him sick. For some unfathomable reason they chose to lace it with warfarin; an extremely dangerous course of action. If there was enough in the booze to kill the kid who drank it – and I can't imagine he drank a great deal from the bottle, being that young – there'd certainly have been enough in it to kill Pete. So I believe Pete was the intended victim; it's interesting that anyone pouring the bourbon from the bottle into a glass would have seen the discoloration, but someone drinking from the bottle wouldn't, because of the disguising quality of the bottle's colored glass. I believe the firefighters meant Pete harm, and believed he wouldn't spot the fact the bourbon was tainted; it seems they actually thought it through. Which is chilling. If I wanted to give them the benefit of the doubt, I'd say maybe they brought the rat poison with them from the US for controlling vermin at the cabin, and possibly, after a few beers and riling each other up, it seemed like a good idea to do what they did. They must have put the tainted bottle somewhere Pete could see it, and steal it. And once it was gone, even if they'd thought better of their actions in the sober light of day, it would have been too late to do anything about it. Luckily for Pete he wanted a pair of sweatpants more than he wanted the bourbon, so he swapped it, never knowing it was poisoned. The barman probably did the swap as much out of pity for Pete as having an eye for a bottle he could sell on for more than the value of a pair of old sweatpants he was possibly glad to get rid of. He sold it on to the kid he knew, who drank it and died of warfarin poisoning. With a dead body at the wheel, the boy's car ran into a tree, and the retired American firefighters are close by; they leap into action, not knowing of the connection to the bottle they laced. When the boy's real cause of death is finally reported, they make the connection, and they never come back. I'm guessing the cabin's for sale?'

Bud nodded.

'Any of the suspects talking?' I asked, doubting it.

'Our colleagues south of the border are fully aware of our suspicions and are carrying on a gentle form of harassment. They think one of the retired firefighters might crack someday, but you never know with these things; the ties that bind these guys from their working days are strong, and it might be that none of them ever spill the beans.'

'But how did you know, Cait?' wailed Lottie, exasperated.

'Because she's a clever, insightful woman,' replied Bud on my behalf. Then, rather surprisingly, he continued, 'You know, Lottie, some people find themselves in situations where they can sink or swim; Cait has faced that choice – and she swam. She's here carving out a new life for herself, and she's using her brains and her understanding of human nature to help not only herself but others too.' Bud flashed a smile at me, then looked gravely at Lottie as he added, 'Earlier you asked if the police were still keeping an eye on Cait; I'm guessing you were alluding to the death of Cait's ex-boyfriend Angus in Cambridge.' Lottie blushed pink to the roots of her hair, and Jeremy's eyes began to slide toward the exit.

Bud continued, 'Maybe you thought I wouldn't know about that; maybe your sly comment was aimed at showing me you knew something about Cait I didn't. Whatever your reason, what I can tell you is that Professor Cait Morgan was investigated and cleared in the UK, before she left. And, to be absolutely clear, there's no way she'd have gotten the security clearances she needed to be able to work with my team if there was even a hint of complicity in any crime in her past. I've given you the chance to see Cait at work, maybe you'd now like to get on with your vacation and leave us to enjoy the beauty that surrounds us.'

There was no doubt Bud had read the situation from the first seconds of our meeting; and he'd chosen to act like a knight in shining armor.

Lottie pushed herself out of her seat, still flushed in the face. 'I think you're very rude, mister policeman, and I think you and Cait are well-suited; I'd always heard she was too sharp for her own good, and she's obviously found a kindred spirit in you. We won't stay where we're not wanted, will we, Jer?' Jeremy was quick to leap to his feet and nod in agreement. 'We're off. Goodbye.' Lottie marched toward the stairs leading to the street below. Marty sent them on their way with one deep growl.

After she'd gone I took a moment deciding what to say. 'That was a bit mean, Bud, don't you think?' I ventured.

'Mean is what *she* was, and spiteful. I've met her type before. You don't deserve that, Cait. I hope you don't mind me speaking frankly' – I shrugged – 'so I'll just say, in you I've found a person who has all the attributes I wish I could find in each of my officers, but it's all coated with a hard shell. Of course I know about Angus and Cambridge; I had to get you checked out and cleared before I could invite you to work with my team. I know what happened; I scanned the police records of the case. Had to. So I know the facts. What I can only imagine, however, is how it must have affected you; it must have been a horror show. And I don't just mean the relationship with Angus himself – though your statement, his record, and the police investigation painted a picture of a brute. That must have been awful for you, yes, but what I mean is these newspapers need some more rules and regulations to control how they can track people down, and make their lives a misery. I'm not being patronizing when I say I think you've done a great job since you got to Canada; you got your promotion to full professor, and you really are using all your considerable skills to make life better for others. But you know what, Cait?' I dreaded what might come next. 'You need to start living a life, not just having a career. It's true a healthy dose of cynicism is handy in our line of work, and I'm only too well aware that investigating the worst in life can make a person more than somewhat untrusting. But you need to learn to trust some people, good people, and allow them inside the walls you've built around yourself. It's quite clear from the little I know about you that you have no real friends. Why not mix a bit more? Join Jan and me – and all her yomping friends – for lunch today? I know you've met her before, but a stuffy rubber-chicken banquet doesn't let you really get to know a person; I think you two would get on.'

I hesitated before I replied; I'd built a pretty good working relationship with Bud, and I didn't know how to tell him his lovely – but hobby-crazy – wife, Jan, just wasn't the sort of person I felt I could warm too; honestly, she was so well-organized she frightened me a bit. 'Thanks, Bud, for everything. Maybe not lunch today, but I'll happily join a slightly smaller group if you and Jan are entertaining sometime. I just don't do well with large, organized groups. And that's nothing to do with the legacy left by my relationship with Angus, it's just never been me. Not likely to become me, either. But I don't see any harm in you, me, and Jan spending some social time together – so long as that's not crossing any lines because you hire me as a consultant; I don't want to jeopardize my chances to work with your team. I'm finally getting to put my theories into practice, on real cases, and maybe to even do some real good. That's what I care about most; the chance to help seek out justice for victims of crime. But, if we can all have a coffee or two without that coming to an end, that would be lovely. Thanks.'

Bud stood and smiled down at me. 'Good answer.' He looked at his watch. 'Jan and her gang will be back before too long, and this one –' he nodded down at Marty, who was already on his feet and wagging his tail – 'needs to attend to his business before I meet them. But, before I go, I have some news; just for your ears. The local cops in Kelowna found the boyfriend of the girl from Maple Ridge. And thanks to you pointing us in that direction they managed to save the father; he was hanging on by a thread – a few more hours and he might have died. In fact, the boyfriend thought he already was when he left him in the trunk of the car he'd stolen. So today you saved a life, Cait; that girl will see her father again, thanks to you. Who knows, she might even come to her senses and drop the violent thug she was going out with. I don't need to tell you how that can release a person to live a new life, do I?'

Bud wrangled a bounding Marty toward the exit, and I sipped the dregs of my coffee; it was cold, and I was a little chilly, but I sat for a while and I looked out at the sunlight glinting on the lake, and the brooding trees covering the surrounding hillsides.

I told myself Bud was right, but I couldn't find it in me to know what to do about what he'd said. It felt wonderful to have saved a life – maybe two, in a way – but what about my own life?

They say the first step toward solving a problem is to recognize you have one. Okay, I have a problem; I'm lonely. I'm heart-achingly lonely, but I'm too frightened to give myself to someone ever again in case they do what Angus did to me – beat me into submission physically, and goad me into subservience psychologically. I admit it – my relationship with him led to me losing some part of the essence of myself. I changed. I became less, diminished. And the awful thing I have to acknowledge is that I let him do it; I could have thrown him out long before I did. But I believed that he would change; I believed him when he said 'never again'. How stupid was I? It's all well and good for a professional like Bud to praise my intelligence, and my membership of Mensa proves I possess more of that than most – but where was it when I needed it? Why did my so-called insights fail me when I was the one who needed them?

Maybe the first step toward solving a problem isn't just acknowledging you have one, but accepting you can't do anything about it if you keep trying to find answers to questions that will remain unanswerable from where you are.

Sitting there looking out over Harrison Lake I made myself a deal; I'd walk around the lagoon, get myself home, and continue do my job the best way I knew how, but I would try to find some 'outside interests' too. Maybe I should travel more? I used to enjoy that, in my pre-Angus days. I promised myself I'd give it some serious consideration.

OCTOBER

The Trouble with the Turkey

If I hadn't undercooked the Thanksgiving turkey, Jake might not be dead. It was my first one ever. Now maybe I'll never cook another, given the way it's all turned out. Which is a shame, because I love Thanksgiving, and everything it stands for; I love the way we celebrate ours here in Canada in October, when it can also be a harvest celebration, not like them having it in November down in the States. But now? I guess it doesn't much matter when it is; it'll always remind me of this one.

To start, there was the problem with the gravy. That should have been a sign, I guess. The package said to mix the powder with cold water and heat it up. I did just what it said, but it went lumpy. And the potatoes didn't roast properly. Pale potatoes don't look good next to undercooked turkey when they're covered with lumpy gravy.

The carrots might have added some color, but Jake was right about me throwing those out; they were ruined. If our kitten Mindy hadn't distracted me by bringing that mouse into the kitchen I guess I'd have noticed the smell of vegetables burning, but she looked so proud of herself that I had to make a fuss of her. The gash she gave me when I took the limp little body away from her will heal up just fine, and I don't reckon I'll even have a scar. But the burn I got on my arm when I took the carrots out of the oven will surely leave a mark.

And there weren't any beans on the plate, either. Who runs out of green beans right before Thanksgiving? They've gotta have some kinda idiot doing the ordering at that supermarket. Everyone has green beans with turkey for Thanksgiving, don't they? They sure do around here anyway, so I guess that's why they sold out. Fresh, frozen, even tinned – all gone.

Maybe the real problem was that Jake didn't finish putting up the new lights in the kitchen until yesterday. With his mess lying about the place I couldn't get ready for today ahead of time. The lights hang from the ceiling above the counter, so bits kept falling down until he was done, then I had to bleach everywhere to be sure it was all good and clean. Who knew a liter of bleach could spread so far on a tile floor? If only I'd bought the small rubber gloves instead of getting the big ones with a money-off coupon, my fingers would have fitted into the handle of the bottle, then it wouldn't have slipped out of my hands and gone everywhere. I even had to pull the gas range away from the wall to mop it up. The trouble I had pushing it back into its spot was something I hadn't expected, but I managed it without having to tell Jake. That said, even though I thought I'd done a good job of it, I needed to give it a final shove this morning just to get it right back in there before I put the turkey into the oven to cook. And the smell from all that bleach is still so strong, even today. Yuk!

No wonder when the guy came to fix the dishwasher he asked what I'd been doing to the place. He was such a gentleman; so good to fit us in the Friday before the Thanksgiving weekend, and quick too. He said maybe something had dropped down inside the machine and trapped the spinning arm, so he guessed that was why the motor had been working too hard, which made it catch on fire. Well, it only smoked a little, then I switched it off – but he still said he couldn't fix it. I'll have to wash dishes by hand now – which won't kill me, I guess.

Won't kill me? Ha, that's a laugh in itself.

Poor Jake. Maybe if someone hadn't smashed into his truck outside the bar in downtown Maple Ridge last week he'd have been able to get all the stuff he needed for the kitchen lights sooner. But we've been sharing my old car, and when he broke the back window trying to get the ladder to fit, it took a whole day to get it fixed. The glass went everywhere; I thought they did a good job of vacuuming it all up at the repair place, but they must have missed the bit Aunt Dorina sat on when we went to church. If she hadn't tried to brush it off her good coat she wouldn't have ended up with that gash on her hand.

I've gotta say, the emergency room at the hospital was full of the weirdest people for a Sunday afternoon. In any case, she seemed fine when I dropped her off at her condo afterwards. Tired, but at least the stitches didn't hurt, she said.

I guess we were lucky she wasn't here last Monday evening, like she usually is, because the TV fell off the wall onto the mantel. Jake was out with the guys at the bar when it happened. I was taking a bath, but the noise was enough to get me downstairs to check what the heck was going on. It was a shame about the TV – we paid a lot for a real thin one that was just the right size so Jake could sit on his big chair and watch his football in comfort.

We brought the TV from our bedroom into the family room and put it on a table beside his chair ready for the weekend. When the plumber came on Tuesday he said it looked 'cute'. That was before he saw the mess I'd made upstairs by dropping the handheld showerhead over the side of the bath when I rushed to investigate the noise down here. I'd cleaned up best I could, but he reckoned that was what had dripped through to the laundry room below. Who knew getting water into a dryer would do that? He said I didn't need a plumber, but a new dryer. It was an old one anyhow – and it hadn't been working right for weeks.

That's a long list for the upcoming sales: a dryer, a TV, a dishwasher, and a new computer. That was getting old too; last week – after I printed out the recipe for the turkey – I got nothing but a black screen. I told Jake I hadn't been fiddling with it, but he wasn't happy. First he shouted a lot. When he calmed down he said there's a guy at the bar who might be able to rescue our wedding photos and video off it before we dump it. I hope so. I'd like to have something so I can remember Jake looking so handsome.

He made a real effort for our wedding; he trimmed his beard, and you could hardly see his neck tattoos because of his new shirt. He doesn't understand why folks don't care for them. He says it's tough to get jobs because folks judge him. Sometimes he delivers stuff with his truck for some of his friends, but it isn't easy to keep money coming in, he says. I've been careful with the cash he gives me, and he gets odd little windfalls now and again; he says he plays pool at the bar and wins cash there. My part-time job at the local convenience store helps, and I get good discounts too.

Jake says I'm nuts about keeping the house as clean as I do, but I think it's important, and having the right kind of supplies isn't all that expensive. He says I should chill out, but Mom brought me up to believe that cleanliness is next to godliness, so I like to have a clean house because it respects her memory. She kept this house in real good shape, and now it's mine – well, mine and Jake's 'cos we're married – so I want to do as good a job as she did.

He sure was glad I had that big bottle of stain remover when he came back from one of his all-nighters with the guys. All I can say is I was pleased it wasn't his blood on his shirt. His leather jacket even had a little tear in the arm, and it looked like the edges were scorched. I cannot imagine what would have done that. Maybe he leaned on something hot?

I guess the guys he hangs out with are all okay, really; they're always polite when they call in on their motorcycles. They don't stop for long, you know, but quite often. He's got a lot of friends. One of them, Dave, sure has been good to us. He showed up one day and handed me a wad of cash – just like that. When I gave it to Jake and told him Dave said it was 'his share from the last lot, and not to spend it all at once', Jake laughed. He's got a great laugh when he's happy, has Jake. But he shouldn't have laughed at me. Or the turkey. That was not polite.

I should call the cops soon, I guess, though I don't like to disturb them on Thanksgiving. And I wouldn't want them seeing the place looking like this. If the dishwasher still worked I could push all the pots and pans in there and have them cleared away before they get here, but I guess I'll have to wash them by hand. I could do with some old rags to clear up around Jake, 'cos they'll have to go out into the garbage after I use them. I think there are some in the garage, but that's Jake's private place, and he keeps it locked. Sure, it's okay for his friends to go visit him there, but not me. Says it's his 'man cave', which would explain why the guys are always running in and out of there through the side door. I think he keeps the key on the chain in his pocket. I'll check.

But first I'll have a glass of milk and some cookies, because I'm real hungry. I didn't get to eat any of my meal before Jake began to laugh at me, and I was up early, trying to make things nice for our first Thanksgiving together. Dave's girlfriend makes coconut flavored cookies, and I always feel good and relaxed when I've eaten a couple of them. They're a kinda funny color, but they taste just fine. Kinda earthy. I guess that's the coconut. Brought over a bagful for Thanksgiving they did, which was nice of them. Yes, I'll do that, then clear up . . . then maybe I'll call Aunt Dorina to wish her a Happy Thanksgiving and ask how her hand is coming along. She'd like that. We've been close since Mom died. I won't mention what's happened to Jake. She'll be upset, even though she didn't like him. Always said he was no good. But she didn't know him like I did.

Thinking about it, Aunt Dorina kinda played a part in what happened today; I was following that turkey recipe off the Internet and it didn't work out the way they said it would. That's not my fault, right? Why couldn't Jake see it that way? Laughed and laughed, he did, but it was when he waved that big old electric carving knife in my face I got real scared, and kinda lost it. Aunt Dorina gave us the carving knife as a wedding present; if she'd given us the coffee maker we'd asked for, the knife wouldn't have been so handy. But she didn't, so it was.

I still don't know why I did it. In fact, I don't even know how I managed to stick the knife right into Jake like that. It just kinda slid in. I do know it's a sin to kill, but Mom always said, 'The Lord moves in mysterious ways, Ellie,' and it could only have been Him who gave me the strength to do it, right? I've been getting awful tired with everything that's been going on here these past weeks, and I've been working hard to keep it all together. But when Jake laughed at me with his not-nice laugh – the one he uses right before he swears at me, and shouts, and hits me – I just kinda snapped. Then there he was. Dead.

There's nothing for it but to give myself up. Maybe they'll be kind to me; it's been such a stressful time lately, and Jake hasn't been at all nice to me since we got married. I thought he'd be happier when we were a real couple; he said how great it would be to own Mom's old house with me – to have a real home he could call his own. And I've really done my best to make everything comfy and cozy for him. Until today.

I know it was wrong. I know I'll be punished – there's no getting away with this, no matter how much people might think he deserved it. I hope they aren't too horrible to me. But all I can do is tell them the truth, and put myself in God's hands.

MAPLE RIDGE TIMES
LOCAL HOME EXPLOSION NO LONGER A MYSTERY

The cause of an explosion which ripped through peaceful Alder Drive, Maple Ridge on the afternoon of Thanksgiving Sunday has been discovered.

The Chief of local Fire Hall #1 announced the home's gas range was the source. 'Evidence shows the gas was turned off after the Thanksgiving turkey had been cooked in the range's oven, but it continued to seep into the home because of a small tear in the line leading to the appliance from the main supply. We believe a flame or a spark ignited it,' said Fire Chief Polley. 'The electrical system in the house was found to be compromised, which might account for a stray spark. Cables had been re-routed to service the illegal growing of marijuana plants in the attached garage.'

Jake Trent, 26, was killed in the blast. His wife of just three months, Ellie Trent, 20, remains in stable condition at Ridge Meadows Hospital. She suffered severe burns and lacerations but is expected to make a full recovery. The couple had no children. The family cat was found by first responders, unharmed, hiding in a neighbor's garden. It's being kept at the BCSPCA animal shelter on 104th Avenue.

'Ellie will come to me when she's on the mend, but the cat? I can't have it, I'm allergic,' said Mrs Dorina Wells, aunt of the injured woman. Mrs Wells added, 'I don't think my Ellie knew anything about what they say was in the garage. She wouldn't have had anything to do with drugs. She's not that kind of girl. She was well brought-up by my widowed sister. She works hard, always kept a lovely home, and never missed church on a Sunday. I can't believe it of her.'

The deceased was known to police, and rumored to have gang affiliations. When this reporter told her about the dead man's police record Mrs Wells said, 'I never took to him. He turned my niece's head and she doted on him. She's a true innocent, and couldn't see him the way I could. He treated her very badly.'

No adjacent properties were damaged by the explosion.

In a strange twist, authorities also revealed they believed Mr Trent had just finished slicing the Thanksgiving turkey when the explosion occurred; he was found with an electric carving knife embedded in his chest. The RCMP liaison officer dealing with the case reported this was likely the result of the effects of the explosion: 'Given the poor condition of the body, it's all we can surmise.'

The authorities have not yet interviewed survivor Ellie Trent, who has been sedated since what they believe was a tragic accident. 'We're not sure what she'll remember,' said Constable Linda Meeker. 'The medics tell me she sustained a concussion when she was blown out of the kitchen door, so maybe she won't be able to remember anything about the incident. If she cannot throw any light on matters, the case is likely to be closed very quickly. Mrs Trent has lost everything in the explosion, including the family home where she was born and raised. We're happy to wait to talk to her until she's in better shape. Victim support services are standing by to offer her the guidance she'll need following such a tragic accident.'

Constable Meeker declined to comment about the activities of Jake Trent, other than to say, 'Finding the grow-op came as no surprise. That part of the investigation is ongoing, and we're undertaking interviews with the deceased's known associates.'

NOVEMBER

Miss Parker Pokes Her Nose In

Annie Parker had just pulled off her soaked mac when the first call of the day flashed on her switchboard. As she grappled with the earpiece that was her constant daily companion she thought to herself, *A woman doesn't want to be juggling earrings and earpieces in her mid-fifties, she just wants to be comfortable, and cool.* At that moment Annie wasn't either; the tube station had been a zoo, it was raining cats and dogs, and her blinkin' earpiece wouldn't fit. She was sweating already; now she'd never cool down.

'Currie, Fox and Knight,' she announced professionally, settling herself behind the grand reception desk in the marbled entrance to the venerable firm of Lloyd's of London brokers.

'Annie, it's Carol. Tonight's off, sorry.' The disembodied voice of Annie's good friend and usually bubbly wine-quaffing companion sounded flat. Annie's immediate response was to be annoyed; she hadn't taken anything out of the freezer that morning, thinking she'd be eating out. What would she have for dinner?

'What's up?' she asked. It wasn't like Carol to cancel at the last minute; Carol was reliability personified.

'It's Christine's granddad; he died last night. Of course she's not up to going out, and I said I'd go over to her place to give her a hug, and a bit of support.'

Annie was embarrassed that her thoughts had flown to her stomach so quickly. A friend had lost a relative; that was very sad.

'Sorry, doll.' Annie's voice was full of sympathy. 'Anything I can do?'

'Not really, not right now, thanks. You know Christine and I have spent a fair bit of time together since my company started working with hers, and I know you two hardly know each other, really. Well, you know, what I mean. So do you mind if I do this just on my own with her?'

Annie had to agree that sharing Christine's company for a few boozy evenings at various wine bars in the City of London ranged over a year or so hardly constituted a deep and meaningful friendship, so she let Carol off lightly.

'No worries, Car, phone me when you've got a mo' and we'll sort it for another time. Got to go now; lots of lights blinking on me board, and Mr Currie just got in. Soaked. They've all got a big meeting here in half an hour and I've got to do the teas; you know what these City broker types are like, their brains don't kick in till they've had a couple of cuppas! Give Chrissie my love, alright doll?'

'Yep, see you soon. I'll e-mail.' Carol was gone, as was any thought of a spare moment for Annie for the next eight hours. By four o'clock she was just about getting her bearings, and she managed to check her personal e-mails for the first time that day; she waded through the rubbish and opened a message from Carol.

'Hiya,' it read, 'got 2 B qwik. Christine's in bits. With her mum right now. Funeral's on Friday @ 2 in City can u come? Up rd from yr office. PLEASE? Cxxx'

Annie dashed off a reply saying she'd be there, wherever 'there' was, and got back to clearing out the dishwasher before packing things away for the night. It was a busy time in the City of London; October and November were always crammed with fancy dinners for this, and presentations for that. Annie understood that, for Messrs. Currie, Fox and Knight – her bosses – it was especially so this year; she knew CFK was making a significant push to show itself off as an attractive proposition for acquisition, all three partners having agreed they wanted to finally retire and enjoy the fruits of their many years of labor. Annie had been with them for over thirty years and was just about as loyal as an employee could be; this relationship meant it wasn't difficult for her to get time off to be able to attend the funeral, especially when she dropped into her request the fact that Christine Wilson-Smythe – her grieving friend – was the daughter of the Viscount Ballinclare, a man well-known in the City.

When she arrived at the church where the service was being held for Christine's grandfather, Annie slipped into a pew next to Carol. Christine was seated with her family in the front row, and Annie smiled and blew a kiss as she caught her eye. Fumbling with her order of service she observed to Carol, in a loud whisper, 'Not many here, eh?' She counted no more than twenty people scattered about in the gloom.

'Not a lot,' agreed Carol as they cast their eyes around the somber scene.

The coffin sat in front of the altar; it looked tiny within the cavernous space of the rather austere Wren edifice. The candles flickering beside it did nothing to brighten the surroundings, and the dampness of the rainy afternoon outside seemed to permeate the very air within the church, mixing with the stale smells of dust, old hymn books, and brass polish. Annie felt her own mortality tap her on the shoulder as she wondered about the man who had died; the setting only served to confirm her dislike of churches and she shivered . . . then jumped as a shrill voice sliced through the silence.

'I will *not* be told where to park – I'm going up the front!'

Every head in the church turned to see who had shouted so rudely, and loudly. Annie was startled to see a small army of elderly men, all uniformed in green serge, glinting with brass buttons, and sporting jauntily-angled black tricorn hats. A shriveled man in a wheelchair was at the head of the group, creating the havoc that had shocked the mourners.

'Tiny would have wanted me at the front. Our beddings were next to each other for donkey's years. Push me faster. Don't be such a ninnie!'

Annie could hear a sharp intake of breath from Christine's mother, then her sobbing resumed. Christine held her mother close and started nodding wildly at Annie and Carol, which Annie took to mean she should do something about the noisy and cantankerous old man in the wheelchair. Being a natural organizer she leapt to her feet and rushed toward the annoying little person.

'This is a funeral service, you know? Could you please be quiet?' Annie used her 'don't mess with me' voice, just to be sure he understood she was instructing, not requesting.

'What did you say? What?' squealed the little man as he cupped his hand to his ear.

Annie deepened and strengthened her voice as she bent toward the man's face. 'This is a funeral service – please keep your voice down!'

Polite coughs rippled through the congregation and people looked relieved as they saw that, thankfully, someone else was dealing with the unpleasant situation.

'Yes, miss, I know it's a funeral – it's *Tiny's* funeral – and we're all here for him. He's been at Battersea Barracks with us for a very long time, and we've all come to say goodbye. Haven't we chaps?'

As Annie looked up she saw the small band of Battersea Barrackers, as they were known to the world, had been nothing more than a vanguard; at least sixty or seventy more of their number were pushing into the church out of the rain. She spied a couple of double-decker buses at the kerb outside, and realized they must have brought the old soldiers from their barracks to the City.

Carol approached and pulled at her sleeve. 'Christine says it's alright; they all lived in the barracks with her granddad, and this chap is to come to the front. Her mother says it's okay.'

Annie stepped out of the aisle and backed into a pew to allow the little man to be shunted forward. He continued to shout instructions to the smartly uniformed colleague who pushed him, parked him, and even passed him a handkerchief when he started to cry, loudly, during the first hymn.

By the end of the service, and all the speeches, Annie had pretty much worked out who was who, and what was what.

Christine's granddad, 'Tiny' Wilson, had been a corporal in the army and had become a Battersea Barracker when his wife had died about thirty years earlier. He'd celebrated his hundredth birthday the previous January, and had now passed away unexpectedly – if you could call it that for a man who'd lived a whole century. The loud man in the wheelchair was 'Lofty' Teddington; he'd not only served in the same regiment as Tiny during the Second World War, but also in the same Company as him for most of the time. They'd been privates together, had moved up to lance corporals at the same time, and had both finished their service as corporals.

It was the annoyingly shrill Lofty who'd encouraged Corporal Edward Albert Wilson – to give 'Tiny' Wilson his proper name – to join him at Battersea after he'd been widowed. So Tiny had moved himself over from Ireland, where he and Christine's late-grandmother had lived, and had taken up residence at the Battersea Barracks. The parade of elderly men who'd stood to speak during the service – all fondly – of their late companion, had told how Tiny Wilson had enjoyed reliving old times with other servicemen, and how he'd thrived at Battersea by involving himself in the many groups that partook of activities and hobbies.

Annie further learned that Lofty and Tiny had 'beddings' – as the Barrackers' little private rooms were called – next to each other on what were called the Wide Wards, and sat next to each other for every meal in the mess hall. She found it hard to imagine how boring that might become as the decades passed, but, apparently, it had suited both men admirably. She also heard how the pair had enjoyed a comradely competitiveness on the bowling green, and at the billiard table, while they happily exchanged stories and memories of military engagements and training camps, variety acts, and girls they'd met at the seaside.

It was Lofty himself – speaking from the nave of the church, as he was unable to make it to pulpit – who explained why he, no more than five feet five in his youth and now shrunken to a smidge under five feet, and Tiny, at fully six feet tall, had been given their respective nicknames.

As a few more insights about how Tiny's daughter had made him so proud when she married a viscount were shared by the eulogizing priest, Annie could see Lofty's small frame shuddering with emotion in his wheelchair. She felt his loneliness. She shared his grief. She wept for Lofty. Carol passed her a paper tissue.

'What are you so upset about?' Carol sounded puzzled.

'Lofty; poor old bloke. He in't got long himself, and he knows it. It must get really hard to go to funerals for people when you know you might pop your own clogs any day.'

'I've been thinking more about Christine and her mum,' replied Carol, throwing Annie a slightly accusing look.

After the service Christine slipped away from her mother, who was being comforted by her husband the viscount, and the priest. She grabbed Annie and Carol and hissed, 'There are drinks at the pub on the corner now. You two are coming, right?' She looked desperate.

Carol nodded but Annie shook her head. 'Chrissie darlin', I'm sorry, but I've got to get back to the office.' Annie's Cockney accent seemed to be at its broadest when she whispered.

Christine's finely cultured tones almost boomed in the now-empty church. 'Oh come on, Annie, there'll be free drinks and sandwiches and such like, you'll enjoy it; can't you just tell them at the office that I need you?'

Annie felt annoyed; Christine came from a titled family and worked as an underwriter at Lloyds more to prove a point than because she needed a job. Annie, on the other hand, had dragged herself out of the East End of London, where her parents had migrated from St Lucia so any children they bore would stand a chance of a better life. By becoming indispensable to her employers over decades she'd secured herself a pretty good income, but she knew she couldn't risk their wrath; she had to be as reliable as they expected her to be.

Annie watched Carol nibble her thumbnail as her eyes darted between Annie and Christine. Poor Carol, thought Annie; she was so lovely, in her quaint Welsh way. Raised on a farm, Annie reckoned Carol would never completely lose her rural innocence, no matter how far up the ranks she rose as a computer systems manager for a massive reinsurance company. Always the peacekeeper, she avoided conflict at almost all costs; Annie, on the other hand, rather enjoyed a bit of conflict . . . as long as she finally got the upper hand.

'I'll just pop back and see if they can do without me for a bit longer,' said Annie eventually. Carol sighed with relief. 'I'll get back as quick as I can.'

'Thanks awfully, Annie. You're a brick,' called Christine as she dragged Carol out of the church.

Annie tried to live up to this solid reputation as she 'explained' a difficult situation to Mr Fox, who was the only partner she could find at the office when she got there. By the time she rushed out with her coat and bag, the switchboard flipped through to the youngest spotty youth in the accounts department, Mr Fox was wishing her friend a speedy recovery, convinced the Hon. Christine Wilson-Smythe was almost catatonic with grief, and Annie was the only person in the world she trusted to be by her side.

As she bounded into the Liveried Lizard pub, Annie was treated to the final stanza of a particularly bawdy version of 'Bless 'Em All', where the word 'Bless' had been replaced by an Anglo-Saxon alternative. She noted the song had Christine's mother looking apoplectic, with Christine herself running around trying to stop the Green Serge Army from starting up yet another ditty incorporating as many swear words as possible, while generally sticking to a rhyme or two along the way.

'Please make them stop, Annie,' Christine pleaded before Annie'd even had a chance to catch her breath. Annie wondered why Christine thought she'd have a better chance of success than the granddaughter of their much lamented colleague, but she promised to try.

Immediately realizing any success would only come about as a result of having Lofty on her side, Annie located his wheelchair, brought him a replacement glass of port from the bar, and knelt at his side shouting above the melee, 'Maybe you blokes could sing a few songs that don't have any swear words in them? Tiny's daughter in't too happy about the language.'

Lofty heard her well enough, Annie could tell that from the flicker of a wicked smile that danced across his face, but he put his hand to his ear and played deaf. 'What was that, miss?' he squeaked, all innocence.

'You 'eard me,' retorted Annie in a deeper, darker voice, and she gave the old soldier a warning wink as she passed him the fresh drink. 'Tell your mates to clean up the songs, pronto, or there's no more where this came from.' She nodded at the glass. Lofty very sensibly realized she wasn't joking.

'Boys! Let's keep it a bit more proper. Ladies present!' he shouted, and the clamor of smut calmed to a gentle humming of 'Tipperary' from a distant corner.

'Ta, doll,' said Annie. She patted Lofty on the arm as she pushed herself upright.

'You're a very persuasive young lady. Where are you from, then?' smiled Lofty, his dentures glistening with pink stains.

'Just up the road. East End, me. Why?'

'No, I don't mean that. Where are you *from*?'

Annie knew exactly what the elderly man meant; she was black, so where did she *really* come from. But she wasn't going to play along.

'Mile End, like I said,' she replied loudly. 'Proper Cockney me. Don't you recognize the accent?'

'So where are your parents from then?' pressed the tiny man.

'I see,' said Annie slowly. 'You mean why have I got this dark, silky skin, and such a lovely complexion? St Lucia. They came over back in the Fifties. You know, when all you lot were all so welcoming.'

'Oh, your people are some of them. I see. English now, are you?'

Annie did her best to not let her annoyance show. 'Yeah, having been born here, that would be right. Nice, that glass of port, is it?'

Lofty raised his drink to her. 'I likes a drop of port now and again, and it's only really beers we run to at the barracks.'

'Well, let's make sure we don't bite the hand that feeds us, eh, Lofty?' replied Annie, nodding toward Christine's mother as she spoke. 'She's the one what's buyin' it for you, and I'm the one what can keep bringing it to you from the bar.'

'Right-o,' chuckled Lofty as he raised his glass toward Annie once more and shouted as loud as his tired lungs could manage, 'To Tiny!'

The toast was taken up around the room, and led to the subsidence of all singing; the relative calm of a low rumbling of old stories about Tiny and his escapades took over. Annie saw Christine was patting her mother's hand as she glanced over and mouthed, 'Thank you.' Annie pushed her way to the bar where she grabbed two glasses of Cabernet Sauvignon, reasoning it would save her a trip. She weaved her way through the throng of old soldiers to a table where Carol was fielding tales of basic training nightmares being batted between two octogenarians – one sat either side of her, and both were obviously hard of hearing.

Dragging a chair to be able to sit opposite the threesome, Annie spoke across the table to Carol, 'Mr Fox thinks Christine is dissolving with grief and desperately needs me to be with her; I hope he don't stop in for a quick one on the way home.'

'Hardly likely,' replied Carol, 'he wouldn't be seen dead in here I shouldn't think.' Annie laughed as Carol's facial expression told her she'd just realized that her remark was hardly appropriate, given the reason for the gathering. Annie giggled. 'Mind you,' added Carol, 'he doesn't know what he's missing today, right?'

'You're not wrong, doll!' replied Annie grinning, raising her glass toward her old friend. 'To Tiny,' offered Annie. The toast was, once again, echoed around the pub.

The two men at Carol's table raised their glasses toward Annie. One of them – a particularly desiccated example of manhood – licked his lips after taking a sip from his glass, then motioned at Annie, beckoning her to draw near.

'You a friend of the granddaughter?' he asked, loudly. Annie nodded. 'Well, you'd better tell her to get to the barracks for Tiny's stuff PDQ; a couple of the older ones have popped off in the last month or so, and word is some of their stuff's gone missing from their beddings.'

Annie was confused. 'You mean if Christine and her mum don't get to the barracks quick, some of Tiny's things might walk off of their own accord?'

'All I'm saying,' replied the man, 'is Stumpy Webber went a while back and his son swears he always kept a pile of money in his room, but when he come to get it, there weren't none. Then Milky Evans went too, and his grandson says as how there's a silver plate he won for playing cricket gorn missing. Now there's Tiny; not that he had much, mind you, but they'd best get there quick. Haven't seen hide nor hair of them at our place yet, we haven't.'

'I think his daughter's been a bit too upset, and too busy getting things sorted out for today, to come to the barracks yet,' offered Carol.

'Shouldn't be too busy to get his stuff,' replied the other old serviceman, who looked to Annie as though he might once have been a redhead, if his freckles were anything to go by. 'But don't listen to this one about stuff going missing. It's all in his head.'

'Is not,' said the wrinkly man. 'And someone should be tryin' to find out why all the old 'uns are droppin' from their perches so soon after each other,' he added.

'What do you mean?' asked Annie, immediately curious.

'Shut up, Willy,' snapped his colleague.

'No, I bleedin' well won't,' retorted Willy, 'someone needs to say it!'

'And it would be bleedin' typical it would be you, you stupid old arse,' replied his so-called friend.

Annie stifled a chuckle.

Willy pushed himself to his feet, leaning heavily on the table with one hand, his beer sloshing about in its glass in the other; he swayed when he stood. He slammed his beer glass onto the table as he leaned forward and shouted at his fellow Battersea Barracker, 'Old arse? Who are you calling an old arse? You're older than me; I'm only eighty-two, you're nearly ninety. And anyway, everyone knows that all the *really* old ones are dropping like flies. But none of us says nothing. Stumpy. Milky. Before them? Fred. And now Tiny.' As Willy swayed and shouted, a hush fell over the pub.

Realizing he had everyone's attention Willy straightened himself up as much as he could and added, 'I wouldn't be surprised if someone was bumping them all off, I wouldn't. And I bet I'm not the only one thinking that. All for a bit of silver here, and a few quid there. Killin' 'em for mess money. That's what I say!'

Willy's friend stood. 'You've said quite enough, Willy Cooke, and the less you say when you're in this state, the better. As we all know. Come on, boys, help me get him into a taxi; I'll get 'im back safe. You can all follow along in the buses.'

A general hubbub ensued, which eventually resulted in all the old soldiers agreeing it was time they got back to the barracks. Annie watched with amusement as they generally seemed to further agree that they all needed to use the gents' before they left; the entire process took quite some time. The slow-but-sure activity allowed Annie to enjoy her second glass of wine.

When all the veterans were safely boarded on their buses, Christine decided it was the right time to usher her mother to the dark, sleek car waiting to whisk them away.

Just before they left for their pile in an exclusive, leafy square in West London, Christine dashed back into the pub and sat down next to Annie, gushing, 'Look, Annie, I know it's a lot to ask, but could you find out if it's true – about all the really old boys dying off, and all that? Mummy's horribly upset at the thought that maybe somebody did something to Granddad. I'm sure they didn't; I mean he was very old and these things *do* happen when one least expects them, but . . . well, she's right I suppose, he always seemed so *healthy.* They don't know exactly what killed him; because he was over a hundred, Mummy made a fuss about them not cutting him up, so they didn't. So I dare say something *could* have been amiss.'

Christine seemed so lost, Annie couldn't help but reassure her she'd 'sort it all out' and it would 'all be alright'. Christine left to join her mother while blowing kisses to Annie and Carol, and thanking them profusely.

Carol stared, open-mouthed at Annie. 'So,' she began, immediately they were alone, 'what are you going to do now, then, Miss Annie Parker?'

Annie knew Carol's natural Welsh accent always became more pronounced when she was cross; what Annie couldn't work out was why her friend had any reason to feel that way. She was puzzled. 'Well, as I understand it, there's at least one bottle of Cab-Sav with my name on it behind the bar, plus a couple of curried chicken sandwiches; after that I'm going to treat meself to a taxi home, and have a lie-in in the morning. Having a funeral on a Friday's very civilized. What about you, doll?'

'No, I don't mean that; I mean what about Tiny's death? What are you planning to *do*? You can't just waltz into the Battersea Barracks and start interrogating old soldiers. What on earth did you mean by telling Christine you'd sort it all out? Are you bonkers? You know she'll hold you to it; City rules – your word is your bond, and all that.'

Annie quaffed nervously as she sorted it all out in her mind; she'd meant to offer Christine soothing platitudes, but Carol was right, she'd actually promised to *do* something, to *find out* something. And she was stuck with it; you couldn't work in the City for thirty years without knowing your word really *is* your bond there, and it's a bond you don't break. There was nothing for it – she'd have to do what she'd promised, no matter how unpleasant.

Annie raised her empty glass toward Carol. 'To Tiny Wilson, and finding out all about his death, then.'

'You're going to go through with it?' Carol sounded amazed.

'Of course. It can't be that difficult,' replied Annie with the courage that follows on the heels of a couple of glasses of wine. 'I mean, they're an honorable bunch of old men who've all served King, or Queen, and country; they might like to sing the odd dirty song, but they're good men underneath it all, Car. They were all prepared to make the ultimate sacrifice, so they must be prepared to help me find out if anything untoward is happening to their comrades, don't you think?'

Carol didn't sound at all convinced as she muttered, 'Ridiculous,' at her friend's back as Annie wriggled her way toward the bar. Eventually Annie returned to the table with a fresh bottle of red, two glasses, and a plate of sandwiches.

'You know I only drink white,' sulked Carol.

'Silly me,' giggled Annie. Almost immediately a barmaid appeared and placed an ice bucket containing a bottle of Pinot Grigio onto the table in front of Carol.

'That one's for you, I suppose,' said the server to Carol as she left the women.

'Oh I couldn't – not a whole bottle!' Carol gasped. 'I've got to get home and cook David's dinner.'

'Oh come off it, little miss goody two-shoes; you've drunk a whole bottle in an evening loads of times before,' goaded Annie.

Carol grudgingly agreed, 'Well yes, but when it's a glass at a time it doesn't seem as bad as having the whole thing sitting there in front of me. And David's not expecting me to be too late.'

'Oh for heaven's sake, give me that bottle.' Annie took charge and all but filled Carol's glass. 'Phone your wonderful husband, tell him you're with me, you'll be late, and when you do get home you'll be incapable of boiling an egg. You can pick up kebabs on the way home, and lay the paracetamol on the bedside table ready for the morning. Dave won't mind.'

'Oh, I don't know about that,' replied Carol as she sipped her drink nervously. 'I know he *does* mind it when I'm out with you, and he hates being called *Dave*. And, by the way, you know I hate being called *Car*; I am not a motor vehicle. Why do you always have to shorten everyone's name?'

'Gordon Bennet!' snapped Annie. 'What's put your nose out of joint all of a sudden? Sorry, Car*ol*. You know what I'm like; it's a form of endearment. And anyway – changing the subject back to one that actually matters – how are you going to help me with this?'

Carol spluttered wine across the table. 'What do you mean, *help* you? Why should *I* help? *You're* the one making all the promises. And David wouldn't like me to be messed up in any funny business.'

Annie smiled sweetly, one of her most dangerous facial expressions. 'Do I have to remind you that *you're* the one who's really Chrissie's friend? Like you said, I hardly know her really, so you must want to help *your* friend.'

Carol's face told Annie she was regretting her comments that Annie and Christine weren't close.

Annie was on a roll, so kept going. 'You know, you're like a human bridge between the upper classes and the hoi polloi; there's crusty-yet-pretty Chrissie on one side, and amiable-but-common Annie on the other, with Carol the Constant Calmer in between. I'm not the one who's become all pally with a girl who wears one of them signet rings on her little finger, has a house near H.A. Rod's, and a father who seems to own half of Ireland. It's taken me *years* to make a real woman of you, but I think I've done a pretty good job, and that Dav*id* of yours should be gracious and give credit where it's due. He'd never have married the girl I met all those years ago, hiding in a corner of a wine bar with a fizzy water, and frightened of her own shadow. Now you're hiring men like him to work for you – if it weren't for all that confidence I helped you build, you'd never have been given the top job at your place, so you probably wouldn't have met Dave at all.'

'Now hang on a minute, Annie—' began Carol, but Annie wasn't about to be interrupted.

'No, you hang on, Car*ol*, it's my turn to talk. Remember when we first met? Someone's birthday party in Balls Brothers as I recall. Me? Out with all the posh girls who swan about CFK looking busy all day, but getting me to do all the work. You? Sitting in a corner – literally in a corner – nursing a glass of water with a bit of lemon floating about in it. Come on, Car! You were acting like you were sixty-something, not in your twenties. I took you under my wing that night, and I've brought you on ever since. You can't tell me I didn't help you overcome all those problems you faced coming to London from Wales – you know, like putting the fact you were raised on a sheep farm behind you – can you?'

Annie wondered if she'd pushed Carol a bit too far, as her friend's eyes began to get glassy. 'It all seems like such a long time ago,' said Carol, wiping away a tear.

Annie buckled. 'You alright, doll?'

Carol sipped her wine. 'Yes. But I'm not pregnant.'

'And that's a problem, right?' Annie wanted to check her facts before she reacted.

'Yes. It is,' replied her friend miserably.

Annie'd never had the slightest interest in having children, so wasn't sure how to proceed. She decided to say exactly what she felt; she usually did. 'Well, at least you can have a good old drink with me tonight then.' She added a friendly nudge, so Carol would know she was trying to cheer her up.

Carol rolled her eyes and said flatly, 'Not really the point, but you're right, I can.' She drained her glass.

Regrouping, Annie said, 'Look, doll, we go back a long way, you and me, and I know you're up to helping me out with this. Besides, you're the link between Chrissie and me – there's no way she'd have anything to do with me without you in the picture. You've *got* to help me!'

Carol said nothing, but refilled her glass. 'I agree when I first met you I was a complete wimp, and you helped me – no, hang on a minute – you *bullied me* into standing on my own two feet, and all but forced me to apply for the systems manager job at work. So, I suppose I have to accept there's no way I'd have exactly the life I do now without your influence.'

Annie felt vindicated, but could tell her friend hadn't finished.

Carol continued, 'But I don't know what I could possibly do to help, Annie; I'm no detective. Nor are you, for that matter. We're just us.'

Annie was ready with her answer, 'Well, for a start you can tell me all about Chrissie, her mum and her granddad, and what that Willy and his mate were talking about before I turned up at your table. Then we'll come up with a plan. It's exciting, in't it?!'

Annie noted Carol didn't look at all excited, but realized she rather liked the idea; the prospect of getting to stick her nose into peoples' business because someone had asked her to do exactly that seemed very appealing.

Matron Mavis MacDonald glanced up from the papers on her desk to see an odd-looking couple of women walking along the corridor toward her office: one was tall, gangly, and black, with a fuzz of cropped hair hugging her shapely head; the other was short, almost round, and pasty white, with a mass of unruly blonde curls. The experienced army-nurse pegged the black woman in her early fifties; she had a sweaty glow about her that spoke volumes. The white one looked to be in her early thirties. She wondered which one of them was the woman who was now exactly twenty-three minutes late for an appointment; she stood to welcome them with an outstretched hand, and as open a mind as she could muster.

'Hello, I'm Carol Hill, I believe we spoke earlier. This is my friend

Annie Parker. We're almost half an hour late for an appointment with the matron.'

'I'm Matron MacDonald; good to meet you. At last. I'm sorry Corporal Wilson's granddaughter didn't feel up to coming herself. This *is* rather unusual, you know. Normally we only allow the family to remove possessions from the hospital. But Corporal Wilson's daughter, the Viscountess Ballinclare, telephoned to alert me to the fact you would be acting on behalf of the family, so I suppose there's no problem there.'

'You work in beautiful surroundings,' commented Annie. Mavis was a little amused to see Carol glare at her friend.

Thinking the friend-of-the-friend was seeking to curry favor, Mavis replied, 'Aye, we're fortunate that William III wanted to outdo Charles II. With his marvelous barracks buildings already sitting across the Thames in Chelsea, they had to push Wren hard to come up with something quite different here in Battersea to best it. I like to think he took the spirit of the Greenwich Hospital and the practicality of the Chelsea Hospital, and gave it all to us here. What do you think?'

Mavis was delighted when Annie answered with what she judged to be genuine enthusiasm, 'The Battersea Barracks has always been one of my favorite buildings in London.'

'Born here, were you dear?' enquired Mavis, smiling politely. She noticed the woman's shoulders sag a little, and wondered if she might have heard the question before.

Annie's rote response suggested to Mavis she had. 'Born in the East End, within the sound of Bow Bells, so a true Cockney through and through. Moved to Plaistow with my parents, who came here from St Lucia in the Fifties. I live in Wandsworth now. How about you?'

Mavis noted Annie smiled as she answered, then she stuck out her chin with defiance as she asked her question.

Mavis decided to trot out her own story in a similar fashion, to show she couldn't be cowed. 'Born just outside Glasgow, married a soldier, he got invalided out while I was raising our two boys, all grown now. I got my qualifications in Scotland later in life than many, then became an army nurse. I've been Matron here for five years now, and I intend to stay until they retire me. It's the most fulfilling post I've ever had, though tragedies like Tiny Wilson's passing are hard to bear and yet are, unfortunately, bound to happen given the average age around here.'

'All old are they?' asked Annie conversationally. Mavis noted she wasn't letting Carol get a word in edgeways.

Mavis replied, 'I'd say the average age is about eighty. However, a few months ago we had four Barrackers over 100, all gone now I'm afraid, so the average has fallen a little.'

Annie jumped in again. 'At Tiny's funeral, one of the other blokes who lives here, Willy something, was saying that – going on about how all the "old ones" were dying off.' Annie leaned toward Mavis, who caught a whiff of Lily of the Valley scent, and added, 'Mind you, he'd had a few, and seemed to be a bit confused about things.'

Mavis had a sense the woman had baited a hook, and wondered if she should bite. Curious to discover where Annie might take the conversation, she decided to allow it to appear as though she'd done just that. 'Willy Cooke can't hold his drink, and if he was with Jimmy Taylor – which I'll wager he was, those two being as tight as ticks – then they'll have goaded each other into a near-riot, no doubt. But confused? Willy? Not usually; he's got one of the sharpest minds around here. So sharp I'm surprised he doesnae cut himself on occasion. What was he saying, exactly?'

Annie and Carol exchanged what Mavis judged to be a significant look, and she sensed Carol Hill was about to do more than introduce herself. She was right, but wasn't ready for the near-stream-of-consciousness that ensued.

'Annie's not wrong,' said Carol quietly. 'Willy got a bit hot under the collar and his friend tried to shut him up, but then they got into a bit of name-calling and I suppose you're right that they goaded each other on – so eventually Willy mentioned that stuff's been going missing from the rooms of the recently departed, and went so far as to suggest someone's bumping off all the old blokes here to get beer money – or some such. Anyway, his friend finally managed to shut him up and no one seemed to pay him much attention really, but it did give us cause for concern, and then Christine's mother got very upset at the idea her father's death might not have been quite as natural as we all thought it had been. Does Willy go off on one like that very often? I mean does he run around shouting "murder" here? Or is that just when he's out and about in the pub – 'cos it was a bit unsettling.'

By the time Carol finally drew breath her sing-song Welsh accent had thickened considerably, and Mavis was wondering if she was anything more than an empty-headed chatterbox. Mavis noticed that Annie looked horror-stricken, and wondered if Carol's behavior was normal for the woman. Her friend's expression seemed to suggest not. She wondered what was going on.

Mavis assessed how to respond. 'Let me assure you, Mrs Hill, Ms Parker, that Corporal William Cooke has never mentioned the word "murder" under any circumstances of which I am aware. As I have already mentioned, he is possessed of a very particular mental acuity. I cannae imagine what would have given him the idea that people are being murdered. True, we have lost more Barrackers than usual over the past few weeks, but September and October can be difficult months for the elderly and frail. All our deaths have involved men over one hundred years of age; an age when we must expect the body to be more prone to little infections and illnesses.'

'So we're safe 'ere then, eh? They all died of natural causes? And it's Miss Parker, or Annie, by the way, ta very much.' Annie almost snapped at Mavis.

'Of course you're safe, Miss Parker. You can take my word for it; all the cases were quite unconnected with each other, and all above board. Sadly, such things are to be expected within such an elderly group, as I have said.'

'Well,' continued Annie, 'at least it's not that 'orrible flesh-eating thingy they get in 'ospitals these days.'

Mavis wasn't going to stand for that. 'Miss Parker, I cannot be held responsible for the sanitary conditions at other establishments, but I can assure you my staff maintains the highest level of cleanliness at our infirmary. Besides, all the conditions that led to the Barrackers' deaths were contracted outside the infirmary, not inside.'

Mavis wondered just how stupid Carol might be when she said, 'But the whole place is a hospital, isn't it?'

Mavis sighed inwardly, and wondered about the quality of schools in Wales. 'My dear Mrs Hill, the Battersea Barracks Hospital is not a "hospital" in the sense of the word as it is used today. Back in the 1600s when it was built, and in the early 1700s when it was opened, the word "hospital" was used in a much broader sense; it simply referred to a place where men who had served their country lived in a caring and common community. Our infirmary is our "hospital" if you like, the hospital being the whole barracks.'

Mavis was somewhat taken aback when Carol Hill checked her watch, nudged her friend and snapped, 'I know we were late, and I'm sorry about that. Annie couldn't get away from her office as early as we'd hoped, so now we're in a bit of a rush. I really need to get home as soon as I can. I wonder, matron, could you take us to Corporal Wilson's room to collect his belongings now? Or to his bedding, rather? That's what you call them, I believe.'

Unable to shake the feeling that some sort of funny business was going on between the two women standing in front of her, Mavis decided it was probably best to let them get on with the task for which they'd visited, and get them out of her way – so she could get back to work. She rearranged her shoulders, straightened her back and replied professionally, 'I agree. Let's walk together.' She set out along the corridor.

As Carol and Annie scampered behind her, Mavis continued, 'Indeed we do call them beddings, Mrs Hill. The name goes back to a time when almost all that was offered to those who lived here was a bed. Nowadays, of course, each Barracker has their own little room with fitted everything, and as much privacy as they want. A far cry from the times when fifty men shared a privy at the end of the corridor – that being the easiest place from which to empty the earth closets.'

Carol wrinkled her nose, and Mavis allowed herself to laugh at her expression.

'Och, my dear, don't panic; the Barrackers have very nice bathrooms these days. Why they even have lifts and ramps to give access to all areas for those in wheelchairs – the television lounges, Internet rooms, and even the allotments, you know.'

'So do they all live on one floor here?' asked Carol.

Mavis checked the watch pinned to the top of her crisply starched nursing apron and said, 'On three. All the same as each other. You'll see when we get there,' and she marched on. Deciding she should do her usual bit to educate visitors about her place of work, Mavis took great pride in pointing out the fabulous Grinling Gibbons limewood carvings at the end of the corridors above doorways that had once led to the infamous earth closets. She further explained that, while William III had been responsible for approving the Wren design and paying for the majority of the building work, it had been planned that the barracks would be finally opened during what turned out to be the end of Queen Anne's rule, in 1714; delays had meant it had not been occupied by the old soldiers it was designed to house until 1717, but the magnificent statue of the female monarch standing guard over the Barracks Square had not been replaced by one of the then-monarch, George I. It took the women no more than ten minutes to reach the third-floor beddings of Tiny Wilson, but during that time Mavis felt she'd given Carol and Annie a comprehensive history lesson about the building, the changes made to it during its three centuries of occupation, and the plans that lay ahead of it.

Mavis finished her mini-tour by explaining the entire building was soon to be fitted with WiFi to accommodate the 'Silver Surfers' who lived there. She also told the women how Tiny and Lofty had been almost joined at the hip since Tiny's arrival, and that Lofty was taking the death of his old friend very hard indeed – to such an extent he'd been moved to an area of the infirmary reserved for those who needed some extra attention.

Mavis was surprised when Annie asked, 'Could we see Lofty before we leave, matron? He's such a character, in't 'e? And I feel we bonded at the funeral last week. It would be nice to look in on 'im; maybe there's some little memento of Tiny he'd like to keep? We wouldn't make him too tired, or nothing.'

Mavis suspected Annie would make anyone tired, but nonetheless agreed she'd send someone to accompany them to Lofty in about half an hour – which was the amount of time she felt they'd need to collect together Tiny's belongings. A large green plastic wheelie bin was already positioned outside the oak-built cubicle that had been Corporal Wilson's home, but Mavis felt she had to make a few things clear before she left the women to their task.

'As the person ultimately responsible for not just the health but also the well-being of the Barrackers,' she began, 'I am the only one who can allow you access to Tiny's bedding. So, if the sergeant-at-arms comes along and makes a fuss, you tell him I said you could be here. He hasn't got any real authority; it's an ancient title and he likes to sometimes take a stand because a woman is in charge of domestic arrangements. So feel free to tell him to phone me, or you phone me yourselves if you have any questions; there's a phone inside each bedding, you can use that. My extension number is 1000; just push the red button, then the numbers.' Mavis looked at Carol and added, 'It's quite simple.'

Mavis hoped the dim-looking Carol understood, then continued, 'Just remember all the fittings are fixed for a reason; they're ours. As is the television set, the sheets, bedding, and all the towels. I'll get a sweep – which is what we call our cleaners – to come and sort all that out later, when you've left. Everything else is Tiny's and you can take it, or leave it behind, and we'll donate it to a local thrift shop, after it's been made available to the Barrackers who might need or want it.'

'Are they all so poor they'll take hand-me-downs then?' asked Annie in what Mavis judged to be an inappropriately cheeky tone.

Before Mavis could answer, Carol added, 'Do they have any opportunities to make money around here? That would be a good idea.'

Mavis was beginning to get annoyed. 'All retired soldiers receive a pension that's transferred directly to us, here. We only have non-commissioned ranks at Battersea, so none of them tend to come from monied families. Tiny's daughter has a title, but married it; there aren't many like her. As for their circumstances, aye, well they'll all be in a slightly different boat; some of my charges have chosen to sell everything they own, give the proceeds to their next of kin, and live out their years here, surviving on their pensions. They have everything they need here, and companionship too. Of course, they can sell the fruit and veg they grow at the allotments, and some of them enjoy making things as a hobby which they can then sell at our open days and seasonal fairs. Some of the warrant officers make a pretty penny advising television companies about historical details and so forth, and I know one particular Barracker has become quite famous as a figure about London – someone the news people like to interview a great deal; I believe he's quite in demand. I suppose some of our wards might have a tidy sum tucked away in the quartermaster's strongroom; the quartermaster here is the keeper of our own internal banking system. You might be surprised to know we even have our own cheque books; of course, they're only of any use here. By the way, I've already made enquiries, and Corporal Tiny Wilson had seventy-six pounds lodged with the QM; you can collect it and sign for it before you leave.' Mavis hoped her emphasis on her final word meant Annie and Carol were in no doubt she hoped that would be sooner, rather than later.

With that, she left the women alone, and bustled efficiently along the corridor, the starch in her apron almost crackling as she headed back toward her office to get on with some work.

Carol looked at Annie, then they both peered apprehensively into the space they'd come to search for 'clues' – though neither of them had the faintest idea of what that really meant.

Measuring about nine feet in every direction, Tiny Wilson had lived in an oaken cube; oak paneling on the walls, oak boards on the floor, and even an oak ceiling made the place feel like a coffin – or so thought Carol, and she said as much to Annie.

'It is a bit claustrophobic,' agreed Annie.

Neither woman seemed too keen to enter the little room. Carol was relieved when Annie eventually took the plunge. 'Come on, doll, we've only got half an hour before we get shunted off to see Lofty, so we'd better step lively,' she announced.

Carol followed; the tiny space felt immediately full. 'It's not exactly the Ritz,' she observed.

'Wouldn't know,' answered Annie.

Carol's eyes swept the room, and she decided it was best to start by pulling open the doors set into one wall; they revealed wardrobes, drawers, and even a little built-in desk. She'd received specific instructions from Christine's mother, who didn't want any of her father's clothes, just his uniforms, medals, and cap badges. The only other items Christine's mother had said she wanted were any papers, photo albums and suchlike, as well as any paintings or pictures that might be about the place. Carol had been told to make her own decisions about any remaining items.

Carol made an instant mental inventory of the room while Annie stared at the bed, transfixed. Carol gathered up some papers, and a bundle of old letters tied with red ribbon, from the desk drawers; a few family snaps in cheap frames sat at the head of the bed, and she found a battered old album in a desk drawer; one watercolor showcasing the Albert Memorial hung on the wall. Personal toiletries, five shirts, various undergarments, one pair of highly polished boots and two uniforms – one in green dress serge, and one Carol assumed was an everyday uniform – were tucked away in the little wardrobe. A few towels and a raggedy tartan dressing gown hung on a hook behind the door, but otherwise the room was bare.

As she stuffed items into several collapsible storage cubes she'd brought in her large tote, Carol wondered if any of the items might provide a clue that would lead them to the truth about what was happening to all the 'old' Barrackers.

Meanwhile, Annie was still staring at the bed. 'D'you reckon he died there?' asked Annie hesitantly, pointing toward the mounded duvet.

'I expect they took him to the infirmary, Annie. Don't keep staring at it; it's just a bed.'

'But it *smells*,' hissed Annie under her breath.

Carol agreed with her. 'The whole place stinks of disinfectant and old men – but what can you expect? It actually *is* full of old men, so maybe the disinfectant is a blessing.'

Both women jumped as a loud knock rattled the partially open door.

'Anyone in there?' called a gruff voice.

Annie pulled the door fully open, crushing Carol against the bed as she did so. Carol squealed and pushed back, so the door slammed into the face of the tall, stringy, bald man who was trying to peer inside.

'Car!' admonished Annie as she pushed her friend to one side, pulled the door open again, and apologized profusely to the man who'd been inadvertently thumped by the door.

'Young lady—' was all he could manage as he staggered backwards into the hallway.

'Oh, heck, I'm sorry,' called Annie as she pushed through the narrow door and tried to catch the teetering man. She failed. He fell. Luckily his cane broke his fall a little, but Carol was in no doubt he was of an age when falling could be very dangerous; visions of emergency hip replacement surgery floated through her mind's eye as she, too, rushed forward to try to help the man to his feet, but it was too late – he'd already pushed the alarm button on a device around his neck and a high-pitched squeal was being emitted by the flashing orb. Along the hallway a light began to pulse high above a bedding doorway, and a bell began to peal.

As frosted heads appeared around doors, the sight that met their eyes brought expressions of astonishment and glee in equal measure; flailing on the floor, thrashing his cane in the air, was their sergeant-at-arms sporting bedroom slippers, a long-sleeved undershirt, and trousers held up with bright red braces; on her knees and trying to get hold of him was a black woman in a long raincoat who was using her very large handbag to fend off the blows of the cane; trying to pull her away was a short, stout woman who had thrown her own handbag to the floor in an attempt to get a better grip, causing its contents to skid across the shining oak boards.

The short, round woman was squealing at the tall, thin one; the tall, thin woman was barking back at the short, round one; the sergeant-at-arms was growling at them both. Above all this noise the alarms were ringing, and, pretty soon, the cheers of many of the residents were encouraging the man and both women to 'give it what for'.

This was the sight that met Mavis MacDonald's eyes as she came running, with two nurses in tow, into the corridor, and Carol could tell by the look on the matron's face, she wasn't having any of it.

'What on earth is going on here?' Matron shouted above the melee. She fired instructions at the two nurses, 'You, shut off that alarm, and you, pull those women off the sergeant-at-arms.' Carol watched as the matron scurried along the row of little rooms shouting, 'Barrackers – there is nothing for you to see here.' Carol suspected the matron's words were falling on literally deaf ears in some cases.

Once they were disentangled from the sergeant-at-arms, both Carol and Annie stood quietly as Matron established that her elderly charge had suffered no immediate ill effects from the encounter; she sent him along to the infirmary with the two nurses so he could be thoroughly checked for bruising. She then unceremoniously pushed Annie and Carol along the corridor toward her office. Carol noted the knowledgeable tour guide had disappeared; Matron MacDonald was a guard dog, on duty.

By the time they reached Matron's office Annie and Carol had assumed the demeanor of two schoolgirls brought to see the headmistress in disgrace; Carol could tell Matron MacDonald was angry, and she was filled with dread; she heard Annie trying to stifle a giggle and thought she might have to kick her friend to shut her up.

Matron began, 'I will *not* have my barracks turned into a rowdy-house – do you understand?'

Carol felt her tummy tighten. She and Annie muttered, 'Yes, Matron,' as they bowed their heads in shame.

'This is unforgivable; I allowed you to go to Corporal Wilson's bedding for the express purpose of collecting his personal belongings on behalf of his family – much against my better judgment, I might add.'

Carol didn't think Matron needed to add that at all; she'd made her feelings quite clear from the outset.

'And you have the audacity,' she continued, in her increasingly-strong Scottish accent, 'to cause uproar from the minute I leave you alone; you even attacked the sergeant-at-arms. Poor wee man. He's almost ninety, you know.'

'Now hang on a minute—' began Annie. Carol thumped her on the arm.

'No, I will not hang on, Miss Parker,' snapped Matron. 'You are a troublemaker; I could see that in you from the moment you arrived. I had hoped Mrs Hill here would be able to keep you under control, but she is clearly not equal to the task, are you, Mrs Hill?'

This didn't require a reply from Carol, but she shook her head resignedly in any case.

'But we didn't attack that man—' began Annie again.

Matron bristled. 'I don't care to hear the specifics, Miss Parker; all I am concerned with is the outcome. Corporal Wilson's daughter, the viscountess, or even his granddaughter, will be welcomed if they wish to visit his bedding, but you two ladies will leave now, and you are not to return to my barracks, ever again. Do you understand?'

Carol nodded meekly, and she felt tears prick her eyes. She and Annie managed to exchange a fleeting glance, and she knew she should have spoken up, but was feeling so unwell – following her unexpected physical run-in with a nonagenarian – that she didn't. But she suspected Annie wouldn't take her telling off easily. She was right.

Annie leaned across Matron's wide desk and planted her hands there. 'Now you listen to me, Matron Mavis flaming MacDonald – I've been told off by better than you, and barred from better places than this in my life –' Carol believed this to be true – 'and I won't stand for being ripped a new one for something I didn't do. Carol neither. That old geezer waltzed in and we didn't mean to push him over; it was an accident. I tried to stop him falling, and Carol tried to help too, then *he* had a go at *us*. We're the ones who need examining for lumps and bruises, not him; he walloped us something rotten with that stick he had. Assault with a deadly weapon, I call it.'

Matron drew a breath as if to reply, but Carol could tell Annie wasn't going to give her the chance. She continued in a quieter, more menacing tone. 'What you don't know, Matron, is we're not even really here to get Tiny's stuff, are we, Car?'

Carol's heart sank. 'Annie, I don't think Christine would want us saying—' She didn't get any further.

Annie pressed on. 'No, we're here because his blessed daughter wanted Carol and me to have a bit of a snoop about for her. Now I'll admit we don't know exactly what we're looking for, but I'll tell you this much – you've got an old soldier running around the City shouting "murder" and you're not taking any notice. Well, Chrissie and her mum took notice – and we're going to do all we can to find out if old Tiny was killed. On purpose. And we don't care who knows it, do we, Car?'

Carol wanted to sit down, and glanced about for a chair.

There was a moment of total silence as Annie's words hung in the air, then it seemed to Carol that the matron softened in some way; she brought a chair to Carol – appearing to have telepathically deduced she needed one – and nodded to another indicating Annie should use it herself. Finally she took her own seat behind her desk.

Carol thought Matron looked suddenly tired; she noticed she placed her small hands on the desk in front of her and spread her fingers, lifting one after the other, as if to make sure they were all still there.

Carol also noticed the matron didn't look at them when she spoke. 'I have been thinking about the comments you made along those lines when we met,' said the suddenly less-acerbic Scot. Carol watched as she tapped lightly upon the desk with her right forefinger, then seemed to make a momentous decision. Carol almost held her breath.

The matron sighed so hard, she almost shuddered. 'What I can tell you, ladies, is that Lance Corporal Frederick Walsh passed away in August; he had been our oldest resident, by a matter of months. At the ripe age of 103 he was still incredibly healthy; he was one of those small, wiry men who seem to have boundless energy, and Fred, in particular, had a real zest for life. I liked him, which meant it was especially difficult for me – even after all my years of experience – to find him writhing in agony in his beddings one day. He told me he'd been ill since the night before; I asked why he hadn't used his personal alarm to call for help, and – characteristically – he said he hadn't wanted to be any trouble. Ach, men. Soldiers. Anyway, we got him to the infirmary, ran some tests while making him as comfortable as possible, and discovered he was suffering from an acute case of botulism poisoning. It's not something one sees often, and not something one ever wants to see; it's a very rare, and extremely deadly poison. In 1922 eight fishermen from Loch Maree, in the Highlands, died of botulism poisoning contracted from duck paste sandwiches. One of those men was my very own grandfather's brother, so believe me when I tell you I come from a family that has always been obsessed by cleanliness, and has always been fastidious when it comes to the hygienic preparation and storage of food. I have brought those habits with me to Battersea Barracks. After some careful investigation and sampling, I was convinced Fred had not contracted the botulism from anything with which he might normally be expected to come into contact at the barracks. And Fred never went off barracks; he liked it here because he was usually the center of attention, even more so this year because he was due to lead our Barrackers in the Remembrance Day parade at the cenotaph, and lay the wreath there too. With this year being our tri-centenary, the Battersea Barrackers get to march ahead of the Chelsea Pensioners – not something that usually happens.'

Carol shifted in her seat, and noticed Annie do the same; she wondered if her friend was sharing her increasing sense of doom. Carol wasn't certain she knew exactly where Matron was going with all this insight and history, but she knew she was talking about someone named Fred – one of the names mentioned by the ranting Willy at Tiny's wake.

'I'm afraid we couldn't save Fred,' continued Matron. 'We were all saddened by his death, and alarmed by the appearance of the poison in his system. Of course, the doctor in charge reported his cause of death, and a major investigation and cleansing process was undertaken throughout the barracks. We managed to keep the news of what we'd found under our hats. Then, when Private Webber died – known by all as Stumpy, due to the loss of three of his fingers thanks to an incident involving a hand grenade – early in October, I was again puzzled. This time I wasn't puzzled by his cause of death – a small cut he hadn't reported had become infected, then septicemia set in and he was gone in a day. No, I was puzzled by why the cut had become so virulently septic in such a short time. I'll be honest and tell you I put it down to his advanced age; once again we were all sad about his demise, but we moved on.'

Carol noted with interest that the matron looked up at the women for the first time as she said, 'I honestly saw no connection between Stumpy's death and any others at the barracks. And, no, we did no' test his wound for botulism.'

Matron paused, and Carol felt she was composing herself again.

'Then Corporal "Milky" Evans passed away. Once again a small wound was involved, but – because he at least brought it to our attention – we caught the infection in time, and were pleased, though not surprised, when he recovered. Sadly, Milky then suffered a violent bout of food poisoning and that, given his weakened state, sent him over the top. His body simply couldn't take it, and he passed away peacefully. Another sad loss, again of a man over the age of 100, so not really a surprise, but this death gave me pause, so

I carried out some tests of my own, and – lo and behold – Milky Evans had botulism poisoning too. I shared my insights, and panic spread throughout the higher-ups; we didn't tell the Barrackers, but we began an extensive schedule of swabbing, testing, and cleaning the entire complex – not easy, and not cheap. It's been a major undertaking I can tell you – all of us working long hours, and none of us feeling comfortable about not telling the men what's going on. After all, they live here and have a right to know if their lives are in danger.'

'So, do you think you've got a serial poisoner in your midst, Matron?' Annie's voice sounded cold. Carol didn't like it.

'Yes, Miss Parker. I do. The more research we carried out, the clearer it became to us that the deaths weren't caused by an accidental encounter with *clostridium botulinum*, the cause of botulism. I have, painfully, come to believe there is someone systematically killing off our oldest residents. And that's one other thing that's particularly odd, and truly awful; the men who've died, have died in age order, the oldest first. I cannae be sure yet whether Corporal Tiny Wilson's death is connected to this pattern; he most definitely suffered heart failure, and we have detected no botulism in his body, from the minimal testing his daughter allowed us to carry out. But, what I do know is, he was the latest in the line of men due to head up the Cenotaph Parade, because he had become our oldest resident. The parade takes place on November 12th this year, just over a week away, and we're all on pins about whether the next man in line will make it.'

'Who is the next oldest?' asked Carol; she hardly dared ask, but knew she had to.

'Corporal Lofty Teddington,' replied Matron, gravely.

'Do you think someone's going to try to kill him too?' was Carol's next question. She clapped her hand in front of her mouth as soon as she uttered the words. Before Matron could answer a knock was heard at her door.

'Enter,' called Matron clearly. A tall, thin nurse poked her head around the door.

'It's Corporal Teddington, Matron. He's taken a definite turn for the worse, as we feared.' Annie, Carol, and Matron exchanged horrified glances.

'I'm on my way,' replied Matron, then added, 'you two, come with me; not a word, mind you.'

With that, the diminutive woman shot out of her chair and began to march rapidly toward the infirmary; Annie and Carol cantered to keep up. By the time the trio reached the all-white cubicles, Carol was out of breath, and she could see Annie was sweating profusely.

Lofty Teddington looked much older and more withered than he had at Tiny's funeral; Carol was shocked by the change she saw in him. He looked uncomfortable propped within a nest of crisp white sheets, monitors attached to various parts of his crepe-like skin. Tears were rolling down his hollow cheeks. Carol thought a light had gone from him.

'Doc's on the way,' the thin nurse informed her superior as Matron took an electronic tablet from the nurse's hands and cast her trained eye over the charts and figures displayed there.

Lofty's voice crackled. 'Come here, dear.' He looked straight at Annie. 'You're the one. I have to talk to you. Now. You lot? You can all bugger off.'

Matron nodded as she drew back, and Annie moved toward the sick old man; Carol was rather glad he'd picked on Annie, not her, and wondered what he had to say to her friend that was so urgent.

Annie Parker had sat beside her uncle's bed when he was dying; she knew what death smelled like, and recognized it now; Lofty reeked of it. She almost gagged.

'I'm dying,' stated Lofty in a hoarse whisper.

'Yes, I know,' replied Annie, calmly. Lofty was the only one who seemed to not be surprised by her answer. The moment she'd seen the expression on his face she'd known; and in that instant she'd also known more than that he was dying.

'Only needed a week more, didn't you?' she said.

'I'd have been Top Dog,' he whispered. A wry smile wrinkled his face.

'It wasn't worth killing them all, was it?' replied Annie gravely. Carol looked puzzled; Matron hovered, and a look of horror crossed her face.

'I don't know about that; I got a couple of extra beers in the mess after Tiny went. But I didn't have nothing to do with him; he just went natural. Which was good; I liked him. The others were just old farts.'

Matron made as if to move forward, but Annie's eyes warned her not to interrupt.

'It was all just so you could head up the Remembrance Day parade at the cenotaph, and carry the wreath, weren't it?' asked

Annie flatly.

'No "just" about it,' replied Lofty, with as much emotion as his weak frame could muster. 'I'd have been cock of the hoop for a time; on the telly and everything. My whole life I've been a nothing; I gave everything to this country, and got bugger all for it. The pension is pitiful. They should do something about that. At least if I'd been carrying that wreath at the cenotaph my family could have been proud of me. I'd have left them that, at least; the memory of me on the telly, something for them to boast about. Haven't got nothing else to leave them. But now this stupid heart of mine has given out. Why couldn't it have kept me going for just another week? I know what's happening; they said this morning my kidneys were all messed up. Always the beginning of the end that. That's right, isn't it, Matron Mavis?'

For the first time Lofty directly acknowledged Matron's presence; she nodded her agreement with Lofty's prognosis. 'Aye. No point lying about it, Lofty, not now. I cannae say things look promising for you. I suggest we get you the chaplain, and let you make your peace with your Maker.'

'No need, Matron,' Lofty gasped. 'It's too late for all that guff. I'll make my confession here and now to you lot – and you can pass it on to him if you like. I've killed a lot of men in my time – most of them because it was my job to kill them, so I suppose I might get away with that lot. But the ones here? No chance. I expect I'll burn for them. All done for pride, see. They say it's a deadly sin. I reckon I'll know for sure, pretty soon.'

Annie looked into Lofty's eyes. She had to know. 'How did you do it exactly, Lofty?'

Again there was a smile playing around the man's cracked lips. 'Honey, fish paste, rotten root vegetables, and garlic oil. Easy enough, really. Smelly though, and you've got to be patient. There was a story about it on an anti-terrorism website I came across by accident one day on the Internet. Maybe if I hadn't read about it I wouldn't have come up with the idea. I don't know. It didn't seem too difficult, so I gave it a go. It's one of the most poisonous substances known to man, you know? But women get injections of it in their faces in spite of that. Can you believe it? The things women do. Never understood them, I haven't, and there's me with two daughters. Anyway, I took my time, and gave it a go on old Fred. They say babies can't cope with honey because their insides haven't developed; I dare say it's the same with us old 'uns, except our insides have given up the ghost. Anyway, off went Fred, nice and peaceful, like. Then all I had to do was scratch Stumpy when we was over at the allotments and put a bit of the stuff on his cut. Off he went too. Milky was more difficult. He needed two goes, but I never touched Tiny, honest. That was Him Upstairs that was; saved me a job I didn't much fancy, because Tiny would have had to have gone eventually. Planning to put it off till the last minute, I was. As I said, I liked him.'

Lofty coughed; his entire, withered body shook, and he took a sip of water offered to him by the thin nurse, who clearly didn't know what on earth the man was talking about.

'Where is it, Lofty? You know it's dangerous.' Annie spoke quietly.

'Shed, at the allotment,' Lofty gasped. He coughed more, this time so violently that Matron had to act; she and the nurse pulled Lofty to a fully seated position, rubbing his back to try to calm the convulsions he was suffering.

'Where's the doctor?' called Matron toward the open end of the ward. 'What's keeping him?'

Almost magically a doctor appeared, and Annie and Carol were ushered away from the deathbed of Corporal Lofty Teddington, Carol shaking her head in disbelief and Annie feeling something in her heart she wasn't used to – a mixture of anger, coldness, and utter indignation.

Matron called, 'Back to my office, you two, and not a word to anyone; I'll be there as soon as I can.' She nodded her head toward Lofty's cubicle. 'He's no' got long,' and she turned on her heel, her apron crackling.

Three months had passed since the death of Tiny Wilson, closely followed by that of Lofty Teddington. Annie and Carol had managed to convince Christine's mother that Tiny's death had, truly, been from natural causes, but they'd given Christine herself the full story, swearing her to secrecy – as Matron MacDonald had done to them. No matter how diligently they surveyed the news media, none of them ever saw or heard a single word about Lofty's killing spree.

This was a special night; Annie and Carol had arranged to meet with Matron Mavis MacDonald and Christine Wilson-Smythe at the Liveried Lizard pub. Christine had chosen the venue; Carol had thought it a poor choice.

Sitting quietly with a glass of wine each, neither Annie nor Carol remarked on the matron's entrance to the pub.

'Hello girls,' said the small woman, hooking her bobbed grey hair behind her ears. She beamed as she approached their little table.

'Oh Matron, I didn't recognize you,' replied Carol lightly, and she sprang to her feet. Annie would have said Carol sprang to attention.

'Please, call me Mavis; they've retired me and I'm no' "Matron" any longer.'

'Hello Mave,' said Annie with a warm smile as she raised her glass toward the woman, who looked smaller than Annie remembered, and rather drawn.

'No dear, it's Mavis, not Mave, thank you,' admonished Mavis, with a tone that sent Carol back to her schooldays in an instant.

'Mavis,' Annie hissed into her glass, rolling her eyes toward Carol.

'I keep telling you people don't like it when you shorten their names,' said Carol, emboldened by Mavis's presence.

'Carol, darling,' gushed Christine when she entered a few moments later, 'it's been ages. I haven't seen you since you brought all of Granddad's stuff to the house.' She hugged Carol. 'And Annie . . .' Christine bent over to try to hug Annie, but Annie pulled away, leaving Christine to hug an empty space. 'And you must be the wonderful matron who looked after Granddad so well.' This time Christine wisely held out a hand in greeting, which Mavis shook vigorously.

'What does everyone want?' asked Christine, then set about ordering drinks at the bar.

When all four women were finally settled, each with a fully-charged glass in their hands, Christine rose and made a toast. 'Ladies – I give you Tiny Wilson – Granddad.' The little group accepted the toast and drank.

Christine broke the slightly awkward silence that ensued. 'I can't believe it's been over three months since Granddad died; Mummy's still very upset, of course, but she and Daddy phoned from Barbados today, and Daddy said she's rallying a bit.'

'I reckon I'd rally too if I was lying about on a beach in Barbados,' replied Annie sulkily.

'Now, Annie,' admonished Mavis, 'there's no need to be like that, is there?'

Carol looked from one woman to the other, and could see that – for at least this evening – Mavis would rule the roost, and Annie would probably toe the line a little.

'I have an announcement to make; it's worth a toast too, I think,' dared Carol. All three women gave her their attention.

'Well, you can't be pregnant, Car, or you wouldn't be drinking,' quipped Annie; she shut up when Mavis arched an eyebrow in her direction.

'You're right, Annie, I'm not pregnant,' said Carol glumly, 'and that's the problem; my specialist says I'm not likely to ever conceive if I keep living such a stressful life. So I've handed in my notice. David makes enough for us to live on, if we cut a few expenses, and I'm going to give my body a chance to do what I want it to: make a baby.'

Annie was dumbstruck; she couldn't imagine anyone actually wanting a baby so much that they'd give up their career.

Mavis patted Carol's hand. 'Good for you, Carol; I'm sure the doctor's right, and I am equally sure you'll fall pregnant when the time is right for you and David. Just give yourself a wee break and it'll all come naturally.'

'And have as much sex as possible,' added Annie, grinning and raising her glass toward her friend. 'You tell that husband of yours from me that you two have got to go at it like rabbits.'

Once again Mavis's warning glance quietened Annie, but only for a second or two. 'Okay then,' continued Annie, 'since it's a night for announcements, I have one of my own.'

Carol looked surprised. 'What haven't you told me?'

Annie winked. 'Haven't had a chance to tell you, doll. Sorry. Only just found out meself. And I certainly don't mean to steal your thunder Car –' a stern look from Mavis followed – 'sorry, Car*ol* –' she rolled her eyes – 'but I suppose you'll all know soon enough so I'll tell you now. My bosses have sold the company to some Swiss gazillionaires who are going to assume all our business and leave yours truly high and dry without a job. Cheers!' Annie raised her glass and half-drained it.

'Oh, I'm so sorry, Annie,' said Christine and Carol simultaneously. Annie knew they were both being truly sympathetic, but she also realized only Carol really understood what this meant for her; she was almost fifty-two and without a job – not a good position to be in, whichever way you looked at it. What not even Carol knew was that Annie had never really come to terms with the concept of 'saving'.

'Any sort of package?' asked Mavis directly.

'Thanks to the luvverly laws of the land, I get about twelve grand in redundancy money, and the Swiss lot have offered a golden handshake of ten grand more,' replied Annie glumly. 'I know it sounds like a lot, but it's not really.'

Mavis nodded. 'I have a fair pension, but I'm not going to enjoy living on it.'

'And I'm not going to like living off David,' added Carol even more unhappily.

Christine looked around the table at the three sad faces and tried her best to cheer them. 'Oh come on, it's not *that* bad, really, now is it?'

All three women were thinking roughly the same thing: *Yes, it is, and you have no idea, oh you twenty-something, pretty, rich, independent daughter of a viscount.* But none of them said anything.

Christine continued in her cheering attempts. 'Maybe you could all band together to do . . . something . . .' Her uncertainly showed in her voice.

'Great idea, Chrissie,' replied Annie tartly. 'And what could we three do? I'm a receptionist, Carol's a Brainiac computer systems manager and Mavis is a nurse – okay, a matron – what could *we* do?'

Mavis sounded surprised as she said, 'That's what you did, Carol? Computers?'

Carol nodded.

'Frighteningly clever with them, is this one, but lives in her own little world,' said Annie, slapping Carol on the arm.

'That would explain a lot,' said Mavis.

Christine looked nonplussed, her normal ebullience leaving her for a moment. Her brow furrowed, then her expression cleared. 'You could poke your noses into things – you're all good at that.' She looked gleeful as she added, 'Carol's always calling you Miss Nosey Parker,' she said to Annie, 'and Annie says you can find out anything by using computers,' she said to Carol. She concluded by raising her glass toward Mavis and adding, 'I don't know what went on when these two met up with you at the Battersea Barracks, but they both said how you frightened them and made them do as they were told, and that they would have confessed anything to you just to keep you off their backs, so there's that.'

Annie, Mavis, and Carol all looked aghast; Christine looked triumphant as she concluded, 'Daddy's always saying he's looking for a good investment – I bet I could talk him into investing in you. Hang on a minute; he'd certainly invest in *us*.' She adopted her most innocent look as she sipped her wine.

Annie managed to divert her anger into a hissed, 'What do you mean "us"?'

'Well, being an underwriter at Lloyds of London is a bit boring, you know; all those *men* all hovering around me all the time, and I just won the award for best underwriter of the year, so I suppose I've finally proved to Daddy that I could do what he always wanted me to do – become a success in the City. If we all worked as a team, I could help; Daddy's got a little office building in South Kensington we could use. I'm sure he'd let us have it for free, and we could be private investigators. It would be *such fun;* you lot managed to find out all about that mass murderer, after all, didn't you?'

All three women glanced about and 'shushed' Christine at once. She continued in a loud whisper, 'Well, you *did.* I think we'd all be really good at finding things out about all sorts of things.'

No one said anything. All three women knew whatever they said next might have implications that could change their lives forever.

Carol broke their silence. 'Christine, I don't think you understand that Annie and I didn't really find any clues or anything, you know; Matron – Mavis – had done all the medical investigating before we ever got there.'

'But you said Annie just sort of *knew* he'd done it,' retorted Christine.

Annie jumped in. 'I *knew*, Chrissie, but I don't know *why* I knew. You can't run a business on that basis.'

'Ach, you knew because you're good at spotting people for what they truly are, Annie Parker,' interrupted Mavis. 'I had my suspicions, and I pride myself I'm a good judge of character, but I couldn't work out how on earth he'd done it; he'd managed to make one of the most dangerous poisons in the world, right there, in his allotment shed. Who'd have thought it?'

'In any case,' said Carol, determined to make her initial point, 'David and I have agreed it's best for me to take a break; we desperately want children, and I'm not getting any younger. I'm thirty-three now and my biological clock is ticking very loudly.'

'Oh rubbish,' interrupted Annie, 'you've got years ahead of you for childbearing, and you could be our office manager, you'd be good at that. Just stay at the office and keep us all organized, and do all the computer research; it would be like falling off a log for you after running the office for that huge company.'

'Well, I'd have to talk to David about it,' Carol was hesitant.

'I've a good knowledge of humanity,' said Mavis firmly, 'I've raised two boys, managed to get my nursing qualifications later in life, and have nursed all sorts – so I sort of know people, inside and out; that's useful. And despite the fact I'm a good deal older than all of you, I'm no less sharp than I used to be.'

'You're also great at putting people in their place,' added Annie, hurriedly followed by, 'now don't get me wrong, Mavis – I mean that in a good way – but I bet you can be a charmer too, if you need to be.'

'Ach, I'd leave the charming to this wee thing,' replied Mavis, nodding her head toward Christine. 'I bet she'd get anything out of any man in five minutes flat.'

Christine smiled, blushed, and replied, 'It might take ten.' She giggled.

'And what about me?' asked Annie loudly. 'What am I good at then?'

'You?' asked Mavis. Annie nodded. 'I suspect you'd be good at just about anything you put your mind to. You certainly know people, and I'll wager you've acted like a concierge for your bosses all these years – I bet there's nothing you can't find out about, or get hold of in a pinch, is there?'

'And you're a natural natterer,' added Carol. 'Something about you makes people want to tell you all sorts of stuff. That's got to be useful for an investigator, hasn't it?'

Annie thought about it for a moment and answered brightly, 'You know, you're right. Without me, those idiots at CFK wouldn't be able to find their own backsides with two hands and a torch; I've fixed things they thought couldn't be fixed, got hold of un-gettable delicacies and gifts for their clients, wives – and even mistresses – over the years. You're right, Mavis, if there's anyone who can work out how to find the right person to ask about something, it's me. But I don't know about what you said, Carol; I just like chatting to people. Everyone's got a story, in't they? But ta, both; I've been feeling a bit lost since they told me I'm out on my ear, and you've perked me right up.'

Annie patted Mavis's hand with real gratitude, and Mavis's face broke into a broad smile – the first one Annie had seen her crack since they'd met.

'See,' chimed in Christine, 'I knew I was right; we could all work together and it would be fun. We've all got the time on our hands, and if it's Daddy's money, we're not taking much of a financial risk, are we?'

'Do you really think he'd let us have an office for free?' asked

Carol tentatively.

'Daddy'll do pretty much anything I ask him to,' replied Christine in a matter of fact tone.

'So, if we're going to become private investigators,' added Carol, 'don't we have to get qualified, or something? Join some sort of an association?'

'A-ha!' exclaimed Annie. '*That's* why you should be the business manager – business first!'

A general chuckle ran around the table.

Christine was excited. 'So, Annie can do finding things out and knowing people; Mavis can do medical stuff and putting the frighteners on; Carol can run the business end of things and using computers, and I can wangle things out of people we need to "use". It all sounds great, ladies. So, what shall we call ourselves?'

'Now hang on a minute,' replied Annie tartly, 'don't go designing the letterhead when we haven't even agreed—'

'Ach, come on, live a little,' interrupted Mavis, unexpectedly. 'I know you all think I'm a bit of an old witch, but I believe we could make a go of it. And I think we should call ourselves . . .' She hesitated then suggested, 'Something Scottish; it'll have a trustworthy ring to it.'

'No Mavis,' replied Annie, 'we'll be based in London, and we're all English except you, so it should be something English – something like English Rose Investigations, except that's far too floral and girly—'

'Hang on a minute,' said Carol firmly. 'You should know better than to say that, Annie. I'm not English, I'm Welsh. So what about something Welsh? Daffodil Investigations? Or what about The Four Dragons?'

Christine replied, 'I'm not convinced by anything anyone's said so far, but it's just dawned on me that – with me being Irish – we could do it like the rugby: Four Nations Investigations. Oh, that sort of rhymes. How about it?'

'It doesn't rhyme, dear, it scans,' replied Mavis, 'and it's not four nations any more, it's six now, as any real rugby fan would know, so that wouldnae make sense.'

'What about our initials?' asked Carol. 'There's P,M,H, and W-S for our last names; no that doesn't work because of you, Christine. What about C,C,A and M? Can we make something of that?'

'I know – WISE Investigations,' said Christine with enthusiasm.

Annie remarked, 'It's not very *personal*, Chrissie, is it darlin'? I like Four Nations meself.'

'But it *is* four nations,' replied Christine enthusiastically. 'Wales, Ireland, Scotland and England, W.I.S.E. And it means – well, wise . . . you know; clever. People would want to hire clever investigators, wouldn't they?'

All three women stared at Christine with surprise.

Annie's felt compelled to comment, 'Clever *girl*, Chrissie.'

'Oh, it's nothing really,' responded Christine shyly. 'Daddy's always made me play word games with him, and we do them sometimes at Mensa meetings too—'

'You're in Mensa?' exclaimed Annie on behalf of the three women who found it hard to believe Christine could be so pretty, so rich, so dizzy, *and* so bright.

'Yes. That's not *bad*, is it?' Christine suddenly seemed uncertain.

'Ach, no, it's no' *bad*, my dear,' replied Mavis gently, 'we're all just wondering what other hidden talents you might have.'

'I knit rather well,' offered Christine, 'but I can't see how that would be useful for a private investigator.'

The little group laughed, and Christine suddenly felt a level of acceptance she'd found it difficult to achieve her whole life. She liked it. These women were going to let her be herself; how wonderful.

Mavis said, 'Anyway, as for the name – WISE Investigations – aye, I like it, but should we no' make ourselves sound a bit more ladylike? What about making sure our potential clients know how careful we'll be about their information? I think it's better if we offer to make enquiries, rather than to merely investigate.'

'And we should say something about confidentiality in the name, too,' added Carol.

'Don't you think that all becomes a bit too much?' said Annie. 'What about WISE Enquiries? Just that.'

'If we're going to incorporate, we'll have to get a name search done,' said Carol.

'Aye, well let's do at least that much then,' agreed Mavis, and held her glass toward the center of the table. 'I'm up for it – what about you lot?'

As Christine, Annie, and Carol also raised their glasses they let out a joint cheer – 'To WISE Enquiries!'

'Oh – and another thing,' added Christine as she rose to return to the bar, 'my second cousin Sophie is having a weekend party at her estate in Northamptonshire for Valentine's Day and she was wittering on about jewelry going missing when she was at some parties in Northumberland at Christmas, and in Leicestershire at the New Year; she was asking me what I thought she should do about it. How about I get us all invites and we go and check it out? David could come too, to keep an eye on you, Carol. It might turn out to be the first case for the women of the WISE Enquiries agency; what do you think?'

The women looked at each other and could feel the excitement crackling between them – Valentine's Day was just a couple of weeks away – could they do it?

DECEMBER

Tidings of Comfort and Joy

'John Evans is dead. It's in the newspaper. It must be true. Poor dab.' Gladys Pritchard waved the *South Wales Evening Post* in front of her husband.

'Good riddance,' muttered her spouse.

Gladys gave him a sour look over her glasses. 'Died peacefully last Thursday in Morriston Hospital, it says. We only visited him the night before.'

'I know. I was there with you.'

'Looked bad then, he did, with all those tubes poking out of him. Service is in a fortnight. It'll take all that time because of Christmas, I expect.'

Ivor Pritchard shoved the sleeves of the baggy sweater Gladys had knitted for him many Christmases earlier up his desiccated arms, exposing the dark blue stain that had once been an impressive tattoo of an anchor swathed in a chain. 'We're not going,' he said with finality.

Gladys made a small 'O' with her lips as she took off her glasses. 'What will people say if we don't go, Ivor? He lived next door to us for nearly forty years. It'll be expected.'

Her husband dropped his spoon into his dish, atop a mound of golden carrot-coins – the remains of his lamb stew. 'If you think I'm going to sit in that blinkin' crematorium in the middle of winter and listen to people going on and on about him being a wonderful person, you've got another think coming. Half of Swansea will be there. They won't miss us.'

'Half of South Wales will be there, given the number of choirs he belonged to over the years. They'll all turn out for the singing, if nothing else. And they *will* miss us, Ivor. Everyone in the street will go. We can't not go. They all thought we liked him. They wouldn't know anything about the wall. No one has any idea about how much of a misery he made our lives.' Gladys folded her arms as tightly as possible over her ample bosom.

'Next door but one down. She probably knows.'

Gladys shrugged. 'Well, she might. They shared a wall too. Mind you, she's as deaf as a post nowadays, so it makes no difference to her any more. Not like me. My hearing's so sensitive. Eat those carrots; they're good for you.'

Ivor knew his wife was right about her hearing; Gladys could have heard a pin drop onto the sheepskin rug in the next room during a thunderstorm. He suspected she might be right about the carrots too. 'Never got it as bad as us, though, did she? They had his stairs between his living room and her wall to give her a bit of a buffer. Always stood right next to our wall, he did. Scales? I'll give him scales.' Ivor dutifully chased the remaining vegetables around his bowl.

'Now, now, Ivor, stop it. John's dead. Gone. No more scales. No more rehearsals of three or four lines of one song for hours on end. No more "la-la-la, ne-ne-ne, la-la-la" exercises. Just a nice bit of peace and quiet in our own home. Lovely, isn't it?' Gladys Pritchard sat back with a look of pure pleasure on her face.

Ivor wiped his mouth with the side of his hand and arched his back in the creaking chair. 'Fan-flamin'-tastic. If he'd sung that "Myfanwy" once, he'd sung it a thousand times. I never want to hear that song again. I used to love it; now I can't even stand the thought of it.'

'You can't say he didn't have a good voice.' Gladys folded the newspaper and placed it on the table.

'I can, and I will. Maybe years ago it wasn't so bad, but since he turned seventy? Terrible! They'd have chucked him out of the choir if he hadn't been their treasurer for umpteen years.'

'Oh, I don't know, Ivor, they were always short of tenors. They even asked you once, remember?'

Ivor laughed loudly. 'Indeed I do. I suppose they must have been desperate; I couldn't carry a tune if you gave me a bucket. Besides, that last concert they gave at Tabernacle Chapel? Modern rubbish. Nice bit of Ivor Novello never goes amiss. You think they'd know that for the likes of us around here. And I'm not saying that just because I'm named after him.'

Gladys cleared the kitchen table then rolled the dishes around in her new yellow washing-up bowl. 'I wonder what his boys will do with the house,' she mused. 'Sell it, I expect. They've got their own places, so why would they want his?'

'You're right,' replied her husband. 'Not boys now, though, are they? Got to be in their fifties these days. They've both got posh houses down near the Mumbles, I hear. What would they want with one of these little terraced boxes? Good enough for the likes of us, they are, but them? No way. Gone up in the world they have.'

Gladys smiled, placing the clean dishes on the draining board. 'They've done very well for themselves, have David and Gerald. Both married nice girls, and all their children always seemed well-behaved. You know, when they used to visit.'

'Never saw any of them at John's flamin' concerts, did you? All but forced us to buy tickets, he did, but he let them get away with not going. You'd think his family would be a bit more supportive of him and his blinkin' singing, wouldn't you?'

Gladys filled the kettle, and put it onto the gas ring to boil. 'Go through to the living room, love; I'll bring you a cuppa when it's brewed. Take the paper to read while you're waiting for the local news on the telly. I'll wipe these dishes and put them away so I can sit down and enjoy *Coronation Street* later. Go on now, out of my way.'

The aged couple shared a companionable hug, then Ivor shuffled out of the kitchen on carpet-slippered feet. He was no longer the imposing man he'd been when he'd worked at Swansea Docks; decades of labor had wrecked his back, though he still did what he could around the house. They'd bought it a short time after they'd married, forty-eight years earlier.

'Not long till it starts,' said his wife, finally settling into her armchair beside her husband. 'Look forward to *The Street*, I do.'

When the doorbell rang, the couple stared at each other with surprise.

'Who can that be at this time of night?' snapped Gladys.

'Why don't you answer it and find out?' mugged Ivor.

'You do it, Ivor. I don't like to unlock the door after dark. It could be anyone.'

Discarding the newspaper, Ivor pushed himself to his feet and lumbered to the front door. His wife also stood, hovering out of sight in the living room, straining to hear who could be calling.

'Oh, it's you,' said Ivor. 'We've not long finished tea, and we were going to watch a bit of telly, but I suppose so.' He turned and shouted, 'Gladys, company!'

His wife tottered forward to see who it was. 'Really?' Her expression softened from surprise to sympathy when she saw their late-neighbor's elder son. 'David. Hello. We were sorry to hear about your dad. Just talking about him, weren't we, Ivor?'

'We were,' said her husband truthfully enough.

'He'll be missed. That's what we were saying, wasn't it?'

'It was.'

'Had a lovely voice on him, didn't he, Ivor?'

'He did.'

'The choir will miss him terribly, won't they, Ivor?'

'They will.'

David Evans watched the couple shuttlecock their comments back and forth, then smiled wearily. 'Thank you. You're both very kind.'

'Come in for a cuppa, will you?' asked Gladys tenderly. 'Let's not stand here with the door open, heating the whole street. It's cold out. Only to be expected, so close to Christmas. Come on in.'

The unexpected guest carefully navigated the narrow spaces between a worn, overstuffed suite and poorly-varnished, dark-wood furnishings draped with crocheted doilies until he sank into a well-used chair. Gladys reached past him to press the 'Record' button on the TV's remote control before switching off the set.

'Tea or coffee, David?'

'Tea'll be fine, thanks, Mrs Pritchard,' he replied, removing his cap. He rubbed his balding head. 'But only if it's not too much trouble. I can't stop long; they'll be expecting me at home.'

'The kettle's just boiled, so I'll be quick.' Gladys bustled out of the room.

The electric fire sitting in front of the painted hardboard-covered grate hummed mournfully in the ensuing silence, the yellow light dancing behind the plastic coals doing little to make the room appear welcoming, or feel warm.

Ivor cleared his throat. 'We saw the notice in the paper tonight. Funeral's in two weeks, I see,' he said in appropriately solemn tones.

'Yes. It was the earliest we could get it booked. They're backed up at the crematorium. I suppose it'll give a lot of his old friends the time they need to arrange buses to bring them down to Swansea from the valleys.'

'Gladys reckoned there'd be a load coming. Will the choirs all be travelling together?' Ivor tried to sound interested.

David nodded. 'I believe they'll try to consolidate into just a couple of coaches. It'll be good to see them there, and lovely to hear them, of course. Singing was Dad's passion. He always said you couldn't beat a male voice choir, but I suppose you know that.'

'We were saying as much before you got here.' Ivor searched for something more to add. 'They'll miss him.'

'They will,' replied the dead man's son. 'The grandkids have taken it hard, too.'

'They would,' agreed Ivor, summoning as much sympathy as he could muster. He and Gladys had, sadly, never been blessed with children.

Ivor beamed when his wife arrived. 'There she is now.' His tone suggested he'd been waiting for several hours to be rescued from a terrible fate.

Gladys pushed her fancy 'hostess trolley' through the door, bearing the best china and the teapot they never used. Ivor shot up from his chair as fast as he could, and noticed the sugar was in a bowl, not the usual bag, and the milk was in a little jug. There was even a plate of biscuits.

When they were all finally holding cups and saucers, Gladys said, 'It's lovely to see you, of course, David, but . . .' Her unasked question hung in the air above the digestives.

'They told me at the hospital you visited Dad the day he . . . on his last day.' David's hand trembled as he blew across his steaming tea.

'Not exactly,' replied Ivor. 'It said in the paper he went on Thursday. We were there for evening visiting hours on Wednesday.'

'He actually died on the Wednesday night,' said David gently. 'We put Thursday in the announcement because that's when my brother and I arrived at the hospital, and it seemed . . . well, the right thing to do. Neither of us had been able to visit him since the Tuesday, you see. My brother Gerry had to go to Scotland on business first thing Wednesday, and I went to watch my two girls in a school concert that evening. It's that time of year; one thing after another in the run-up to Christmas. The doctors had told us he was improving, so we thought it would be alright to miss a day. It seems you were the last visitors he had, and Gerry and I wondered how Dad had seemed. We knew he'd never have been the man he once was, but we were shocked when we were told he'd passed. We wondered . . . well, was he was in good spirits? Did he seem content? With neither of us being there at the end, it would be a comfort to know.'

Ivor thought David looked just the way he had when he'd kicked his rugby ball over the garden wall on so many occasions all those years ago, when the Evanses had first moved in. Even though he'd been a teenager at the time, he'd always had that lost-little-boy look about him.

Ivor and Gladys exchanged a glance as David sipped his scalding hot tea.

At an almost imperceptible nod from her husband, Gladys said, 'To be honest, your father wasn't at all well, David. Though I have to say, that evening we saw him at the hospital, he did finally have a bit of color in his cheeks. We'd been in and out of next door with food for him for about a month, and I did bits of shopping and so forth, just to keep him ticking over, so to speak. He'd not wanted to go out much. Not feeling up to it, he said. That last heart attack did for him, though.'

David blew across his steaming cup, his eyes wide and sad.

Gladys continued, 'In a way it was lucky for him that he'd managed to get himself out and about a bit when it happened, otherwise – well, who knows how long it would have been before someone would have found him in the house. I dare say that would have been me, too. But, as it was, that nice man Sooly – I can't say his whole name, because it's too complicated, so he lets me call him Sooly – he saw what happened. Do you know the man I mean, him at the shop on the corner?' David nodded. 'Well, he did the right thing phoning the ambulance when he saw your father fall down on the pavement.'

'Yes, I understand it was his quick actions that saved Dad that day,' said the grieving son.

Gladys nodded. 'It was. And him not speaking much English, too, poor dab. Well, enough to run a shop, I suppose, but, you know, not much real conversation. I happened to be coming back from town, and I was walking from the bus stop. And there was your dad being carted off by the ambulance. I could tell just by looking at him that he wasn't good, but I'd been thinking that for a couple of weeks. He'd reached the point where his teeth looked too big for his face. Never a good sign, that. And he was getting on, after all. Eighty-five, wasn't he?'

David smiled sadly.

'Good innings, really,' said Ivor.

David put down his tea. 'So they say.' The man didn't sound convinced. 'The thing is, Gerry and I were wondering if Dad had – well, just given up, I suppose. You see, the doctors said they were puzzled that he went as fast as he did.' He unzipped the top of his plaid-lined, waxed-cotton jacket a little. 'He'd been doing well, they said, and then he was gone.'

Ivor rallied. 'Well, what do they know, these doctors? Just youngsters, all of them. When it's your time, it's your time. As the wife said, he was obviously not a well man. She might be right when

she says he had a bit of color about him, propped up in that bed
there, but I don't know. Maybe they just filled him full of drugs to
make him look a bit perkier. He was weak, but in good spirits, mind
you; talking about when he could come home and get back to his
singing. We chatted about this and that, didn't we love?' Gladys
smiled. 'How things were around here, could we keep an eye on the
house for him, that sort of thing. But then he got tired, and asked if
we could pull his curtains around him, 'cos the lights were a bit
bright, and we left. He was a bit quiet but – you know – alright, I
suppose.'

'So Dad seemed quite . . . happy in himself then?' asked David
with the eyes of a hopeful child.

'As happy as he ever was when he wasn't singing,' replied Ivor.
Gladys nodded.

David stood, grim-faced, the dark circles beneath his eyes telling
the tale of his grief and loss. 'Well, thanks for that at least. I suppose
you're right; even the best of doctors can't always be certain of
things, can they?' He forced a smile. 'We'll see you both at the
funeral, of course.' It wasn't a question.

'Wouldn't miss it for the world,' said Ivor, also rising to his feet.
'Have you made any plans for next door yet? Gladys and I were
saying we thought you'd probably sell up.'

David shook his head. 'Actually, we think we'll hang onto the old
place. Gerry and I talked about it; his eldest is at university now, just
started here in Swansea, so we thought it would be a good idea to
keep it. His son and a couple of fellow-students will live there for
the next few years. It'll save them paying rent to someone else. Of
course, they won't move in until the new term begins, after
Christmas. Then, when they're all finished, maybe Gerry's younger
son will use it. After him, then my girls will be about ready for it. If
they all decide to go to university or college in this area, of course.'

Ivor felt Gladys reach for his hand. She gripped him tightly.

'Young people living next door? That'll make a change, won't it,
Ivor?' she said quietly. 'I hope they're nice.' She forced a laugh.

David's reply was warmed by genuine affection. 'He's a good kid,
is Gerry's eldest. He's studying geography, but he's a wonderful
musician too. Got a lovely voice he has – must have inherited it from
his grandfather. And he plays the bassoon. All three of them who'll
be moving in are musical types. Classical, of course; none of this
rock-band stuff. Bassoon, clarinet and violin, they play. It'll be nice
for them to have somewhere they can rehearse in the evenings.' He

pulled at the collar of his jacket, and tugged the zip upwards, flapping his cap onto his head as he left. 'See you at the funeral,' he called, as he slid into the leather-upholstered seat of his large, sleek car.

Once the front door was locked, Gladys burst into tears. 'All those years listening to John singing – and now more noise? I don't know if I can take it, Ivor. I thought all that was behind us with him finally gone.'

Ivor put his arm around his wife's heaving shoulders and steered her into the sitting room, where he settled her into her chair. His heart was thumping. He'd seen the same horrified expression on his beloved wife's face when John Evans had perked up in his hospital bed, and had begun to talk happily about getting home, and starting to sing again.

Then Ivor had spotted the huge syringe with a long, thin needle lying unattended on a little cart beside the man's hospital bed. He knew that injecting a whole container full of air into the tubes plugged into a person's veins killed them in a way not even the doctors could always spot. He'd seen it on one of Gladys's TV programs a few months earlier; she liked to watch those 'real emergency' ones, where they save people's lives – or don't. In one of them, a nurse had talked about how, sometimes, little air bubbles weren't really dangerous at all, saying how they got it wrong on telly all the time. She'd even showed how much you needed to pump into a person to be sure to make it fatal. It was quite a lot. Handy to know.

So that was what Ivor had done to John, to stop him coming back to the house next door to sing again. He'd fussed about a bit at the side of the chattering man's bed, and had pushed the air in the syringe into one of John's tubes. All he could think about at the time was that he wanted Gladys to be happy; that was all Ivor had ever really cared about.

It only took him a minute to do it, while Gladys was picking up something the man in the bed opposite John's had dropped onto the floor. Then Ivor had said goodbye to John for the last time, and had closed their soon-to-be-late neighbor's curtains around him. It had been surprisingly simple, and he hadn't felt so much as a single twinge of remorse since he'd done it. Quite honestly, until Gladys had told him about the notice in the newspaper, he hadn't even been sure it had worked.

It seemed he'd got away with murder alright, but now?

Music students? Next door? For years?

The news couldn't have been much worse. And just before Christmas, too.

Afterword and acknowledgements

As you can see from the copyright page, some of this work dates back to 1988. The story 'Dear George' was written in a car park on Baker Street, in London, in 1987, and won the right to be published because of a competition being run by a women's magazine. The launch of that anthology, 'Murder and Company', brought me into contact with some 'real authors' for the first time in my life and – though I enjoyed it tremendously – I couldn't turn my attention from the business I had just established, despite the further boost I received when the story was selected to join others by well-known authors like Peter Lovesey and Ruth Rendell in a collection being put together specifically for the English GCSE syllabus in the UK.

I ran my business until 1999, then sold it, and moved to Canada where I taught at the University of British Columbia, then Simon Fraser University. It was while I was teaching there that I was approached by the wonderful Martin Jarvis, OBE, and Rosalind Ayers, asking if they could produce 'Dear George' for BBC Radio 4. Of course, my family all almost burst with pride when my words were broadcast for the world to hear; the death of my father soon thereafter gave me the kick up the backside I needed to get back to fiction writing, and I produced, and self-published, a collection of twelve stories called 'MURDER: Month by Month' in 2007. Quite a few of the works in this anthology first appeared there; they have been reedited to allow me to apply what I hope is some useful learning, acquired by writing what I estimate to be more than 1,500,000 words as I have crafted The Cait Morgan Mysteries and the WISE Enquiries Agency Mysteries.

In 2008 I produced a collection of four novellas; 'MURDER: Season by Season' joined my first volume when I approached a Canadian publisher with the idea they should 'release my characters' via a ransom note – you know the sort of thing . . . letters cut out of a newspaper and all. They then published what has become to date eight books in the Cait Morgan Mysteries series. Thank you to TouchWood Editions in Victoria, BC for having faith in me. The first time Cait made an appearance in print was in 'MURDER: Month by Month' in the story 'The Corpses Hanging Over Paris', which is in this collection; when I revisited these first three Cait Morgan stories I was amazed to realize she'd truly 'found her voice' in them, back in 2007; from that voice came all those other books. Indeed, the main reason for republishing these works is to allow those who have read about Cait Morgan and the WISE women to find out 'how it all started'.

I was also pleased to discover that my original tale about the four women who set up the WISE Enquiries Agency also showcased the women readers have come to know through the, so far, four books in The WISE Enquiries Agency Mysteries, published by Severn House Publishers. That said, there were more changes for me to make when rewriting 'Miss Parker Pokes Her Nose In' because, through four books, I have developed the characters' backstories in ways this 'genesis' story didn't acknowledge.

Other stories that appeared in that first volume haven't fared so well, and do not appear in this collection; it's quite amazing how the passage of just ten years can make some key elements of a story seem anachronistic. Those 'missing stories' will be reworked, and are likely to appear in the future – freshly minted for a new age.

As for now, I have no idea where my writing life will take me over the next few years. My first novel was published in 2012, and here I am five years later re-self-publishing my earliest works. Sometimes we need to step back before we can march forward. I hope you'll come with me on that journey. I've met and worked with so many wonderful people in the past decade – the decade since most of these stories first appeared. Thanks to Anna Harrisson (editor) and Sue Vincent (proofer) for this collection. Through it all my family has cheered, and my husband has supported me. Thank you to everyone for the learning, enjoyment and fulfillment.

Cathy Ace, November, 2017.